A
STRANGER
CITY

ALSO BY LINDA GRANT

Fiction
The Cast Iron Shore
When I Lived in Modern Times
Still Here
The Clothes on Their Backs
We Had It So Good
Upstairs at the Party
The Dark Circle

Non-fiction
Sexing the Millennium: A Political
History of the Sexual Revolution
Remind Me Who I Am, Again
The People on the Street: A Writer's View of Israel
The Thoughtful Dresser

LINDA GRANT

A STRANGER CITY

virago

VIRAGO

First published in Great Britain in 2019 by Virago Press

1 3 5 7 9 10 8 6 4 2

Copyright © Linda Grant 2019

The moral right of the author has been asserted.

A CIP catalogue record for this book
is available from the British Library.

Hardback ISBN 978-0-349-01050-2
C-format ISBN 978-0-349-01049-6

Typeset in Goudy by M Rules
Printed and bound in Great Britain by
Clays Ltd, Elcograf S.p.A.

Papers used by Virago are from well-managed forests
and other responsible sources.

MIX
Paper from
responsible sources
FSC® C104740

Virago Press
An imprint of
Little, Brown Book Group
Carmelite House
50 Victoria Embankment
London EC4Y 0DZ

An Hachette UK Company
www.hachette.co.uk

www.virago.co.uk

For Ben, Farnaz and Talah

A
STRANGER
CITY

Part One

February 2016
Manor Park, East London

1

She was buried at 9.30 in the morning and as soon as the earth was filled in by the mechanical digger, fog obscured the spot. Sleet was forecast for early afternoon. The four pallbearers, the clergyman and the undertaker watched her go under, standing by the grave in black leather gloves and smart black overcoats. The film crew stood apart; they shot the figures of the six men as bulky separate shapes in the whiteness of the morning.

One of the pallbearers was trying to start a conversation about classic cars. He was bidding on a 1965 Triumph Herald convertible on eBay. It needed a lot of work and he was looking forward to its restoration. 'Very unusual colour combination, olive and cactus. Last tax disc was 1979 so it's been off the road a long time. I think there's plenty of potential there for a lovely motor.'

His boss gave him a hard look. This chat was out of order. Poor woman, dead and buried to a threnody of leather interiors and nostalgia for string-backed driving gloves.

'Come on now,' he said, 'someone loved her somewhere. Must have done. Show some respect.'

The pallbearer apologised but went on thinking about whether the paint was original.

'You'd imagine so,' said the priest, 'yet here she is and it's just the six of us, who don't know her from Adam, not even her name.'

My name is Father Gerry Cutler, he thought, *and over there is Kevin Redmond the undertaker with his professional AIDS ribbon, though there's fewer of them dying now, thank heavens. That's Geoff Stott, on his phone the whole time, and the others I've been intro-duced to but I can't recollect what they're called.* All had families and friends who loved them and a wider circle than that. Father Cutler had his parishioners. The undertaker had many custom-ers, if that was what you called the bereaved. It was the same for the others, he had no doubt; and this poor lady with no one, not a soul in all the world except for God who must have known her.

The day was ashiver. The sky looked sleety though it hadn't yet started to rain. Miserable time of year. The Christmas lights were all gone from the shops and only the Easter eggs to look forward to.

'Let's get in to the warm, shall we?' the undertaker said. 'We've done all we can.'

They walked back in from the cold. He made a pot of tea and opened a packet of biscuits. 'Help yourselves. Keep your strength up. Only gingers, sorry about that; we finished the last of the chocolate digestives yesterday.'

The door banged, letting in a blast of freezing air. The police-man arrived; icy drops glittered on his beard, his pale blue eyes gleamed in a worn face wrapped against the cold in a navy Crombie overcoat. He was heavy set, but not fat; he came in with the confidence of a man with a provable identity, no hesitation.

'Blimey, did I miss it? I'm so sorry, just couldn't find the place. I don't know this part of London. Never even knew it was here.'

He introduced himself. Detective Sergeant Pete Dutton who had led the investigation.

They were way out east at Manor Park by Wanstead Flats.

The drive had taken forever. The Thames rolled along from the soft Surrey hills under the fancier bridges, Richmond, Putney, Chelsea. Pete had set his alarm for six and went out with his Crombie overcoat collar turned up when everyone else was in bed. The streets were still black, there was little early traffic until he hit Chiswick High Road then it choked up. The coffee shops were opening, figures slinking in like wraiths under fluorescent lights. He had his own coffee in a flask.

'Too late; she's gone, I'm afraid,' said the undertaker. 'Wasn't much *to* miss, to be honest. Just us.'

'No one else turned up? I was hoping someone might have read that piece in the local rag and finally twigged.'

'Not a living soul. Just the camera boys.'

'What a crying shame. Seven months' work and all over in five minutes.'

'I know. Have a cup of tea, warm yourself up. There's plenty of biscuits if you're peckish; only gingers, though. Your gingers are the ones which always get left over, don't you find? They're not a popular biscuit, even the Rich Tea get eaten up quicker and they taste of nothing.'

To drive all this way and not even see her last moments, coming in from Surrey when he didn't need to, not out of a sense of duty but a feeling – not even of respect, just wanting to be here, for he might be all she had in the world to worry about her and think about her and not let the matter drop though it wasn't in his hands any more and nothing left to be done. He had seen her not long after she came out of the water. Six hours earlier she had been alive, walking through London. He felt once more the sharp, tearful resurrection of that distress he had felt when he had arrived at the incident and said, 'What have we got here?' He was looking down at her, drowned, mud-plastered, bruised by sea chains. Pretty only a few hours ago, blonde, slim, well presented, now something a dog dragged up from the water.

5

He drank his tea and ate a couple of biscuits. The others in the room were johnny-come-latelies. They had no idea about her. He had picked a red flower from the Christmas cactus by the television in the lounge at home, placed it gently in a freezer bag and transported it all the way across London with the intention of dropping it on to her coffin and now he'd lost his chance. Nothing to be done. The flower was in his pocket, he'd throw it in the bin. More waste.

'Do you not think sometimes,' the undertaker said, looking round the room for support from his colleagues for an idea he had always wanted to express in public but somehow never had the opportunity (the subject hadn't come up, or not in the right way or at a time which seemed appropriate), 'that throwing yourself off a bridge must seem quite seductive? The death it offers has a kind of grandeur. I don't know, you could call it a return to the elements.'

'Nah, I wouldn't say that it was grand at all,' said Geoff Stott, who had taken out his phone and was checking the bids for the olive and cactus Triumph. Still sluggish; this might be his lucky day. 'Because if you think on it, there's no one to see you do it. I mean, where's the gesture that would get you noticed? If you wanted to go out with glory you wouldn't just slip away like that.'

The starting point was not known. CCTV had first caught her near Moorgate station. They had searched for her image in the tunnels and on the escalators but she emerges out of nowhere past cliffs of pale implacable buildings, walking, walking, walking. By Mansion House, Bank of England, Old Billingsgate, St Magnus the Martyr, London Bridge. She had climbed on to the balustrade and thrown herself over unnoticed. Did she hover there? Could a passer-by have talked her down or did she go straight off? No witnesses had come forward. According to the pathologist she had been in the water five or six hours when she was found so it would have been around ten at night when she

6

jumped, a time when transport was roaring through streets and tunnels and people were coming out of theatres and cinemas and still eating in restaurants; the city was not bleak, it was engorged with pleasure. A warm night in July when people were moving from one gratification to the next, a veil of humid happiness lay over the good city.

'Listen, let's have a bit of reality here,' said Pete Dutton. 'She would have been dead in about six minutes. In fact, I'd be surprised if she lasted that long. My brother's got a boat moored out at Teddington Lock. We're river people us Duttons, grew up on it, Strand on the Green near Kew Bridge, *Wind in the Willows* kids, so I know quite a bit about the Thames and its peculiarities. Even on a warm day, and this *was* a warm day, or had been earlier, you're struggling immediately, the fall itself completely knocks the wind and strength out of you, no matter how big you are or how young. And she was a female not some strapping lad who might swim his way out of trouble. Very soon you start to lose control of your arms and legs, the cold gets into you.'

'Even on a warm night? It was very warm – humid high summer, if I recall,' said Geoff Stott.

'Oh yes, a few inches below the surface and it's cold, the water isn't stagnant, the tides are always running, you see. So knocking the wind out of you with the chilly water is enough to make you start drowning anyway, then you've only got to start taking one mouthful of water and it's game over. So maybe not even as long as six minutes.'

'Yes, that's exactly my point, if you want to make a *statement*,' Geoff Stott said, closing down the eBay app on his phone, 'you'd be better off throwing yourself under a train during the rush hour. Person on the line. Disruption on the track. All that temporary inconvenience. People late for job interviews, missing their connections, never turning up for a date. But she just slipped over the sides and no one saw her. You wonder if she changed her mind on the way down, tried to save herself but didn't stand a chance.'

'But why did they find her so quickly?' said the priest. 'You hear of people chucking themselves off and nothing is ever recovered, not a scrap of clothing even, doing a Lord Lucan.'

'Yes, she was lucky,' said Pete. 'Or not, as the case may be, depending on what she actually wanted. Did she hope she'd be found? We'll never know. In the early hours of the next morning they spotted her, I mean the river police patrolling for smugglers, it's all drugs and bodies in that line of work. The poor woman only got herself tangled in the chains of HMS *Belfast* and that stopped her progress downriver.'

The others had seen the posters of her after she'd been cleaned up. The police forensic artist had carefully opened her eyelids for the colour of her eyes, to see whether they were dark or light, for that would make all the difference to the face and how he might make her appear as though she had once been alive. They were pale blue. He closed them again, pressing his finger against the ice-cold lid with brown lashes long cleansed by river water of any cosmetics, went to the sink to rinse his hands, thinking as he soaped them that whatever he did he could not capture her and that was partly his own failure being no Rembrandt and partly that something had gone, leaving the premises of her flesh vacated.

The undertaker had prepared her body after she had lain all alone in the freezer drawer like a long bag of peas so he had come very late to the case, as had all the others at the funeral apart from Pete Dutton who thought, *What do they know or care despite their professional pieties?*

It was all so bloody mysterious. Her clothes when they found her, everything down to the knickers and bra, were from Marks & Spencer. That wasn't a particularly cheap shop, the company still prided themselves on quality; Pete Dutton bought his own undercracks from there, not shirts or suits or jeans, though. He had some self-respect, even at fifty-two he preferred something a bit more interesting; there were fantastic shops in Richmond if you knew where to look. Still, good old Marks & Sparks. It meant she was not a homeless person, not a vagrant, not a rough sleeper. The investigation had checked with the company, she was wearing jeans and a top which were in the stores a few months before. Her jacket was only a year older than that. Her shoes were Nike trainers with silver flashes. She had no tattoos and no rings or mark of a ring. Her ears were pierced but the holes were empty. Her light mousy hair was dyed with blonde highlights: not all that long ago applied, judging by the roots, three or four months' growth. She had no money at all on her, let alone a wallet, nothing at all in her pockets.

Dutton explained all this to the others, who took it in with a lowering sense that the day could only get worse.

What is my connection to my fellow man? thought Geoff Stott. *Is it no more than something at the end of my fingers, some pixels on my phone?* And maybe he would not walk out of the room tonight into the kitchen to make a cup of coffee when his wife began her nagging about spending too much time with old cars and not enough time with people. But no, he would have forgotten by the time he got home, he knew he would. A leopard can't change its spots. I like cars, he would tell her. They're my thing. He hoped his wife would be the person to make sure they didn't lead him to a bridge and water. She'd see him straight. *And how long before I shake off this morning, this frozen corpse, this buried box, or will it stick around like a dirty toilet smell?*

The radiators were warming up, they were reaching their temperature set point. The office by the chapel was cosy and the men ate more biscuits. Outside in the paupers' graves the dead were laid on top of each other until the hole was full and they started a new one. Below the ground lay blocks of wooden studio apartments each with their sole inhabitant. In death, maybe they kept each other company, maybe they had parties down there, bringing bottles from one coffin to another, lonely people finding sociability only when they were turning to compost.

'What do you think happened?' said Geoff Stott. 'Who was she? You must have your suspicions, clues, leads?'

''There's always theories, of course there are.'

'And?'

'Not my case any more. Let's see what the next round of publicity throws up. The camera boys are on it now. Fingers crossed.'

Outside the TV crew had been silent and respectful. They were still at the grave and had not joined the others for tea and biscuits. They filmed the digger at first from a distance; when the paltry funeral party moved off they came in closer. Beneath the ground the unknown woman was buried deep, like the victim of an air raid. She was London's daughter now.

Pete Dutton went out and said hello to Alan McBride with his camera and crew. They shook hands. 'Not as cosy as when we last met,' Pete said. 'You found it all right? I had a hell of a job, got lost, missed the interment.'

'Sorry about that; it was terribly sad.'

'I had a flower for her. I feel like a right pansy myself for getting so upset.'

'Poor woman.'

'I know. And nothing to identify her in death, not even now.'

'There was something – a plaque on her coffin.'

'What did it say?'

'Just the date of her death and DB27. I don't know what—'

'Oh that, it's not what you think. It just means she was the twenty-seventh dead body we pulled from the river last year. There were more, of course, as the year went on. Most quickly identified, reported missing, looked out for. We're all a set of numbers one way or the other: National Insurance, credit cards, bank details, and all the rest they've got on you, but at least we've got names. She had one, don't forget that, we just don't know what it was.'

'Thanks again for your help, thanks for everything. I really appreciate it, if it wasn't for you—'

'No, it was a pleasure. When's your show going out?'

'We haven't got a transmission date yet; they're talking about July, the anniversary. I'll be in touch as soon as I hear.'

'Let's hope it jogs someone's memory. You never know.'

'I mean, it's *got* to.'

'Yes, you'd think.'

'Would you mind if I filmed you for a minute or two walking towards the grave? Is that okay? Do you want to hold the flower?'

'I think I'd rather chuck it if you don't mind.'

'Okay, whatever you feel comfortable with.'

Alan watched him march down the dead avenues. He was sorry the policeman had not arrived on time. He seemed the only human link in this unpeopled story. The fog was clearing, the sleet was starting to make itself felt. Conditions for filming were difficult. It was hard not to be moved by the bleakness and poverty of her funeral, the indifference of its attendants.

When Pete had performed his walk, his hands in his coat pockets, feeling the dying flower encased in plastic, chucking it in a bin by the gates of the cemetery, angry with himself and her – her for being so conclusively lost, himself for being unable to make her not matter – he got into his car and drove west. The journey home was long. The sleet was definitely moving in from the north now. He passed along the A12, by Stratford and the Lee Valley Park, through Hackney into central London, braking for a few minutes by the site of the recovery of the body, looking out once more at London Bridge, undistinguished, concrete and steel, box girder construction and only forty-odd years old. An unromantic structure apart from its famous name. What made her do it here? The river was black and cold today. It seemed scummy and foetid. Along the bottom were the bones of sailors and of fallen women. Hardly anyone knew of Dead Man's Hole, the old mortuary where they kept the bloated corpses of the suicides pulled from the river. He had seen the long pole, the row of hooks. The sight sickened him. Had she known . . . ? But maybe the undertaker was right and the glamour of the plunge, the exhilarating drop, had drawn her. How decisive it was, death was certain.

It was his river. Now she was its property and so she was also his. It was beyond his ability to explain to anyone. It was his secret. He had talked about the case while it was his case, but when it ceased to be there was no longer any reason. She lodged herself inside him. She had become a part of his life. A shrink would want to get to work on that and ask him a load of questions he'd struggle to answer except to say, *Well, you know, something had happened, I was already poleaxed, and she just turned up.* And was it disloyalty to his wife? How could you two-time a living woman with a dead one?

He gave up the struggle to work it out, he wasn't a deep thinker, things were churning, which was to be expected in the current circumstances. Slipping the brake, he drove on, passed through the West End, skirted Buckingham Palace, drove down Brompton Road. In Chiswick he stopped for a late breakfast.

Alone at his table he ate bacon, sausage, egg and chips and wondered how long this would go on, the dreams he woke up from with a sudden rush of longing to return to sleep, and to her. Who can you talk to about such matters? No one, you're not that kind of guy, unless HR spotted his odd demeanour and sent him for counselling. So you keep it to yourself, go to Sunday lunch with the in-laws once a month, bid for punk-era badges and other paraphernalia on eBay, go shopping in the West End, thinking back to your youth and how there's no one braver than a teenage working-class dandy in the age of punk with a few quid in his pocket to spend on clobber and records. The shirts he used to have! The beautiful shirts, the reckless T-shirt slogans, the Doc Martens, the drainpipe jeans.

In the dream world there she is, though she had lain for so long, freezing cold in the morgue, naked, her M&S outfit in a plastic bag in storage. A body in waiting. Now she is buried and it is over until she comes staring blindly out of a TV screen and someone says, *Look, it's her.*

All he can do is wait. Go home to a sick wife and be a cheerful face around the house, filling the dishwasher and emptying it, all the weary routine while Marie, upstairs, tries her very best to get better, giving it her all, all for life and for living.

Part Two

Seven months earlier

2

A terrible shock came over the girl's face. A moment ago she was yakking on her phone. 'I'll call you when we get there but don't bother coming if the party's shite, if it's shite we'll come over to you no don't worry I'll get the address off him but it might be shite and we won't bother I'll call you soon love ya babe love ya love ya,' and she had looked up to say something to the guy sitting opposite – starting to ask him for the address, the postcode, she would text that to her, but only if the party wasn't shite. Then quietly he spoke, this verbal atrocity. Her face had collapsed in on itself, no comeback, no *how dare you, what are you talking about*, or laughing it off. Said it not loudly or aggressively but as if he was making a quiet, reasonable complaint about the infrequent timetabling of weekend trains, for they were very bad at the moment on this line, and she sat and took it, a machine gun to the chest.

'And what's your best record now for giving blow jobs at parties? Seven, or was it eight?'

Alan McBride, sitting on the other side of the aisle, ear cocked, witnessed it as if it were a close-up on his camera's screen, seeing the full force of the impact on her collapsing face.

The scene was as ugly and sad and disastrous as he'd ever known in all his years of eavesdropping on strangers.

Later, at home, the incident rewinding and replaying in his head, capable of being summoned at will for examination, he began to talk it over with his wife Francesca.

'You know, if someone told me my mother was blown up by an IRA bomb, which was one of those messages you were always dreading when I was a kid in Belfast, coming home from school and your mum not there and your auntie running in to break the news, just coming out with it, no softening up or preparation, *oh my God your mum's been murdered by the Provos,* I'd have looked just like that girl, though maybe I wouldn't at first be able to take it in but she'd absorbed the whole thing at once, it knocked her system right out, poor kid.'

'Oh, come on now, you're making it up, it couldn't have been that bad.'

'But you saw her yourself.'

'I did not, I was looking at the house on my phone. What was she like?'

'Tall girl, statuesque build, big bones, Irish by the way, one those self-confident lasses always with a smile and a joke. Dublin accent, I'm pretty sure, with a really cheap-looking pink handbag. Not tarty, by the way, not even dressed up when they were supposed to be going to a bash of some kind. I felt sorry for her with that bag even before he opened his mouth. It was shapeless and it had the kitchen sink in it.'

'They must have come from the park. Loads of people got on there.'

'I know, it's a fine park.'

'Yes, nothing wrong with the park.'

'And walking distance.'

'I *know.* You don't need to keep reminding me like I'd

18

forgotten, that's the whole point of looking there. There's no argument about the *park*.'

'That's all I'm saying. The park is grand.'

'Well, we agree, so shut up. I'm not going to argue with you about the *park*.'

A crowd had surged in from the platform, reddened by the sun, on their way home after a long day out, an open-air music festival, and this pair were going on to a party without even returning home first to change out of their park clothes, for the party might be shite. And what did it even mean that a party was shite – not enough booze, bad music, no one interesting to talk to? He'd half-forgotten. No one they knew went to parties any more. No one even gave parties, it was not something married people did, apart from housewarmings and baby showers. The last stag night he went to was more than a year ago. You look up, he thought, and everyone is married, all your mates, all the guys, the ones from school, the ones from uni, the ones at work – young fathers, young home-owners with cordless drills and the discovery that they had the skills to do something so completely surprising to themselves as put together from flat pack a baby's cot without even ardently wishing they were at the match.

And even if you sometimes have the impulse to run, you actually love it, this married life, because nothing could be more depressing than heading out to a party that might be shite and its only redeeming feature some random girl going down on her knees in the room with the coats, or out in the garden by the trellis, or on the balcony, and you unzipping, full of shame, yet thinking sod it, coming sooner than you'd like into her warm wet red mouth and watching her pick up someone's jacket and wipe her face on the lining. Which overturning the laws of statistical probability turns out to be yours.

Had the guy really said that?

Blackish tinges of pain had darkened the girl's face. You think

19

you're one thing, a vivacious girl who loves her friends and will not inflict on them a party that is shite, and the guy you are with has called you a slag. As if you picked up your coffee and took a sip and an acrid unexpected taste made you cry out, I'm poisoned!

Alan thought, *Is she going back through those seven maybe eight guys she gave blow jobs to, or is it that there were no blow jobs at all and he has just said the most hurtful thing he could think of for absolutely no reason but cruelty?* Or had she said something to him first that Alan had missed, drowned by a train announcement, and he was lashing out. There must be a whole story behind it and he might never know what it was, it was killing him! The guy was a suave bully. Good-looking, well-groomed, he was out of her league, even without hearing that thing he'd said, you could tell they weren't a couple. A metrosexual smoothie with an olive complexion and wavy dark hair full of product. He was looking at her as if nothing had happened, imperturbable. He might have just said, 'Is there a shop to pick up a bottle where we get off?'

From what he could read of the girl's face, it wasn't only hurt, it was way beyond that, it was the atomic glare of self-revelation: that he thought she was a slag when she believed that she was someone who was friendly enough to give a blow job at a party. (Though what was the pleasure in it for her Alan couldn't really say. Thank God for a wife and weekends fruitlessly viewing property they didn't want or couldn't afford or their offer beaten by someone else, and then an early disappointed supper with friends.)

The cheap bag lay on her lap sloppily and her phone was falling out. Still she went on absorbing the damage. Alan looked at the guy and thought, *You little shit, I'd like to . . .* But he didn't speak. If his wife had not been with him, he might have done, tried to comfort the girl, but they were getting off at the next stop and anyway people don't like attention being drawn to their personal tragedies and she'd have said, *No way! There's nothing the matter. You think he said what? Oh bollocks now, he never did, you heard it all wrong.*

Francesca, opposite him, scrolling through the photos and the floorplan of the house, hadn't heard a thing about blow jobs or observed the girl at all for she was facing the wrong way and had not looked up from her phone since they got on the train. Now, forehead down, she was studying the house again and finding not as many flaws as she had expected, for there was very good storage space, you couldn't fault it for that, and the kitchen work-tops were actually quartz, which lasted a lifetime, plus there were French windows leading to the garden which was well planted with climbers over the fence that now, in high summer, were flowering madly, the clematis and japonica. *But the railway line; what about the trains shaking the foundations?*

For yes, it was fine to be a couple of minutes' walk to the station, that fabulous overground connection that led straight to the City, if it *was* true that all that you heard was the low thrum of the rails in the distance on hot nights when the bed-room windows were open and the rest of the time, which was almost all of the year, through the double glazing, nothing. But for the lines to be a few metres away and the station itself, its platform and ticket office and waiting passengers clearly visible from the window and maybe they could even see *in* – that was humiliation.

So no, they would not make an offer for the house, she would put her foot down. There would be other houses, there had to be, and she would make Alan understand that she could not live there, and it was nothing to do with what her friends would think, though a few were actually managing to buy in Hackney overlooking Victoria Park, but most were, like them, looking in these outposts of London, these strange, double-figured post-codes.

Alan had said, 'Put your phone away, we're here.' She had looked up dazed, hypnotised by property, dropped it into her own bag which was not a cheap one, a Mulberry, her thirtieth birthday present from him, a classic he had been told, though how that worked he had no idea, like cars maybe, but shopping for it had given him the eye to tell what really cheap looked like, and he had seen how terrible the girl's bag was, and felt sorry for her.

He thought that they had left behind the drama of the train but the geezer was behind him and the girl stayed in her seat, transfixed into a wand of pain. The geezer was shouting to her, 'Get off, we're here.'

Alan badly wanted to loiter on the platform, to witness the next scene in the tragedy of the party that might be shite (and whether it was or not, this situation was definitely shite), but his wife took his arm, said, 'What are you just standing there for? Now, listen, I've made up my mind, we're not going to make an offer whatever you say, it's too close to the railway line and to the station. You'd think you could never be too close to a station, but there it is.'

She dragged him away up the steps and over the bridge towards home, into the humid street, the heavy shade of London planes burdened with coarse-fingered leaves, the gardens turning jungle, pots of geraniums and Michaelmas daisies and night-scented stock on balconies where people were having dinner or sitting on walls drinking wine and smoking. The street was full of music, here someone on the piano, a pale girl's arm stretching along the keys seen though the shadowed slats of the venetian blinds. Skin that had caught the sun in the day peeked rosily from bra straps. Like mercury the pair glided along together. They passed the high escarpment of a five-storey block of flats and every window was open and couples leaned out into the air. Then the street shrank back again to its rows of double-fronted

Edwardian houses with panels of stained glass depicting palm trees, coats of arms, weeping willows.

'I think you're wrong, you know,' Alan said. 'I think it's a pretty good house. It's better than all the others we've seen and it needs hardly anything doing to it. We wouldn't need to knock through or reconfigure the bathroom or any of that expensive stuff. Even the garden is nicely planted. I think we'd be mad not to even *try* to get it. What's the harm in putting in an offer and seeing what happens?'

'So why hasn't it already gone? It's been on the market six weeks and they haven't even *had* an offer even though loads of people came to the open day. That tells you something, doesn't it? If it was any good it would have been snapped up by now. What about the foundations? They must be *crumbling* under all those vibrations.'

'Don't be ridiculous. That street's been there a hundred years. The houses are still standing, aren't they?'

'Well, what about rats, then? Rats come up from the tracks, have you thought about that?'

It had been all about the neighbourhood when they first started looking in Wall Park. If you searched online, and Alan had done ages ago, you could find old footage of the high street taken by members of the local ciné club a few years after the war. On his iPad housewives with wicker baskets over their arms, turbans tied around unwashed hair or hats with perky feathers pointing purposefully to the radiant future, wheeled infants in coach prams. There was a carefree air about these people, a cheerful cheeky innocence, an absence of any awareness of irony or cynicism – briskly strolling, smiling to each other, waving, men darting forward to shake hands. His grandmother in Belfast confirmed that was what life really was like after the war: 'You won't believe it but I was young, I was happy all day long, always laughing, not a care in the world. We'd made it and that was all that mattered.'

He didn't believe this. People had to be suffering from post-traumatic shock at the very least and were suppressing it; the country was awash with looted guns taken from the corpses of enemy soldiers, an arsenal of animosity. The population must have been eaten away by the effects of anxiety, loss, grief, sorrow, anger and pent-up insubordination, a mental health crisis unrecognised and untreated by doctors who handed out bottles of nerve tonic consisting of coloured water and a few vitamins. Yet here they were in the midday sunshine casting no shadows at all, exchanging their ration coupons for an ounce of cheese. It seemed propagandistic and probably was: a whole community volunteering to put a good face on itself.

By the seventies the street had become a thoroughfare of dead signs and semi-derelict frontage shuttered and abandoned. The toy shop failed and no one took it over. Its faded dusty stock remained in the window, a museum of long-lost childhoods of jigsaws and balls and dolls and golliwogs and train sets and colouring books. The tailor walked away from his shop leaving the styles of yesteryear displayed in the window: trousers with flares, suits with over-extended lapels. In the back room of the chemist, mice fed on out-of-date antibiotics. The Lyons café closed. There was nowhere any more to stop for a cup of tea and a rock bun or a plate of garibaldi biscuits. The abandoned street took on the manner of a retail Miss Havisham, forever dressed in the rotting fascia of its high-water mark.

During the civil war in Cyprus the Mediterranean began to extend its warm breath along the street bringing with it a general atmosphere of abroad, of sunshine and tanned shoulders and exotic delicacies. Litre bottles of olive oil, beige garlicky pastes and pungent blocks of salty white cheese appeared in the shops. Triangular pastries studded with sesame seeds were openly eaten by figures lounging on the pavement. The essential Englishness of the street had been permanently breached and was now yet

24

another inner-London neighbourhood of ethnic diversity. A shop opened selling Greek Orthodox iconography at the same time as the parish church was turned into flats. Only a record shop had survived into a new millennial era. And now a new breed of customers were arriving, young pioneers in search of commuter-land.

They had viewed five houses in the neighbourhood but none as close to the railway lines, and had been out-bid on each they had made an offer on. Together they had viewed this house twice. He had gone back secretly on his own after the first viewing to have a chance to consolidate his first impression. The road ended in a cul-de-sac at the fence separating off the line and a deep no-go zone of brambles, sycamore saplings, buddleia, weeds, foxes, abandoned pieces of machinery, pizza boxes, Tesco carrier bags. Along it a narrow pathway allowed a shortcut to the station. 'Poo alley, over there,' Francesca had said, holding her long nose between two index fingers as if she was pinching her nostrils with a nutcracker (and he had tried not to laugh at her). 'All the dogs in the world must come and take their shits. You *know* they do.'

On this path on the way to meet the estate agent, the toe of Alan's shoe had stumbled into the corpse of a rat. An out-stretched body, not yet stiffening, complete, no blood, suffering internal injuries beneath the bloated fur. The sight momentarily sickened him. So yes, she was right, there were rats, and yes, if you stood on the station platform you could indeed just about see the windows of the house, though it was ridiculous to think you could snoop inside, for it had venetian blinds. He had stopped a woman with a buggy walking up the path to her house and asked her if the trains bothered her and she replied that 'Oh, with double glazing you heard almost nothing and what you do, you get used to.' He knew she must be right. He wanted to get on the property ladder. He was nearly thirty-five, he should have started all that years ago. His father would ring him and say, 'Still renting? That mug's game. But all for art, eh, lad?'

'Don't be ridiculous,' he told her now. 'There are no rats. You're imagining it. We'd have heard if there were.'

'I bet I'm right, I just bet I am,' she said, her face dismissive. 'Rats are everywhere.'

He said nothing. He must take her mind off rats.

They had stopped off for a drink at the pub that might become their local after the viewings, and now they were both hungry. Francesca made pasta. When she cooked she tied a scarf round her heavy dark hair, her hands were greasy with olive oil and salty with capers. She licked her fingers. This gesture ignited an erotic flare-up in her husband. *Venus among the pans*, he thought. It was ridiculous how easily she could arouse him.

She washed her hands and undid the scarf. Her hair fell back to her shoulders. She brought the plates to the table.

'This is very good,' he said, sauce around his mouth.

'I've made it before, don't you remember? Almonds and anchovies are in it.'

'That's right.'

His body was a stick, she was feeding him up, giving him bulk. He was too skinny, she said. Three years into their marriage he had developed a small pot belly. His jeans had started to feel uncomfortable, though he refused to shop for a larger size, being a thirty waist, just as his eyes were blue and he was in his origins a Belfast boy and would never lose the accent.

A motorbike passed the open window. He said something she didn't catch about the girl on the train.

'Go on, tell me about it again,' she said. 'I wasn't really paying attention.'

Now she was interested, now she felt sorry for the poor cow and her bullying companion.

'I wonder where she went. I wonder where she is now. Probably gone home. I bet she didn't end up at that party.'

'Which was almost certainly going to be shite.'

'They so often are. I'm glad we're not at a party.'

The day had been, she felt, a dead loss, but now, eating pasta together at the dining table, all the windows wide open letting in the sweet evening air, something at least had been redeemed.

'Any pudding?' he said hopefully, for he had a sweet tooth and kept chocolate bars in his office desk.

'I think there's some ice cream.'

'I'm happy with that.'

Yes, they were happy. And they went to bed, not late, and fell easily asleep.

After midnight they were woken by the sound of fireworks. 'What fresh hell is this?' Francesca said. 'What are they doing letting those things off, this time of year?'

'I don't know, maybe it's somebody's birthday.'

He got up and pulled back the curtains. 'Come and look,' he said, 'they're quite magnificent.'

Together they saw St Paul's turn crimson then fade, revive. London inflamed and hectic was pricked out along the water-front: Shard, Gherkin, Oxo Tower, a panorama part-obscured by the towering arms of crimson cranes, crawling prehistoric creatures of the twenty-first-century riverbank. A new block of flats was going up, it ascended in front of the Shard's base. By autumn their flat would have lost the view. In the foreground the thousand streets, the low brick terraces, beneath them old farms and market gardens, remains of cottages, bridle paths, drovers' roads, manor houses, wolf tracks in the snow. It was impossible, Alan thought, to tell London's story; it was too large, too ancient, too many layers obscured it, its stories were too contradictory, that the poor lived, in the journalistic phrase, cheek by jowl with the wealthy was a shallow simpli-fication – the place simply defied narration. Once, they had had dinner with friends at an Indian restaurant in Peckham, and like a reversed image in a mirror, saw young couples just

27

like themselves, exactly like, young millennials whose brains mapped the city upside-down.

The fireworks should have felt like a glorious finale to the lovely evening, instead they had spoiled everything.

'We'll never afford a view like this, will we?' Francesca said. 'Not unless we win the lottery and you don't even buy lottery tickets and I never get around to it even when I mean to.'

'I'm not superstitious about numbers, I wouldn't know what to pick.'

'So where does that leave us? What *is* there for us?'

She had been expensively educated at a private girls' school in Highgate, had studied art history at St Andrews and met people who had grown up in actual castles with ancestor paintings on the walls. Was invited for the weekend and hadn't anything like the right wardrobe, the right walking boots or rainproof jacket and had stayed in the library by the fire and read (hogging the heat, apparently – was not invited again). And now she was expected to live along a rotten railway line with rats and shaking rails and noisy neighbours behind not one but two party walls. And yet the opinion of the castle-owning family to whom she had already disgraced herself was not the real source of her objection, though the postcode continued to rankle. There were deeper reasons. Alan knew what they were, he ought to try to understand what it felt like to be the child of an immigrant family whose only purpose was to do better than the previous generation, as her father with the detached house in Hampstead Garden Suburb had vastly improved on his own parents' rented flat in Hammersmith. But how possible was that these days?

'That house,' Alan said, '*that's* for us.'

Now she spoke to him even more sharply. 'Oh, for fuck's sake, you're not still going on about it, are you? I said no and I meant it.'

'Come on, babe, it's not like we'd have to live there for ever; when we have kids we'll have to get a bigger place anyway.'

'So not that house, there must be other houses.'

'Not ones we can afford.'

And he began, calmly and in point form – one, the price; two, the location near the station; three, the proportions of the rooms – to enumerate its virtues, until he had achieved fourteen, with his leg pressing ever closer and more intimately to her cushiony thigh. But there was a separation between them, she wasn't responding as she usually did, sensing he wasn't quite there, and nor was she, deep in her own anxieties about her place on the map of London, that shifting series of postcodes and their meanings.

He was remembering the girl on the train, a twanging thought as he calmly countered his wife's position about the rats and the noise.

Was the party shite after all? And did the girl even get off the train or had the doors closed without her and had she hurtled on past to home, or another station and another life? How was he to know? This atomised London – they were all chained together, part of its vast invincibility.

3

But it had been a grand day in the park, such a grand day with all the bands playing, and she had eaten two hamburgers in the end and a bite of his because the first was so good but wouldn't another one be even better and she did not care if he said she was a fat pig as he always did as soon as food appeared any-where near her mouth, and even if he took mincey little bites of everything and went to the gym and his body was a temple she had that metabolism that burns up calories fast. They had a bottle of wine between them and she'd drunk as much as she liked and, oh God, she had danced, everyone said she was an amazing dancer and had a sense of rhythm like no other, she'd danced in the park last year to the Arctic Monkeys and someone had spotted her and filmed her on their phone and she was on YouTube now with hundreds of comments, some of which were cheering her on and telling her she had such spirit while the rest were the usual shite.

Would he spoil the day? It was only half nine, was she sup-posed to go home now and cry with her bedroom door locked like some snowflake, couldn't take a knock, a ruined Saturday night, for even if the party had turned out to be shite they would have gone to Dee's place? She had her sister over who had just come back from holiday in Greece with a bottle of ouzo, that fire in your throat, and they would find a way all right to make a night of it.

No way was she going to Dee's because *he'd* turn up, looking for her, pretending he'd said nothing or she'd misheard or wasn't it only the truth? Better to stay on this fucking train and see where it got to now it was past the stop they were meant to get off for that party, which didn't sound too good anyway, just some random geezer from his work who was inviting everyone, all the neighbours and then some. And they'd not know a soul and have to make conversation, talk crap about nothing such as the music you liked and then when that ran out maybe you'd start dancing and someone would recognise you from YouTube – it had happened before. Was there supposed to be a garden? He hadn't even known that, when it was a sweltering night and if they were kept indoors you might as well be at home where at least there was the roof terrace with all the summer flowers out, the pansies and geraniums and whatnot, the decking littered with butts and bottle caps from, now you think of it, going back last year. Dee had a garden, just a strip of weedy grass out the back with enough room for a little barbecue, a patio table and a few chairs, but there was no going to Dee's now.

On the platform, his mouth open like such a gobshite as the doors slid shut, and the train moved off with her on it. She laughed and the shock went away for a minute like a black cat passing by in the night as her gran used to say of things gone and lost. He was standing there, saying something, then shrugging. Her phone rang the next minute, it was him, but she turned it off. That'd teach him. Not there at his beck and call like she usually was, being taken for granted – oh Chrissie, can you drop in at the offy and pick up a nice bottle of wine, you know the one we had last week, with the floral notes? Floral notes, my arse, he'd been on a weekend wine appreciation course at some country house hotel and came out with this bollocks.

What was she to do now? And where is she going on a July night, when there's still some light in the sky? Time enough, time enough later to think whether it was seven or eight blow jobs at parties, to count them up in her head, to try to remember back to the very first which was when she came to London and only knew her cousin Paula, sleeping on her couch till she got a flat-share, so you went out of your way to make yourself what Daddy called agreeable, though obviously he didn't mean it like that and would kill her, flay her hide if he knew, now wouldn't he just?

Here goes the train, Finsbury Park, Drayton Park, Highbury and Islington, Essex Road, Old Street, Moorgate. When they had got on at Ally Pally it was all in the open air, a commuter choo-choo come down from Hertfordshire, a little toy-town thing, and now it takes the plunge and goes underground, down into the dark tunnels and doesn't come up again for air even when it reaches its destination. Dark when she comes out, the days no longer at their zenith but plenty of summer ahead. Out on the street, no idea where she is, never been to this bit of London before, only knew the retail parts, Oxford Street and the two Westfields, and where she worked at the hospital, which was all traffic and furniture stores and the big railway stations.

God, it was quiet here all right in the evening, nobody about hardly because they worked in their glass banks during the day and went somewhere else at the weekend. She had no idea where she was going, just walking for the sake of it and trying not to think about that thing he said, his nastiness, how quiet his voice so she had to strain to hear him, give him her full attention. That was a mean trick he was always pulling. She knew why he said it, it was obvious now, to *smash* her because she'd laughed at him yesterday when she came in on him in the bathroom soaping his willy (so he should have locked the door!) and she'd crooked her little finger before she knew it, it was just one of those things you did, didn't mean nothing by it, but she'd never seen him before without his clothes on and he certainly didn't want to take a peek at her. She thought he must be gay at first, but it wasn't that, he just didn't fancy her. Which was all to the good when you're sharing a flat but still, it's nice to be appreciated even a bit. He'd taken offence at her finger; why did she have to make a nasty crack like that, implying his was a tiny little thing? But she'd done it without thinking, it was just a joke they had at home when they were trying to bring a boy they knew back down to size when he got too fond of the sound of his own voice, let some air out of his tyres. She shouldn't have done it, maybe. She'd learned her lesson, keep that one for your girlfriends.

All around her these white walls: cliffs of shut-up buildings with no lights on, nobody home at all. Not many women on their own walking, like her, just that one right ahead in that top she'd seen at M&S last week and tried on but it was a bit pricey and anyway, let's face it, they'd run out of her size and the next one down was straining under the arms. Lost sight of her when she turned down past the church, wandering in circles, then the black cloud coming down, that thing he said, like a little animal, a rat inside her stomach. The shame of it, she'd never look at another fella again, or not in that way, be a demure creature like the nuns, but no, why should she? Wasn't she a young woman in the prime of her life, only twenty-four and in London which is the capital of the world really? Where everyone comes and everyone is here, you meet all sorts, people from countries she'd never heard of – Central African Republic, where the fuck is that? It's not a real name, is it? And now the poor refugees from Syria, the little kid drowned, washed up on the beach, she'd signed that petition.

Is there some lack of self-respect in her – what do you call it, low self-esteem? But she has the highest regard for herself in the world or she wouldn't laugh off those comments on YouTube, they were just cunts saying cunty things like cunts always do, she'd seen that all over Twitter, which is why she took it up for a week then deleted her account and no going back to that stupid place. At work you saw terrible tragedies that would break their hearts if they had them, babies with wires sticking out of them and tubes in their noses and old men who no one came to visit in their beds even when you'd rung their nearest and dearest and said it won't be more than a day now. Why be a cunt? If those people on Twitter had seen what she'd seen, they'd be so shocked it would wipe the malicious smirks off their faces, though she'd heard they were just lonely fat men prescribed too many pills for depression, or a spotty kid under the thumb of some bully at school and taking it out on someone who couldn't touch him. She had *wonderful* self-esteem, everyone said she was a ray of sunshine in the wards, cheerfulness itself. And her attitude to the human body was matter-of-fact, no mysteries, so why can't she just *enjoy* giving blow jobs, the thing in her mouth? Not everyone does; Cally said, 'Oh no, no, always the fucking hand on the back of your head.' No accounting for taste.

When she didn't turn up at the party after being expected, he'd have told them with his innocent good-looking baby face that he bought all those scrubs and creams for – how was I to know she'd get so upset about a joke? Just a bit of banter between friends, flatmates, I thought she'd laugh it off, I had no idea she was in any way sensitive; who would, to look at her? She can lift an Alsatian dog, you know, I saw her do it. Poor doggy, are you hurt? Took the thing up in the air in her arms, must have weighed a ton.

He never saw her pick up her patients, now did he, lift them on to the trolley or to the commode or turnover for a bed-bath. She was big because the work needed her to be. And all his girlfriends were built like birds, fragile creatures with not much make-up because he said he preferred the natural look, and was not able to see how it was you got that in front of the mirror with five different brushes and powders and creams not to mention Botox. Men can be so stupid.

The river was close. She could see it between the buildings. What was that bridge now? London Bridge, which isn't the one you think it is, that's Tower Bridge, the famous one from the films. The big wheel alight, probably still revolving though it goes so slow you can't see it move, and over there the Shard, Mordor from the *Hobbit* films with elves and hobbits coming up on it to expel the evil spirits.

The river lovely in the moonlight, but making her feel bleak as hell. Couples are walking across it hand in hand, and she was all alone. The water dark, with a gold necklace of lights shining on the surface, it might be warm on this July night, a temptation for the reckless to swim. The wine curdled in her stomach. Oh, she was a fool, she'd ruined everything with that finger and now he would tell everyone, word would get around, she'd have to slink back home, he might as well have kicked her in the stomach when she was pregnant, not with a kid but with her *own life*, here in London, the place she came to *live*, like you always heard. They were supposed to be friends as well as flatmates but she was nothing to him, was she? He despised her and maybe she really was despicable, just a slut, a piece of shit. Look at your toenails, aren't they a disgrace now, the polish all chipped and the nails too long anyway, you could see the growth from the cuticle, they were disgusting, a slut's toenails. How long since that pedicure she'd treated herself to, months, and the red was half-flaking away; she should have had gels like they said, last longer.

A police boat was rushing now. What do they do those patrols, look for smugglers or something? The river was older than everything, older than the city, a crack in the landscape. Before there were boats people spent their whole lives on one side or the other, that's what her father had told her once. Imagine not knowing what was a hop, skip and a jump away – cottages and churches and you'd never see inside them or meet your neighbours over the water. The Thames was nothing like the Liffey. This here was a river that meant business, on it went being half poetry, half bluster and oily and dank. She rummaged in her bag for her phone but it had fallen out long ago, somewhere near Moorgate.

4

Now it is late October. That summer evening might never have happened; long days belong to memory, perhaps they're even imaginary. London has resorted to its natural condition of leafless trees and puddled wet pavements. In the cellar room of a pub on Fleet Street, fires in the hearths, real fires, burning real coal, barmen in burgundy jackets and the burgundy house tie, and alone at his table was not the solid bloke Alan expected, in coppers' off-duty uniform of North Face jacket and Timberland boots, but someone who reminded him of a sepia tin-type photo from the American Wild West. DS Pete Dutton, with goatee beard, tweed cap and chestnut-coloured Doc Martens, quite a dandy, with a face like a mince pie, round and freckled, a bit pushed-in around the eyes, as if he'd recently had bad news and was still struggling.

The two men eyed each other up. Pete was there because he had an agenda. He wanted to implant in the filmmaker an interest in a case he was no longer involved in, having officially retired from the police force last month. The case of a drowned woman who no one seemed to know or recognise. He had reached a dead end in all his inquiries before he left; no one would have the same passionate curiosity. Alan was his last hope, who had contacted him about a film he wanted to make about missing persons; he had found him through a Facebook forum for retired officers. Going through the Met press office was a weary and bureaucratic endeavour, he'd have to consult them eventually. At the moment he was looking for an off-the-record background chat before making formal requests.

At home, Marie was having one of her good days; in fact, she'd had three in a row. Pete would have cancelled the meeting if she hadn't been feeling well. He had warned Alan about this, it could be very last minute that he wouldn't be able to turn up, but she hadn't minded him coming. She would lie on the sofa and read her magazine, that would be fine. She said that after all the tumult of the diagnosis, the second opinion, the start of the treatment, an afternoon's peace and quiet was just what she needed. She would catch up with her soaps and her celebrity gossip, which was all her exhausted mind could handle and he wasn't to judge her for it. He had brought the Teasmade from by the bed down to the lounge and put it on the coffee table. 'You just have to reach out,' he said. 'Oh, do stop fussing,' she said, 'I know how to make a cup of tea with the bloody thing. Now go away and leave me in peace.' Which was not fair or kind, but the kind of thing you took like a man, if you were one. He was glad to get out of the house, if he was honest. And they both knew that. She was happy to get rid of him.

'Interesting place you've chosen,' Alan said.

Everything about him was concave, Pete thought, his chest, his face, with just a beak of nose like a rugged outcrop of rock.

'I know, a lot of history.'

Pete might drone on about the famous men who had drunk there long ago; he'd gone on a walking tour of the historic pubs of Fleet Street and could remember a fair bit about what he'd learned, but the young guy wouldn't want to hear about any of that, they never do. Alan was fiddling with his phone.

'Mind if I record this? It's just easier than frantically scribbling notes.'

'No problem. Is that what you're using, no tape recorder?'

'This is fine.'

'Brilliant what you can do with them now when only a few years ago, and I'm old enough to remember, you just used it to talk.'

A few formalities, and the phone was propped up next to him. It was the latest iPhone; Pete had an Android which felt slightly inferior, these media types were always one-upping you.

'Okay, so let's get started, how can I help?'

'I know it's not the first time by any means that someone has addressed the subject, there have been other documentaries about missing persons but there's new interest because of strangers on social media getting involved where it just used to be posters. Now there's Twitter and Facebook alerts to spread the word.'

'Fair enough.' The thoughts rattled through Pete's head as if he was typing them. It was just like a briefing session, he knew this stuff backwards; he had spent four years dealing with those randoms, as the younger guys called them. A lot of officers would groan when a missper came over the radio, it was a donkey job. Old sweats like him were supposed to find it beneath them, and it generated a lot of paperwork. He had been shunted over to misspers when he turned fifty.

'Well, the internet has definitely changed a great deal for us, though you'd be surprised how plain old policing still plays its part. Misspers cases are pretty standard and the methods we use to deal with them are too; it's just a matter of how you prioritise. Obviously if a kid goes missing it's sirens and squad cars from the word go. The one you were asking about in your email, the young lady – I can't discuss it in detail, you'll understand that – but consider, if you like, a couple of flatmates out together on a Saturday night, on their way to a party. They have a barney, he gets off the train when they reach their destination, she doesn't, she stays on, even though the train is taking her out of her way, into the City on a Saturday night when everything's shut up. He rings her, no answer. He goes to the party expecting she'll be there, or she'll ring him, or she'll be at home when he gets back. Next morning she's not in her room, no sign of her, phone's still off. He assumes she's at her mate's but he hasn't got the number because they're just flat-sharers and don't have pals in common, they weren't friends to start with, just answered an ad off the internet for a room. So, it's not till the Monday night when she still hasn't come home and he rings her work, the hospital – she was a nurse, you see – and finds out she didn't turn up there either and her phone's still going straight to messages that he thinks maybe he should call the police because you never know, she might have done something stupid after that row they had, though he doesn't think she's the type and more likely something has happened to her, against her will.

'So, we put out a Twitter alert. Now these are people who are social media savvy and all their friends and friends of friends are on social media and they're all retweeting like crazy because they don't know about the row, think she's been abducted by a bad man, imaginations running wild. That's where you saw it, you say?'

'Yes, but you see I recognised her. I saw her on the train, I actually overheard the argument.'

'Oh, I see. And did you ring us? Offer to help with our inquiries?'

'No. Because by the time I caught up with it she'd already been found.'

'Quite right. Once she'd turned up the investigation was at

an end. No harm had come to her, that's all I'm prepared to say, it's their business. It's just one example of a very, very typical scenario. These cases arouse people's curiosity, and then they feel dissatisfied because they never do find out the whole story. And yet the story is always much the same, to be honest, the same old patterns over and over again, there's not a lot in that line of policing that ever surprises you. Almost always they turn up, that's the true answer. Where were they? The relatives don't want to say and the person you were looking for, the one you've been hunting, tells you, "I just had a moment and you don't need to know any more; it's all sorted now, we're all happy." So you'd say, "Look, *are* you happy? Are you trying to get away from him? If there's any concerns you can come and speak to me, don't do anything silly." And they'll say, "Nah, everything's all right." So that's the end of it. And that's what happened with the girl on the train. She turned up. We asked a few questions. The end. Because he wasn't her boyfriend, she wasn't frightened of him, she said they'd had a row and she was moving out and he didn't seem all that fussed about it either. They'd just come to the end of the road, no bother.'

'Don't you feel frustrated that all these people are wasting police time?'

'Frustrated, yes. But to be honest, it's the runaways from children's homes that are the meat and potatoes of our work, they're the ones that sap so much time. They're still vulnerable, I get that, but when you've dealt with them ten times and they always come back you're not going to spend hours and hours of precious resources on them. I'll say, "If he's not back by noon, yeah, we'll start." But then that can turn out to be wrong too because now there's the issue of gangs and grooming.'

'How depressing.'

Pete sucked at his pint, the beer was in the hairs of his moustache. Marie said, 'Don't lick your upper lip like that, it's gross.'

But what did she know about gross who had never seen a dead person pulled from the river after three weeks submerged?

The time had come. And here *she* came, up from the deep into a tourist pub in Fleet Street. His lady. He inserted her into a comfortable pause.

'Have you ever thought,' Pete said, 'about people who are found, but aren't missing, if you see what I'm saying? I mean the unidentified.'

'No, I hadn't. Do you get a lot of that?'

Now he marched across even terrain, for it was all on the internet if you knew where to look.

'Oh yes, there are unidentified bodies all over the place, washed up on the coast mainly, in a state of decomposition. Sailors from foreign lands, people who threw themselves off a cliff or into the sea. There are probably hundreds of unclaimed bodies; we keep their cases open because you never know, a long-lost brother could still turn up out of the blue. That's why we don't cremate them, incidentally. One of the saddest goes back to the late eighties, we found nothing more than a right foot inside a sock and a shoe and then a bit later we found the matching foot and sock and shoe, that's all, size four. A lady. All that was left of her. She could have been any age, we just don't know. This was in Lancashire, thirty years ago. And that case is still open. What do you think of that?'

The idea of not being missed startled Alan. His life was thick with relationships of many kinds, not just his wife and friends but his mother who used to expect a phone call every weekend and now demanded Skype, and his father wanting a response to his cantankerous emails asking what he thought of this or that gobshite on the national political stage, a contempt for politicians choked and swallowed through thirty-five years of broadcasting on Radio Ulster, burning bile causing debilitating bouts of acid reflux. Francesca sending him pictures five, six, seven times a day of a sofa she'd seen or a paint colour, or a mirror for the far wall and did he think they should buy a new mattress? His in-laws also had his number, sometimes they texted him because they had not heard from Francesca for a day and a half.

'Well, that is the very opposite of my life,' he said. 'Tell me more.'

'Oh mine too, without a doubt. And yet it happens, it happens. We had a case this year, the odd thing is, it was the very same night as the nurse you're interested in, and she had been on that bridge at much the same time but seen nothing. We'd hoped we might have had a witness but she was too full of her own preoccupations. Pity. Because we've spent months investigating and come up with sweet Fanny Adam. You've got a person who is self-evidently missing but no one appears to have missed her. The description goes out in the police gazette, nationwide, has anyone checked their data base for a female of this age? You look at the body, the face, and you're thinking, *Who are you?* And the answer comes back, *No idea.* It can drive you mad. They're not on Facebook, they're just a blank. They've got no ties to anything, no financials on them, they've never been in trouble with the police and then they go and jump in the river. This woman jumped. The river police saw her body caught up in the chains of HMS *Belfast* last summer and the diver went in and brought her out and she was cleaned up and we put out our appeals and yet we're no closer. She was well dressed, too, all M&S labels, a well-nourished woman in her early forties, no rough sleeper, and that's all we've got. Pathetic.'

Alan started. His heart jumped. A story, fully-formed, was irresistible. One had an instinct for these things.

'But what's just as pathetic, worse maybe, is the number of calls that came in from people who thought she might be the one they were looking for even though the description didn't match but I suppose they think, *Maybe she's changed.* They're thinking,

She was about that age when I last saw her, and they don't realise how long ago it was. I heard some terribly sad cases, schoolgirls who'd done a runner twenty years back, Mum still puts a dinner plate out for her with the evening meal. Someone's missus who'd scarpered and never come back, clothes all still in the wardrobe. A long-lost sister and even a long-lost mum. They've seen the posters and the tweets and all that social media stuff and even though the description doesn't match at all, they're still hopeful it *might* have been the one they're looking for even when there's no match at all. But we do live in hope, don't we? It's just human nature, and where would we be without it?'

'The same night? What a coincidence.'

'Is it a coincidence? I don't know. How many people were on that bridge that evening, and how many were feeling low and looking down and thinking, *This is it for me?* Though the nurse certainly wasn't. She was no suicide. It's just a glitch that they both came to public attention at the same time, but that's London for you.'

'I see. And do you think you will identify her in the end?'

'Yes. Of course I do. I mean, I've got to. I firmly believe that sooner or later something is going to come to light, someone is holding back, they'll come forward eventually for how can a woman of all people be so detached from human society? Women gossip with their mates, their families, for heaven's sake, they're naturally sociable, don't you think?'

'I suppose so. My wife certainly is. So what's your guess about what's happened here?'

'The usual assumption is maybe she's had a falling-out with her relatives, or she's had mental health problems and become a recluse. And still I ask myself – because I've got a wife at home and daughters not long left – what recluse dresses in this season's clothes, all from M&S, everything up to the minute? Women *care* what they put on. I don't know about you but I've never met one who didn't so it has to be ... it has to be ... I don't know. All I can say is that someone is staying silent, someone who's seen the posters, and the TV appeals. Suppose she told a friend what she planned to do and they hadn't been able to talk her out of it, in fact agreed to respect her decision and stay quiet? Or she could have been brought up in a children's home like so many runaways, as I said, those poor kids are hardened to running away, cutting their losses. Their sense of identity is never that strong to begin with. That could be her grown up now. That's my best suggestion for the time being, unless we come up with anything else.'

They talked for a few minutes about confidentiality, all of this being off the record and just for background. The conversation began to get a little ragged and inconsequential. It seemed rude to Alan to be the first to leave but he did.

Pete stayed behind and bought another pint. How had it gone? It had gone okay; he thought he had sounded more or less professional. He had imparted information, had mostly managed to mind his language. He wasn't interested in the nurse. She seemed a bit of a slag, already shacked up elsewhere two days after the call had gone out. DB27 was where it was at. The consequence might be that McBride would make a show about her and someone would finally come forward and then she'd be his girl no more. Which when all's said and done was a good thing. Marie deserved not to have to share him, even if she'd not a clue that she was sharing. She was at home now, probably fallen asleep on the sofa with a cup of tea growing cold and her magazines around her on the floor, looking a bit crazy with her mouth slightly open, and that scar in her chest from the lump he had found.

And why was it him who had to find it? Why couldn't she have found it herself in the shower or something? Why did he have to jump with horror like he'd touched something disgusting, lifted a cushion and found a dog turd, and say, 'What the hell is *that*, Marie?' And she said, 'What the hell's what? What are you talking about, Pete?' And he had to guide her own hand to her own breast and say, 'Can you feel it?' Her face just dying in front of him, even with the lights off he could see well enough that she touched her own death down there in the soft tissue. And it was Friday night. So nothing to be done. And the long weekend to wait, worst two days of his whole life, moping around the house trying not to think about it, watching crap telly. Marie just sitting in an armchair staring into the distance and a weak smile saying no, she was fine, nothing a cup of tea wouldn't sort. He took her himself in the car to the doctor's first thing Monday morning and waited by the door till the receptionist unlocked it and pushed her through to the counter with his hand on her shoulder.

'We've found a lump, I want her seen right away.'

He had smashed a window once, climbed through it and had to step over the dead body of a mother stabbed five times in the chest, to pick up her nine-year-old kid and pass her out to waiting women PCs, the girl rigid in his arms, like a wooden doll, too traumatised to speak, her father raving on the pavement delirious with hallucinations. Saw a young lady's lungs being removed at an autopsy after a drug overdose. Fought a murderer and multiple rapist armed with an eight-inch carving knife. The worst case was one he'd only heard about back at the station, not himself involved, but still it gave him nightmares, a young mother cut off from her family who had a heart attack and dropped down dead and her four-year-old, unable to get out of the locked flat, had starved to death. They found him two weeks later with his arms round the decomposing body of his mum.

That's what policing is, he would say, it isn't all clues and puzzles like you read in books or see on the telly. Policing is dealing with the dregs, it is dealing with damaged people and broken lives. He was tough, he could even take on a wife with breast cancer, nurse her round the clock. But you cannot help your mind turning to other things; it's not possible, is it? The thing about this unknown and possibly unloved woman was that it was *wrong*. She didn't look like she should be a police number. She looked like a bird you could fancy, or your wife's best mate. She seemed to him to be a person he could very easily know, yet nobody knew her and that was off somehow. It didn't add up. Compared with the dead kid hugging his decaying mum, this was nothing, but it was something to him. He wanted to do right by her. He wanted her to be restored to her loved ones, for he did not believe for one moment that she was unloved.

5

Way back in the summer when she lived a different life from the one she's living now, and still it pops up randomly on Twitter and the whole thing starts all over again, because people don't check, do they? They don't clock the date or scroll down to see if she was ever found, so there she is, missing all over again, and the whole thing resumes its momentum because His Arseness put up that YouTube video of her dancing to the Arctic Monkeys with the original tweet and then the police tagged it. So as well as everything else, the video has had a load more views and a load more thumbs-up and thumbs-down, some nice comments (hope-you're-found-lovely-lady) and the cunty ones saying the usual shite. A few are even spelled properly so not just by morons with an IQ in two digits.

That had been a crazy few days in her life, hard now to remember how she felt. You're always afraid that if you didn't have your mum, your dad, your big sisters, your mates, your work, your flatmate saying now you do this, now it's time to . . . you'd fold up. That's what life is, just a load of obligations to other people and trying to find the good times in them apart from all the boring shite you have to put up with. And hoping you'll find love, which is something you see in films, it's always happening at the movies, and to your friends too, they talk about it, love being something different from a crush. Though hard to nail down how because she hadn't felt it herself yet and no wish to, once that happens you're saving for a ten-thousand-pound wedding and buying *Brides* magazine and arguing with your mum about the guest list for there's always some old auntie from Leitrim you have to invite and that means you can't ask the girl at work you've been boring for months about the kind of canapés you want. This was what happened to her sister and she'd cried during the speeches, the wrong kind of tears, not happy laughing ones.

What you *really* want is to be dancing to the Monkeys in the park but with no one filming you, no one even looking at you, just doing your thing in your own sweet way, but people are always looking and holding their phones up and you're being seen. And they upload to Instagram and tag you and that's it, you're public property.

At first she was just walking aimlessly, but then she was on the bridge where she'd realised she'd lost her phone and that feeling of terror and almost dissolution at first, like a soluble aspirin in a glass of water, until she'd thought, *No you're okay, you've got money, you've got your keys; what do you need a fucking phone for anyway? It's not like you feel like talking to anyone.* So that was good, that was the beginning. And she was feeling so generally up for it, up for anything, that she walked off the bridge and instead of going back down to the trains she kept on and eventually she got to Shoreditch where everything was happening this time of night. She'd been here before, of course, but only during the day to the market and to look at clothes at AllSaints. There was some big church with flaming torches burning outside and people standing out on the steps smoking and inside there was a party which she'd crashed and nobody minded because the free drinks were over, it was a pay bar now. And everyone was pissed and she'd talked to some guy for a bit, usual bantz, he bought her a vodka martini and she drank it and then she'd had enough because she didn't trust herself not to add to the number. (*Was it eight or was it nine?*) Didn't have to wait for anyone or get permission or say goodbye to the host, no idea who it was anyway. This is freedom.

No phone. Didn't know what time it was, who wore a watch any more? She got one for her twenty-first from her grandpa and never put it on once, it was an old-lady little thing, gold with a dial you could hardly see. Then there was a homeless man she came across who was taking a big shit in a shop doorway, a mad old fella not right in the head who pulled up his pants and then walked away as if he had nothing to do with it but she saw the shame on his face. Where do the homeless go to do their shits? She'd never thought of it before and it made her sad to think how embarrassed they'd be, bowels boiling, and trying to go into a McDonald's or Starbucks and being chased away. Because there used to be what they called public conveniences in the olden days, her dad said, but you never saw them any more. To go now you had to have the price of a latte or some French fries, which wasn't cheap when you come to think about it.

Outside she saw a girl with a gashed eye, went straight over and told her to get herself to A&E because that needed looking after, don't leave it till the morning, and the girl said, 'What do you know, are you a fucking nurse?' and she said, 'Yes, right, I am. Go to UCH, say Chrissie sent you, maybe you'll get seen a bit quicker.' And the girl said, 'Oh, okay,' and headed off in the wrong direction but what can you do?

Eventually, the night bus home, no idea what the hour, could have been one or two. She always loved the night bus in London, it felt like family. She took it from the hospital, all the sleepy workers and the party revellers, the drunks, the homeless, the people you saw again and again, and they told you their story. That trans girl she'd never have thought used to be a fella, hadn't even heard of such a thing till she came to London and she was a dainty little miss with fine delicate bones, lovely wrists, so wouldn't have worked as a guy anyway. People sad, people drunk, people asleep, but plenty who thought coming home was another chapter in the day. Old people think of morning afternoon evening and night, which is when you go to bed but in the real world there's many parts to the night and only a bit is sleeping. On the wards people died, most often four in the morning, that's when the heart gives up at last, when there's no hope of dawn ever coming. She's sat by them and watched them leave and gone to tell someone who'd make the call to the family. Then you'd hear a bird cheeping out in the half-dark and you know morning is on its way and they'd missed it for ever now and you were still here with everything in front of you.

Yusuf reading his French newspaper. Little cap on his head, made him seem a bit gay, then that melting milk chocolate smile when he looked up, lovely jeans he had on, Edwins, not cheap, all to do with a Japanese selvedge or something. Got them from the factory outlet in Hackney, saved up.

They started to chat, he was a sous chef in a big grand restaurant in the West End where the rich ate stuff you wouldn't want to put in your mouth, bits of pigs you didn't even want to think about, bleugh, and plankton! How was that a thing to eat, something you did in biology lessons? The one thing they didn't want was steak and chips, he said, and she was amazed to hear it wasn't even on the menu. Do you spit in the soup? Dip your dick in it? she asked him, because everyone knew that was a thing in restaurants and her uncle wouldn't set foot in one for that very reason, but he looked shocked, said he couldn't do that to the food.

So she missed her stop, yakking all the way, and it was Wood

Green now and he said he was getting off and one way or the other she went back to his for the night. That's what happens on the night bus, or it could.

Everyone had gone to bed, there were four of them sharing, two of them were Romanians and one was from Brazil. It was a good flat. They even had a garden; he took her out there in the dark, among the bushes and flowers under the moon and it was even more humid now, she was dripping, nearly two in the morning, not a breeze in the air. They sat on the garden seat and nattered away until she thought, *Should I do him? Does he expect me to? Am I to go down on my knees again?* The hand on the back of the head is coming, isn't it, it always does. But no, the hand went to her face, cupping it like in some silly film, and he kissed her. He smelled of sweat and maybe tomatoes or they were growing in a pot somewhere near and she was picking it up that way.

Bed. A very tidy room. All shipshape. He went down on her with his tongue. She'd come like a jet taking off from a hot runway and woke everyone up, the shame of it, but he thought it was cool, so it was. It was a grand night.

The next day he had to work but said to her don't go, which wasn't what she expected at all. And what was she going home for? Marco wouldn't notice she was gone, would he? He didn't give a shit about her. She went to the big Marks & Spencer on Oxford Street for new clothes because the ones she had on were starting to smell and found that top she'd tried on, the one she'd seen the woman at Moorgate wearing, and they had it back in her size and it fitted like a dream.

And that was Sunday and he had Monday off so she didn't go into work either, or even ring, because when you've got no phone you can't, can you? That was what she told herself, and felt terrible about it a couple of hours later, worried they'd fire her, but who fires nurses for not turning up once in a blue moon? Nurses are gold dust. This was the essence of the situation, of her new freedom, this dissolving act she'd done and finding it grand and Yusuf so lovely and asking her no questions until that evening when he showed her his phone and there she was, missing, but also dancing to the Arctics.

That was the summer, and she'd not gone back to the flat except to get her stuff and moved in with Yusuf and the other boys. Then the days wound down, they got damp and the skies turned into a grey bowl over your head.

This TV guy got hold of her, said he was making a documentary about missing persons and did she want to be part of it and she said, 'Whoa!' He said she was a modern phenomenon, someone who had a life on the internet different to who she really was and that seemed to her true. He said he wanted to tell the story of that night and what it felt like to find yourself famous and she said, 'Only for about fifteen minutes, though, it's not like I ever did anything like be a model or someone on the telly.'

When she thinks about it, she's lost and gained something. The internet has deprived her of her right to privacy, to be anonymous and like her dad said to her that's a precious thing to lose, but on the other hand, she's also never going to be forgotten, is she? People die and all that's left of them is some bones in a box but she exists now independent of herself, which is quite a thought.

And why not do it? She could speak for herself at last, except not of course to say why she'd run off from Marco, she'd have to make something up about that and make sure he had nothing to do with the thing, with his big mouth.

6

A rooftop bar in Dalston, mid November. Up in the sky police helicopters grinding through the wet clouds. In the distance the city blurred and blotchy in the rain, a vaporous haze enfolding London.

Online, Marco was merely an abbreviation or a punctuation mark. He was like everyone on screens, an avatar, and he'd chosen a man with a shoe balanced on his head. What did it mean? What was the code? Was it a symbol, an in-joke, a cultural reference Alan didn't get, an ad or logo? Or something personal? Which could mean that there could plausibly be more to Marco than a remark on a train, stated in a quiet, even, pleasant voice with a pickaxe in it. A complication he hoped to observe emerging from their conversation.

Marco had already arrived, seated on a banquette beneath striped vermilion awnings like a barber's pole and his hair was slicked by showers. He retained what Alan recognised as his smooth plasticity, his attentive polite smile as he rose to introduce himself, to shake hands, the old formal gesture Alan never used.

Francesca had said of Alan that he could go anywhere because he was so anonymous, he drifted about like smoke. He never had the right clothes but they were wrong in indeterminate, harmless ways, the style of a perpetual detached observer with no skin in the game. He said he had plenty of skin, she said, 'You don't *look* it, that's all I'm saying, but I'm not suggesting it's a bad thing, it helps you get around. You're never incongruous, you fit in everywhere. That's good, isn't it, I mean what you're trying to achieve?' 'You're saying I'm boring?' 'I don't mean that.' But he had a nagging fear that he was a yawn.

Marco wore expensive jeans, rolled at the ankle. His crossed legs revealed no socks. The skin was olive, polished and lightly haired. No one had ever fitted in better to this present environment than Marco. He seemed to Alan now to have been on that hot July train by mistake, all wrong on the train as he was so right here in a rooftop bar in Dalston that it was difficult to imagine the place even opening up without him sitting there, drinking a complicated cocktail which might have been invented ten minutes ago.

'Nothing like Dalston, is there?' Marco said. 'Drug dealers' paradise and twelve-quid cocktails. Ridiculous. We just did the PR for this place, we got editorial in the *Guardian*, did you see it?'

'No I'm afraid not. I'm married, we don't go out much, we just bought a house. We've got a mortgage.'

'Nothing wrong with that, I'm thinking of switching careers myself. It's guys like you who make me think it's time to move into digital.' He smiled his pleasant agreeable smile and seemed for the moment as if he had insufficient grit in him ever to rub anyone up the wrong way.

'Isn't everything digital now?'

'Of course it is, but I was thinking about how you could take the essentially analogue going-out experience – I mean bars and clubs and restaurants – online, so people like you who can't get out much or live off the scene in the provinces could sample it anyway.'

'But how could you do that? You might as well just be watching TV, sofa Glasto.'

'I know what you mean but I was more thinking you could, say, download a customised set list from a top DJ on Spotify and order custom cocktails and canapés which would be couriered to you, maybe a link-in with ASOS for clothing. Invite a few friends round, it would be your own VIP room, or just stay in on your own if you don't have any. There'd be welcome messages from celebs, a whole package experience, personalised for you and your mates.'

'I can sort of see the point of it but it sounds a bit sad.'

For Marco's 'parties' would, he felt, make people even sadder, and they'd go to bed drunk and in tears.

'Does it? Why? I mean it's true that most parties are crap, but that's because the music and the drinks are usually terrible and you're making chit-chat with strangers. Parties don't really work any more because they can't compete with clubs, but clubs are expensive and you can't always get in, they hold you back or turn you away, and fat girls *never* get in, and suburban-looking guys, who wants them? You make a club night for them and their mates so they feel they're cool. It would need to be priced up so it was like an event, maybe something you saved up for.'

'No dance floor, though.'

'True, you'd have to improvise, but maybe you could hire somewhere, a room above a pub or a church hall, something like that, there's always places. Look, everything is virtual reality now, we all live online so why not *actually* live online, does going out matter any more? I mean clubs *are* great, but they're not democratic, they can't be, the essence of their situation is that they're for an elite. And you can't get a table at a top restaurant unless you've got a line to the maître d' through the PR company. Nothing is worth having or experiencing unless there's a wait list of some kind, without that exclusivity you might as well be shopping at Lidl. But that means the majority of people are never going to have access to those experiences and what I'm envisaging allows them to take a leap out of the ordinary to share the big new thing everyone is talking about without the people who the big new thing is *for* seeing it watered down and made so accessible it's meaningless. Do you know what I'm saying?'

And Alan thought, not for the first time, there was a solidity which was vanishing before his own eyes, although he was only thirty-four. Life had become insubstantial. What was real? The house, the neighbourhood, the trains themselves, segmented diesel snakes that rattled the rails and brought people down from York and Durham, staring blankly out of the window or down at their phones. It was worth remembering all that, not allowing it to be squeezed out of your recollection because this corporeal reality, in which a real person could go missing and be missed, or be found and not seem to have existed, was what remained when you had to sit and listen to this shit coming out of Marco's mouth.

'What I really want to know is why does your avatar have a shoe on his head? Is that actually you?'

'Long story, personal.'

'Still interested.'

'I think we're here to talk about Chrissie. So can we do that? I'm sorry, I've wandered off the point before we even got on to it. She went missing and she was found. What else would you like to know?'

'What I'm interested in, the underlying theme, is to do with those who disappear in a city, how you can vanish without trace, be forgotten altogether, or, as in this case, develop a second life online as a result of being searched for.'

'I see. Of course, it's true I played a part in her running away. It was my fault, did she tell you?'

'No, she didn't say anything about that.'

'So she doesn't want the whole story told, fine, that's fine, I mean, whatever. You probably look at me and think that I'm the kind of guy who doesn't have regrets, that they would take me to places I couldn't really handle.'

'Why would I think that? I just met you five minutes ago.'

'I may not have been as kind as I should have been to her. We were just sharing a flat. She irritated me. She was so crass, maybe she's changed, I don't know, I never saw her again after she disappeared, she came back when I was at work to collect her stuff. She'd paid up to the end of the month and I got someone else in quickly enough, it's not hard to find a flatmate. Chrissie is very . . . how can I say? Unpretentious. A little bawdy, I think that's right. Crude, vulgar, but what they call salt of the earth, not a malicious bone in her body, just doesn't really *think*. She'd leave her knickers drying in the bathroom, she always wore thongs, can you imagine, with her big arse hanging out? It was embarrassing, she was someone you wanted to give a good shake or a slap – no, I don't mean I wanted to *hit* her, I'm emphatically not the type to resort to violence in any situation and hitting a woman is beneath contempt. I just wished she'd engage the brain before she opened her mouth. And maybe I caught that from her, maybe I let the mask slip once and said what I really thought. And whatever you might assume, I'm embarrassed now. It wasn't a nice thing to do and I'm sorry, I genuinely am. Sorry and ashamed. The whole business was in all likelihood my fault.'

He wants me to ask him what he said, Alan thought, *and then he'll tell me, the little shit. Just see if I don't thwart him.*

'I don't believe that the exact catalyst is really necessary.' He smiled dismissively. 'I understand you had an argument of some kind, that's all I really need to know.'

'I was just mentioning it for background, that's all. I assumed you'd want to understand what happened.'

'I'll take it on board if I need to, but not at this stage.'

'Okay.' His face turned petulant for a moment, then he returned it quickly to his plastic smile. 'Well, let's just say that I made a remark, not a very nice one, about her behaviour, her . . . social life, if you see what I mean. If it doesn't matter to you, then not another word.'

Marco described the events leading to his contacting the police and how they had handled it, the visit to the flat, the search of the premises, 'as if they thought I might have done her in and was hiding her body, but that's just procedure they said. At first I wasn't really too worried about her because I felt that whatever happened she could always take care of herself, but once two days had gone by and I'd heard nothing, then I really started to panic. That's when I put out an alert on Twitter tagging the video of her dancing, which you would have seen because it went viral. Once Nigella retweeted it, well, obviously it became *huge*. Chrissie, as you know, is a big strong girl but she's completely uncoordinated, she shouldn't dance at all really, not if she doesn't want people laughing at her. After she was found her sister rang me from Dublin and she was livid about that, why couldn't I have just gone with a nice photo of her at her graduation or a wedding, she could have sent me plenty, but I only had to go and bring up that old thing again and she knew why. I said, "Why?" and she said, "Because you want to make a show of her," which was unnecessary, because I was genuinely worried by this stage and only wanted to help. But then Chrissie went into a police station in Wood Green and announced she was alive and well and the copper said he'd enjoyed the video of her dancing, because at the end of the day, Alan, Chrissie loves that video and she's proud of it. Which is a good thing, really, isn't it? Admirable, in fact. And that's why I'd thought that if anything bad had happened to her it would have to be *really* bad.'

'I must say, when I met her, I thought she was a thoroughly decent human being, she just lost her phone, that's all, and wanted a break from everything. Maybe she'd had a touch of sun. It happens.'

'Aren't you prejudging your own story?'

'I'm looking for at least one sympathetic, likeable personality, someone who doesn't have mental health issues or is running away from an abusive relationship and she seems that way to me. That same night Chrissie went missing a woman threw herself off London Bridge and she's still unidentified four months later. It's so odd, because this other woman wasn't the homeless type, she was well-dressed, definitely couldn't have been a rough sleeper. I've been talking to the policeman who investigated the case. There's a fascinating link between them because it seems that they were actually both on the bridge at around the same time, though Chrissie has no recollection of seeing her. They have lifebelts on the bridge and she told me if she'd seen anyone go over she'd definitely have thrown it in, because who knows, the woman might have panicked and changed her mind and grabbed it. I've got a boy who ran away that night too from his foster home, they found him in Brighton, he managed to sneak on to a train without paying, just a kid, too, but he wanted to see the sea. Poor little lad. So it's all about one night last summer when three people disappeared. Chrissie is a particular type I'm interested in. Nomadic flat-sharers renting, with no roots in a community, recent arrivals in London who move around a lot and if they have any permanent place it's actually in that most ephemeral place of all, online. What exactly sparked her running off doesn't have to be spelled out. It's the extent of how she became, if you like, notorious on social media that interests me, and whether it's even possible now to live a private life. But the suicide woman had a life so private that nobody knows who she is, no one has even reported her missing.'

'Wow, you have to be a bit clever these days to have a private life. I mean, you have to hustle and know how to play all the games. I'd definitely like to be involved, certainly under the right conditions. And if I agree to come on your show will there be a fee?'

'I could say that no, we don't pay because it might affect the integrity of the programme but you wouldn't believe that. So the answer is no, because we don't have the budget.'

'We?'

'I have a business partner, Johanna, she does all the financials and admin. I can't get much past her, to be honest.'

'Okay, but I can see we might have further interests in common. I mean, I'll need a film-maker for my digital project. Let me sleep on it.'

But what did he dream, Alan wondered, as he descended in the lift. What on earth could lie on the flatlands of his unconscious? Marco's slickness depressed him. He was a few years younger, not even half a generation, yet he seemed to have been formed from pixels, not flesh and blood. He supposed that Marco must have some kind of inner life, everyone did, or maybe not. Perhaps he was just a shallow current. The nurse was the real thing.

Part Three

7

'That's a high-stepping woman you're marrying,' Alan's father had said to him the night before the wedding. 'Are you sure you know what you're doing?'

'What do you mean?'

'What do you think I mean? Just watch out, that's all I'm saying.'

'Watch out for what?'

'My mouth is shut, you'll only put words into it. And are you a philosemite, now? It was popular years ago, sympathy for the Jews and their terrible suffering and admiration of their cleverness.'

Alan hadn't known that was a thing, but he thought that maybe it was his thing. For yes, she was a high-stepping woman: not just her clothes and her hair but literally the way she walked. She walked, he understood, expensively with an arrogant strut, was prone to pricey purchases and possibly, he feared, affairs. She was famous for being tactless, abrupt, some of his friends didn't like her. But how can you explain why a woman excites you, one he had first seen shopping for Christmas cards at the National Gallery on another wet, early evening in late autumn and wearing of all things a violet trilby hat with an emerald feather? He noticed the brightness of her fingernails when she waved her hands about as she talked, ten scarlet ovals jabbing the air. He was with a commissioning editor from Channel 4, they had just had a lunchtime meeting in the café. She said, 'Oh, Francesca, how funny seeing you here.' Francesca said, 'Why? I'm always coming here, it has the *best* presents.' And so they had stood and talked and he asked her would she help him find a wedding present for a friend, she had laughed, seeing through his risky awkwardness. She had made him wait weeks for their first date, she had worn an orange scarf and a nutmeg-coloured cashmere sweater, a study in the careful matching of shades.

After that meeting at the National Gallery when she was still thinking of him more as a spare man for dinner parties, she had found some of his documentaries online and watched them. Two had won awards. One was about people their own age in, of all places, Hampshire, who lived in the 1940s, or as if they were alive then, the women's hair in a workday turban or night-time Victory roll, the men in zoot suits, dancing on lino to swing bands. It was a cult, as those who re-enact Civil War battles dressed up as Roundheads or Cavaliers, but also a performance they had committed themselves to for life. They lived this way, they explained, partly because they liked the style, the music, the décor: utility furniture, mannish shoulders, painted stocking seams, jazzy ties, peek-toed shoes, and underpinning it philosophically, a belief, perhaps naïve and romantic, that the forties were a time of greater moral clarity and certainty, an age of national purpose. They did not want to be regarded as freaks and generally avoided publicity. Francesca, at first disbelieving, then mocking, by the end of the hour was verging on admiration for their implacable self-confidence, their self-belief. Alan had handled them with delicacy and sympathy. They seemed to her now to be genuinely heroic, if impenetrably batty.

For Francesca the film revealed in Alan a serious intelligence and non-judgemental curiosity that could touch everything it gazed at with a radiant illumination. She began to realise that he looked at *her* this way. She began to see it even in the photos he took on his phone, in which she appeared deep in thought – thoughts so deep she had no idea what they could have been. He seemed to know the real her (he didn't) and what women does not want to be gazed at as if she is intimately understood? 'But I mean in a *good* way,' she told her friends. 'He seems to bring out the best in me, I don't know, it's difficult, he just . . . ' She felt the immense wattage of his attention and was flattered.

At the office, Johanna, his business partner, thought Francesca was a flake. At home in Hungary she had made her own films but there was no money in them. You could not get foreign distribution apart from festivals who paid next to nothing. The best you could hope for was a foreign-language Oscar, and hoping for that was like spending a couple of euros on a lottery ticket. She had lost interest in being an artist, it was all bullshit, who cared? Better to have a nice flat and nice clothes and go out to bars and restaurants.

If Alan did not know why Francesca was attracted to him, Johanna had her own theories. Francesca was not a serious person, but thought she ought to be. The girl had aspirations towards gravity which he fulfilled by proxy, an intellectual authority from working in television and making documentaries about sad and weighty subjects. Johanna had said nothing to him about this observation. It was not her job to save him from a bad marriage. Her role was to get his films on TV, make money: money so she and her husband could buy a flat out in Stratford and rent it as an Airbnb. Let Alan pursue his destiny with the lady with the stupid hats and wobbling bosom. Men are fools. Always.

Adding to Alan's significance in Francesca's eyes, was the louring presence of his father, George McBride, a radio presenter with a three-hour morning show. He was known in Northern Ireland as the heavyweight Wogan. The first time Francesca had flown over to Belfast to meet the prospective in-laws he had said to her, 'Let's have an argument, choose any subject you like.' She had managed to evade it by producing a box of Fortnum & Mason macaroons in various pastel shades. The old man, like his son, had a sweet tooth. 'Ah, isn't this the nicest little thing?' he had cried. 'I never saw these before. French, you say?' Francesca, whose mind was a clutter of florist's flowers, expensive art books, shoes and hard-to-obtain French cheeses, was nervously attentive to his opinions about a range of subjects she knew nothing about. Fishing treaties, assisted dying, traffic-calming measures, food additives, penal reform – the usual blather of phone-ins. 'Oh, I *see*,' she would say. 'How well you've explained it.' Who wouldn't be flattered? Not him, who assumed everyone listened to him like this. He was as beguiled as Alan.

Even Alan's mother, who had spent her married life adjusting by increments and degrees to the presence of a larger than necessary personality, thought that Francesca was actually the kind of wife her son needed. She was not what she had had in mind, not someone as bold as brass and with those sultry dark polished looks ('so much lipstick, and so bright!'). But at the end of the day, she told herself, this girl was someone who would allow her son to make something of himself, give him a push, keep pushing.

And Francesca had educated him into seeing that the corporeal as well as ideas had value, aesthetic value. Alan did not experience art as she did, as a kind of wave that passed through her, an intense barrage of emotion, but he could now see, dimly, what she saw. What she was most aroused by was the decorative and the ornamental. 'A society deserves the art it gets,' she said, as she examined, for what seemed like an hour, a lace cuff on an 1850 dress in a glass case at the textile rooms in the V&A.

When you walked into a house arranged by Francesca, you could certainly tell the difference, something to do with proportions and symmetry and what she knew about paint was nobody's business. You could show Alan three shades of off-white and he could see that they weren't the same but he had no idea why you'd go for this one or that one. But she knew. When he visited her flat the first time, nothing jarred or seemed out of place. It was relaxing to be in an environment designed to make you feel at home. In the flat he felt lulled and luxurious. Even her wine glasses were beautiful, small, cut glass, slightly saucer-shaped. Above the marble fireplace hung a gilded mirror in front of which she would fasten her coat and spend minutes arranging her scarf, this odd, staring action, its attentive scrutiny, which made Alan feel that he did not know her at all. 'But all women do it,' his father had told him. 'They go off in a world of their own and if you ask them they'll tell you they're not doing it for us, it's some set of rules only they know about. They've all got a secret, women do, your mother included. You can never know a woman and that's a fact.'

He found she'd made his life very comfortable, not only because she was an excellent, experimental cook, never nervous of new ingredients. He couldn't wait to move in with her, to leave his basement apartment off the Holloway Road: tidy, undecorated sparse rooms too neat and soulless for the human heart to flourish, he now recognised. She gave him a set of keys, and arriving at the flat from work before her, he would open her cutlery drawers and examine the shining arrangement of her silver soup spoons, teaspoons, forks, knives, all with fern decorated handles. The radiance of them made his heart pound. He picked up a spoon and licked its curved interior, then rinsed it under the tap, dried it and carefully replaced it with the others. An hour later he was holding it to his lips again, bearing a mouthful of her delicious vichyssoise dotted with the spring-like green of chives. Cold soup. He'd never get to the bottom of her surprises.

In the early months of their relationship he would, as all new lovers do, ask her what she was thinking. She was often thinking about how she might do her hair, or if ankle boots with a mid-length dress made her calves look chunky, or how to season a dish of creamed mushrooms on brioche toast, or what colour top would match a cobalt-blue jacket she was looking at on a high-end fashion sale site (or if cobalt might, as it were, frighten the horses at work).

'You can't ask me that.'

'Why not?'

'You might not like the answer.'

And assuming that she was thinking critical thoughts about himself, he felt insecure in her affections and pressed her to tell him what had he done wrong, had he hurt her? But she smiled, showing that monster row of gleaming, even teeth behind rose-pink lips and winked.

She had started to read an Italian novel in the original language. She had studied Italian up to A level and taken a number of advanced immersion courses in Florence in the summer to facilitate a future career in the art world. The project was very slow going. She kept an Italian dictionary by the bed and managed two or three pages a night. The novel was set in Ferrara before the war, in and around the villa of a Jewish family, almost a ghetto itself, but one offering luxury, and the luxury of being able to live lives of a higher purpose. She was entranced by passages describing walled gardens, tennis parties and, of course, unrequited love. It began with a discussion of Etruscan tombs and the observation, quite acute, she felt, that the Etruscans had been dead so long they might as well have *always* been dead. When Alan asked her what she was thinking, now she recounted to him the silly conversations between these pampered characters who had no idea what was coming, who would all quite literally disappear from the face of the earth.

A third of the way through, bedtime had turned into her retelling the pages she had just laboriously read, the exploits of beautiful, longed-for Micol, her sick brother Alberto and their sequestered parents, Professor Ermanno and Signora Olga. She was Alan's Scheherazade.

Thus *The Garden of the Finzi-Continis* became what Alan thought Francesca was thinking about.

She had once loved a man with Spanish eyes, and was going, it turned out, to marry a man with eyes the colour of an English summer sky on a good day. She had never really been attracted to alpha males, preferring weeds and poetic types, but on the other hand, and this had been a surprise to her, he could confidently drill holes in walls, assemble furniture from flat packs, fiddle with electrics and plumbing, had been up the ladder to the attic to examine the beams and the loft insulation, could explain what caused subsidence (tree roots, clay shrinkage in dry summers). If he was in the market for a new toaster he would spend an hour online reading customer reviews and going to price comparison sites until he had found the cheapest deal and she was cringing at the beige plastic items that arrived from obscure bargain suppliers. When he shopped his long face became fox-like, his mouth was set tight in a refusal to be taken advantage of.

'But isn't it so tiring? Don't you get worn out by all your bloody consumer research?'

He had stood for twenty minutes in the lighting department of John Lewis reading reviews of bathroom wall fittings on his phone.

'And do what instead? Spend money like water?'

'I'm greedy for luxury, for nice things. I am what I am, take it or leave it. Cheap stuff hurts my eyes. I have a more developed aesthetic than you do.'

Every purchase was a battlefield; mostly she won, for she would just buy it anyway. Her salary at work rose comfortably each year. 'But why can't we pay extra for good design? What about this one, it's lovely?' 'Because seventy-eight quid for a *toaster*?' 'Well, look.' And she clicked and paid. 'It's done now.'

His hand light on her hair. His fingers stroking the nape of her neck to calm her. A slight alteration in sensations. He loved her skin, he loved the way she felt, how she shivered at the approach of his fingers, how easily aroused she was, how eager, and how the erotic charge of merely hearing her key turn in the door announcing that she was back was enough to saturate him with her physical presence vibrating a few metres away. There had been no one else like her in his life, so gloriously fleshy that the sight of her bending over to fasten the zip on her long leather boots, the calf muscle constricting at its approach, was enough to make him kneel and cupping her ankles, take the zips between his own fingers and pull them up himself until they were closed and his hand continued on, past the dimpled knees to feel the lace at her crotch.

And if she had been unsure for many months after they started seeing each other whether or not she loved him – being without that flash of revelatory certainty one read about in novels and magazines – it was when he was away filming, occasionally for weeks, that the pang of missing him was so intense she would feel winded. Without his attention, she felt depleted. Was this love? Or was she merely a narcissist? He was not her type, he was – but he wasn't there and she held tightly to her phone waiting for his calls and his texts. He had slipped into her, he had made himself at home in her complicated life. When he nervously proposed marriage at a room in the Wallace Collection, taking from his pocket an antique ring and smiling with such a boyish, heart-rending appeal to her to make him utterly happy, she experienced a surge of joy, that in some indefinable way, she was home. It was over, all the stuff of being single in London, in her particular world. She had caught and landed a bona fide British fish. Was safe, finally.

Alan's father had said to him, 'It's sex, I suppose, the old bojangle. That's what you see in her. You look like the cat that's got the fucking cream.'

'No, listen, Dad, you should hear her in an art gallery, she's so absolutely knowledgeable, honestly, provenance and all that stuff, she can see things in a picture that hardly seem visible to the naked eye, but when she points them out, you—'

'What bra size does she take now, 38DD? Am I good guesser?'

At the wedding, breathing loudly in his lounge suit, he walked around the flower-wreathed marquee saying, 'Ah, the auld bojangle!'

And could they build a lifelong marriage on the foundations of their libidos? Alan was sure there was more to it than that. Her world was nothing like the granite Protestantism of his childhood. She was waste and luxury and spiced dishes and strong French perfumes, with a top note of mouthwash and minty toothpaste, for both her parents were dentists and she flossed morning and evening. He adored her.

In the end, through sex and other means, he had talked her into buying the house by the railway line. She had capitulated. They had made an offer and after some haggling, which she was in charge of, better at bargaining than him, they had got it. Now on the day of the move she was losing her ground.

She had pestered the vendors of the new house to be allowed to come over, not just for the usual measuring up for the sofa and curtains but to actually bring with her in a taxi small items of furniture and place them in the long room taking photos on her phone, until the vendors blocked her number and told the estate agent she was not to make any further contact except through the solicitor.

But finally, after all the legal squabbles were at an end, they shut the front door of the old flat, dropped off the keys, took a taxi following the removals van, picked up a new set of keys and opened the door to an empty house whose walls bore the dark marks where earlier in the day Ikea pictures had hung, a generic inoffensiveness that made her skin crawl. The old flat had been partly furnished, she had taken it originally because there had been a rather marvellous vintage oak dining table from Heal's, Ercol, she believed, with a matching sideboard. Leaving behind these two items had made her cry. The landlords (a couple working in Dubai) had not been prepared to part with them and Ercol these days, especially vintage Ercol, cost a bomb.

The new house was one of a row of early twentieth-century railwayman's cottages. Alan told her that whole families had been brought up here in the two cramped bedrooms. The bathrooms were extensions added to the rear flank, jutting out into the garden. They were houses for workers, for men who went to work in flat caps and women who prided themselves on scrubbing the front step. What dirt did railwaymen bring home on their boots that the step must be kept so clean? Probably horse's dung. Motor cars would have been a rare sight up here. As they pulled up in a taxi, he saw at once that the vendors had taken the venetian blinds from the downstairs bay. Until they ordered something to replace them, anyone could see in. She'd kill him.

The lock was fiddly, there was a system, a turning, then a pulling. It took him three goes to get it right, everything moving in the right direction to itself.

'Well, I think it's great,' he said, reaching for her hand as she stood, holding a basket of wrapped china she would not trust to the removals men.

'Do you?' She hadn't taken a firm enough stand. She had let him talk her into it the night they'd come back from the second viewing when she had lain beside him in bed listening to his calm reasoning and thinking she only had prejudice to counter him. Something about rats.

Tears surged.

'When can we go home?' she said, unable to keep the stupid words in her mouth and conscious that she was being petulant and babyish and that only for another, say, forty minutes would Alan put up with it before saying something a bit sharp to which she would have no good answer that wasn't even more petulant, and he hated that mood, and would go all tight in the face. She knew he would do anything to please her, put up with her storms and tantrums, her ridiculousness for even longer, though there would always be that point at which he'd turn, snap – she had learned to try to stop a hair's breadth before he got to that point.

'Come on, babe, it was never our home, it didn't belong to us, you know that.'

'But it felt like ours. I loved that flat.'

'I know you did, it was a great flat, we'll never beat that view, you were clever all those years ago to find it, I loved it too, but this is our home now, we're going to live here for a few years and everything is going to be fine. Come here.'

Now in the new house, which was uglier than he remembered, having not seen it for so long, not since the July evening on the train, he said, 'Don't worry, you'll get used to it, we'll change everything you'd like to change, if not immediately, then later when we have more money.' For he was sure he could make it work for her, if he tried hard enough, earned enough.

He kissed her. He comforted her. She was soothed.

In the night she said, 'I can hear trains.'

Alan said, 'There are no trains. You're imagining it.'

'No, I'm *not*. Please, just listen. It's not so bad in the day, I will concede I didn't notice them then, though maybe that was the removal men drowning out the noise. This house is full of noises, it's creepy. *Listen*.'

'That's the pipes. It's normal.'

'And what about the roof?'

'The rafters creaking.'

'Are they supposed to do that?'

'You didn't hear it in our old flat because we were on the middle floor. You heard the neighbours moving round, you heard the toilet flushing and the shower running and the sound of their TV and you weren't bothered by it. You have a fixation with trains. You're just suffering from house-hate. You haven't settled in yet.'

'What the fuck is house-hate and why *should* I have settled in? We haven't unpacked a single box.'

'We will, we will tomorrow. Tomorrow we will unpack everything and the paint can start to go on and the new furniture will start arriving and the next day we'll have a supermarket delivery and you will see this is a very good house and the trains are nothing.'

He was determined their marriage would not end in anticlimax then failure. It was to be a romantic odyssey.

'Go on, shall we make this the first time in our new house?'

'Oh, for God's sake, I'm exhausted, it's the last thing I want. Are you mad?'

(He would leave her when he was sure she was asleep and stand amongst the packing cases with his tube of lubricant. The problem of being married to her, sleeping with her every night in the same bed, cupped together, her cunt pressed into the small of his back, was that sex was always on his mind, and when he could not get any from her he had to find other means. He had wanked more since he moved in with her than in all the years before they had met.)

To punish her he said, 'There goes another train.'

'I *told* you, you wouldn't listen.'

'There was no train. I made it up. To show you it's all in your head.'

'You're nasty.'

'No, I'm not, babe. We're going to love this place. We are going to be very happy here. They'll have to drag us screaming and kicking out of it.'

Next morning, at lunchtime, after the delivery of the new furniture she had ordered, she said she was starving and would go out to buy food. Beyond the limits of the awful house she thought she might feel okay; after all, they had always liked the neighbourhood which was up-and-coming and she felt that they were arriving there at the point where becoming was the operative word, the whole place was in motion after decades of neglect and abandonment.

Around three years ago the street had undergone another alteration. A Dutch couple moved their micro-brewery into an abandoned pair of buildings. After the micro-brewery, a small café opened offering a fashionable breakfast of avocado and chorizo on sourdough toast and in the evening cocktails, craft beers and live music. A graduate of Central St Martins took over a redundant shoe shop and sold her own designs of children's wear, little retro pinafore dresses and matching babies' cotton sun bonnets. A branch of a Shoreditch vintage clothing store was rumoured to be coming. Alan (and eventually even Francesca who had stumbled and grazed herself badly against the double digits of the postcode) understood that this forgotten enclave behind the railway line was a tiny sequin in the fabric of London, a high street whose original wooden frontages had not been ripped out and replaced by neon and plastic but formed a reversible decay of quirky, arty, hipster individuality.

At the delicatessen a woman with a mole on her cheekbone cut cheese and meats with thin, gold-ringed fingers. The shop was scented with dried sardines, bunches of coriander, mint and parsley, lemons, gritty slabs of halva and coffee.

Francesca did not know what some of the items were, and

pointed to rolls of salami studded with cubes of fat, unidentifiable cheeses, olives in oily brine, tins of beans she recognised from their illustrated shapes on the label.

'*Endaxi!*' she said as the woman cut the salami. 'Enough slices, *efharisto.*'

She had flown over Cyprus once, en route to Israel to attend a Gehari family reunion of exiled Persians in Netanya, returning four days later with a kilo of gold jewellery in her hand baggage. Birthday presents of precious stones were routine in her family. Her father had a slightly flashy gold watch.

She left with a carrier bag of foods she had no idea if they would want to eat, it was all trial and error, but as she walked home her future life came to her without conscious thought or reflection but as memory of events that had not yet taken place, but now would.

Alan was assembling a mink-coloured sideboard. They worked all day. The previous owners had lined up everything against the walls as if they were living in a corridor. Just by placing the sofa with its back to the window she negated the impact of the railway line. The new dining table stood now in the centre of the room and a mirror on the far wall reflected the whole long arena of pictures and lamps and candles and vases of flowers and rugs and six dining chairs and another item on which she had agreed to cave – the unit on which Alan's turntable stood and his vinyl collection below. To Alan it all looked pretty good.

Still, the constant feeling of dispossession, of what she had lost in a flat they had been living in only yesterday morning: an unbearable parting with the south-facing balcony, the butler sink and the ice-making machine in the fridge. It made her cross. She was imagining her grandparents' faces when they first visited, their smiles of congratulation freezing and their stumbling, fragile attempts to look on the bright side, the housewarming gifts, the food and the flowers still in their hands as the car pulled up on the street outside the railwayman's cottages (a concept they would not begin to understand). Her grandparents were everything to her. No one's opinion was more important. They were her lode star. Her mother and father, the dentists, were fainter, dimmer beings.

'How quiet it is,' she said now. The cars in the street were all home, no one passed their window.

'I told you.'

Too tired to cook, they sent out for pizza. The delivery man knew the house. He said, 'I worked out it must be new people, different order from usual.'

'What did they have?'

'Meat treat. Every time. And a tub of ice cream.'

8

Halfway along the street the German family were getting ready for bed. They spoke quietly to each other in their own language; though their English was perfect it was reserved for the daylight hours of work and school. The little pig-tailed daughter was having her pale plaits combed out and swooning as the brush passed again and again through her hair. A nightlight in the shape of the moon shone over her tired face. Her father was in the kitchen getting her schoolbag ready, cutting the sandwiches for her lunchbox, slicing an apple into segments and putting them in a bag. Chinks of light fed into the street from their venetian blinds. They had ordered unpainted pine shutters and were waiting for them to arrive. After the child was asleep they sat on the sofa together and researched loft conversions. Adding a third bedroom, they agreed, was cheaper than moving.

9

Further along the street, Mrs Simarjit Kaur Khalistan was waiting for her taxi to take her home to Southgate, safely in her
handbag the tube of Bourjois lipstick she had received for her
birthday. The two women wore the same shade, as dynamic as
if their lips were two pairs of coral-coloured tropical fish. They
had matched colours like teenage best friends since 1966 when
Mrs Khalistan had come into Mrs Audrey Shapiro's husband's
chemist shop asking for aspirin for a child: a sick son at home
with a temperature. Mrs Shapiro had noticed the timid manner,
an expression which suggested that she feared she might be
turned away, or greeted with a sneer or a raised fist (which had
already happened in the chandler's two days ago), but she also
understood that the fear of walking into a shop populated by
complete strangers was a breeze compared with a mother's terror
of a child's overheated forehead.

Bernie Shapiro had come out from the back and led her
through a series of questions about the little boy's condition,
which was nothing but the usual, and nothing to worry about,
and carefully wrote down in block capitals on a bit of scrap paper
the dosage instructions. Horror fell from the woman's face, she

began to emit a volley of frenzied thank-yous in English and longer expressions of gratitude in her own language. There was an impulsive moment, lasting for a few seconds, when Mrs Shapiro reached into the Rimmel display, took out a lipstick and handed it to Mrs Khalistan. 'On the house.'

Mrs Khalistan looked at the lipstick as if it were a miniature hand grenade.

'What is this?'

'Never seen lipstick before?'

Mrs Khalistan said nothing, put it in her handbag. The next day she returned emblazoned with Hawaiian Fire and took out from her shopping bag home-made samosas wrapped in a tea towel. Bernie Shapiro. It reminded him, he said, of a fried knish but hot, even though she had toned down the spices to suit the pallid English taste.

It was the forty-ninth anniversary next month of the meeting. Bernie was under a marble star in Golders Green.

'Who are your new neighbours?' said Mrs Khalistan.

'A young couple; he's as white as a bed sheet, she's got a bit of life in her.'

'That's very nice. You should take an interest.'

'Don't worry, I plan to.'

'Always from the beginning, you put yourself out.'

'Why not? What should it cost me?'

The taxi sounded its horn out in the street. The two old women embraced by the door.

'Oh, Simi, Simi! Don't forget me, will you?' cried Mrs Shapiro in anguish, for her friend was a sister and her own sisters, like Bernie, were in the other world, the *yenne velt*.

'Audrey, like I ever would. I'll see you next week, same as usual, my house, the samosas will be piping hot.'

'I'll bring the honey cake. Oh, here he is with his bleddy dogs. Make sure you don't leave any mess in my garden, fella.'

Half an hour later, after cold-creaming her face and brushing her teeth and putting on her peach nightdress, the nylon lace trim feeling a little crisp and old these days, Mrs Audrey Shapiro kissed goodnight the photographs of her husband and of her mother and father who came as children from Bessarabia, an unknown place caught for ever in her imagination in a grey fog: a river, a town, a forest, men on horses carrying swords, a soundtrack from *Fiddler on the Roof.*

10

Down past all their houses the old dog man came walking with his two Afghan hounds, great shaggy animals which pawed the pavement like impatient horses. He wore a round-collared polka-dot shirt and plum-coloured jacket. His long white hair was tied back in a pony tail. He walked down the road three times a day, until reaching the end he turned left at the passage along the railway line and disappeared from sight. It was nine at night. 'Girls!' he cried as the dogs smelled dead rodent flesh and strained on their leashes. 'Oh my lovely girls, don't leave me behind now, will you?'

11

A month later, Francesca had lost her job.

Before Alan met her she had been selling Persian carpets for her great-uncle Farki to wealthy customers in Belgravia. For high net worth individuals it was not enough to invite them to the shop, bring in silver pots of perfumed tea and tiny sugared cakes and roll back the rugs for their inspection. The rugs must be conveyed to them to examine, laid out on the floors of the rooms in which they were to be eventually placed, accompanied by a commentary on the history and symbolic language of each one. She was in command of the van and two sweating assistants. She wore a navy knee-length Chloé dress and a double strand of pearls. Her heels were always higher than were comfortable. In the winter she had an emerald-green bouclé wool coat with a matching dyed mink collar and exuded wafts of Miller Harris iris scent.

Carpets were everything, they had led her to art, to painting and sculpture. She had learned their symbolic language as a child in her grandparents' flat in Hammersmith, guided by her grandmother, as if they were a picture book: a lozenge of flowers for example was an oasis in the desert. Each colour had its own meaning: red for wealth and courage and fertility. A camel was strength. A peony was rank. All this must be learned and remembered and identified.

At her grandparents' flat the child lay on her belly staring down at reddish tufts of wool, outlining patterns with her finger. The more she learned about the rugs the more mind-blowing they were, a kind of dictionary and thesaurus of stars, flowers, hands, numbers, birds, combs, jugs, amulets, fruit, trees, snakes and mythical beasts each with a coded meaning. Combined, they sent messages that she could not yet understand. Carpets, her grandfather told her, were an image of a garden of paradise full of living things, a wool utopia, an oasis of abundance at the heart of heaven.

After four years working for her great-uncle, she was taken on by the textile department of a West End auction house: from her grandparents' threadbare flat to writing the catalogue entry for a seventeenth-century 'Polonaise' silk and metal thread rug from Isfahan (or possibly Kashan) which had been part of the estate of King Umberto II of Italy and which would sell for a quarter of a million dollars. When she left work each day it was after many hours of research and exactitude. Everything was, of course, always up for dispute, new information was constantly becoming available, but her considered opinion about a carpet contained as much as there was to be known about it at that date to establish a guide price. Part of the rug's great age was the long track of imperfection – fraying, fading, loose threads, errors in the weave itself. The carpets had not been created in a factory with machine settings designed to eliminate error, nor had they been intended to become historical objects. The art of carpet weaving had begun in order to cover the floors of nomadic tribesmen, protecting them from cold and damp, and the finest were still made in the villages. They were functional items, designed not for the wall but the soles of the feet.

Then the error. A carpet she had authenticated had been wrongly, fairly disastrously dated. She had not been fired but more, she felt, gently shoved, as if by a hand in the small of her back, into voluntary redundancy. She was certain that none of her colleagues would have been treated this way, the types she had known at St Andrews whose jobs were invariably arranged through contacts: a phone call between a godfather and a cousin. Perhaps she was being unfair and they were genuinely talented, or maybe their upbringing had assumed such talent must exist and so it necessarily did, but they seemed to her to ascend without effort.

If she was Lord Peregrine Occasional-Table's daughter they would have given her a brief wrist-slap and allowed her to carry on. Alan was inclined to agree with her, he couldn't stand the auction-house world and its patronage, but did not want to encourage her to brood over grievances.

'They never liked me,' she said. 'It was probably – what do you call it? – constructive dismissal.'

'I don't really know what that is, but look, think of it as an opportunity.'

'You sound like a fucking life coach.'

'I'm sorry, I don't mean to. I'm just trying—'

'I *know* you are, but it just hurts so very much, do you understand?'

'Of course I do. Come here.'

Her face was a tragedy mask. He had no sense of what she would do next. As long as she was working she had occupation and prestige, now she had a redundancy payment. He knew her anxiety was rooted in the understanding for her family that life was a perpetual game of snakes and ladders. For though she might be the daughter of not one, but two dentists, at a low point in the early eighties her grandfather had driven mini-cabs round West London, the A–Z open on the seat next to him as he

87

crossed the alien city, a homesick foreigner, an unreturnable refugee. He had scrambled back up again – he had started various moderately successful import-export businesses in partnership with other Persian Jews, had got into wine for a while, then it was mobile phones. Something was always changing hands in his world, it was all about prices, the goods were immaterial. Wine, phones, carpets, the transaction was the point. Still, he missed carpets and was thrilled that his only grandchild had reconquered their territory. And now expelled.

On a visit to see how the new house was shaping up, her English mother Hilary was so genuinely impressed by the transformation, the way Francesca had somehow managed to turn the interior into a kind of elegant uncluttered Aladdin's cave of delights – behind the brilliant radicchio red of the front door, a terracotta-painted long wall, a pair of canary-yellow armchairs facing the window – that she tentatively wanted to suggest that her daughter start an interior design business. The Gehari family she had married into were sensitive, opinionated, emotional people, easy to get on the wrong side of. Her husband, who had been practising Englishness since his twenties and tried to stay aloof from these storms, would suddenly go under and begin to cry at nothing. She knew it was all too easy to get embroiled in a row with Francesca who was cut from a very particular type of cloth and had from an early age been difficult about her bedroom curtains, carpet and bed linen, never mind screaming if a dress was put on her of a colour she disliked. Hilary's own aesthetic tendencies were limited to the cosmetic appearance of the mouth, the creation of gleaming slabs of even teeth, but their daughter had this talent for remaking other people's rooms, walking into a kitchen and being able to rearrange it in her head, so she might say, a little abruptly, 'Have you thought of putting the table over there and painting this wall, say, a *very* pale pistachio green?' It was quite clever really, and people were often surprised and grateful and actually did what she suggested and were happier.

Hilary had sounded out Alan first who said he wasn't quite sure what she'd make of it. But Francesca had been open to the idea and even investigated going on a course, but halfway through the application she realised that she was not going to be able to accommodate herself to other people's taste. She would spend too much time arguing with them, trying to persuade them that they did not want what they thought they wanted. In other words, she couldn't, she explained to her husband, take a brief.

No, he said, then that wouldn't work. Shame.

When he was out filming or editing or researching and she had time by herself to think, she asked herself what her Persian grandparents would do in such circumstances, for they had conquered a greater loss than she ever would. Their example must, she felt, provide her with some clue as to her future direction, a game plan to make a bad situation work to her advantage.

It was not that they had come here with just the clothes on their backs, far from it. They had arrived in London as tourists, each with a pair of matching suitcases carried by the porter from the hotel lobby lined with clubman's brass-studded leather armchairs and bowls of peanuts on the bar tables, up in the swooshing lift to their room. Kensington is so delicious, they cried, and spring did seem to come to this part of London earlier than to other, rougher neighbourhoods, the cherry-blossom anticipated warmer weather, as if the rich were owed nicer seasons. They unpacked, hanging mohair suits and silk dresses, folding cashmere sweaters into drawers, checking the amenities, examining the room service menu, ordering up sandwiches which arrived correctly on silver doilies and ate them from a tray. After an hour's rest Younis rang down to the concierge to enquire about which were the best West End shows and could tickets be obtained.

The following morning, breakfasting in bed, drinking coffee from a silver-plated pot, watching the news on their own in-room television, they felt a massive lurch in their circumstances, as one who misses a step in the dark and trips. For overnight their status had changed.

'Of course it's a good story,' Francesca said, 'a modern parable, but you don't believe it, Alan, do you? God, I hope not. You're not that gullible? Why do you think they had already sent my father ahead to London to finish his education? They knew what was coming.'

For in the bazaar everyone knows everything. Her grandfather had an early-warning system embedded in his brain, people like him were heat-seeking missiles for trouble. His nose smelled changes in the political atmosphere as rural people could detect, by sniffing, the onset of rain when there was only a cloud-fist in the sky. Nothing took him by surprise, only the ferocious total-ity of it was amazing, how the people longed for something so completely alien to his own impulses and reasoning – wanted a uniformly devout society. Later, he heard of secular women who put on the chador so they could act as undercover agents against the Shah and then found, like a mask that cannot be removed and sticks to the faces, that the black sheet had moulded to their skin. The Shah was cruel and despotic and greedy, but his impurities were what made him preferable to the religious ecstasy of that monster, the Ayatollah Khomeini.

No, Younis did not believe in goodness. He preferred things to be more or less half right, then there was wiggle room. Looking out of the window at Kensington, calculating how many taxis they would be able to ride in before they were reduced to the tube station, he thought that he was in for a long exile. The people had once again gone mad as they periodically did. He would have to get used to rain and women whose colouring did not attract him.

Eventually, when it could be put off no longer, Francesca invited her grandparents to the house for lunch. Her parents had driven over in the Audi to pick them up. The boot was loaded with Persian dishes – a stew flavoured with pomegranate and walnuts, rice with dill and fava beans, aubergine and tomatoes. Her grandmother, Mamani Amira, had not made these herself (since they had moved from their flat in Hammersmith to sheltered housing they lived on supermarket chilled meals), but were bought in from a Persian restaurant. Once they arrived, wherever you parked it was not possible to hide the railway line, the chain-link fence, the dog shit. The two old people were shaking as they stood at the front door, finding themselves in *terra incognita*, an alien landscape of hunched railwayman's cottages and the pulsing sound of car alarms on the street.

Francesca had done everything she could to make lunch resemble a Persian banquet, decanting the containers into her nicest china and laying them on a white cloth on the dining table. Her grandparents had each drunk a very small glass of red wine from doll-sized glasses meant for liqueurs. Eventually they began to reminisce about a nightclub in Teheran they had once visited, the band, the miniskirted girls on the dance floor.

They had paid many formal compliments on the house, how the exterior was deceptive for look how beautiful she had made it inside, and Alan had said, 'Exactly, that's why we've been suggesting—'

But Francesca cut him off. 'It's just a starter home, you know. We'll soon move on.'

'Of course,' everyone replied, as if this was self-evident, or had better be.

It was her grandfather who said, picking at a faint brown tea stain on his shirt cuffs that embarrassed him in his granddaughter's presence, so particular about everything, 'Well, *azizam*, have you thought of a shop? Do you remember setting one up on the stairs and serving your dolls?'

'Oh yes, I remember that,' said her mother. 'You took all sorts of things from round the house and wrapped them in tissue paper. You were so funny, you wouldn't even take invisible money, I had to empty out my change for you.'

'No, I don't remember that at all.'

'I can show you photos, darling.'

'A shop,' cried her grandmother. 'You must open a shop, of course!'

Francesca felt that she could detect an air of falseness in her grandmother's enthusiasm, regretful that she would no longer be able to drop the name of the auction house in conversation and say as she so often did, 'Where our granddaughter works, of course, they think very highly of her.' Uncle Farki was dead. The business had been handed on to his son who had sold it. He worked in something they knowingly called 'high tech', and was above commerce. It was to do with the encryption of digital . . . but they had run out of words. It was a shame Farki could not advise her about this proposed enterprise, they said. 'Yes, a shop!'

At the door, her grandfather, reaching up to kiss her cheek, had whispered, 'You belong in the bazaar, you know what we called it back home? The place of prices, under a vaulted roof.' He winked.

When they left, Francesca said, 'Now they've gone what do you think?'

'It went quite well, I thought, they—'

'No, about having a shop.'

'I'm not sure, you always seem to me to thrive amongst masses of people. I'd worry you'd be a little lonely.'

'Couldn't I have an assistant?'

'Maybe, but perhaps not at first, you'd have to build up the business before you could afford one. I do know about how these things work. All the bloody admin you have to do, the budgeting, the business plans, the bank loans.'

'Doesn't Johanna do all that?'

'She does now, but in the beginning I had to do it all myself. I hated it.'

'That's true. Yet, I do like the idea; I could sell anything I liked, couldn't I?'

'Yes, though inevitably you'd need to find a market for whatever it was you were selling.'

'That's completely obvious, credit me with some common sense. But you know, I do think that if you're offering something *really* strong, people will come: they'll just see that there's been something missing up to now that only you can fill. I really believe that, don't you?'

'Well, perhaps.' For his experience with commissioning people in television was that they always wanted a duplicate of the last success.

He might take his chance and tell her a shop was a ridiculous idea, it would never make any money, but she did have quite a bit of redundancy pay. Perhaps the experiment could be time limited to, say, a year. He wanted to please and support her, to be seen to be on the same side as her beloved grandfather.

'And wasn't I actually selling at the auction house? I mean, I was doing valuations and catalogue copy. I was assessing the market, just not doing the actual sales.'

'You wouldn't find it a comedown?'

She blushed a brutal blood-black red. 'Well thanks, just thanks. For reminding me.'

'I'm sorry, I'm sorry, I just meant—'

But what he meant she was unwilling to find out, for she put on her coat and left, out to walk along the darkening high street though nothing was open, apart from a single lighted window in which the old dog man was filing his sleeves of vinyl according to categories of his own invention.

Expulsion.

No more to emerge into the light at Green Park with Bond Street to your left and early-morning window shopping for frocks and shoes and coats and handbags behind the shuttered glass. A restaurant, local, not cheap, but not snobbish either, which had been there for decades, a place where men took their mistresses for discreet lunches and the waiters welcomed the smartly dressed girls from the auction house who wanted no more than a salad and occasionally, if they could not resist, a serving of île flottante.

Oh, snap out of it, you silly bitch, she told herself, not aloud but thinking it so intently on her face that the old dog man, locking up, believed that he could actually see someone in the process of changing from one thing to another and it was an interesting sight and she was interesting, or at least it was to him, who had the resignation of the shopkeeper who stands and waits.

12

An eclectic mix of interior design items incorporating my passion for the rugs of my Persian heritage as well as innovative design from Italy and Scandinavia, a curated collection for the contemporary lifestyle with always an eye out for affordable luxe.

Mrs Audrey Shapiro had no idea what any of that palaver meant but was going to make sure she found out. She watched Francesca process down the street carrying a brand-new fuchsia-pink broom, a dustpan and brush and some black plastic sacks.

Alan, waving her off, thought she held them more like fashion accessories than cleaning aids. She marched like a soldier with a pink plastic rifle and in this context she seemed faintly ridiculous. Really, she was right, she actually did belong only in certain postcodes, all within zone one of the tube. He thought there was something almost heroic and adorable about her being anywhere else. This adorability had lately started to get on his nerves but that was because she was always hanging around at home with nothing to do. The shop, as ridiculous as it was, he accepted, would sort that out.

Inside the abandoned chemist Francesca pushed the broom across the floor. The bristles left brown trails of mouse shit. A stink arose, releasing chemical vapours of waste and rodenty unpleasantness. A clatter on the counter, a mouse running across her silk headscarf, its feet pulling at the threads. She lasted ten minutes before going outside to look at her phone. She sent a series of texts: to the estate agent, to Alan, to her best friend Sasha and her second-best friend Zoë. These messages she felt were so reasonable no one could disagree, their recipients would concede that she was in command of the situation and had its true measure. That this had all been a colossal mistake, that she had now realised the absurdity of an ambition that had no basis at all in reality – what the fuck was she thinking? – and it was best to ruthlessly cut your losses rather than blunder on into catastrophe. She knew herself well enough to acknowledge that she had *no* perseverance when it came to the realm of the physically disgusting, the cheerful rolling up of one's sleeves and getting on with it.

Alan texted back, *Can't you get a cleaner?*

She had not suggested it because she thought he would laugh at her, not knowing that he was already laughing at the sight of her pink broom and matching dustpan and brush. Sasha and Zoë texted back, *Well why not just get a bloody cleaner of course you shouldn't have to do it yourself, are you mad sweetie find an agency, there's loads of them ring around xxx.*

Mrs Audrey Shapiro turned up with her shopping trolley having started to put her coat on and do her lipstick as soon as she saw the fuchsia cleaning set trail along the road.

'Now what are you doing sitting on the step, dear?'

'Well, I've taken the shop or maybe not.'

'Yes, I know you have. What do you mean maybe not? Everyone knows you're turning it into something nice.'

'Do they?'

'Just look at you. It's going to be something fancy, am I right?'

'Interiors.'

'That's what I thought it might be, or dresses. Knick-knacks, I'd say.'

'And Persian carpets.'

'Ooh, lovely! I always wanted one. They make a room look very smart, not like your dreary Axminster.'

'I don't know if I'm going ahead, to be honest. The place is a disaster, do you not think? Have I made a completely stupid mistake?'

'Listen, dear, this used to be my husband's premises. We had the place thirty-five years till he retired. Lovely business, I worked behind the counter and every Sunday morning when we were closed I went in and put furniture polish on the wood. Dusted and polished. Shining. It could be like that again, somewhere you'd want to come into.'

'But have you seen it recently?'

'Well, no; I heard but I daren't look.'

'Help yourself, go in if you like.'

'Oh, I couldn't. It would break my heart.'

Francesca was distracted from her troubles by Mrs Audrey Shapiro's lipstick painted on in a cupid's bow. No grey roots were showing through the lacquered helmet of waves. Her whole appearance was a study in the effortful exercise of getting dressed in the morning: the coffee-coloured tights, the low-heeled court shoes with gold snaffles, the comfortless girdle flattening a sagging midriff, the brassiere like a pair of pale pink ice-cream-sundae cups, the navy skirt and gilt-buttoned blazer with white piping at the collar, an outfit finished off with a scarf knotted at the neck and held in place by a butterfly clip which spread its wings and threatened at any moment to fly off and settle above a pencilled eyebrow. She had, Francesca thought, managed to avoid the humble self-effacing drabness of old age. She liked and admired these defiant old ladies who did not succumb to the premature coffin of beige clothes and Velcro-fastening shoes.

'I don't blame you. The smell is bad enough.'

'You should get yourself a cleaner.'

'That's what everyone says.'

'Well, take their advice, dear. Why cut off your nose to spite your face? You want someone who knows how to roll their sleeves up, enjoys hard work. You don't seem that type to me, not that I was myself. My line was selling the Rimmel lipsticks, everyone said I had an eye. You look to me like you've got an eye.'

'Thank you; that's what I was trained to do, actually.'

'In that case, get yourself a charlady. Do you want me to send a woman round?'

'Do you know someone?'

'I know people.'

'Well, that would be brilliant.'

'Look out for her at lunchtime, her name's Jean Riley. You can't miss her.'

'But how do you know she's available?' She felt that Jean Riley could not be up to much if she was free to turn up at the old woman's bidding.

'I saw her half an hour ago, taking out the bins.'

'And how much does she charge?'

'You can ask her yourself. Goodbye, dear, and good luck.'

Francesca watched her walk off with her Black Watch tartan trolley, fairly briskly for her age, past the last shop, and turning left disappear from view. Her sense of the atomisation of city life, the granular quality she had always taken for granted, people plotted on a map like stick-pins, was being replaced by clusters of which she and Alan were members without being aware of it, part of defined groupings of individuals unknown to them but with common purposes.

At twelve thirty she came back and found, sitting on the

doorstep smoking a cigarette, a wiry woman in her forties dressed in skinny jeans, a grey T-shirt with Elvis's face on her flattish chest, worn-down leopard-print ballet flats on her feet and rolled up next to her a nylon overall. Her blonde hair was tied back with what looked like a J-cloth and her fingers ended in a chipped blue manicure. The sight of her on the step smoking inspired confidence in Francesca, she seemed designed for the function of cleaning while dressed in a way that both dismissed the activity with a flippant contempt and gestured to it as if she was a drawing by a cartoonist.

They exchanged formalities and agreed a price. Jean appeared to know her own value and brushed aside any attempts to bargain. 'It is what it is. I'll do a good job. You won't have any complaints.' Francesca felt there were always grounds for complaint, it was in the nature of life for there to be the potential for improvement. But across the street in the Greek shop the woman in the white coat was observing the transaction and she could not afford to be seen left high and dry by a charlady who would, it was obvious, simply walk off if she didn't get what she asked for.

'I know this gaff like the back of my hand. My old mum used to clean for Mrs S years ago and sometimes during the school holidays I'd have to come with her and sit in a corner being quiet and Mrs S would let me try on the lipstick testers. You should have seen her on the high holidays when she used to walk along the street on her way to the synagogue in a hat made out of silk flower petals and the old man walking behind her carrying his velvet bag with his whatnots in it.'

'She seems very nice.'

'A lady, you know what I mean? Hats and gloves and make-up on before she leaves the house, every single day. No slacking. We're lazy, we let things slip, she used to call me a little scruff. Which is true, as it happens.'

Jean had cleaning products Francesca had never heard of. She carried them in a plastic pannier: they dealt with mildew, limescale, stains, and restored wood to its original high slippery shine. She estimated she'd need three full days' work to get everything shipshape, she would start at once and get in a good four hours. Francesca left her to it and went home and read *Vogue*. There were moments now, crossing the bridge over the railway line, which left her feeling fraught and breathless. It would come back, it would keep fucking coming back, that she was no longer a person who travelled every day into the West End, who ate lunches in Mayfair restaurants, was privy to all the gossip of the art world – whose prices were going up and who was a busted flush. There was something about her generation, she felt, that was constantly being picked up by the legs like frogs or cats and *flung*, flung out of jobs and flung to the margins of the city and out into the distant countryside or south-coast commuter towns. Central London was hollowing out, the real London was constructing itself in these edgelands: neighbourhoods and postcodes no one at the auction house had ever heard of, streets of double glazing and satellite dishes and untidy bins, always seen at a second-hand distance through the glass of a taxi taking you to Heathrow.

In the middle of the afternoon she decided to take a walk. Past her shop (which was currently Jean's shop, and she could see her in there on her knees, thank God, really going at it), there was a turning which led to the – what was it called exactly? A river, a canal? An artificial waterway, Alan had said, built in the seventeenth century to bring fresh water down from Hertfordshire to the city and still doing so, finishing in Clerkenwell. Locked metal gates periodically shut it off to pedestrians along its route. Up here it was a straight shallow channel with steep grassy banks and bushes congested with the open-mouthed white trumpets of strangling bindweed wrapping itself round buddleia and saplings and concrete posts. It seemed to her ridiculous that there was no path at all along which baby buggies could stroll, no benches, no amenities of any kind, only the dirty steep ground to sit on. One had to watch one's step. On the other hand, there was a tantalising view of other people's lives, which were always of interest. Gardens descended to the perimeter, and some had low fences and an uninterrupted view of the water so she could see lawn chairs, a child's paddling pool, barbecues and swing seats. Perhaps there were so few walkers that it did not matter that they were overlooked.

Soon she passed under road bridges, stopped at a baffling iron device on the bank jutting an arm out across the aqueduct. She took a picture of it on her phone; Alan would know what it was, and if not, his father, with his industrial archaeology hobby, would. She passed a corrugated tin chapel standing roofless and naked and grey. It began to rain but only lightly at first, a damp frizz of drops on her hair.

Abruptly the bank reached the North Circular and she could go no further. The rain came down heavily, a drenching shower. Turning back she sheltered under a tree by a bridge. The leaves dripped pellets of rain down her neck, it seemed to her worse than being out in the open, the rain was sliding down the foliage in sheets. Her feet squelched in her sandals. The bridge offered a couple of metres of shelter but it was low and dark and smelled of rotting vegetation, mould, the wet fur of scurrying small animals, none of which she identified separately but as a musty mix of decay. Looking along the wall she could detect a brick archway framed by brambles covered in hard green fruit. They were not ready to pick yet, she would come back another time when they'd ripened. She took another picture on her phone to remind her.

Through the arch was a passageway which might be a short-cut leading up to the road and she would not need to make her way back along the soaking grass and slippery bank. She pushed along through the tunnel. After a few steps she reached daylight and a yard and a back door. There was a flaking sign on it which had long ago been painted with a rough hand. ENTRY 1d. Was it a flat number? A maisonette? There seemed to be no access to the street except through this house with its a privileged entry to the water. It was annoying to come all this way and find herself forced to go back to the squelching bank. One might, she thought, knock, plead being soaked through and could she take a shortcut? Yes, she could, really, she had the chutzpah to do it, could put on the haughty privileged manner of the girls she'd been at university with, the gracious condescension of knowing how to speak to the lower classes in a way that carried enough charm to make people give way to obedience when they didn't have to. She'd seen them do it, could make that work. And she was soaked.

Later, in bed thinking back across the day, considering the irrationality of the passageway, she tried to re-create the moment at which she had raised her hand to bang her fist on the gate. She knew because Alan had once explained it to her that memory was not a filing cabinet or the rewinding of a recording, it was the act of creation and re-creation but though it had seemed to her, in the moment of being about to knock, that the noise that made her jump out of her skin could not be what she thought it was – the distant crashing, trumpeting sound of, of all things, an *elephant*, it was simply too ridiculous – but now, at the rim of sleep, it came back clearly to her as exactly like an elephant. And she had jumped, lost courage.

She had walked back along the tunnel until she reached the bridge and the bank. The rain died down into a series of occasional spits. The clouds were clearing fast to reveal huge hurtling patches of aquamarine sky and the sun sliding about above the trees. A pair of Afghan hounds were coming towards her, off the leash, bounding and playful, their hairy coats

102

steaming. She was frightened of dogs, their black teeth, their thrashing tails. The old guy was wearing a tweed deerstalker cap but his flared green velvet trousers were soaked with rain almost to the knee.

'Halt, girls!' he cried and the dogs screeched to a shambling stop. 'Don't take fright, darling, they wouldn't harm a fly, they're full of beans because they've been cooped up all morning. And look at you, soaking wet. Did you walk far?'

'Just up to the North Circular. What's that great big iron thing on the bank?'

'Any guesses?'

'I've no idea.'

'A lot of people have a go but they never get it. You need to understand the management of the waterway. It's a launching crane for a weed cutter boat. It gets rid of weeds and algae. Keeps the water fresh. They bring the boat to the crane by lorry, then pick it up and swing it over and into the river. The weed is lifted, moved to the side, and dropped into a skip then the grab returns for another pick-up. And this is rather macabre but I was told that someone who sadly drowned here was found in the skip, but that could have been a bit of inventive story-telling by Thames Water.'

She thought Alan would find this more interesting than she did and that she would have forgotten the details by the time he came home.

'There's a passageway under the bridge, too. That's all a bit odd.'

'Yes. It's a shortcut.'

'How do you get through?'

'You knock and you pay. My girls are enjoying themselves, aren't they? They love this walk. Sometimes I take them up to Ally Pally and sometimes down the old railway line to Finsbury Park. In the winter they just go all around the houses. I know where you live, no offence, I'm not stalking you. I'm just round the corner, I pass your house with the girls every day. Your old man comes into my record shop, doesn't he?'

'Yes. I'm opening a shop too.'

He had a wolfish smile and long yellow teeth. He might have chosen his dogs to match himself.

'Everyone knows that. We could do with an injection of West End glamour. The place has been run down for too long.'

And though she was terrified of his dogs she held out her hand and gingerly patted some fur.

13

Only when Younis was dressed in his pyjamas and Amira in her nightgown lying under pink sheets and rabbit-coloured waffle blankets, a fringed lampshade casting a rose-coloured flush on their old faces, did they whisper to each other in Farsi. The night outside the curtains was a protective fleece; the moon could not overhear them, the stars were cold indifference.

A man born into the bazaar always knows before anyone else when something is happening, when there is an alteration. To Younis it was something he could smell; an idea concentrated into an odour. He had sniffed out that their days in Persia were coming to an end, yes, even after thousands of years, and now once again he could smell that life here in England was going through a process of transmutation into something different. The order changes. What can you do but prepare?

'You don't think this will pass?' Amira said in his ear. 'I thought you always told me the English were puddings.'

'Sometimes you put your spoon in a pudding and something you didn't expect is there.'

'Yes, remember the first time we had their Christmas pudding?'

'And they set it on fire!'

'So funny.'

'You were frightened, you tried to put it out with a wet dish cloth.'

'I thought the woman was mad, I thought she was an arsonist.'

'They've set fire to themselves now.'

'We have been here for forty years and never did I suspect that they—'

'I know. They are always capable of surprising me, but never I thought *this*. What are those small animals that run in a great herd to the edge of a cliff and throw themselves over?'

'I don't know, I never heard of them. They must be mad.'

'No one knows why they do it, it's a great zoological mystery.'

'People do go mad, you know.'

'Yes, but the *English* of all people? Who drink their tea with their little finger crooked!'

'Though we do not really see this happen any more, do we? Perhaps in the past. Not now.'

'Good manners have slid away, that is true.'

'When we moved into this building I thought perhaps there would be afternoon tea in the lounge with cakes and sandwiches.'

'I would have liked a library.'

'I know you would.'

'Instead they complained about the smells of our cooking, as if one could possibly mix up a Guerlain scent naughtily escaped from its bottle for a stew!'

In his own language, talking to his old wife whom he had met when he was twenty-two years old and she was seventeen, Younis felt he could speak as eloquently as Spinoza if he wished and had the thoughts. But when he spoke to strangers in English he was a tongue-tied fool. After forty years their English was still that of illiterate children, stumbling for words, resorting to the clichés of speech they learned from the newspapers, phrases which Younis noted down on scraps of paper for future use.

At home in – but there was no longer a home for them in Persia and no Persia either, except in the memory of its exiles. A small, continuously depleting population of Jews, mostly elderly, remained, barricaded into their synagogues or guarding the tomb in Hamadan of the mighty Queen Esther. The young people had all gone: to London, Paris, California, Israel.

When they first arrived in London, checked out of the Kensington hotel, ceased being tourists, they had fallen rather low, and risen, with his brother Farki's help, to take a rented flat furnished with the contents of a house-clearance job lot from the saleroom. They had moved into the dead lives of bona fide English people lock, stock and barrel, and would have eagerly bought guns for shooting blameless birds from the sky if such items had come up for sale at the auction, enthusiastically discharging them at pigeons and blackbirds in Hyde Park. Canteens of silver cutlery radiated out in complicated place settings laid on tea-stained Madeira tablecloths. Pouffes and foot stools were arranged around the room, wicker magazine racks held copies of the *Daily Mail*, *Woman's Own* and the *Radio Times*. 'I know these are not really *quality*, but we find the English in them much easier,' Amira said apologetically, knowing she must seem quite primitive compared to her son, her English daughter-in-law and educated granddaughter. 'The articles, you see, are shorter with uncomplicated words.'

Since he retired from the efforts of running his businesses, which began so optimistically and always ended with only patchy success without actually bankrupting him, their lives had contracted down to their little flat in the sheltered housing block and these occasional outings: sitting waiting for the sound of their son's car brakes, the slamming door, the figure outlined in the glass, the impatient jabbing of the general bell to take them to a party across London.

In the car Younis asked his son about the animals who commit mass suicide.

'Oh, lemmings, that's a misconception,' he said. 'It's not a mass suicide at all but the result of their migratory behaviour. When population density becomes too great they aim themselves at a body of water looking for a new habitat. Largely they survive the fall, but often they don't survive the swim. They *can* swim, but the destination might be too far.'

'How they know that the population is too large?' asked Younis.

'Not enough to eat.'

'That easy?'

'Yes.'

'And how you know these things, my clever son?'

'Wikipedia.'

'I have heard of this. A miracle, but can you trust it?'

'You have trust issues, you don't trust anyone.'

'Why should I trust?'

This rudimentary primitive warning that it was time to move on interested Younis. In his case the neural connections had been rather more complex. There are locations where gossip and rumour thrive; in the bazaar people come to trade not only foodstuffs and household goods but the precious metal of information. The merchants of the bazaar hear everything, and being mercenary, they judge everything according to whether it is to their own advantage. Gossip, like gold, is a currency, it has a precise coinage. In the bazaar the man who is a master of his own circumstances knows how to distinguish between a story that is just that – an entertaining anecdote embellished as it is passed from hand to hand until it exists as a timeless immortal thing, going back to the days of King Nebuchadnezzar – and what is considered valuable information you would pay for in *rial* notes or the granting of licences, favours, discretion, etc., etc.

In the bazaar a man might discuss the great affairs of the day with his fellow traders but his chief study is human nature for all types come to buy, and a deep understanding of the human condition is necessary to sell to them: an appraisal of who likes to bargain and who is more concerned with the quality of the goods over their price. In the matter of carpets there are always know-it-alls who boast of their familiarity with the subject, pronouncing genuine articles as fakes and believing that they have discovered an overlooked masterpiece amongst the cheap rugs. Such individuals, men and women, should be flattered. Closed-faced or boastful, they could be braggarts or the type who say little, a miser of words. No layperson knew more than Younis did. He had handled carpets every single day and felt a spiritual connection with the many feet that had once walked upon them. But the carpets were not more important to him than the life of the bazaar itself, and he knew that what he was selling was not wool woven into patterns but his own true self which could be exchanged day after day for certain sums of money, yet never depleted.

This morning he had said to his wife, 'We will no longer speak in our own tongue, outside this bed we will talk only their language even if we sound like fools.'

In the car his son asked about life in the building, were they still satisfied? Were there any complaints that should be raised with the management? Was everything clean, the warden pleasant, the lift always working, the other residents courteous?

The other old people were all nodded to and some brief pleasantries were exchanged. A few days ago, after the *big thing* happened, the thing that had so surprised their son and his English wife, there had been a brief surge of what he considered to be *glee* amongst some of their neighbours. He detected a rising emotion of cheerful satisfaction with what had been an unexpected outcome and an optimism that things would be 'different, very different' now. How things might be different he and Amira were unclear about. Some old bore was certain that they would be returning to pre-decimal currency, restoring the glory of pounds, shillings and pence with their florins and half-crowns and sixpences. All of this was sheer silliness, one might as well turn off the internet then see how they liked not being able to do their online shopping or pay their bills on a screen which Javad had shown his parents how to do on an easy tablet he bought for them, a child's toy full of the wonders of the world which attracted and frightened them, like drug addicts.

In their flat they were able to hear conversations taking place in the corridor. Their front door was near the lift and leaks of dialogue would seep through the cracks. The complaint about the smell coming from their flat had taken place some years earlier and the old lady who had made a fuss had moved on to a nursing home. What they heard outside now was a rising up of the general tone, a ratcheting up of complaints, so where before one had heard only pleasant comments about the Polish handy-man, now the residents grumbled that his work was inferior, his attitude surly and the motives for him coming to London in the first place in question. Was it true that back in Warsaw or wherever he was from, he had a criminal record? It seemed to Younis that something had been unleashed, the residents given permission to give in to their basest instincts.

The cleaner had been called a 'fat black bitch'.

'It's not what it used to be,' he said to his son. 'I don't like to say anything else.'

'Don't worry about causing trouble. I will deal with any trouble.'

'Well, you know what is going on as well as we do. You must see it.'

'It is worrying, I agree.'

Hilary said, 'It's certainly worse than I expected. Everyone is hearing stories now. We used to talk about people living in their own bubbles: well, they're all starting to pop.'

Amira said, 'I don't think there is any real harm in these people, we just need to continue to be polite. What harm *can* they do to us? Beat us up? They shuffle along on their walking frames and with their cataracts; if any of them had a gun they would aim at a picture on the wall by mistake!'

Everyone in the car laughed.

The old people were excited about this evening out. A party! How often was one invited to a celebration these days, Younis in his linen suit with a magenta silk spotted handkerchief arranged in his breast pocket, Amira in a lavender silk dress. The car was filled with the scent of Nina Ricci L'air du Temps, a perfume from the time of Dior's New Look, and associated in Amira's mind with romance and being courted by a young man with patent hair and a devastating smile who sat beside her now, with little hair but excellent dental work due to his son's attention. Implants were an absolute marvel.

14

Mrs Audrey Shapiro in front of the mirror in bra, pants, coffee-coloured tights and half-slip examining her figure.

'Oh, Audrey, you still got the legs. If you got the legs you keep them. If you ain't got the legs, you'll never get 'em. But you got 'em!'

A flush of pleasure rising, falling damply back down again, a slight dizziness – blood pressure? Long ago a feeling like that was pure sex, Bernie coming up behind her and cupping his hands on her breasts, twiddling with her nipples so she screamed, 'Get off me, you beast!' And they had rolled around on the bed, her tights round her knees, the lipstick all over her face. You never told anyone about these things, even Mrs Simarjit Kaur Khalistan had no idea. Working in a chemist shop you were exposed to the gross materialisation of the human body, you knew about suppositories and condoms, a woman with her face burning red would come in for the jelly for her Dutch cap. Bernie was clever at school, he was at Hackney Downs with Harold Pinter. 'I'll tell you about him, he wasn't afraid of anybody, not the bully boys, not the fascists, and I was the same but he was our leader.' Brainy Bernie, crude and animalistic in bed. And not always in bed, one time on the floor in the lounge with the TV on and the newsreader looking at them in their disarray, her left shoe halfway across the room and her knickers ripped at the gusset, looking up at the dust on the light fittings.

The dress she took out of the wardrobe was kingfisher blue, square neck, bows at the hips, sewn of stiff sateen and purchased from Fenwick's in Brent Cross for Bernie's retirement party. A diamanté bow-shaped brooch was pinned near the shoulder. Was it vulgar? Bernie said no way, for Bernie liked a woman to put on a show, he lived to spend an evening in a maroon cummerbund. *I have had a wonderful life*, she thought. *Nobody can say any different.* Since the retirement party the frock had been worn for her grandchildren's bar and bat mitzvahs, worrying each time that she was a little overdressed for the occasion in synagogues where the men and women sat together and she felt deprived of that eternal female natter in the gallery. Downstairs you had to pay attention to the rabbi and his nonsense. Her children were all over the place. Colin in Highgate, David in Leeds, Rochelle in Geneva working for the United Nations, a carousel of all the nationalities, living in a luxury apartment overlooking the lake, in a stagnant affair with a married coloured gentleman from Sierra Leone whose wife was stowed in Freetown. She was forty-one, so that was it, she had lost her chance.

Was an evening bag all right or too much? Was the whole thing going to be jeans and gym shoes? But Vic said he was definitely going and he never lost an opportunity to put on his velvets and one of his kipper ties. The bleddy dogs would be there too. His wife had been a nice woman, she came in in her wheelchair to get her prescription filled, then he came in for her when she was bedridden. Back in the day when they first turned up on the high street migrating east from Muswell Hill, she had had long glossy flicked-up hair like Sandie Shaw and little miniskirts and a lovely smile and had taught English to refugees at a centre in Camden Town. Vic had made a wonderful carer.

The guests thronged along the high street in their excitement and curiosity. A Saab pulled up and an elderly couple were assisted out by a younger man and a woman with fine blonde hair pinned up in a loose chignon, her neck free to form a showcase for pearl and diamond earrings. They all had wonderful, very white teeth.

There was a glance of recognition from the vantage point of the pavement as Audrey studied these people. Were they not (the old couple and the younger fellow, not the pale-face lady) what Bernie would have called 'our cousins' and might she try a sly shalom on them to establish their complicity? For Jews, she felt, shared a secret, though she was never sure what it was – not some big conspiracy, but a feeling that there was always us and there was always them, and them were the English with pale skin and smells of roast pork rising from their kitchens.

No doubt about it, the old couple were *cousins*, for their features had that aspect of exaggeration, the lips too full, the hair too heavy, and the nose, always the big hooter. The younger man had all these characteristics but his voice sounded to her like someone had taken out a steam iron and given it a good press.

This must be the girl's mizpochah.

The party from the car managed to navigate its way through the door of the shop. She followed it in its swell. Inside, she looked round at a transformation beyond her expectations. Bernie's many years of making people well or helping them to swallow the bitterness of death through the dispensing of a harmless panacea that could not cure but gave them hope was gone, the proportions of the old room remained as far as she could tell but their identity had been eradicated, as if she, Mrs Audrey Shapiro, should wake up one morning and looking down at her own limbs and then her reflection in the mirror, find that she had turned overnight into – she tried to think of the most unlikely person she could be. Elizabeth Taylor? No, she had once had a certain look of her.

Kate Moss.

Years ago, when the children left home, she and Bernie had downsized from their four-bedroom house two streets away to a two-up two-down and on the day of the move, the rooms empty of their marriage, she had cried her eyes out. For what was left was the tiled fireplace which preceded them and had endured the ignominy of being fitted with a gas fire, then been ignored altogether when they got central heating and finally photographed by the estate agent and flagged up as an original feature with a note that it could be fitted with a wood-burning stove. Apart from the conservatory their own tenure was junk. Their floral-patterned carpets would be turfed out on to a skip. Her duck-egg blue Formica-topped kitchen units would be for the chop. The house sat silently awaiting its next alteration. It broke her heart. But Bernie, not on her wavelength at all, said, 'I'll be glad to see the back of that damned boiler, won't you, always playing up?'

No more would a prescription for antibiotics be measured out in his back-room dispensary. All the lights were on, the place was almost too brilliantly lit, though she couldn't see where the illumination was coming from, there were no pendant fittings or fluorescent tubes. Light washed down from the walls propelled by invisible thingumajigs. In the centre of the ceiling a black glass chandelier was burning pink candles emitting a faint rose glow.

Three carpets attached to the walls were explained by small cards as if in an art gallery. The whole shop was lurching, tilting into the category of the fantastic, the made-up. The mahogany display counter behind which she had presided in her powder-blue nylon overall five days a week seemed to stand there with an expression of surprise and resentment at the service it had been pressed into, filled with little glass birds, complicated coffee pots, Parisian notebooks, German pens and other tchotchkes.

Vic had tied up the dogs outside, they were resting quietly for once in their lives when she had passed them. Inside he was talking to Jean, both of them holding flutes of fizzy wine. Scrawny Jean, the doyenne of scrubbing, who was solely responsible for fumigating and cleansing the shop, had arrived in a mangy emerald-green rabbit-skin jacket worn over a Morrissey T-shirt and her usual New Look skinny jeans and worn-down ballet flats. Towering over her, Vic in his velvet jacket and high-collared polka-dot shirt reminded everyone of a certain age in the room of a former member of Pink Floyd whose name they couldn't quite put their finger on.

The young Germans were with their little girl, who was overexcited and drinking orange pop from a champagne glass.

It was known on the street that the child had come home from school last week eyes swollen not with hay fever but anxious tears – another child had asked her, not even cruelly her mother later established, but with the clinical interest of the curious: why are you still here, aren't you going home now?

Gaby's notion of home was the poster on her bedroom wall of the universe and all the constellations and a corner insert of her own solar system radiating whizzy planets. Her father Caspar had put her on his knee, an old, childish thing by now, she squealed with remembered pleasure. This *was* their home, he said – look at all the nice people around them in the other houses who had smiled so sympathetically or spoken encouragingly when they saw them in the street or at the station, even though they had never uttered a word before or even registered that they were neighbours. This child who had said such a thing must be troubled and unhappy and probably even jealous. Jealous of *dein goldenes Haar*! They would speak to the teacher tomorrow and it would not happen again. Now they would talk a little less

German in the house and they would no longer chat in German outside it but that was the only difference, there was nothing at all to worry about. And these precautions would only last a short time, he was certain, while things settled down.

These people, he said to Elfriede, when Gaby had been put to bed that night, are rather like those little cartoon characters, aren't they? The minions. Depressed, restless and unmotivated without a master to serve. They have always existed and always will. Sometimes minions rise en masse and cause trouble under a malign influence then sink back down into a temporary decay. We need not worry about them just yet.

For even Mrs Audrey Shapiro, who had once bought a German alarm clock by mistake and returned it to the shop with the receipt for a full refund, had said to Elfriede's face when she saw her along the railway alley, 'You're very welcome, my dear, very welcome,' which Elfriede had thought at first was in response to some service the old lady had believed she had performed but later, when she got home, deduced was an expression of hospitality on behalf of the country itself. Caspar thought it could mean anything, that she was talking to herself, or becoming senile. Next time she saw her, Elfriede called out, 'We are staying, no question of that!' Mrs Shapiro said, 'Staying where, dear?' So the encounter was inconclusive.

The Greeks from the deli had not had time to dress up having come straight from across the road when they closed, confirming what everyone suspected: that they were no longer local but had moved to more prosperous neighbourhoods in Hertfordshire, to houses with drives and garages and conservatories. The other guests appeared to have risen up from the flat paper of magazines Audrey read at the hairdresser's: young, their faces smooth, their foreheads like billiard balls, and wearing mostly, thank God, dresses; plain but with interesting touches – a Liberty print collar on black velvet.

117

Francesca came to greet her. 'Oh, Mrs Shapiro, you came! I'm so glad. Now please do have a glass of fizz. Alan, babe, will you please look after our guest of honour, find her somewhere to sit.'

She was not sure she needed or wanted to sit but the husband guided her towards an empty corner of the room.

'Not massively comfortable, I'm afraid, I could get you a cushion if you like.'

'What's not comfortable? There's nothing there.' For he seemed to be propelling her to put her bottom down on thin air.

'Sorry, can't you see it? It's a stupid thing really. I don't know why anyone buys them.'

He reached her hand out and guided it to a solid surface. If she concentrated hard she could see the outlines of a rigid arm-chair which seemed to float in and out of invisibility. Perhaps she should have worn her glasses.

'What the hell is it?'

'It's what's called a ghost chair, they're very fashionable. Made of clear plastic.'

'Why?'

When she had gone to the hairdressers that morning and had a cut, shampoo and set she had thought she was prepared for anything, but not for a chair you couldn't even see.

'I honestly don't know, you'd need to ask my wife, I'm sure she could explain it, but it would still be bloody uncomfortable. Now can I get you a glass of fizz?'

'I don't mind if I do, given the occasion, though I'm not normally a drinker. But I've got to tell you, I saw your programme, what a sad story, did anyone turn up? The one who was in the river, I mean.'

'No, not yet, I'm still hopeful, early days yet. People are on holiday, they might catch up with it later, who knows?'

'I can't credit it myself, why not a living soul in all the world recognised her. It doesn't make sense.'

'Unless they did but wouldn't come forward.'

'Oh, that's even worse. Anyway, you're a very talented young man.'

'Thank you, you're very kind.'

'It made me a little misty-eyed, if I'm honest, and I'm not normally one for the waterworks. My friend is, oh, she had tears coming down her face when we watched it together. She's an Indian lady, known her for donkey's years, and she said it made her homesick, of all things. Can you credit it? I said, "Simi, what are you weeping about? What's set you off all of a sudden? Your home is here, you came when you were a young married, didn't you?" And she said, "Oh yes, but for how long do they want me?" I thought, *Now I don't know the answer any more.* What can you do?'

He installed her with prosecco and a napkin of canapés. The other elderly party were on the other side of the room seated together on a bench decorated in what looked like offcuts of old carpet, and they were staring round, their heads cocked, looking appraisingly at the scene as if they were pricing up the stock.

Vic had spotted her now and was coming to join her, raising both his hands in that open-palmed gesture which indicates both amazement and acceptance.

'So what do you think of the old place, Mrs S?'

'And what should I think? What is it to do with me any more? More important, you've still got a shop, what do you think?'

'I have to say I think it's going to be good for the neighbourhood; if it increases footfall, I won't complain.'

'I wish her well, I wish her all the luck in the world, which she'll need because the moths will get those carpets.'

'She says she knows all about that. She's an expert.'

'Then good for her.'

'Everything is changing, I'm afraid, look at the Greeks.'

'What about them?'

'They're not happy.'

'Because a knick-knack shop has opened? They should be so lucky not to have anything else to worry about.'

She and Bernie had been there before them, had watched them arrive bearing odd foods and cans of olive oil, escaping from a war, as everyone will do in the end, he had said, 'We're just taking a breather from it.'

'They don't like the atmosphere,' Vic said. 'They want to go home.'

'Well, can you blame them?'

Standing by the door, Johanna and her husband saw, with the force of cynicism, the fragility of the enterprise. These people, she said to him, had no idea. She might have warned Alan that they were throwing money away on nonsense, but it was his wife's money, not his. *His* money she would have locked up away from such stupid investments. Johanna and Galon were selling their flat in Crystal Palace at the top of the market; prices had to slump now. They were buying two more Airbnbs. Then, Johanna said, we will see what we will do with this ridiculous country. We give it a few months.

But Francesca had tinkled her gold bracelet against a glass to ready everyone for a speech.

Alan thought she looked amazingly beautiful. Seen from certain angles her face could appear a little lumpy but now it was a smooth oval. She had put on a necklace of gold and pearls and her skin had that glow he recognised from moments when she was ready for sex but not yet acknowledging it to him.

Francesca, looking out at the room, seeing at least three people from the editorial side of magazines, and one feature writer for the *Evening Standard*, was experiencing a surge of righteousness. She had propelled West End glamour to a neglected high street in north London, had made to walk over the railway bridge the actual people who defined where glamour lay, who laid down the very rules on, say, knee-length boots, a fringe swept to the side, where one went on holiday this year, the new singularity of a lip.

At the edge of the room her grandparents had risen to their shaky feet to gain a better view. Her father had worked the crowd on her behalf, introducing himself, explaining the rich heritage of his daughter's Persian culture and actually, this had gone down rather well, because Amina and Younis were surrounded by what appeared to be a pack of acolytes brought forward one by one by her mother for a formal introduction.

Francesca felt weirdly bouncy, like a Zebedee toy that moved about on a single spring instead of legs.

She spoke. She paid tribute to those in exile from the bazaar, the spirit of which she hoped to create, the revival of the high street, asking Mrs Audrey Shapiro to rise and be applauded, which she did in that dress, that amazing, vulgar, unapologetic dress. The woman from the *Evening Standard* was taking notes. The room buzzed, broke into applause, some guests began to retreat to the street to smoke. Alan was filming everything, the whole event would be edited and online tomorrow on her website. The night was golden. Everyone left with a small gift, there was a priceless feeling about the line of people getting into their cars and taxis or walking to the station swinging a little carrier bag or standing on the pavement smoking and looking round at the closed shopfronts, saying, '*This is magical*, how clever of her to have ... shouldn't we do a feature on Persian rugs?'

Yes, Wall Park high street was in the ascendant. In a few months it would be mentioned in *Harper's*, *Tatler* and *Vogue*.

15

In the spring Alan had contacted Pete with the transmission date for his film. Pete felt flickers of nausea that the private world of what he thought of as 'my lady' was to become public, that she was to be re-created in forms he had no idea he would like or approve of. Marie wanted to watch it. She remembered him returning from the funeral and clamming up when she'd asked him how it went, as if the unknown woman was someone he knew and not just an unsolved case, for he hadn't needed to be there and had only gone, he said, because no one else would apart from the TV people. But this was what it was like being married to a copper, they saw and felt things others didn't. They had another life you really didn't want to know about.

The film opened with some classical music Pete didn't recognise, and a reconstruction of DB27 walking through the City played by an actress, and the actual nurse herself walking, their paths crossing for a moment though exchanging no looks, no eye contact, as if each was invisible to the other. Then there he was, doing his staged walk through the cemetery, ice on his beard, looming out of the fog like some old wartime movie.

Marie laughed. 'Don't you just look like Jack the lad. You've got to dress up even for the most godforsaken occasion.'

'It's my thing, you know that, always has been.'

'I do know, and I love you for it.'

Next DB27, in an artist's impression.

'So that's what she looked like.'

'Not really, to my mind it's too generic, I don't think he's got anywhere near. Loads of women look like her, he's not managed to convey anything special. There's some spark missing, I can't say what, but as soon as I saw the poster I knew it was right off. I don't mean the wrong colour hair or anything like that, it just doesn't look like her.'

'I see what you mean. You could mistake her for half my book club, it's the pointed chin and the highlights. And at least three people I know had that M&S top last year, I tried it on myself, it was a bestseller. She could easily be mistaken for Julie Pearce or Emma Gleeson and neither of them is missing. Poor woman, what a bloody life she must have had for it to end like this with no one caring about her, whether she lived or died. Unless someone did her in, of course.'

'We don't think so. There were no marks on her of a struggle.'

'A lonely death, then.'

'That's about it.'

'And maybe a lonely life.'

'But you'd know better than me, what lonely woman has those streaks put in her hair and buys the top everyone's buying?'

'Yes, it's unusual. I don't have an answer.'

The whole programme had done all its missing people justice, he felt, and had asked what it meant to be a person from somewhere who was now apparently nowhere. Even though, obviously, you were somewhere, just not where your friends thought you were. Apart from DB27 who was a person from nowhere who was now a person from somewhere: the bridge and the river and the pauper's grave. Chrissie made the point that she'd always known where she was, it was other people who hadn't known, and then the shock of seeing herself all over the internet like that. And was the internet somewhere, or not? It was hard to tell, really. She couldn't say.

Alan had added nothing Pete had not already known. There were no surprises. DB27 was half in the world now, it seemed inevitable that the phone would start ringing and someone would come forward, his own possessive grip on her memory would be undone. How could she not be known? It was impossible.

With the screening of the documentary Pete felt calmer; someone would identify her, she was passing now into the known world. He dreamed of her less often, Marie was flourishing, had a strange post-cancer bloom and energy. They went for walks together in Richmond Park, she liked the sense of wide-open spaces, he didn't mind them. Somewhere in the park were herds of actual deer. It was bucolic. And sitting down on a bench with squirrels scampering around their feet, Marie said, 'Pete, love, don't be funny about this but I've taken a fancy to leaving London.'

'What?'

'I'm just saying what about moving to the West Country to open a café or something. A little tea room serving scones and what-not. Home-made cake, jams, crab sandwiches. Doesn't that sound appealing?'

'No it doesn't. It sounds like shit. Anyway, you're a VAT inspector, for Christ's sake.'

'I expect Customs and Excise people would run an efficient business. We're good at the paperwork.'

'But you've got no experience of catering. I can't believe this, you're—'

'Mad? No, it's not my hormones; don't patronise me. There's never been a better time in our lives to make a fresh start, you can give me that, surely? The girls are on their way in the world and they'll have a free holiday with us any time they want. What do you do all day but mooch around on the internet and practise your guitar?'

Because of you, he thought, *because you got sick, otherwise I'd still be on the misspers cases, I'd still be looking out for that lady.* 'Fair point, but when did this even enter your head? I don't know where it's coming from. We're Londoners, for God's sake, there's nothing out there for us apart from – I don't even know – *scenery* and what's that got to do with anything? You've got scenery right here in Richmond.'

'Aren't you forgetting the water? Wouldn't you like to have your own boat again? Didn't you always tell me your lot were *Wind in the Willows* people? You could mess about with ropes and tillers to your heart's content. All day long, you'll love it.'

'Okay, a boat would be nice, but what about pubs, I'd miss the pubs.'

'They have pubs.'

'Not the same, there's nothing like a London pub. Anyway, I don't know a soul down there, do you?'

'Yes, I do, as a matter of fact. A school friend moved to Penzance when she got married, we kept in touch.'

'So we're going to Penzance?'

'Not necessarily. We've got the luxury of looking around, finding somewhere that suits us. And we'll make friends. We'll get involved. There'll be volunteering or something, who knows? I've set my heart on this, Pete, and after all I've been through don't I deserve something nice for a change?'

'Yeah, but it's not something nice, is it? It's not like a new car or a foreign holiday or some jewellery, that I could understand. Look around you, this is our home, our house, our neighbour-hood, your friends, your book club, the office.'

His mum used to talk sometimes of getting that 'fiery feeling'.

For a long time he assumed she meant heartburn, but in later life she revealed it was more than that, some other kind of severe ache in her heart, a sense of rage and longing for something she couldn't put her finger on. 'I've always been dissatisfied,' she said, 'and never knew how to tell your dad. It's hard being a woman, Peter, very hard. You men have no idea. Of course, things are very different these days, but I bet plenty of women have that fiery feeling just as much as I ever had.' He had found this conversation enlightening at the time, and he credited it with helping him when he went to interview women who had run away from home, bolted, or just not come back from an evening out. He felt he understood that force which led them to take off, even when the scrote wasn't abusive or hitting her, though he was hearing that there was a way of doing it without laying a finger on her. Coercive control. Making her feel she couldn't breathe, that was it.

He had known Marie since she was seventeen, his sister's pal, dressed up when she first came round to the house for tea one afternoon like Boy George with the hat and a broad pink streak in her hair. He was in his leather jacket and jeans. He was showing off to her about his record collection. A spark of a girl, a little poser. Next time he saw her, years later, she was all in leathers herself, going to an air show on the back of her brother's Norton and her hair under a crash helmet so no idea what colour it was this time. It went on like that, catching sight of her here and there, once in the Co-op when she was shopping after work looking all spruced up, not quite ordinary in her navy jacket and white shirt with the collar turned up, because her tights had a pattern in them. He was in the police by then and going out with a series of little blonde constables. A week later he spotted her in a wine bar with her mates in a tight skirt and spangly top and once again those tights with patterns. She looked really good. She could pull herself together in a way that was cool but not tarty. He wasn't sure how she did it but she did. And these things mattered to him. He took in a deep breath, went over and asked her out on the spot. And she looked up from her glass of Chardonnay and said, 'Oh Pete, you took your time, didn't you? I've been waiting since Duran Duran brought out their second album.'

'*Rio*, wasn't it?'

'Correct.'

When she asked him while they were courting why he had joined the police he told her he had thought it was going to be all nyee-nahs and catching robbers, it had sounded exciting.

'Is it?'

'Yes, but not the way I thought.'

'What do you mean?'

'More like the bloody Stasi.'

And why had she joined Customs and Excise? She said she found high numbers exhilarating. The amount they collected every day in VAT was gobsmacking, and she enjoyed combing through people's books, looking at where they'd hidden their earnings, arriving at the door all innocence, looking dull and bland in her navy office outfit till they caught sight of her diamond-patterned legs. They must let her in and show her everything. She had the power to send them to prison for white-collar crimes and enjoyed using it on middle-class smart-arses with plums in their mouths, sitting there in a nice suit talking down at her, thinking, *She doesn't have a degree, does she? Just some jumped-up little jobsworth.* And yes, she was a girl who in her bad youth shoplifted eyeshadow from Woolies. And no, she hadn't gone to uni, yet still she could send them to Ford Open Prison where there were no Ocado deliveries or tickets to Wimbledon or fine wines. Pete enjoyed these stories of her triumphs against the toffee-nosed elites.

Now her idea of lighting out for pastures new was a fucking

tea shop, the cosy comfort of home-made cakes and finger sandwiches. It wasn't much of a dream, as dreams go, as tame as a box of Milk Tray chocolates. What he remembered of a holiday they had spent in St Ives was the long white miles of the sky. Nothing up there apart from migrating birds and transatlantic air traffic. Birds were of some interest to him, he'd seen kingfishers on the river a few times, he could recognise all the usual breeds. His dad gave him a pair of binoculars for his twenty-first and he still had them in a leather case. But everything he cared about was down on the ground or flowing out to sea. On the river on a hot day he might lie down against his oars and stare upwards identifying the shapes of clouds, cumulus was a very satisfying word like the great bags of coddled gas they described, and it was pleasant. But mainly the sky was an unacknowledged blank grey companion with nothing much up there. It was the river itself that was interesting with a set of very clear-cut rules for watermen; it had its own language and the tide tables were something he had studied. He knew what spring tides were and that they were not confined to the year's first season. He understood that there could be hell to pay in the water if you didn't know what you were doing, and it was his purpose to get to the bottom of it.

So, sure, he could have a boat down there in which he could putter around the coast from inlet to inlet. At a pinch, he might even be able to get across the Channel, but that was hardly the point because what he liked was not open water but the general furniture of the riverbank: power stations, bridges, wharves, footpaths, riverside pubs, the Thames Barrier, container ships, the port of London.

They had been sitting on the bench a long time. The expanse of grass, the rumoured deer, the paths, the squirrels were an omen, he thought, as if the future was rushing towards him, full of birdsong and cows and sheep and muddy boots and olive-green fleece jackets and rural shit like that.

16

Only a month later and the sniff of a storm in the rushing air through the car window.

They had been guided west by old triumphalist signs embedded in all the fields and hedgerows.

Leave leave.

'It's not a very subtle message, is it?' he said. 'Did you arrange all that yourself on my behalf?'

'It doesn't mean that.'

'I know what it means.'

'Well, it's right, isn't it?'

'Do you think so? I'm surprised.'

'What are you surprised by? We've talked about nothing else since – oh, I see. Well, on that score I don't know what I really think, to be honest. But where we're hoping to go, it isn't really going to matter very much either way.'

They drove on.

But the West Country turned out to be not far enough. After

a couple of visits she turned her sights to the Lake District and it took two more trips to make an offer on a café on Lake Windermere. The owners had come to the end of their experiment in the hospitality trade and were planning to do nothing at all for as long as they possibly could, hoping to watch the wallpaper fade in bars of sunlight and, for excitement, observe clouds swell and take over the entire sky in a solid block of grey.

The café had a prime location near the landing stage; the passengers disembarked, ran up the stone steps by the slipway and the café was the first thing they saw, the kids straining at their parents' hands, screaming for sugar. It became obvious to him after a couple of weeks that he had no interest in or aptitude for café life, small children irritated him. His own had got on his nerves when they were this age but he had concealed it from their mother for they were flesh of your flesh, your message to the future and in the end they had grown up to become wonderful girls – cracking company, full of laughs and good humour and getting on with things and that stage in their lives had been overcome. Other people's whiny brats were a torment.

If he heard a kid crying his instinct was not to pick it up and soothe it but to walk sharply off so someone else could handle the situation. At work he had always tried if he could to delegate the comforting of a child in distress to a female colleague. There was a little girl he had to sit with while they waited for the ambulance. She died on the way to the hospital. Her heart had been crushed by a fist. He felt that her last half-hour should have been spent in the arms of someone with more of a knack for infancy, who could let life gently release her without fear or pain. But he was tense and hoarsely breathing, kept barking at her, 'It's going to fine, it'll be fine I tell you,' when he could see that it was no good at all. She was turning a strange colour, her eyes rolled upwards. The psycho was in prison now and so was the mother, the kid under a teddy-bear tombstone paid for by

130

the granddad who had given evidence in court against his own daughter while these living brats screeched for ice creams.

The children trooping in and out of the café with their mummies and daddies demanded not just the homely familiarity of a slice of Victoria sponge or carrot cake but babyccinos and smoothies. Their parents, before they would hand over their money, demanded to know the organic provenance of the ingredients and whether the meat had been humanely reared. The supplier, to cater for these suspicious investigations, had an actual poster in the café with photographs and names of members of the herd producing the milk for the ice cream. It was all so fucking preposterous and twee and middle class, surely they were taking the piss? Taking the piss out of Charles and Allegra and little Fuchsia and little Sebastian in their Boden holiday clothes crying for pomegranates and avocados.

Their own house was inland, in a village. A village by a river, a tributary of some bigger waterway, sluggish and even-tempered in the summer, a docile bit of wetness lined with reed beds and herons and warblers. Early on after they arrived, they had borrowed a boat from a guy in the pub and taken it out one evening after work. It was after eight and the sun was still over the top of the bank. Above the treeline cows ambled about on the hillside and in other fields sheep were grey smudges. Marie had brought a picnic basket and a bottle of wine. 'Isn't this idyllic?' she said. 'Isn't this just beautiful? We'll sort out your own boat for you once the season's over.' He looked around at the placid scene and at his wife, and thought, *It's what she wants so I'll put up with it; it's what she wants.*

She looked very healthy, the shadow of cancer had passed over her and left little mark. Her hair had grown back. She felt, she said, revitalised and reborn as if an electric current had jolted her into a more intense life, one in which she felt she could demand what she wanted, whenever she wanted. It was a licence, she had conceded, to selfishness. 'Of course,' he had said. 'Of course, love.'

In early September he cherished the memory of that high summer evening, they hadn't had another opportunity, and now the days were too short. 'We'll be better organised next year, we'll do it more often,' she said.

She had developed an interest in deserted places.

'You know what else I'm thinking about, buying a nice little camper van and doing a winter tour of the Highlands. Oh my God, you should see your mug. It reminds me of that painting, what's it called? The man with the scribbled face screaming.'

She said they could tour the whole of the British Isles, penetrate up to the Hebrides. It would be, she said, a gas, getting to know their own country for a change instead of two-week breaks in Minorca grilling by the pool and drinking and eating too much at night. She was finished with all that. And he conceded that he too would like a different type of holiday but if he had anything in mind it was city breaks, exploring, say, Barcelona with a guidebook and he bet they had cracking shops she'd enjoy. But they set this disagreement aside until the end of the season, because as they were to discover, the end of the season was both the finishing tape and the starting point for everything in their lives that mattered.

The village contained a church, a pub, a shop selling milk, newspapers, gravy granules, salad cream, Pot Noodles, chocolate and a few wizened vegetables. For as long as anyone could remember there had been a chippie which had recently become a Thai takeaway. The Thai owners did not live in the village, no one knew exactly where they resided, they just turned up every afternoon by car to open up and heat their woks. It was supposed that somewhere there was a community of their fellow-countrymen. After they had doled out the last green curry and pad thai they departed, small and smiling, the smiles snapping shut on their faces as they pulled out beyond the church in the direction of urban life.

In the pub everyone casually, and probably, he thought, unintentionally, rubbed him up the wrong way. There was a certain amount of ribbing he was prepared to take about his appearance: his tweed cap, his goatee beard, his chestnut-coloured special-edition Doc Martens. Working-class dandies always got it in the neck from the sheep who wore Next jeans, replica shirts and scuffed white Nike trainers; he didn't take it personally. Everyone, he realised, had their prejudices, it was the way of the world, but it was what they kept saying about London – no one had actually been there but they all watched *EastEnders* and claimed that this was enough to get the picture.

The days behind the counter in the tea room took for ever; at the end of the afternoon he was exhausted, hungry, itchy with boredom.

At home he picked up his knife and fork and attacked the pie and peas Marie had heated up for their supper, tearing a big rent in the crust and forking meat and potatoes into his mouth.

'They're looking forward to leaving in the pub,' he said. 'Can't bloody wait for the foreigners to go home and there aren't even any foreigners here apart from the Thais.'

'Since when were you interested in politics?'

'What do you mean? I always vote.'

'Oh, voting. It takes you five minutes and you never give it a thought before or afterwards.'

'We've always voted Labour.'

'Not necessarily.'

'What do you mean?'

A husband was supposed, he had read, to enjoy his wife's surprises but he wasn't enjoying the rush of declamatory announcements which had started arriving as far back as when he found the lump in her breast, as if he'd willed them into being with his wandering hands. Who was she anyway? He would watch her in front of the mirror drying her hair and putting on her make-up and her face would become completely strange to him, assuming an expression of severity and coldness, as if she was judging what she saw: the crepiness under her eyes and the mole with the hair growing out of it (a hair which had once been a springing lustrous black and had now turned limp and completely white). She painted in a fuller upper lip rose pink. And he would say, 'You look nice, love,' just to get rid of that face, that expression, it scared and repelled him. She would turn round and say, with surprise, 'Thanks, thanks for noticing.' He would bend to kiss her hair, but she'd grab his hand, 'Don't mess with it, I've only just got it sorted out.'

Now they were having some sort of row about politics in which she said, 'That's between me and the ballot box.'

'What the fuck do you mean? Who did you vote for?'

'Language, Pete. And it doesn't matter because it's not what I'm talking about and I wouldn't tell you anyway if that's the words you're going to use.'

'So what are you saying? You've lost me.'

'You're not even *making* an effort.'

'I try my best. Anyway, what's that got to do with it?'

'That business with the coin you stuck to the floor. Talk about passive-aggressive.'

'Yeah, so what? It was a practical joke.'

He had laughed himself sick watching the kids trying to pick the pound up from the step. One of the mothers had accused him of child abuse, had got hot and bothered and angry and stood for a few minutes outside warning customers not to go in, and this had led to a short-lived rumour that he was a paedophile. In his bravado he'd personally spread it about that he was a bent copper who'd made the money to buy the café from dealing drugs in Notting Hill. One of Marie's waitresses had actually asked her if it was true. He was still approached, as he was closing up, by local youth, trying to buy pills and weed.

'You're getting a reputation.'

'As what? That bent copper thing or the nonce thing?'

'For being a misery guts, that thing.'

'I agree. I'm miserable. I don't like it here.'

A condensed, compacted mass of irritations and blown-up incidents like the coin joke were leading to an explosion. Marie in her floral pinny looked to him the part, the part of someone playing a part but soon she wouldn't be, she'd have become one of them.

He said, 'Getting back to what you were saying, did you vote UKIP, by any chance?'

'What the hell has that got to do with anything? Why are you going on about them? It's you we're talking about, and our life here.'

'You better tell me if you did.'

'I give up, I really do.'

'You wanted to get away from the foreigners, didn't you?'

'Not necessarily.'

'Have I been married to a fucking racist – sorry *bloody* racist – all these years, is that more acceptable language? Or have you just turned that way?'

'I can't believe you just said that. I can't even—'

'I'm sorry, I'm sorry but it just came out, I'm suffocating, I can't breathe here. I'm so bored, every day is forty-eight hours. No wonder my thoughts drive me bonkers.'

'Oh, get over yourself.'

'What's cancer done to you? I don't recognise my own wife any more.'

'Everyone changes, we're not stuck in the headspace we had at twenty, we grow up, life throws stuff at us and we react to it. That's normal, it's natural. We've both said things we shouldn't have said and don't mean. Let's give it a rest, shall we? Get to the end of the season, let's get to the end of October, then we'll talk again.'

And it was his intention to clear the plates from the table, to stack them in the dishwasher, the evening meal she had just heated up for them after a long day with the sandwiches and scones, but instead he got his cap and walked out of the house. The village was empty. In films, deserted tame-looking places like this were always the openers for horror or zombies. It gave him the creeps. He passed along black streets and looked up at the sky where low clouds obscured the moon and stars. At the crossroads a stone war memorial held the names of the dead, the farmers and blacksmiths who went off to war like mugs. His dad had been too young for it, done national service without ever leaving the country and said it was the same tedium without the risk of getting killed. Warned his son against uniforms but he hadn't listened.

Beyond the last cottage was a rugby pitch. Then nothing. A track across a field of sweetcorn. From a hill, a glance at the lake but only in leafless winter.

He turned back and passed through the village again. It was five past nine. The barman in the pub was idle, watching a football match on TV. Everything was depressing. He felt that his marriage was going under like a cartoon character sinking into quicksand.

And he remembered his lovely Thames, her steady inexorable purpose, how she was a watery road through the city, how the Spanish Armada had tried to sail up her and been repelled, how in that film he'd seen Sir Thomas More was rowed home from visiting the King at Hampton Court, how the river brought the plague and how it had become so polluted by industry it nearly died. The coal barges, the sailing ships, the great steel barrier out at Greenwich (beautiful sight in the sunshine), and the bridges, twenty from Tower to Kew, there was a poem about them he had learned at school.

I'd have you know that these waters of mine were once a branch of the River Rhine.

Yes, she could have flowed and ebbed and eddied all the way down to Germany.

Now memory was at a high flood, the memory of the dead woman who had arrived in his life at a time of crisis and borne him away with her. Were they both drowning? He had lost everything, his city, his river, his own real wife, who stood behind a counter with her flapjacks and brownies and Victoria sponge and carrot cake, making chat with the locals, having been entirely consumed with that fiery feeling women get, and made for herself another life, of cake and floral pinnies, a pale-faced existence in a pale-faced land. Sometimes a black family came into the café smelling of cocoa butter and looking all wrong: the woman's weave, the bloke's shaved head, the kids in expensive trainers, as if they were a ship that had blown off course and found itself marooned in the sand banks of an alien port. The other customers stared down at their bowls of leek and potato soup and slices of crusty bread and butter. The men surreptitiously felt for their wallets, the women pushed their handbags between their feet. There was a definite atmosphere. Marie said she hadn't noticed, he was imagining it, he was being unfair. He should take people as he found them.

One afternoon a woman in a hijab appeared, by herself, and ordered an Americano and a Bakewell slice. The scarf was tied like a bandage around her face, a brown oval with kohl-decorated eyes. The place held itself like a cocked gun until she finished, paid, left.

Part Four

17

'Are you lost?' Rob said to the man looking at a map, thinking how unusual it was to see someone holding a paper gazetteer of London's streets as he and everyone in his generation had bought one when they first came to the city and felt they were in the wilderness if they left it at home.

'Well, I know I'm in—'

The map was the fold and the fold was deep in his life.

He had taken his mother to a concert at the Queen Elizabeth Hall. He had chosen it for Beethoven's 'Emperor' concerto, which they were both great fans of, she had been a reasonably accomplished amateur pianist in her youth, but the opening piece was Holst's 'Ode to Death', perhaps a tactless choice, for she kept looking down at the programme notes to read the Whitman poem it was set to. She must think about death a great deal at her age, he supposed. Or perhaps she didn't. The final item was a Vaughan Williams, who was filed away in his mind as a composer of charming, pastoral – what was the phrase? Cowpat music – but the *Sinfonia antartica* was all crash-bang sound effects of wind and storm and ice cracking, terribly atmospheric and the percussion section had its work cut out. Glancing at his mother, instead of being excited, enthralled, carried away, she seemed frightened and upset. He wished he could make it stop. It had been composed in 1952 and it seemed to him to have all the hall-marks of Festival of Britain symphonies for the new Elizabethan age, concrete modernism and Lucienne Day curtains. Was it not his mother's era? But of course she had been a child after the war, and her period was really the early sixties, at teacher training college, drinking instant coffee, listening to Cliff Richard and the Shadows on the Dansette.

Still shaking from the violence of the symphony ('Oh, I didn't like that at all, Robert, wasn't it noisy?') they walked along the South Bank to Blackfriars station. It was nearly ten, the last light going from the sky. He watched from the other side of the ticket barrier as she safely got on her train back to Horsham. Her mood had lightened on the walk. 'I've had such a lovely day,' she said. 'It's been perfect.' So she seemed to have forgotten about the clamorous Vaughan Williams. A taxi had been pre-booked to pick her up from Horsham station and take her home. 'Everything is arranged, Mummy, but send me a text as soon as you're in the car, you will, won't you?' She is not so old, he thought, and could she not join a club or an evening class and meet new people? And what about a widower with a trilby hat and ... But here his imagination failed for he could not really think of where you would locate these widowers who would find his mother alluring. She had settled down years ago into early widowhood, she had decided that like a new fashion it suited her and she would go on wearing it. She would not do well on a dating app, good God no, he'd protect her from that.

He crossed the river and was walking to meet Justin. Then the man with the map.

Days later, when Justin banged on the door of his flat, ham-mering with his fists – 'Where the hell are you, Rob? What's going on?' – he would make him coffee and do his best to explain it, to reassemble the tesserae of memory and perhaps false memory, to form it into a narrative that would work for him. For Justin deserved that, the whole story, as much as he was capable of even telling it to himself, but there was no whole story, just this string, this . . . and the man with a map with a fold in it.

'You know, of all the things that happened to me after he said . . . I mean . . . look, I didn't *see* the van, I just heard the impact and the screams. It wasn't like a bomb going off, that's different, I heard one of those, years ago. In the split second before it there's this . . . tension, a great calm, like the stillness before an earthquake, then a huge . . . I don't know what you'd call it, I suppose a *force*. Yes, I guess so. But this was completely different because there wasn't a bomb, just total fucking chaos. And the van was veering away from us, I was watching it like a movie, as if you could even interpret what it was doing as . . . harmless? But everyone was screaming except me and the man with the map because I don't know about him but I couldn't speak at all. I wouldn't have been surprised if the medics said I'd been struck dumb. I *know*. Me of all people. And when I could speak I was completely incoherent for probably the first time in my life, babbling actually, just making random consonants with my tongue.

'I could see you a way in the distance, looking round wildly for me, I think you must have arrived later because . . . I don't know . . . you just didn't look like everyone else, you seemed to have a purpose whereas I had no purpose, I was just staggering around with this numb tongue. I heard you ask if I was all right and I couldn't get a word out. Someone else, was he with you, I don't know who he was, anyway, he said, "He's shocked, he's shocked!" And I thought, *I'm not shocked*, but I didn't say it. I couldn't say anything. And then the man with the map, who I think must have been a tourist, said with an accent, maybe Spanish, "What a welcome," and he walked away, he just . . . I don't know, disappeared back into the world.

'By now I was finding it more difficult to move. I was filled with terror and I felt rooted to the spot. I heard people shouting "Clear the area" but I felt as if I was invisible. I *wanted* to be cleared but I couldn't clear myself. I couldn't walk and I couldn't speak either. There were a lot of confused shouts and I heard the police crying, "Keep them, they're witnesses!" And someone said, "They won't let us go, they think we're terrorists." The area was cordoned off by now and it started filling up with ambulances and police and medical staff. I think they actually did know what to do; that is, they knew what to do but they didn't know what to do first, so they kept moving us about, shuffling us from place to place.

'And then this big Irish girl came over and she said, "Are you all right? You look terrible, I'm a nurse." I said I thought I was okay, I didn't have any injuries or anything, I wasn't close enough to have been rammed, thank God, and she said, "Well, these things can affect you in funny ways, I'd get off to hospital if I were you." "But I'm just the walking wounded," I said, and it seemed to me, not for the first time, that this was a ridiculous condition to be in, like a hypochondriac, nothing the matter with you, except maybe in your head. As she stood there, in off-duty clothes – jeans and a little sequinned crop top and a jacket and her hair piled high on her head and pinned with velvet bloody butterfly bows, I thought, *But don't I know you?* And she saw my look and said, "Do you recognise me from the telly?" And it came back to me that she was on that documentary we saw about missing persons a while back. "Yes!" I said. "I'm glad no harm came to you."

'"Oh, don't worry about me," she said, "I was always fine, always right as rain."

'"And you've got that nice boyfriend now," I said.

"No, not any more. Wasn't he just picked up by the police one early morning and deported, no work fucking permit? All those lads have gone now, the ones in that flat. Couple of them left after the vote thing, said they were off, knew when they weren't wanted. I told them they were being stupid, if anything happened it wouldn't happen that quick, and I wasn't going nowhere myself."

'I said that was a shame, and then I said, and this was really apropos of nothing, I don't know why I said it, because I was kind of tactless, that this wasn't the first time this had happened to me, it was years ago, it was an IRA bomb in a pub in Covent Garden in the nineties, the Sussex it was called, it's not there any more, it was pulled down and redeveloped, thank God, because I used to have to avoid Long Acre and that end of St Martin's Lane altogether, which was awkward, it meant operas at the ENO were out for years. The press, they want to put words in your mouth about how you feel about the kinds of people who do this kind of thing and I never accepted those words. I think I was trying to say something about her being Irish but she didn't seem to understand. "I mean terrorists," I said, and she said, "Oh, they're terrible scoundrels, the lot of them.

'"But listen," she said, "you should go to hospital anyhow, even if you think you're okay." So that's what I did. I said to you, "I'll go to hospital," and you said – because you'd found me by now and you were standing there trying to hug me and I was shrinking away, "I'm coming with you." I don't know why I told you to go home, it doesn't make any sense to me now. I can still see you standing there looking, looking . . . looking as though I'd rejected your big fat marriage proposal or something but I thought I'd be better by myself, giving me time to absorb everything, it was stupid, wasn't it? I kept thinking about Mum and getting out my phone because I'd told her to text me when she was home but sometimes she forgets and if she'd turned on the news before she went to bed . . . I wanted to ring her but I didn't want to worry her, and of course I'd told her I was straight off home, not going out to a bar and having to put up with her questions. So that was another fold, between you and her and that meant between you and me. Ridiculous. That look you gave me, I'll never forget it. But I don't know, it seemed the right thing to do at the time, to be by myself, I mean with the others who this had happened to. Because we were a kind of pack now, like animals who hunt together, no, this is rubbish, I don't know what I mean.

'I'll tell you what happened in the hospital. I started saying my name and address endlessly, I don't know how many times. No idea. Dozens. They would come up to me, look in my eyes, ask me if I needed a cup of tea and take my name and address. They came in relays, very caring actually, eventually the Irish nurse turned up, but changed into her uniform now and I waved to her and she came over and said hello. I could see her walking very quickly and very calmly from one patient to another and picking people up and hoisting them on trolleys and generally just being one of those angels of the NHS you're always hearing about. I was sorry her boyfriend got deported, and I thought, *Well, she's another who had a fold, from running off from that creep to the guys in the flat and now she's lost her chance of a fresh start.* It seemed a shame.

'We were all looking at our phones, reading and watching the news trying to make sense of what just happened. I can only explain it like this, that I was beginning to feel that the enormity of it was separating me from other people. I didn't ring you because I didn't know what to say. That's all it was. I just ... I know. I *know*. Honestly, I understand why you're hurt. I would be myself. Then they let me go. A copper said if I needed to talk I could ring him any time and he gave me his number, so I went out. Then the nurse started calling out to me, she must have read my name on all the forms I'd filled in, "Robert, Robert, get back here! You're needed by the police." It was just more questions, of course, but now I was beginning to feel suspicious of everyone around me. And then, wouldn't you know it, when they finally allowed me to leave I walked out into the arms of the press.

'You have to understand by this time I'd already told my story over and over and over, and it just seemed as if I had to tell it again, it was mandatory. I thought, *Okay, I'll talk to this guy with the notebook because it's only words, words in a notebook.* Then out of nowhere all these cameras appeared and I'm on the news, I'm on the TV news, and my phone starts going off like a fucking bomb in my pocket with texts and calls and it sounds mad, I realise that, but the phone began to feel like an enemy so I threw it in the bin. Which was a bit stupid because, as I say, I'd told my mother to text me when she was in the taxi and now . . . I can't say I experienced that sense of freedom the nurse did when she found she'd lost her phone, because when I got home I realised I'd forgotten I'd got rid of the landline and couldn't call anyone. Mum was completely inaccessible because she doesn't use the internet, I couldn't even email her. So I'd cut off my nose to spite my face there. I know from later people thought I'd done very well on television, as if I'd given a performance but I didn't want congratulations, I wanted sympathy. And I couldn't get any because I had no phone.

'It's been bad, I can't pretend otherwise. The past few days I've found it really hard to get up in the mornings. I lie in bed for four or five hours and when I do get up I find myself in a room without remembering how I got there. I go to the sink to brush my teeth and stand there, looking at it. My mind is telling me, *This is what you do in the morning, you brush your teeth, you idiot. This is what you do at a shop, you go in and buy something.* But I can't seem to act on that information. I feel floaty, as if I'm high on drugs and I begin to wonder if the attack even happened at all. And I needed a connection to people who'd been through it, to tell me it *did* actually happen and it's not just me and my overactive imagination, or an hallucination. Because thinking that can drive you completely doolally.

'That nurse came round, which was a surprise and an actual

lifesaver, which you wouldn't expect. She wanted to see if I was all right. Turns out after the flat-share broke up she'd moved in just round the corner on one of the other blocks on the estate, she said the hospital kept trying to ring me but, of course, no phone any more until the insurance replaces it . . . no I haven't rung them yet . . . I mean, I haven't got a phone, have I? So she had my address and wanted to look in. Which was nice, wasn't it? Not that I could tell her how I felt, it would have taken ages but she's maybe the only thing from that night that seems real. The guy with the map, the tourist, he might as well be from a fairy tale, did he ever exist? But there she is in a YouTube video dancing to the Arctic Monkeys in some park and I've watched it a few times on my laptop, because I feel a connection to her and . . . Yes, don't look at me like that, I do know that it's going to be a problem between us that I don't feel that about you. I mean, obviously I feel a connection, but not through what happened, because you weren't there, you were late – no I don't mean late in that sense, I mean that it was over by the time you got there, the main thing was over and you arrived for the aftermath, while she was *actually* there on her night off, and I was there. Do you want to see the video? No, not of my interview, I mean of her, dancing. I've got it right here.'

18

There was a girl at school and she was always saying, 'One day I'm going to go to Bangkok.' What a place to decide to go to and no one knew where the hell it even was and you had to look it up and found it was just as far away as it sounded, the capital of Thailand, all palm trees and beaches and willowy graceful golden-brown people but then there had been that tsunami and a lot of people killed so maybe not all it was cracked up to be, sounded dangerous. The girl said, well you just have to stay away from the beaches after all and Bangkok isn't even *on* the beach, it's on the Chao Phraya river. Then what do you know, as soon as she finishes her exams, she's gone to Bangkok and is working in some hotel there so it's possible that you can say this stuff and it's not just words.

'I'm going to live in London.' She said it one day on the bus and everyone nodded, and yes, actually, it was something that you could do, no trouble, not like Bangkok. London wasn't such a big deal, you could get there quick enough and once she'd finished her training off she goes to London. When are you coming back? they said, but she couldn't think that far forward, because what reason was there to *ever* return with the economy back home in a terrible mess and her uncle Eamonn who had that building company out in Wexford shot himself one morning in the garden amongst the rose bushes.

And now the funniest thing was everyone here suddenly finding out they were Irish. Oh, my granny came from Limerick, my dad was from Cork, all this Irish discovery just to get a European passport, and she had been born with one and could marry a million guys, take her pick, just because she had that maroon-coloured book so she could go anywhere instead of being stuck on this tight little island which is how everyone at home used to feel and now the shoe was on the other foot and her brother said he'd be laughing forever at that one. Yes, that was jokes.

Marco would have an EU passport, he'd be okay, as ever. She'd seen his passport and his real name in it, and she'd asked him, all innocent, where that last name had come from and he'd said, 'Well, obviously it's Mediterranean,' which shut her up, so he probably had an Italian grandpa or something. Alan forwarded her a text from him after the show went out, wishing her well. She hadn't replied. Marco was in the past now. They didn't have any friends in common and she'd no idea what he might be up to. But actually, that show had done her good, because she was always getting stopped by people on the street talking to her about the very important point she'd made about social media and all the rest of it, and how we should learn to live our lives more authentically, whatever that meant. Alan sent her reviews from the papers and while she didn't understand some of the stuff they said, she could see that it was pretty positive and that Marco had come across as a bit of a twat.

She'd watched it with Yousef and the other boys, he sat on her knee and kissed her neck, they were all scrunched up in the little living room. That woman, the one who drowned and the sheer coincidence of it being the very night she also went missing so everyone wanted to know if she'd seen her because they must have been on the same bridge at around the same time, but no she hadn't noticed a thing, no person on the parapet, no splash. She thought, *Well, maybe I could have talked her down, or at least grabbed her and pulled her off, she didn't look too heavy at all, I've lifted bigger than that.* And then everything would have been different because the police and the emergency services would have come, someone would have rung them, and she'd be required to say what happened and she wouldn't have wandered off, but gone home back to the flat and wouldn't have become a missing person.

While they were all watching and they were on that bit about the drowned woman, the Romanian boys were pointing at the screen and talking to each other in their funny language and she said, 'What? Did you know her?' But they just went and got more beer from the kitchen and clammed up.

Next day, she said, 'You knew that woman, didn't you? I could tell by your faces.'

One of them said maybe. Maybe at a party a couple of years ago. But they were like Yousef, something they didn't like at all was dealing with the authorities. They didn't trust the police, no way. She'd read on Wikipedia about where they were from, they'd had a dictator once running the country, before she was born, 'Yes,' they said, 'we killed him.' And they laughed. This was London, you really did meet all sorts here, just like her mum would have said, whose idea of all sorts was a Protestant.

Later in the week when Alan rang, she told him and he said, 'Oh, at last a lead,' like it was a cop show, and he would let the police know. But by the time they got in touch a couple of weeks later the boys had gone back home and it was just her and Yousef, and then he was deported and that was the end of that and she had a new flat-share, how many was this since she came to London? She felt a bit like she was of no fixed address, which was how they described homeless people, but she was never homeless, always had a place with a nice bathroom, insisted on that. Good strong water pressure to rinse the hospital smell out of her hair, though the limescale didn't help. Good strong water pressure, that was her number-one ask, which turned out to be not so easy to achieve in London because the mains were so old they were always leaking, leaking away underground, and there were underground rivers she had been told. Beneath your feet there was a lot going on.

She was with a couple of nurses now, so that was easy, both of them from Jamaica, which was very interesting because of everything they needed to do with their hair to make it straight, and the products that they had to put on it, and the gallons of cocoa butter lotion under the sink they sluiced themselves with because when you were dark and you had dry skin, you ended up with ashy legs, ew, you don't want that if you can help it. So now she smelled of cocoa butter too, and when her brother came over for the weekend he told her she smelled like a black person. Maybe she was becoming black from the inside out because it was a while now since she'd had it off with a white boy.

It was a great flat, near Victoria station so handy for the tube, on this big council estate. The flat didn't have a view of the river just the main road going up to the station, but you could get up from the telly in your living room if you wanted to and hoppity-hop into the lift and be down by the river watching the rushing water which it did when the tide was running and all the boats and barges and shit, though she never felt like doing that since the business on the bridge. The others did. They went down there to smoke and laugh whereas if she went down she just thought of past things and standing on the bridge someone would recognise her from the telly and thought she was going to jump, even though it had never been in her head her whole life long to throw herself in the river. God, a lot of people had seen that show and, she'd heard in a text from Alan McBride, it was up for an award, he thought she'd like to know.

Now her dad was calling her every week to come home, the city wasn't safe, all the terrorist attacks, you were protected nowhere, there were no warnings like in his day, when he'd lived in London in the eighties and you had the bomb scares, because the Muslims were all about murdering as many as they could and not even a clear goal in mind, what exactly were their demands? At least the IRA tried. She didn't even tell him she'd come *that close*. That would be oversharing because he'd go mad. He'd get on a plane and drag her back. Indeed it had been a terrible night. The injuries they'd seen, just horrendous, they didn't mention that on the news, people would completely freak out if they knew that surviving was such a terrible ordeal and you would probably never get your old life back. One of the doctors who was from Sierra Leone said it reminded him of the civil war in his country where the dead were in the ruins and rotting above ground. But you kept calm and did what you needed to do, like that gay guy, purely zombie, all by himself, in a much worse way than he thought he was. When she went round she told him he had PTSD and he needed to get some help, gave him a number to get counselling from Victim Support and did he know he might even be able to get some money from the government from a fund they had for victims of terror, it was worth looking into. But he said he didn't need any money, and looking round you could see what a nice flat it was, with no expense spared, apart from the bathroom which was sad and bit down at heel, the mildew in the grout, of course it was clean, but everything was a bit out of date and not like a hotel. Ex-council, like hers, but that was where the comparison ended, all the rooms beautifully furnished with lovely rugs and vases with real fresh flowers in them and actual paintings on the wall, not Ikea posters, which to be fair was always what she'd imagine the pad of an old gay

153

guy would be like. He was forty-nine, he'd have had the time to accumulate all that stuff and the taste to know how to buy it. But when she said how great the flat was, he said, 'Oh, do you think so? I've been living in Scottsdale and I needed somewhere fast so I bought this on first viewing because it was chain free.' Whatever that meant.

She wanted to know why he'd come back from America of all places, who would want to do that? He said he'd come to hate it, he used to be romantic about the US but that was finished, he couldn't stomach the place any more, he had wanted to be back in Europe, connected to Europe, to Paris and Rome and Madrid, which was ironic, he agreed, because it was only a few weeks before the referendum and now they were going to be cut off from the Continent. 'Not really,' she said, 'we can still go, after all.' 'Oh yes, but there's more to it than that,' and he began to talk about courts of justice and so on and he said the worst thing of all was going walking in the park and listening to all the foreign languages being spoken.

'We won't hear that in twenty years. If they stay, their kids will speak English as their first language and no new people will be coming. It'll be a time machine, taking us back to the past, don't you feel that, Chrissie? Isn't it like winter's wind?'

19

If everything was wack –

If David Bowie was dead and Leonard Cohen was dead, gone to the land of wack –

If the referendum was completely wack –

If the *Apprentice* guy was president so wackness ruled –

Then the stay-at-home club night idea was wack, it was for wack people –

'And you know what?' Marco said. 'Most people *are*.'

20

Marco had watched Alan's documentary alone at home on his MacBook Air after work. He drank a negroni whose intense, lacquered redness was a fortification and a statement of strength and confidence that felt less clichéd to him than an expensive brand of Scotch. His days were densely populated. So many handshakes, so much brand chat, that when he came home he preferred to retreat to privacy and peace. He luxuriated in the silence of his bedroom. By his bed was a vase of flowers. There was something ridiculous and unmasculine about this bunch of tulips but he liked their silent drooping, the falling of the white petals on to the quiet surface of his bedside table. The cleaner bought them and he reimbursed her; fresh flowers were always there when he got home from work on Friday night. Next to the flowers stood a framed photograph of his grandfather, Soad Itani, from a city called Tyre in the Lebanon. Tawny skin, gold-tooth smile, oiled quiff under a white chef's hat. Stylish at weddings in his navy stripe Cecil Gee suit and polished winklepicker shoes. 'A man must make much of himself, ' he said. 'It is his duty.'

The sanctuary of the room with its white bedlinen and charcoal throw, the white painted chest of drawers, by the window the cream Mies van der Rohe chair (a copy, bought on the internet), the wardrobe where his T-shirts lay folded in stable towers of snow-whiteness, deep-navy, jet-blackness – the rows of shoes a waiting army ready to march out on to the carpet and out of the flat along the street to take on the city, the charcoal Hugo Boss suit for which he had managed to negotiate a discount, the grey and silver grooming products an accessory to the mirror, all formed the stable cube of his personality. Here, he was most fully Marco, a character he had painfully assembled as boys of an earlier generation put together Lego castles and pirate ships. (For his real name was Neil Geoffrey, which was separated at such a distance from his surname Itani that it resembled a cut-up, one of those cars formed of the front and rear end of two completely different vehicles.)

His new flatmate Joe was out. Joe was staying with his girlfriend. Joe was fine and no trouble, they barely saw each other. His arrival had eradicated the chaos of Chrissie's tenure, the months of her large presence in the flat. She had ended dramatically, with fuss and publicity, but she was gone and what was left was a moment of unearned celebrity. And honestly, he had told his boss at work, she was the last person you'd ever expect to have her fifteen minutes of fame for she did not belong in their world, he could not make her fit with handshakes with restaurant critics, tasting menus and VIP cocktails. Most of all she seemed to lack any kind of inner life or locking mechanism for her thoughts (as he all day must produce a shoal of smooth silvery platitudes like fish) and she would say whatever came into her mouth until he'd finally snapped and blurted out loud what he'd been thinking, because she'd *goaded* him into it. Her presence was flaying his skin with that phone call (*if the party's shite*) and he was thinking, *Shut up shut up shut, for God's sake, everyone is looking and listening, oh you do go on.*

His interview was only two and a half minutes long. He timed it. He had expected to be her co-star, the person she had argued with, and run off from in a fit of silly pique, the one who had in her own best interests, and because of his genuine concern, got the Twitter appeal going, uploaded the YouTube video, brought into being what the film was supposed to be investigating – how one became, unexpectedly (even unknown to yourself, as it was unknown to Chrissie), a viral personality online. This was his work, not hers, and he had talked, pretty lucidly, he felt, about the process by which he had made sure that the tweet was retweeted by significant celebrities in the club, fashion and music scenes, people he actually knew, or whom he followed and had personally requested to hit the little button. That was all his endeavour.

He was lying on his bed. He was in his olive-green silk boxers. Last week he had nearly bought a full corduroy tracksuit, the marketing made him laugh – 'For when you're ready to do road and geography simultaneously.' He admired fashion even when it was stupid, for it was fearless in its belief that it could *never* be ridiculous; if you took yourself seriously enough then the world would respect you. They would be defeated by your self-confidence. There was something out there for everyone, especially if you were brave, and he understood this because he had shown courage, more than anyone else he knew; had the injuries, had the scars. At sixteen he had got a job after school to save for a pair of expensive shoes. Not trainers, he had aspired to something more adult, a classic shoe, a brogue and a polishing kit to go with it, he had read an article about them in a men's magazine he had found in a bin at the bus stop, full of treasure. Of people who stood in awkward positions and looked angrily at the camera. Of the surface of everything being burnished by newness and inaccessibility. He loved it. A gentleman's shoes, he read, were how you judged him. He would never again be judged by scruffy trainers.

He still had them in their original box, though his feet had gone on growing and they no longer fit him, but they were stored on a shelf, a memento of an early commitment to a higher calling. To pay for them he cleaned the school classrooms and cloakrooms in an orange tabard after the school day ended, dragging a bucket around. All day boys and girls ostentatiously sniffed when he passed, yanking imaginary toilet flushes; brush-head was the obvious and unoriginal nickname. There was shame and humiliation but if he had not bought those shoes when he was seventeen and a half who exactly would he be? Not Marco. Still Neil Geoffrey.

I know wack, he thought. *I have a fucking degree in it.*

The negroni rinsed off the day, his phone was throbbing with messages from friends who had already seen him on TV: *There'll be no stopping you now.*

Chrissie had changed. She too had finally started to make something of herself. She had lost a bit of weight, the make-up artist had done an amazing job. Her skin appeared smooth and flawless. She'd had a manicure. Marco was fascinated by her self-assurance talking to the camera, as if she had no trouble expressing a complex thought and she had known all along what she was doing. She spoke instead about feeling free, a freedom you at first might mistake for loneliness but was not the same at all: a disconnection from the world you knew and the possibility to do something else. It had begun at the moment when she realised she had lost her phone, and how losing your phone, she used to think, was the very worst thing in the world that could happen to you – because your whole life was in there, wasn't it, who remembered phone numbers any more, she didn't know a single one apart from her own. But it had liberated her. She actually used that word, was not rehearsed, she was rushing through sentences as she always did.

And knowing nothing about the Twitter appeal, she had

drifted across London, met some guy on the night bus and now she was living with him and they were an item, and he appeared too, saying he had no idea he had taken home a missing person, she was just a lovely girl. The guy looked like a little dog, small enough to sit in her lap.

'It is a fairy tale of the city, this wonderful city!' he had said.

This was shown and almost everything Marco had said had been cut. The show seemed to him to be fundamentally untruthful. Alan had for some reason bottled it, as if he was willing a happy ending for her. And that as much as she had become a temporary celebrity on social media for a couple of days while it was being retweeted and liked, something else was going on during her wanderings across the city – what was the word for it?

'Real', that was what Alan was trying to get at, wasn't it? That real life wasn't online, that your authentic self found its expression when you weren't staring at a screen or living your life on a screen or pretending to be someone else on-screen. But oh, *reality*, Marco said out loud, give me a break. Nobody believes in that any more. For what are we all doing here, smart-arse, but watching your fucking show?

Then there was the body in the river, but he had fast-forwarded her, having nothing to do with him, and the missing kid riding the rails to Brighton to see the sea he had tried to blank.

21

He had a new girlfriend, nothing serious at this stage, he could not quite believe that she was real and not someone he'd read about in a magazine. She was only twenty-two. Her name was Agatha Mackenzie. She interned for an event management company in the kitchens making up trays of miniature hot dogs and pork pies the size of raised pound coins. When he explained his idea for online club nights she nodded and whooshed her long blonde hair with its Sloane Square highlights. She had connections to people on *Made in Chelsea*, two of whom were related to her in complicated ways he could not follow but these blended families were all like that, she said. Agatha wanted to know why the two of them had no Venn diagram overlap; at the very least they should have in common friends who had gone to the same school or the same university. Marco said his father was a supermarket area manager in Aylesbury.

'Really?' she said. 'How strange.'

'It's Sainsbury's.'

'We shop at Waitrose,' she said. 'At home.'

'Of course you do.'

Occasionally he picked up packets of chicken breasts and

sautéed them in olive oil and served them with crème fraîche and Dijon mustard and tried to interest her in a sit-down meal together in the living room, at the table. Agatha mostly ate salad leaves, chopped tofu, avocado on toast, standing up in the kitchen. Her father, she said, 'farms in Shropshire', which was nothing to do with getting up at dawn to milk cows or muck out smelly pigs but involved sitting on the boards of various agribusinesses. She had two sisters, and three half-sisters from her father's second marriage and a half-brother from her mother's relationship with her yoga teacher. It seemed to Marco that people of her class only promoted outsiders into their intimate circle whose standing was that of servants: grooms for their horses, personal trainers, drivers. Supermarket managers were outside their zone of knowledge, except as the recipients of letters of complaint.

In his career in restaurant and bar PR he was constantly invited to openings, to drinks and lunches with chefs and entrepreneurs, journalists and social media stars. He was naturally at home seated in the VIP area. The difficulty about starting a company dedicated to wack was that you could, if you were not careful, become – how would you call it? Shop soiled? Contaminated by the people your product was sold to. In wack times, the world of exclusivity would become smaller and more pronounced to mark itself out and separate itself from what he had created. There was only so much work a Hugo Boss suit could do on your behalf.

Returning home on the tube he would look round at the numb passengers, the general exhaustion of getting through a single day, let alone a week, in London: the careworn faces of girls no older than twenty-five, the signs and signals of their fashion tribes; the African women with splayed feet; guys studying what looked like company paperwork; others staring glassily at their Facebook page (one girl scrolling past a photo of herself, jaw stretched, actually in the act of giving a blow job reminding him sharply of the half-forgotten Chrissie) – all of them with white wires coming out of their ears. In this grubby, tired hiatus between work and the flat it came to him that he should try if he could to marry Agatha, ideally at a society wedding at Babington House, or if he could not persuade her family out of it, some blah country house hotel in Shropshire no one had ever heard of.

Strap-hanging on crowded trains, his copy of the *Evening Standard* jammed under his arm, he saw himself in riding jodh-purs and a crimson coat on the back of a majestic horse, like a Ralph Lauren advertisement, looking handsome and chiselled in the winter sunlight but not having a clue what to do, holding on to the saddle while the beast took off across icy fields.

Agatha had said, 'Oh, I love riding, but I suppose the fox is less keen.'

He had seen foxes at night, attacking the bins, they were grey, long, disgusting creatures; they made him feel sick. Agatha said real country foxes were nothing like that, these were urban crack addicts by comparison. 'Gross. Really gross.' And he said it was a shame that the good foxes were hunted with dogs while the wack foxes were free to roam about city gardens. She agreed that it was somehow the wrong way round.

His father was in London for a meeting at head office. He was a man of limited recreational interests and a dislike of public transport. In the West End there were few forecourts with ruled-off parking spaces, just costly meters and that was if you could find one. He endured the train as if it were a transportation to a worse life, he belonged behind the wheel of a nice, but not flashy car. He enjoyed driving, it suited his need for a lapse into emotional distance from customers and their erratic demands.

Marco met his father in Starbucks. There was a long-standing affection between them that expressed itself in a brief touching of each other's shoulder, a comforting intimacy. His father's wedding ring brushed across his son's jacket. He chose a cake, and a complicated drink with whipped cream. Marco ordered a peppermint tea. His father had practised on the journey calling his son Marco instead of Neil, it was only polite to do so, his wife said. 'He's still our boy, but let him live his own life, Frank, he's twenty-nine, he knows what he's doing.'

Frank Itani had a theoretical understanding of his son's business proposal. When the idea had first been introduced, he grasped that there were many people who did not want to go to the bother of going out: having to order taxis, or driving and not being able to drink, alarm clocks the next morning smashing into a pounding headache. The idea fell into the same category as online shopping. He did not understand much of what his son told him about his life in London. Days after the twitterstorm he had discovered Marco's social media stardom with the missing flatmate; a year later he had watched the TV programme and thought she was a bit of a tart, a surprising choice for Neil to live with, not his type at all. He had learned from him what had provoked her refusal to get off the train and career onwards to Moorgate: to the lost phone, being lost herself, then becoming famous, then found, and now long gone from Neil's life. He understood how something like that would inadvertently slip out, it was only human nature with a girl like her, she sounded exhausting.

Marco introduced the subject of his new girlfriend.

'Agatha? Isn't that an old lady's name?'

'Back in fashion, Dad. Keep up! I'm thinking that if I can get my digital club night idea off the ground she could be my assistant.'

'You wouldn't need to pay her very much, I hope.'

'No, just minimum wage.'

'Ideal.'

'You know the type, Penelope's pony paddock and private school. Connected.'

'Good for you! I won't mention it to your mother, she'll start shopping for a hat.'

His mother at the wedding was something which would require careful planning. He might get her an appointment with a personal shopper to bring out the best in her blocky figure. She would cry too copiously and have forgotten to use waterproof mascara.

'Way too early for that, Dad.'

'Changing the subject for a minute, I don't know what you think about this business of, you know.'

'What business?'

'The country. Whether or not it will all end in tears.'

'Oh, yes, that.'

He felt he ought to be able to understand them, the leavers. He had voted himself, had got on the register and found the polling station, walked past all the Remain posters in the windows of houses and flats and gone in, and they had his name there, and they'd given him his ballot paper and he had stood, looking down and smiling at the idiocy of the question as if only a fool could possibly give the wrong answer, then gone back to work, gone out to a bar, home to bed and the next morning been woken by Joe shouting in the next bedroom at seven in the morning, *'Fuck! No!'* Which was unusual coming from him, a quiet guy who worked in finance, pensions, and read actual newspapers, the type one held in one's hand, which was so retro it might even return to fashion.

In the next few weeks he had wondered if that was an over-reaction, for London, as everyone knew, was in a separate category, a category of luck and money.

'We had an incident last week,' Frank said. 'On the pavement outside one of the branches, we had to call the police. I happened to be there at the time, we were reviewing the freezer sections. People don't want so much frozen any more apart from the obvious, chips and peas and pizzas and ice cream, but we'd had a few requests in for frozen croissants and bags of mixed berries.'

'What happened?'

'We decided to give them a trial run, it was a matter of making some room next to the fish fingers.'

'I mean the incident, Dad.'

'Oh, yes, sorry. You see there's a woman who sells the *Big Issue* outside one of our branches. I'm not sure where she's from originally, Greece? Albania? I don't know. She's a bit funny looking, always wears ankle-length skirts but no headscarf, she might be Muslim but I can't be sure. She's very energetic, much more than the last lad whose pitch she took. He was a pathetic case, the type who comes out of a children's home to nothing, he's not actually homeless, he has a hostel place, but he's not – well, I think he's probably on drugs.'

'They all are, Dad.'

'That's what I thought. Anyway, she did steal his pitch, in that apparently she contacted the organisation and said half the time he didn't even turn up so she got it and as you can imagine that sent him over the edge, so this day he starts screaming at her: what's she still doing here, shouldn't she have gone home by now? She asks him what he means and he says that all the foreigners have got to go home, that's the law, it just happened. Frankly I was surprised he followed the news, he always seemed so out of it, but there you are. He was such a pathetic bedraggled creature, half falling over because he was drunk or sick or stoned, looked like he wasn't long for this world and the woman saying nothing, just staring back at him, much healthier, no way she was on drugs. So then the security guard came out to see what was going on, Charles his name is, big Jamaican, body-builder type, and this lad starts screaming at him, too, saying what's he still doing here, he's got to go home to Africa or wherever he's from.'

'Jesus, that's a bit rich.'

'I know. Well, a customer asked to see the manager, I was in the office as it happens, so I came out and she said she wanted to report him for a racially motivated attack and would I call the police, so that's what I did, I called the police. While we were waiting, the lad starts on me – why is an Arab running the shop? I said I didn't know what he was talking about but he says, "You look Arab to me," and I smiled and said, "Well, my dad was from the Lebanon, if you must know, but the furthest I've got to that part of the world is a week's self-catering in Turkey." So everyone laughed and I think I defused the situation with the customers. They took him away and I don't know whether they charged him with anything, but I haven't seen him since and that was a week ago.'

'Oh, my days. Did anyone take his side?'

'Funny you should ask, nobody actually *said* they did; I mean, I didn't hear anyone saying he was right, but you could see a few people, I don't know, just watching it all, assessing which side they were going to be on. I suppose once the police had arrived, then the law-and-order types will always take the part of the coppers and he was such a pathetic wreck who *could* take his side? But Charles told me that this was nothing new, he was getting it all the time, at his gym and in the pub, and I said, "But don't they understand? *You* won't be affected." And he said that Europeans were only the start. The rest would follow on later.'

'I see. And do you think there's anything to worry about?'

'I don't know, I honestly don't. I feel like we should be taking – what can I say? – precautions of some kind, but I don't know what. I'd press your case with that Agatha girl if I were you and make it sharpish. Those families are like castles, they protect their own.'

'That's good advice in itself, but I'm not sure there's anything to be alarmed about. I mean, I never hear anything like this.'

'That's the circles you move in, they're privileged people, aren't they, not like Aylesbury.'

'Sure, but look around you.'

'At what?'

'People just want to drink their coffee and be left to get on with whatever they're interested in. Nobody's – what's the word for it?'

'I don't know, what were you thinking of?'

'Possessed. Possessed by big ideas about the world.'

'Ideological.'

'That's it. If you were to ask people what they're thinking about, it's always going to be sex, or what they're having for dinner, or the match, or their hair. I'm not sure most people have the energy for anything more complex than that, which takes proper thinking.'

'And yet on the internet—'

'Oh, the *internet*, Dad. Please.'

Later he thought that the incident outside his dad's store was like an itch in an area in your upper back you could never quite reach, irritating, but only, after all, an itch and not a tumour or anything like that.

22

In the weeks after the attack Rob found himself on the receiving end of a story related by multiple mouths in various guises. Remembering his schoolboy Greek mythology he looked for its underlying structure which was not difficult to detect because it was simple enough, only the identity of the personae, the message being conveyed and the action which initiated it changed. It had an *ur* form. To Chrissie it had been conveyed by a radiographer at the hospital who had noticed that a 'Pakistani-looking fella' had dropped his wallet in the food forecourt, and this lady had noticed it, run out and followed him down the escalator, caught up with him, handed it back. He had told her she was a kind person and in return she should take his advice and the following day stay away from—

Rob said, 'Yes, well, unfortunately I heard the very same anecdote, but from someone completely different. A friend who said he got it from the trainer at his gym, and it wasn't a hospital, the wallet had fallen out under the treadmill.'

'But maybe it was the same Pakistani fella and he was telling everyone who did him a favour.'

'Well, if he was, he certainly drops his wallet a lot. You see it's a long-standing urban legend which goes back at least to the Second World War, with someone with a German accent warning people about a bombing raid, and it pops up in America just after Pearl Harbor.'

He considered the story of the warning, the possession of foreknowledge, as a thread reaching back through civilisation, an Everyman (always an outsider, an emissary of the enemy) with inside information. Perhaps in the face of inexplicable catastrophe the yearning to believe that the human spirit was inherently good surged up, kindness could prevail over evil, yes, he felt, it must be that and some people must find it a comfort to believe it was so. The myth might have its origin in the story of the Good Samaritan, a Christian founding parable, but underlying it was the longing that it was possible to evade disaster.

What also fascinated him was how the story was ported across communities through the iron mathematical law of the friend of a friend, the person never known, always at one remove, to whom this had happened, never oneself. You could ask the friend to ask the friend but the friend would say it was their friend and so on, on and on, ever receding. His mother had in her bedroom a cherrywood dressing table with side mirrors like wings. Aged eight she had sat him down on the plush pink stool and shown him how if he looked at the correct angle he would see his image reflected back to infinity, getting smaller and smaller and further and further away until his original self was a dot only visible through a telescope at the far end of the universe, a sub-atomic particle of himself. At the very end of the world the last friend would not be found.

In the nuclear medicine department they told Chrissie that the story had been circulating on every floor of the hospital with a different source for each telling. Out in the world it proliferated and blossomed, it mushroomed in coffee shops and restaurant kitchens, in university cafeterias and on the trading floor of the stock exchange. It was told and retold at Notting Hill dinner parties and in Tottenham benefits offices. She looked it up online and found a site that debunked stories like this one. The story was circulating after 9/11 in New York and again after the tube bombings in London. There was no kindly person and no compassionate terrorist, only a collective craving to be comforted. Since the attack she felt that the city was more perplexing than she had first realised when she arrived with her two suitcases and a job already fixed up: more prone to distortions and misunderstandings. Incidents and events rippled through it from one mouth to another, millions and millions of mouths. When her uncle Paraic asked her last year where she *really* felt at home, she said, without a blink, 'At work. The rest is all moving around.'

In Scottsdale, Rob had watched a neighbour trying to grow roses round her swimming pool and failing. He observed her efforts to create an English cottage garden with hollyhocks and lupins. The angry sun smote them. He could feel, moment by moment, the wrinkles accrete around his eyes and mouth in the dryness of the air. The vastness of the continent, the presence of the desert as soon as you reached the margins of town and the potential, if the energy ran out in a city which could only exist on the say-so of air conditioning, to become a new Ozymandias, a colossal wreck, 'boundless and bare', had expelled him. He came home (reluctantly) to his duties to his ailing lonely mother sitting at her mirrored dressing table where he had first seen his own reflection, her fleecy slippers, her nightdress, her forgotten pots of yogurt in the fridge blue with mould. But really what brought him back was an exhaustion with the New World, a loss of confidence in its fabled capacity for reinvention. And he was a terrible driver. And he had no confidence that he could defend himself with a gun. And there would always be Netflix.

As much as he could he stayed indoors reading and watching films on TV. His mind could no longer deal with the rough

171

handling of relationships, their demands for openness and intimacy, plans for the future, ceaseless arrangements – brunches and dinners and movies, all those date nights. His body felt raw and abraded, his skin was hypersensitive. He was worn out.

His flat faced the river, it was why he had bought it. All day long the river retained its fascination. There was no need ever to leave home.

A few weeks after the attack, when he believed he was in recovery and the flashbacks, the heavy sense of dread and anxiety, had stopped overwhelming him, when he no longer woke from nightmares, and he believed that the resilient, well-exercised brain could combat extreme stress, he woke on a very bright morning and walked in his T-shirt and slippers to the balcony to watch the busy life of the Thames.

As he approached the window and looked out, the river, its banks and bridges, became fragments of a mirror as if he was looking through the eyepiece of a kaleidoscope, lit with rainbow flashes. His world had broken into pieces. He screamed. *My God, this is it*, he thought, *I am dying, this is how the light goes out*. Through the fracturing, a stream of people crossing Chelsea Bridge were hurling themselves off the bridge, hundreds of people throwing themselves over the parapet like a colony of penguins from an ice floe in search of fish. He screamed again. He rubbed his eyes, blinked, nothing changed. He sat and waited for the shutting down of a dying brain. A few minutes later, about twenty minutes, he thought, his vision returned to normal.

What had just happened? This destabilisation disturbed him so much that he was unable to think of a physiological explanation. Exit pursued by demons, either I am going mad or something is happening, something—

His hands shaking as he inserted a coffee capsule in the machine, watching a spurt of dark liquid come down, all normal, nothing awry, the flat as it should be, nothing out of place, no ghosts or poltergeists, he returned to his bed and closed his eyes. A little while later, he rang the optician.

'Oh, I see. No, I had no idea. But you know I didn't have any kind of headache. Really? So that's all it was. Thank you, you've put my mind at rest.'

Justin said, 'Of *course*, optical migraines, I've had them a few times, freaky when you first get them, but they pass very quickly. Something to do with bright light and dehydration, I think.'

'It was a bright day. I suppose I should try to drink more water.'

And he wanted to talk about the hallucination of the people throwing themselves from the bridge but Justin wasn't interested in his auras, his weird eyesight, the single issue they needed to discuss was himself being sent away, shut out when he was supposed to have been sharing the experience with his actual boyfriend.

'Why did you exclude me?'

'Well, because it didn't really happen to you, did it? You were late.'

'That's not my fault, I didn't know. But afterwards, why did you—'

'I can't take all these questions. Can't you just leave me alone?'

'And how long do you want to be left alone *for*?'

'I don't know. As long as it takes, I suppose.'

Justin held out his arms. Rob flinched.

'Oh, my God, so that's how it is. Really? I mean, that's how you feel about me?'

'I'm sorry, it was involuntary. I don't know what's happening to me. It's all a muddle.'

'Let's go over again what happened that night.'

'Please. No.'

'I don't know what to say to you. I don't know how to behave. You're not all right. I'm looking at you and I can see you're not.'

'Yes, but you're not helping.'

'I don't know how to help; tell me what you want, talk to me.'

'I can't, I'm sorry.'

'Why can't you?'

'Will you stop asking me questions? Cut it out.'

'Am I supposed to just let you get on with it?'

'Yes, why not?'

'This isn't a serious relationship, is it? We're really just fuck-buddies.'

'Is that what you think?'

'So it's fine for you to ask me questions.'

'Don't be ridiculous.'

'I'm off. This is going nowhere, I'll talk to you later.' And Justin exited the flat leaving behind a few traces of himself, his toothbrush, some T-shirts, a pair of work shoes and his blend of coffee in a jar on the kitchen worktop. *These fragments do I shore against my ruin*, Rob thought, watching his denim arse leave. *And what do I feel about this?* he asked himself. Peaceful. Free now to eat cheese on toast without being nagged about his arteries, or smoke a joint, or look at porn all day. He did all these forbidden things.

Justin rang the next morning, and for many days afterwards. Rob did not return any messages or calls. And that felt like a relief. For Justin had always been a bit of a drain, he had shown himself up this time for the narcissist he really was. They had known each other in their late twenties, and met up for a drink when Rob moved back to London. Sleeping with him, going out to bars and clubs with him, had been an easy way of re-entering London. As he kept saying to himself now, in the end one is really on one's own. Then thinking it was just existential crap and we are social animals. But could only half remember the theories behind these two schools of thought.

His compassionate leave had been extended until the beginning of next term and he prepared and revised his coursework;

he might surprise them yet with a brand-new module on the novel of terrorism, starting, fairly obviously, with Joseph Conrad's *The Secret Agent*, a lugubrious narrative he had never particularly enjoyed, but would sharply shove his students out of their 'relevant-to-my-personal-experience' and 'relatable-characters' comfort zone. Their lack of curiosity drove him mad. They seemed to aspire to nothing beyond their own limitations, they were not ceaselessly being and becoming, as he had been at their age, away from home for the first time, studying English at Bristol, coming out in one incautious explosive burst at the end of freshers' week with a boy called Jim, looking up at each other, incredulous, smiling, at what they had just done for the first time.

He was certain he would never have sex again, he could not imagine the circumstances in which it could happen. A club or bar was out of the question, a dinner party at a friend's flat in Bermondsey was intolerable, not even travelling there and back by taxi. It was impossible to enter an enclosed space with a total stranger.

He had had a couple of futile sessions with a counsellor who had encouraged him to write about his experiences. The woman had been recommended by the HR department at the university, she wore a grey cashmere sweater, grey wool trousers, pearl earrings. Her cloudy greyness felt oppressive not calming.

'I don't write, I teach writing that's already been *written*.'

'In that case, wouldn't you be particularly well-qualified to—'

'No. I would not. I don't really know why I'm here, to be honest, I can't really see what it's supposed to achieve, scratching away at scar tissue. Sorry, I'm not convinced.'

Chrissie wrote nothing down except texts, WhatsApp messages and numbers in her phone's contacts. She had never suggested he relieve his feelings in the written word. She would turn up, randomly, without any advance notification, carrying a partly eaten pizza, a bottle of vodka and a rudimentary bunch of supermarket flowers.

'Only me! Fancy a bit of a rave?'

There was an unselfconscious lack of awareness that she might not be welcome, that they had nothing in common, that she had not read a book since she left school. Looked around his flat and said the usual thing, 'Bloody hell, have you really read all of them? It's like a library in here.'

'Most, darling, most. Would you like to borrow anything? Does anything strike you as interesting?'

'No, you're all right. I'll stick to my magazines.'

He ate some of the pizza and made cocktails. She was looking around his flat at the Ligne Roset sofa ('is it supposed to be like this?'), the Basquiat screen prints on the wall above the dining table, the silver venetian blinds.

'It's so nice here, river view and everything,' she said. 'Our place is a tip, everything's sticky with leg creams and hairspray. It's a load of fun sharing – or it can be if you all get on all right – but you never really get to watch what you want on TV. And here we are, and isn't it just like a romcom with the single girl and the gay best friend.'

'Can I ask, what made you run off?' he said. 'What did he really say to you?'

'You don't want to know.'

'If you'd rather not—'

'It wasn't a nice thing.'

'Yes, I rather assumed that.'

'I'd just as soon forget all about it, I was just wanting to – you know, I mean how did I come across on TV? Was I all right? Not a div?'

'Very well, very well indeed. Authentic and fresh and down to earth, funny too, I thought. You were brilliant.'

He watched the documentary again on. How odd, he thought,

that of all the pieces of music in the world the filmmaker had used the adagio from Beethoven's 'Emperor' concerto, recalling the first part of that night before the fold. And who had been performing? Was it Stephen Hough? He thought it probably was, for his mother was a great fan ('such a lovely boy, do you know if he's *available*, dear?') but his memory was in rags and patches. Like a blind spot on the retina, portions of the past were lost to the dark. He had bought the programme, stuffed it in his jacket pocket, he believed it must have fallen out somewhere in the hospital. The documentary opened with a reconstruction of the two lost women's walk towards London Bridge. Chrissie's terrible pink plastic handbag swung from her shoulder, the drowned woman was played by an actress. The lost boy was a plaintive minor key. He tried to remember where he had been that July night of the disappearances – still in Scottsdale under a baking sun, looking out on to a cracked harsh garden. Then a sharp cut to the funeral, the policeman's icy beard looming through the fog like an avenger.

But he saw how the artist's impression of the drowned woman seemed to him now flimsy and incomplete, as if only a suggestion of her features had been attempted, and something significant held back. People were specific, she wasn't. She might have been deliberately excluding her own personality from her appearance as if she was trying to pass for something or blend in or be forgotten. There were many unobtrusive women like her that one came into contact with in the course of the day: a fly-by-night barista serving behind the counter in a coffee shop, her back turned to you, tending the hissing machine; a cleaner in an overall dusting your flat trying not to disturb its occupants; or dressed in the uniform of an airline, heavily made-up, checking you in on the computer and handing you your boarding card with a company smile. Who noticed people working in the service industries? He didn't. They might have been powered by

177

artificial intelligence and in the future he thought they probably would be.

He considered the case of DB27. He felt that if you could scrape away the generality of her appearance, if you could animate her face with something – then there might be a flash of recognition. Did he know her? Perhaps he did. But that wasn't the point, the point was not to play the detective but to consider why no one had so far come forward to claim her. The funeral in the fog was so atmospheric, the men in their dark overcoats around the open grave, the tiers of bodies. It was all so . . . literary. Dickensian, almost. It reminded him of the opening scenes in *Our Mutual Friend*, the waterman on the foetid Thames; and the fogginess of the morning was surely a reference to *Bleak House*. Perhaps, he wondered, that might be the problem. If one stripped all this metaphor away, what had everyone been missing?

Part Five

23

A wet street in Gunnersbury at sunset. A mottled sky, indistinct bars of colour on the horizon, dreadnought clouds bearing down over patchy lighted windows. Windows, double-glazed, sash and casement with blinds down or curtains drawn reflect back to the street its rush-hour traffic. When the sun starts to go from the sky at quarter past three, summer seems imaginary. In December you are dreaming that you once sat in the garden with a glass of wine and a bowl of olives, the alliums in the flower beds waving, the geraniums seeming to flower for ever in their terracotta pots. The boiler is forgotten, it will make a loud ominous grinding noise when reluctantly turned on again in late September as the first socks come out of their drawers, and coats return from the dry cleaner's and the winter-weight duvets go back on the beds. Summer *was* a dream. Autumn and winter are the natural condition of England. London is a city made for rain and traffic-clogged roads, umbrellas at the bus stop shaken out on the tube platform, a metropolis of scarves and parkas and boots and bottle-green leather gloves lined with cashmere which Francesca buys every year, the complete pair never surviving until the spring; lost, impaled by a passer-by on a railing, screaming for its hand.

From her kitchen window, in the garden the table and chairs, the barbecue are shrouded in plastic covers. Frost grows along the washing line. Damp leaves moulder under the choisya bush. Snails burrow down into the soil waiting to rise again in wet and warm weather. Mangy foxes shelter in the shed which no one has remembered to lock and no one wants to go out there to see if all is well and though the winter flowering shrubs are ready to put on their frozen display, the garden no longer matters, no one cares what is happening there. (And Pete Dutton doesn't even have a garden any more in his new flat above a nail salon in Gunnersbury and mourns the absence of lawnmowers, shears, his wife's annual autumn bulb-planting bending over in the drizzly rain, her hair a halo of shining droplets – the memory comes to him with a sharp erotic pang.)

On the street where Alan and Francesca used to live, the London planes have finally disrobed their full green dress, the last to go.

Neither of them knows much about trees. Vic Elliott, the Afghan hound man and owner of the vinyl shop, does, has recited a short poem about them.

> Green is the plane-tree in the square,
>   The other trees are brown;
> They droop and pine for country air;
>   The plane-tree loves the town.

He has explained them to Alan who in the summer had been looking into getting an overgrown bay removed from the garden where it cast an unwelcome shadow on the small lawn between two and four in the afternoon. London planes, Vic said, are now half of London's tree population and did not exist as a species until the seventeenth century when they came into being as a union between the American Sycamore and Oriental Great

Plane. They were plants from opposite ends of the world that would never have met had they not been brought together in a botanical garden in Vauxhall and discovered, having secretly and independently cross-bred, by John Tradescant the Younger.

This tree, Vic said, is a Londoner by birth as well as name. As he was himself, having remained roughly on this spot give or take a couple of miles in either direction since he and Ray Davies had started at the same primary school in 1949, and worn the same blazer and cap until they were separated at the age of eleven when Vic went to the grammar school and Ray to the secondary modern but still raised a hand of embarrassed recognition when they ran into each other on the scene in the sixties.

In Gunnersbury, the onset of a London winter is celebrated and glorified by Pete Dutton, who gives praise for it to a god he has not believed in since he was eleven and challenged any supernatural being to smite him down if he stole some sweets. Or perhaps the punishment, he later thought, was to damn him to be a copper, to catch the miscreants, the wrong-doers and the pure evil. This train of thought carried him along on the District Line on a wet evening before Christmas when passengers were steaming in their coats, faces slack and dreaming, consumed with inner panoramas of what they might have for supper, or badly needing a stiff drink, or considering what they should have said when they had said the wrong thing, or had said nothing at all. Thinking of sex and football and maybe go back and try on that dress, what to watch on telly tonight, and how the avenging master of all would smite his enemies, with bombs and suicide belts, and with landmines and with drones. All the faces were opaque. All looked at their phones. The evening paper was scanned and discarded on the seats. The train stopped for a few minutes in a tunnel between Earls Court and South Kensington and an enveloping silence came down in which you could hear a cough or leaking hip hop from tinny bud headphones. And now everyone's eyes are raised, staring at each other in a kind of amazement that they were not, after all, alone but sharing a tomb with the dozing Bulgarian builder in plaster-dusted jeans and a bag of tools, and a relic of the Sloane Rangers in late middle-age passing from Fulham to Chelsea in navy pullover, piecrust collar and pearls, like a teenage Lady Di now with coarse pepper-and-salt hair, a double chin and a mastectomy scar beneath her Rigby & Peller bra.

An announcement came at last, a bored explanation of signals and lights and they would be on the move soon and then they were.

So far, it seemed to him, nothing really had changed apart from himself: no longer a family man with a house and a garage but a single guy who had run away from his responsibilities and commitments, and from a woman he had always considered to be the love of his life. Because he could not rot in a village. He had failed over and again to explain himself to Marie who said how could he love a place more than he loved a human being, that it identified a coldness in him she'd never noticed before. There were whole opaque areas of his personality that never came to light, like dark patches on an X-ray.

'What are you *talking* about?' he said. 'I'm a sheet of glass, me.'

'You know what I mean. You hide everything away, we never talk.'

'I'm dying inside!' he had shouted, actually picking up his reading glasses from the table and hurling them across the room.

'You're selfish, that's what you are.'

'*I'm* selfish? It was you who dragged us up here, never gave me a say.'

'You had plenty of say. We talked it through.'

'It was an ultimatum. It was cancer talking, not my wife.'

With that, the glass of their marriage shattered.

She would accuse him of having another woman in London

he'd been with behind her back all along, and that was what was pulling him back, some tart. He admitted to himself there had been at first a kind of tidal tug, that much was true, of the memory of that dead woman whose identity he had sought and failed to find. Marie had seen her, she had not thought her in any way remarkable and he had not been able to explain why he felt such yearning and curiosity. They had never talked about it again. Had they done so she might have accused him of preferring a corpse to his living wife. But it wasn't the woman in the river who brought their marriage to ruins, it was a thick mass of grievance and homesickness and feeling not right and the moral high ground of his wife's fucking cancer, a stick she would use to beat him with as long as they both should live.

Alan, not having known about the exile to the Lake District, sent him a message asking if he'd like to meet up for a pint in town and Pete accepted the invitation because for one night out he wouldn't have to talk about the failure of the move and of his marriage with concerned mates who wanted to tell him he was bananas: London was finished now, was he really going to let a girl like Marie go, who had stood by him through thick and thin?

Alan had chosen a pub near Victoria station, five minutes' walk from his office, a space now empty of Johanna's forceful and energetic presence and clearly too big and too expensive for his current needs. It had always been a strange and unfashionable location; as a newcomer to London, he hadn't known that when he'd first taken it. On the one hand you had the gardens, lawns, flower beds of Buckingham Palace hiding behind stone walls crowned with barbed wire, maybe the Queen in one of her hats was out there with a watering can tending to the hydrangeas and snapdragons. On the other hand, streets thronging with people with suitcases dragged along on wheels looking for trains to take them to the south coast's stony beaches and grey waves crusted with brown foam. Commuters with their briefcases heading to those Home Counties stations which had always mystified him, the belt of middle-class smuggery that surrounded London. Victoria seemed to Pete, too, to be a bit of a dead zone and he had no idea what hinterland the pub could possibly serve. It seemed artificial and strange, with none of the camaraderie you'd expect from your local for it could be no one's real local, just people waiting for trains, and office workers in no hurry to go home and maybe the domestics who worked in those shuttered white mansions owned by absent Russians and Arabs. Somewhere near here last summer, there had been a terrorist attack, not bombs but a lone man with a truck driving into crowds of people making their way to and from the station. Up in the Lake District they'd watched it on TV and Marie had said, 'See? That's what we're supposed to be missing, that's what you call home these days.'

But Pete felt that surge of adrenalin when something is happening. *What's going on?* In their village, nothing. Absolutely nothing. The darts cup was reported missing, maybe stolen. It turned up in someone's cupboard under the stairs. In London a nutter who spent too much time on Islamic sites on the internet worrying about the world's woes and pumping up his sense of grievance like black tyres until he was popping with rage and ill-will rented a truck and drove it into a crowd of harmless people. Not many killed, thank God. The murderer had bombed himself, he was literally in bits, a finger here and a nose blown out of the window rolling down the pavement. Gruesome, but satisfying.

The pub had kept its original features, engraved glass, wood panelling, wrought-iron railings. It was as a pub should be: someone's correct idea of a pub, accurate and authentic apart from the clientele. There was a good selection of ales; he bought himself a pint. He saw his reflection in the mirror behind the bar, his watery green eyes, his long upper lip, his beard sawn off in a straight line at the chin, hardly recognised himself. He found Alan sitting at a table drinking a glass of white wine.

It was good to be in town, bad to be in a part of town so motley and inconsequential that it hardly mattered what he wore, when everyone else was in a cheap office suit or sitting with luggage next to them in overcoats and parkas while he was wearing some expensive jeans he'd bought online, rolled at the bottom so you could see the selvage above his boots, and he'd put pomade in his moustache. In the corner a Christmas tree was piled with fake presents, which always promised, he thought, more than real, clumsily wrapped presents. These were anonymous gold boxes which looked as though they'd contain something really good (electronics or a cool shirt). The Christmas music playlist was too loud, but they were always too loud. Christmas bore down on you like a teacher with a cane, Christmas threatened you with loneliness and solitary tears if you didn't get your act together and make up with your nearest and dearest. He was spending the day with his brother and sister-in-law in Kew. Marie was going to be in the Lake District with the girls. If you could eliminate Christmas, separation would be tolerable, but that was not an option. He must buy presents, he must start that.

Alan asked if he was up to date on the consequences of the film, or the lack of them.

'No. I'm out of the loop. Nobody tells me anything any more so I'm relying on you to fill me in. As I said in my email, I thought your show was very good, very realistic and honest about the work we do, or at least I used to do, and respectful too, I mean of the people involved. That girl on the train came off pretty well, I thought, and you had the measure of the bloke. As for our DB27, the filming of the funeral was very nicely done. You got the atmosphere of the day down. I can still remember it, even though I was so late. So any good news to report?'

'Not really, I'm afraid. We had a lot of calls. People did get

187

in touch but the problem was we could rule most of them out altogether immediately – women who had gone missing years ago at around her age, but they'd be in their late fifties now. Or they looked nothing like her, timewasters perhaps, but also relatives and friends clinging to shreds of hope that it *might* be her when in fact they were miles out. Then we had callers asking about identifying tattoos when there were no tattoos, or scars or moles or anything like that. We did come close, we thought we had her, I got very excited. From my point of view, as stories go, it was a dream. She was matched with a missing person's report. A cranky little religious community in Wales, based around the teachings of some defunct Indian guru. They were trying to trace a member who had grown up in the sect since she was a teenager and left eleven years ago. Not heard a word since she took off. They were sure it was her. But she wasn't that hard to trace, alive and well, married and living in Manchester. Wanted nothing to do with the lot of them. The thing is, most of the calls we got were along the lines of: *I knew someone who looked a lot like her and I haven't seen her for a good while so it could be her.* You've no idea how many of those there were, because what I came to realise is that she looked like anyone, I don't mean really anyone, but she ... I can't put my finger on it.'

'I can. My wife said the same thing. She looked like everyone's best friend, the hair they all have these days with the highlights, the pointy face, the clothes anyone could walk into a shop and buy.'

'But a kind of blurred person who seems to have erased her specific identity. I don't really know how she did it. She had good teeth, didn't she?'

'Yes, excellent. Not a filling, no dentures or implants. She could have been a dental hygienist.'

'If she was, wouldn't someone have remembered her, with her face peering down at you?'

'She'd have a mask on, though, wouldn't she?'

'Oh, you're right, maybe she would.'

'Was that really all? All you came up with?'

'I didn't feel, and your colleagues certainly didn't feel, that there was anything that represented a lead.'

'Huh.'

They had finished their drinks, Alan offered to buy him another pint. Pete had no idea why he was here when there was nothing really, no new information. It was hardly worth coming into town if you were only going to have one drink so he said yes to another IPA and waited at the table while Alan pushed through the throng at the bar, useless at it, he should have gone himself, the guy had no technique, and this of course was why you stood instead of sitting at a table, maintained your spot, so the barman had you in his eyeline.

The chandeliers were blinking, a couple of the bulbs were going out. Pete thought that this was what it must feel like when a bomb is about to go off, though he didn't know why, or how long they would blink. He looked up to see if they were swaying. Everything was normal, Alan returned to the table.

'Did you hear about the conspiracy theories?' Alan said.

'No way!'

'There was one about her being an obscure member of the royal family, some third cousin twice removed of the queen shoved away in an asylum when she was born, they dyed her hair, put new clothes on her, pushed her over the bridge to get her out of the way, orders of Prince Philip, apparently.'

'Are you serious? That doesn't make any sense.'

'I think Princess Diana came into it somehow. There was another one about her actually *being* Diana, who didn't die but – well, you know what's coming.'

'People haven't got enough to do with their time, have they? Or they've got a screw loose.'

'These are strange times.'

'You can say that again.'

'Look at this, though. Human nature never changes.'

The pub was emptying out. The commuters and office workers had left, pools of light spread on the lily and ivy patterned carpets. Beneath the table a woman had kicked off her high-heeled navy court shoes and was running her toes along the tongue of her companion's highly polished brogue. His tie was loosened, the woman's lip gloss was bruised round her mouth. Alan could smell the violent torrents of her perfume from where he sat. Everything about this tableau seemed to him to be blindingly obvious, they couldn't go back from here, it had gone too far; they would walk the sordid streets of Victoria until they found a cheap and sordid hotel. He wanted to cry out to tell them to stop, that no good could come of this, that he had watched his father with a raised red welt across his cheek where his mother had slapped him with such force that their son thought she must have killed him, and the smell the next morning at the breakfast table, of the sweet stench of shame rising from the toast and porridge and tea.

This isn't going to end well, is it?' Pete said, thinking it might as well be his own ending.

The woman was in her thirties, next to the table lay her briefcase. If they left now, she would forget it. She might work in a bank or a finance office in her blue suit and white shirt, the gold chain sliding down beneath the undone buttons towards a pale pink bra. But she would need the briefcase in the morning.

The pair stood up unsteadily. Gallantly the man took her hand to raise her. She put her shoes back on and he put his arm round her shoulder, she leaned in towards him, stumbling against his arm. She was in the hinterland between tight and drunk, it might go either way, she might pick up her briefcase and walk out with him and raise her hand for a taxi, she might disappear towards the tube, weaving along the pavement then righting herself, righting her morals, Pete thought. Or they would be unified together and disappear, looking for a room.

'She's left her briefcase,' Alan said. 'I should go after her.'

'I wouldn't bother.'

'I'd be saving her from herself, don't you think?'

'No. Leave her be, she knows what she's doing.'

She might wake up tomorrow morning, the mascara smeared down her face, and wonder where she was: this unfamiliar hotel room, the stale-smelling body snoring in the bed next to her, the silent TV mounted on a bracket high on the wall, the Gideon bible in the drawer, the trouser press, the empty folding stand for a suitcase, the curtains they had not bothered to draw and the room service menu thrown aside from the pillow. She would try to wash her face with a miniature bar of soap, he would stumble in behind her, grab her tits as she was working out how to navigate the controls of the shower. She would attempt to recall what had led them here, and how many glasses of wine had washed her away. She would dress in her grubby white shirt, zip up the side of her skirt, look around for her briefcase, search under the bed and in the wardrobe and not finding it, would sit down on the chair by the window and cry.

24

'I'll tell you, when I first moved into my flat my next-door neighbour was a black drug dealer with a BMW and five years later – ha! – yeah, well five years later my next-door neighbour is a *white* drug dealer with a Bang & Olufsen TV and an off-shore account. It's like living next to a minor oligarch and obviously he only deals in the best stuff so you don't get any pathetic junkies sniffing and picking and scratching at themselves on the stairs. A lot of the stuff is couriered, he has an account with Addison Lee and you see lines of bikes and vans parked outside waiting for the bags of coke.'

'What? And the drivers know that?' Marco said.

'Of course not. They just have to drop off in Spitalfields or Notting Hill. I mean, whatever people are taking here tonight, probably came from him. He wants to buy my flat and knock through to make a super-apartment. Crazy, eh?'

'Ha ha! Hilarious. Where is this?'

'Dalston, where else?'

'Oh yeah, of course. It's very pricey now. I'm trying to move to Homerton, which is just as bad. I've seen a place near the designer outlets that's coming up in a couple of months. It's a mate who's moving out. Whether the landlord will raise the rent I don't know. It's just a shot in the dark, really.'

'Well, good luck with that. I mean, look, London is impossible. Don't you ever think of moving out?'

'Out of London? No, I'm *from* out of London. I'm not giving up now.'

'Okay, I get that. I'm a small-town boy myself, Cumbria. When I came out my mother said, "Kevin, you can be gay, but you can't be gay in Keswick." Still, there's always Brighton, you can definitely be gay in Brighton. And it's possible to commute.'

'I know but not with my job, too many late nights.'

'What do you do?'

'Bar and restaurant PR.'

'Oh, so this is in fact your party?'

'Correct. And how do you—'

'My flatmate is the maître d'. So don't you need to work the room, make sure everyone is happy?'

'I think by this stage they all are, don't you? The cocktails are still coming out, that's the main thing. We've managed about two-thirds of the guest list, which is excellent.'

'Is there anyone I should recognise?'

'A couple of *Made in Chelsea* girls and a former Doctor Who. A few models. Professor Green was around earlier.'

'How long do you have to stay?'

'Sorry?'

'I was just wondering—'

'*Hello?* Are you hitting on me?'

'I was, actually. Yeah. Is that a problem?'

'Ah, no offence. Not my area of interest. Always flattering to be asked, though.'

He turned away and smiled at the man's presumption, thinking he might go off with someone holding of all things a *pink* drink. He had no idea there was anyone left in London who drank a Cosmopolitan and they were being served tonight in a retro spirit so that people would exclaim that they had not seen one for years but you weren't expected to actually take a glass from the tray. And he despised soft-bellied men. It was the third proposition that evening. What was so special about tonight? You could call it luck but it felt like something more motivated, less random. Luck was just a superstition and if you made your own, then what was the machinery for its creation? He had no idea but he was going to take responsibility: put it down to his new jeans and the session with the sunbed, the manicure and pedicure and waxing, all the grooming products laid out in the bathroom, the lustre of the deposit of his annual bonus into his bank account that morning. Agatha had been here earlier, she had witnessed him in his pomp, then gone off for dinner with her girlfriends to Hoxton. 'My days,' he whispered.

The night was lovely, there was no other word for it. Loveliness cast an innocent glow over everything it touched. They might all be moonstruck. Deep breaths of summer air; outside a courtyard strung with lights, candles in lanterns hung from the branches of pot-bound fig trees hung with fruit, banks of flowers real and artificial. Groups were out there smoking and vaping. Something was afoot, a glamorous pall of perfumed mist hung over everything. He was about to step outside.

'These canapés are really good.'

Nick Barclay. That old windbag, holding a miniature pastry shell, raising it to his face, which had in recent months acquired a patchy reddish beard.

'What have you got?'

'I think it's a curried coconut soup, I'm not sure whether to drink it or put the whole thing in my mouth.'

'Go for it. It's one of the chef's signature dishes.'

'The Cosmos are a cute touch.'

'I know.'

'It made me smile to see them; I wasn't sure at first whether they would survive the irony.'

'I'm too young to remember their heyday, to be honest.'

'You are so young, sickeningly young. Still in the same flat?'

'Yes, but hoping to move to Homerton.'

'Bad idea. I'm thinking of leaving, cutting myself adrift from all this nonsense. I'll probably relocate to Paris or Madrid. The country is finished, that's obvious.'

'Don't be ridiculous. It won't be that bad.'

'You're being fooled by all *this*. Our London is coming to an end, what we knew is disintegrating, soon we won't recognise the place. You've got to go with the change, Marco. It's not our fault, we didn't initiate it, but you need to prepare, make plans, have your exit route arranged.'

'Nah, London's a bubble; I mean, look around you. People still want to eat, don't they?'

'Have you ever been to Lisbon? I went there in the nineties, weird burg. In the thirties they got this fascist dictator, name of Salazar, and the whole place just rolled over and died. From a really fascinating, sophisticated city it turned into a fossil, a whole intact art deco fabric that hadn't been touched for sixty years, really run down and neglected. Like, I don't know, ancient Rome. That's what's going to happen to us.'

'Oh, you do talk some bullshit, Nick, you always have done.'

'Go with the change, Marco, go with the change.'

'Have another canapé. Look, a tray is coming in your direction.'

He turned away, exasperated. No one knew how much work PR was; apart from all the handshaking and smiling, it was a continual grind. He lived on a list. And a list of lists. But that did not matter for he felt himself to be at the epicentre, yes, there were other parties going on, there was always an iridescent glittering grid of parties all connected to each other by taxis moving guests across the city but it was not any one party that everything else radiated out from but the web of parties itself. Outside on the rim of London, people were indoors with TVs and takeaways and in his generosity he felt they should not be excluded from the radiance because they were too poor, too ugly, or not connected, not on the guest list, or burdened by babies, trapped by early-morning starts.

A tranche of people were leaving to go on to a club. They coalesced into a new mood and a new intention. He would go home soon, perhaps Agatha would be there, sleeping, or perhaps she too would have gone on, a bright filament in the perpetual motion of the city.

Out on the street, his long day ending, he took out his phone to call an Uber and felt a rush of air coming towards him, as the train racing through the tunnel at an underground station sets up a hot blast and the passengers sway on the platform, going as best they can with the change.

25

Marco thought of the rows of leather shoes in his wardrobe, each with its set of wooden and brass trees, his tightly edited collection of trainers lapping their tongues at the sun below the window, his bottles of Acqua di Parma and Jo Malone arranged in a row at carefully judged intervals on a frosted-glass shelf in the bathroom, the T-shirts he had archived on a top shelf in cloth bags waiting for a time when they had achieved a value he was still mentally setting, and would auction them on eBay. Condoms in the drawer, a tube of KY jelly, luxurious wanks in the bath, steamy mirror, trees rustling against the window, flipping through his mental look-book of slender girls with scrubbed-out faces. The whole of his existence so far from the time he cleaned toilets to buy proper shoes was predicated on these props, as well as his brain, his interests, his degree in Business Studies from Bournemouth University.

He would wake up, he would wake up, he would wake and see the flowers, whatever the cleaner had brought him this week, he couldn't remember, was it roses, was it yellow roses?

When you are asleep you can think you are awake, when you are awake you know you're not really dreaming, the two states feel completely different. And it came to him, that no, he was not dreaming and that he would give anything to get back to the state of being trapped in a nightmare, which was not real and eventually you *would* wake up. He was awake.

He saw his parents through a wall of fire.

26

Was it wop, was it wog? She didn't know, not even sure what either meant but the police said they were treating it as a racially motivated attack so either way it must be such an awful word that came with torture in a bottle. What they had done to him and for nothing, not even for his phone for he had it in his hand tapping at the Uber app and they hadn't bothered taking it. It was completely random, no material motive, the police said, they'd shouted something at him and even in his agony, he had told the police the word.

'Look, he's getting the very best of care,' she said. 'No, you're right, it'll be a long recovery, skin grafts and all that, he won't look the same, but they'll do their best, he's not going to be a monster, I promise you that.'

'Not a monster, thank God.'

The dad holding his wife's hand throughout this conversation, the two of them like bears chained together sent out to be baited, having driven down in the middle of the night half-dressed, asking dazed questions and not taking in the answers then recognising her as she tried to slink past along the walls.

Why did she have to be on duty? Why did they have to bring

him here? She didn't even know him at first, his face half gone, and only because they had his driving licence and she knew his real name could she cry out, "Oh, bloody hell I used to share a flat with him." You wouldn't wish it on your worst enemy and all he was guilty of was saying a nasty thing to her on a train and shouldn't deserve this. His face falling away, the skin melting, could be blinded in one eye. Even when you think you've seen the worst it turns out you haven't really seen the worst, old men dying of cancer a sorry sight and a still-born baby nowhere near term, its lungs not yet developed, can't even cry, it's all sad, and car-crash injuries are terrible, a steering wheel half-stuck in someone's head, but a person you know from on the outside with his face melted away, screaming in the night, and you're in your rubber gloves so as not to get contaminated, swabbing him with cold water to bring down the heat, the burning fires of hell one of the doctors called it. Grabbing handfuls of sterile bandages, trying to tell him it'll be okay but he knows it won't, and all you can say, is – Look, you'll live, it's not the end of the world, it didn't even touch your chest. But it's not his idea of living, is it?

'Oh, thank God,' the mother had cried when they spotted her. 'Could we have been luckier! We've a friend here, Frank. Neil has a friend.'

'Look, I haven't seen one of these cases before,' Chrissie said. 'I'm as ignorant as you are about the actual treatment, to be honest, I just know they—'

'They're talking about a specialist burns unit, there's one not far from us, we'll be able to take him home.'

'Oh, now that's grand. Where do you live now?'

'Aylesbury.'

'Is that—'

'It's Bucks. I'm going to go round to the flat later to pick up his bits.'

'You'll find more than bits, he's got a whole shoe shop in there!'

And this joke seemed to free them for a few minutes and they could speak of their son as if he was still their untouched boy.

'We know, he was always like that, once didn't he have a tantrum in the middle of the street because they didn't have the trainers he wanted in his size, this was when he must have been six.'

'No, they had them, Frank, I just told him that they were too expensive. He was lying on the ground with all the traffic stopped, banging his little legs up and down, lying down in the road. I didn't know where to put myself, I had to pick him up and drag him by the shoulders to the pavement. We laugh about it now, even he does.'

'He was always fussy.'

'Yes.'

But the present came down on them like a burning cage.

'He'll be better off at home, we'll look after him.'

'I'm sure you will.'

'You see, I don't know if he ever told you, we lost one already.'

'What do you mean?'

'Well, he had a brother.'

'He never said.'

'It's a long time ago, dark days, now this. What is this country coming to? What is going on? It's all changed, you've no idea what the neighbours will come out with next, people we've known for years, used to complain about the bin collection, nattering over the fence, now—'

'That's right, you thought you knew them then such non-sense.'

'But that's not throwing acid in someone's face. Words are just words. This isn't words, and his phone in his hand all the time, that new iPhone, he spent a fortune on it. What's wrong with the old one, I said, you've only had it five minutes, there's plenty of life left in it.'

'Yes, but in his line of work you have to put on a bit of a show, don't you? I don't know what kind of show he can put on now. You're our saviour, Christine, you're our guardian angel, everything is in your hands.'

'No, it's the doctors, not me, I'm just—'

'Yes, but we feel better knowing that you'll be there to sit by his bed, a friendly— That stupid business is all in the past now, you'll have long ago made up your differences.'

She said, 'Of course, I'll look out for him. What happened to his brother?'

His dad said, 'The usual story. Running out into the road. It was a very quiet road normally, we're only one street away from a cul-de-sac, but he was hit by a bus on diversion.'

'Oh Jesus, the poor kid.'

'I'd like to say it was instant, but it wasn't.'

'Well, nearly, he died in the ambulance. Neil was ten at the time, this was his kid brother, seven years old. It was nothing to do with him, not his fault, he was out in the back garden but William had come round the side of the house through the gate we never kept bolted out into the front and we don't know why, we'll never know, there wasn't a ball he was chasing or if there was we never found it.'

'He wasn't even *playing* with a ball. There was no ball.'

'No.'

'So we thought maybe him and Neil had had a bit of a kids' fight and William was just getting away from him.'

'But Neil loved his little brother.'

'That's right. He did. He was in a terrible state when it happened.'

'And did he change after that?'

'Yes, he did change, I think he wanted to—'

202

'Make us proud of him.'

'And we are proud. All his achievements, that wonderful job and his beautiful clothes. But I don't know why we're talking about this when Neil is lying there in agony. Will you call him Neil please? That Marco business is just a load of rubbish.'

She said she certainly would, but thinking she'd never remember.

Now the press had come, and they turned to talk to them, to cry out in anguish at what had been done to their boy. Frank said, 'This country has been taken over by the *dregs*. I'm telling you, the scum of the earth are in charge now.'

They wrote it down and recorded it.

People she knew, and herself even, were becoming famous. They blundered into the news without meaning to. They had never done anything to attract attention and now they were stories, the public wanted to know what had happened to them, they were examples of something. It was all so fucking weird. The police kept saying *racially motivated attack* and his dad told the reporters, 'We all know why. We all know what this comes down to, doesn't it, the bad atmosphere that's got into this country, people distrusting foreigners, what's the word?'

'Xenophobic?' said the reporter.

'Yes.'

But Chrissie did not know what it meant and couldn't find out because she couldn't spell it. So that was that, until tomorrow when she'd go and check on him like she promised, and try to make out, as she always did, you had to, that it was all going to be all right.

Her dad called her from Dublin.

I heard they're throwing acid in people's faces, you'd better come home.

But she laughed and said, 'Who's going to think I'm an Arab or something, a great big Irish girl like me?'

27

Before Christmas Francesca had said to the German family at their drinks party, feeling entitled to mordant humour in the circumstances, that if it came to it she would be happy to hide the whole family in their attic and provide the little girl with either a notebook or an iPad in which to write her diary.

The child was in a pink velvet party dress, white knee-length socks edged with lace and T-bar patent shoes. For this special occasion her hair had been unravelled from its pigtails and allowed to fall loose, held back from her forehead by a silver Alice band. She was getting ready to give a short recital on her violin, having been taught from an early age the Suzuki method, her shyness at performing in public overcome by coaxing and flattery until eventually she stepped forward to her music stand with a set expression of concentration, drew her bow across her instrument and began the first notes of Schumann's 'The Two Grenadiers'. It was during the change of sheet music to Weber's 'The Hunters' Chorus' that Francesca made her amusing, tactless offer.

All along the German family had remained optimistic about the situation. A mental mist had descended over the thoughts of some of their adopted countrymen and women but as fog burns away in sunshine, so the light of practicality and reason would disperse this temporary loss of perspective. If Caspar concentrated, and read newspapers that were not his usual cup of tea, he could understand objectively the romanticism of it – not feel it, of course not – but he got that emotions are attached to landscapes, cultures and small things like the coins in your pocket and a particular biscuit. He did not eat biscuits but the English had a huge appetite for them and took them very seriously. The dispute about the correct definition of a Jaffa Cake was something he had followed with great fascination a year or two ago; so many quite eminent people could have an opinion. It was very funny and he had told friends in Germany about it when they asked him to characterise the British.

The couple had come to London because Caspar regarded the city as a supra-state, beyond nationality. It was the type of place they wanted to bring up their daughter, to teach her to be a citizen of the world, fluent in languages, used to seeing headscarves and skullcaps and saris and other signifiers of different races. They felt that the point of London was its capacity to stretch your imagination, even to snapping point. There was nothing one could do that would provoke its surprise. It absorbed atrocities, shrugged them off. In the event of a terrorist attack the authorities took the relevant and necessary precautions, of course, set up exclusion zones, laid cordons, rounded up suspects, but its citizens continued to hold barbecues, or went shopping in the sales, or planned seductions. Nobody talked to each other or made eye contact on the tube; like an elephant bitten by a mosquito, London was simply too big, too absorbed in its own individual business, too intent on getting to work and going shopping and having dates and affairs and planning robberies.

So it seemed to Caspar, and he persuaded Elfriede of this, that here in London the city would not be adversely affected even economically and there was no reason to make any plans until signs emerged that the situation was assuming a form that would be tricky to deal with. Only then they might think of moving to California but it was so very far from family, from mothers and fathers and sisters and brothers all of whom requiring not only constant phone calls and Skype conversations but weekend visits home for a wedding anniversary or a birthday celebration. And here they could be at Heathrow in forty-five minutes on a quiet early Sunday morning and eating Elfriede's mother's excellent lasagne by lunchtime.

Caspar and Elfriede had been cold and affronted and embarrassed by Francesca's joke; she felt she had put her foot in it, as if she were implying they were Nazis, or responsible for the Nazis, sending a shaft of memory down to pierce the pleasant friendly street, re-opening old wounds. Caspar had let them know that during the war his grandparents were potato farmers, 'Mud people, never looked up from the tubers to the sky. I don't think they had a clue about ideology, they just put on a uniform and went off to do their duty, not even knowing what it was or what it was about. Then they came home and dug more potatoes. I'm not so attached to the land, and actually, I prefer rice and pasta.' The conversation had moved on to carbs more generally. Elfriede had tried the Atkins diet but her breath had smelled of pear drops (ketosis), Caspar had told her he could not bear to kiss her. 'And don't you start with that,' Alan had said to his wife.

But the attic reference seemed to be a stone that had fallen into a deep well of social inappropriateness. Down it went, to stone faces. Francesca felt it necessary to bring round from the shop the next morning an Alessi lemon squeezer in the shape of a pointed egg and a hand-made card, as harbingers of the comfort of their insulated loft where they stored their holiday suitcases and Alan's rarely ridden BMX bike, and a reassurance that nothing so absurd was going to happen. They would be pressing citrus fruit for a long time to come in North London, she was sure. But Elfriede seemed to have forgotten about the faux pas and rushed with the wrapped gift to the tree where it was reverently placed with the other parcels. A card, already inscribed and in its envelope with their names on, containing the warmest greetings, was handed over. 'I was going to hand-deliver all my local cards this afternoon, and now here you are.' The two women drank coffee and ate some spiced biscuits iced with green sprigs of holly and the remark was, presumably, forgotten or at least forgiven.

28

After the last Christmas trees had been collected from the pavements and drives and the decorations packed away, the old dietary regime reinstated, lapsed gym memberships renewed and treadmills pulsing again, there was an unexpected alteration in atmospheric conditions. The Met Office informed the public that an anti-cyclone (a circulation of winds whirling in a clockwise rotation) was squatting over Scandinavia blocking the movement of low-pressure areas out across the Atlantic Ocean and forcing them across to the south of England. Strong easterly gales brought snow first to London which spread across the whole country: snow in the Thames estuary, snow in the Scillies, snow moving north to Scotland. Snow, the well-read said to each other with satisfied nods of recognition, was general over the British Isles and also of course Ireland.

The snow was general over everyone. It lasted for seven and a half weeks. Intermittently, and for several days, the temperature in London did not rise above minus five degrees. On a few nights it went down to minus sixteen as if the city had become Moscow and the heavy, blunted figures of commuters like fat sheep in down jackets, woollen hats, thermal gloves and fur-lined boots stumbled out from the tube stations along streets whose grit and salt was buried every night under fresh snowfall. Trains were running to a severely curtailed timetable. Francesca missed the infuriating rumble of normal existence. Alan showed her old film footage of the great ice winter of 1947 when steam trains ploughed through an English landscape resembling the Soviet steppes and navvies in tweed jackets and mufflers, some of whom had advanced on Berlin in army uniform two years earlier, dug the passengers out of white entombment, fuelled by a weekly ration of a shilling's worth of meat.

In the front gardens a population of snowmen had arisen, rows of cold white figures, carrot-nosed. Resistant to melting they stood rigid and unyielding like another species waiting to take over when everything human had died of frostbite. Snowmen of all things, she thought, are supposed to be temporary structures, an idea of a person in another medium and lent our clothes. But they lined up facing out on to the street growing blank and intransigent in their permanence, resisting being knocked down, composed inside now of compacted ice.

The Greek delicatessen was shuttered and up for sale. The owners had slid away without farewells. Later the street heard they were back in the tranquillity of partitioned Cyprus. Francesca believed that cold weather must have finally caused something to snap inside them: that olive oil growing first cloudy then solid in their bottles was no longer sufficient sustenance for their chilled souls, they needed the actual trees, the actual leaves, the actual hard green fruit. Alan told her that Vic in the vinyl shop had heard something about their papers not being in order and they had not so much left as been involuntarily returned. Believing they were of this country they were not, or in not quite the right way. They had come too early or too late, it was all opaque, but their status was wrong, and could not be fixed easily. Alan was collecting material about the Caribbeans and

Cypriots and other Commonwealth citizens who had found that when one asked the age-old question, *what is an Englishman?*, the answer was nothing to do with parliament or the Queen. For without the prop of a passport a person is a disembodied ghost.

Francesca's grandparents had British passports. It was unthinkable for them not to have secured their paperwork. Uncle Farki's son in California had two, which was considered by the family to be the absolute minimum for a secure life. Younis had told his son to make approaches to Israel but his wife Hilary did not like the country and had 'views'. She was, he said, 'a bit of a petition signer'.

On the high street time was spooling backwards. With the departure of the Greeks metaphorically something older and more enduring reappeared in the climate of the country, a return to the sharp clarity of the seasons when winter asserted itself in Victorian form not as dull brown skies and leafless trees but snowfall, robins in the garden, ice-skating on the ponds.

On the telephone from Belfast Alan's mother told him of her own childhood, her mother getting up in the freezing pre-dawn to rake out the ashes from the grate, kneeling on the hearthrug, her hair wrapped in a rag of an old red duster. She recalled her own baby clothes drying on wooden pulleys in the kitchen, steaming in the carbon heat. 'Oh, Alan, winters were very different before radiators. The food we ate, all that stodge, it was just a substitute for central heating but your dad still wants his steak and kidney pud even with the new boiler. And now this. Are you warm enough? Can I send you a fruit cake?'

Everything was going a bit nutsy, a bit frayed and fucked up. For example, Alan had not remotely expected there to be a conspiracy theory about the *snow*. About the council's failure to provide enough pavement grit there were plenty of suspicious stories involving kickbacks and privatisation but who was supposed to be to blame for the weather? Which scapegoat for what the meteorologists called merely 'a prolonged cold snap'? And yet out they all came, as diseased rats from the sewers spread filth and lies and contamination, screeching about an attempt by Israeli scientists to seed clouds with rainfall to irrigate the Negev desert, permanently affecting the climate. When the chief rabbi appeared on 'Thought for the Day' and spoke reassuringly through his soft black beard in a voice at first soothing, then increasingly beseeching, that there was no such experiment and the freak conditions had already been explained by the meteorologists, would pass, were just weather, only weather, then the denial became a cover-up and cover-ups were proof. Francesca's mother had come close to signing a petition demanding that the UN look into it, but was stopped by sharp words from her husband. She had never really understood that side of him which retained an innate foreignness, disguised by what he had so energetically cultivated in his twenties, the flat, placeless tones of what he called his 'international accent'. He took a detached analytical view of politics with no sense of attachment to a cause or a party. Yet now he stood there, shouting, 'Hilary, how *could* you?' as she was filling out her name, and she had said, 'Oh, well, if you're so sure it's wrong. But all it was was a question and is it a crime now to ask questions?'

Alan waded to the end of the garden making deep runnels in the snow. He hoped the blanking whiteness would clear his head of the stupidity of human nature. *People can be so grim,* he thought. There was something almost medieval about how these old libels could be resurrected to suit even twenty-first-century technology. He used to think that conspiracy theories were the effect of a lack of democracy and transparency and a sense of helplessness in the face of the uncontrollable and inexplicable; if the political process was opaque the gaps were filled in by the imagination. Maybe religion was the first, the grandest of the conspiracy theories. Looking up to the sky early humans thought, *Something must be controlling all this*. He found it fascinating. Gazing round, it seemed obvious that all life in the garden was dead, yet at long last the spring would violently make its presence felt again in the form of daffodils and buds on the trees and the flat grass growing and seeding and giving him hay fever. Resurrection myths just tried to make sense of biology, that was all. But now they had the Met Office and still these primitive ideas persisted.

Francesca, watching him brood out there, envied his disposition for philosophy, his Hamlet-like qualities of silent soliloquising, the inner depths into which he could plunge, dive, come up for air, go down deeper. He did not share these thoughts with her. He had, for some time now, ceased to look at her as though she was the subject of one of his films with the enhanced light of his intelligence and curiosity and visual framing. Saturated with his attention when they first met – his consuming interest in her exoticism, the way she dressed, the way she put on her make-up in the morning, a rounded arm lying across the pillow at night, his amusement at how excited she became by the idea of clothes and backchat – his mind's eye had eventually clicked away.

After the high-water mark of the shop's launch and the piece in the *Evening Standard* and the editorial mentions of the high street, it had not been a great success. She had gone on selling carpets, still shuttled round in taxis every month or so delivering rugs to middle-ranking Russians (not oligarchs, just high-earners), but even the lives of the various Sergeys who lived in Highgate and Swiss Cottage were becoming more awkward, as if the oxygen had become slightly thinner and they were finding it harder to breathe. Alan thought her stock was simply too expensive for the households of first-time buyers in their two-bedroom railwayman's cottages and on Christmas Eve the last-minute present-buying rush produced only four sales: a

Murano glass duck; a nude-pink plastic figure lying on its back, its mouth open dispensing Sellotape; a branched vase designed for displaying amaryllis or tulips; and a shoulder bag made from scraps of old non-valuable Turkish carpets which smelled of horses.

There was a distance between them, a rupture of the intimacy that had kept them going for so long. Francesca felt she was now seeing the real man, how he was all bunched up inside, but weren't all men at least a bit on the spectrum? Or it was something to do with his relationship with his father whose radio show was advertised on the side of a Belfast city bus, that glowering sclerotic face lumbering around Stormont? Alan's chief reason for leaving Northern Ireland was to get away from the sight of him, lurching unexpectedly round corners. Was his vagueness, his retreat into nuances that got ever more flimsy, a reaction against the old man's ceaseless opinions?

She had never liked Johanna, the woman's flat white face, like a plate pocked with features. But she had pulled in the work, she had done the contracts. Without her Alan was an auteur without a commission. There he was, out in the snow, looking half-mad. What could you do? The shop was failing, she was failing, he was failing. And he went on thinking his obscure thoughts.

Would this marriage work? They had ploughed together through the whole of *The Garden of the Finzi-Continis*, they had jointly written a long review of it on Amazon, awarding it five stars. They had created a little world between them of merged Alan-ness and Francesca-ness, a territory only they knew about and that was difficult to explain. Now he was alone out there in the snow with his terrible thoughts and she knew she should go out to him, stand beside him in the white length of garden under white trees and white shrubs. She should ask him what he was thinking.

Turning to get her coat, she saw Gaby pulled along to school by her father on a sledge and forgetting her husband she admired the little girl in fat red puffa jacket and woollen hat with ear muffs, waving as if she was the queen riding in a golden coach. Francesca waved back. Caspar was panting and laughing and enjoying himself, they had managed to import to their adopted city the German Christmas they must have known in their own childhoods. They knew exactly what to do, and had salted their path, and then the strip of pavement outside their house until, moving along the whole short road Caspar had in a neighbourly way turned it from ice rink to a walkable route to the station. But then the snow fell again, and again, and hardly any trains ran.

The snow clearance had cemented the German family's popularity. Mrs Audrey Shapiro said to her friend Mrs Simarjit Kaur Khalistan, 'He has a good heart that fella, I can't honestly fault him, much as I'd like to.'

The alley had not been gritted. Caspar felt it was not his responsibility. The Afghan hounds skidded along, Vic walked them wearing a khaki greatcoat purchased in Carnaby Street in 1965, smelling of mothballs and wartime powdered milk. The dogs were agitated by the general whiteness of their surroundings and barked at the muffled trees. Their piss left yellow holes in the snow. Vic fumbled with gloved hands to pick up their shits in a freezer bag. On the fence a cat watched their progress as they turned and began to disappear round the block. The cat seemed to have the measure of the situation, incurious and self-protective. Francesca went out on to the path to call him, having completely forgotten now about her intention to join her husband in the garden.

'How is Mrs Shapiro, have you seen her, does she need anything?'

He turned back and observed her by the gate in pyjamas and bulky sweater, her feet in sheepskin boots. She looked harrowed and unwell.

'You can ask her yourself, here she comes now.'

Mrs Shapiro appeared dressed in a fur coat, odd-looking sheepskin-lined suede booties fastened at the front with a zip, and woollen trousers. The outfit looked ill-at ease with itself, but she had defied its disparity with a peach-coloured silk scarf embellished with sketches of the Eiffel Tower tied around her hair and knotted under the chin, like the Queen out stag-hunting at Balmoral, taking aim beneath a Hermès silk square at an antlered head.

Francesca was surprised by her nimbleness. She stepped with purpose, pulling along after her her perennial shopping trolley. Mrs Shapiro stopped by the gate and said, without preface or introduction, as if she knew what Francesca was thinking, 'My mother was born in Russia, you know. In the winter they didn't sleep in beds but on an iron ledge around the stove. This is nothing.'

'That sounds primitive.'

'Oh, it was! But she knew how to walk in the snow, she taught me. It's just putting your foot down flat and wearing a broad sole. Would you like to come with us, dear?'

'Come where? Where are you going?'

Vic said, 'Somewhere you tried to go before.'

29

A track ran through the snow. The tread of boots and the paw prints of dogs had already stamped themselves on the overnight fall. The aqueduct was partially frozen, miserable-looking water-birds skittered on the icy surface in clumps of feathers and beaks. 'During the war,' Mrs Shapiro said, 'when we had nothing, that lot wouldn't have lasted five minutes. The men came out with nets and grabbed them. Have you ever tried to strangle a duck? Slippery little buggers.'

'No,' Vic said, 'but I've killed a river fish once by bashing its head against a stone, didn't half thrash around. Not even worth it, tasted of mud, disgusting.'

'Then that awful winter, 'forty-seven. Were you alive then?'

'Oh, yes. We couldn't get down the hill, marooned up there, no buses would come even if they had the petrol.'

'I was only fifteen, me and Bernie used to go for a walk together round Clissold Park just to get away from our parents and cuddle under the trees for warmth and he'd make me a million promises about how we'd live one day, and we did, everything that came after was better. We went on holiday to Rome in 1962, by aeroplane, which was a big deal in those days.'

The conversation between the two old people was opaque and confusing. Who caught ducks to eat them? In what primitive London did such people have their origins?

On Audrey pressed, the wheels of her shopping trolley making rails in the snow. Francesca assumed they were taking the garden route to someone's house with a gate to reach the water but they passed the iron structure on the bank and they were at the bridge, and on the other side, the tunnel which led to the backyard door.

'Now look,' said Vic, 'you'll find it a bit unusual. But there's nothing to be scared of. They're just a little odd.'

He banged on the door and felt in his pocket, producing some coins. Eventually, the door was opened by a pair of twin girls with pigtails coiled up and attached to the side of their heads like ring-pulls on a can. They had the air, Francesca thought, of Tweedledum and Tweedledee though neither was fat, but they spoke in chorus. *A penny a penny a penny.* Then they giggled, pointed at Francesca and said, 'Who's she?'

'A neighbour,' Audrey said, 'from the other side.'

Through the gate rabbits slumbered in their hutches in the yard. Even in the chilly air you could smell their rabbity stink, their musty fur, their sour droppings. Their bowls of water were crusted with ice.

The twins led the visitors through the back door into the kitchen where two slices of Welsh rarebit were browning under the grill and through into another room in which an old woman watching *Location, Location, Location* on a portable TV set turned to examine the new arrivals and then point in a derisory manner at the screen, laughing. 'Have you ever seen such rubbish in all your life? What a load of old nonsense.'

The potential buyers were motoring through a chocolate-box village, discussing their aspirations of finding a perfect cottage with a couple of acres of land and an outhouse which could be

217

used as a business hub. They had researched broadband speeds and were hopeful that the next stop would produce their dream home.

'Fucking idiots,' the old lady said. 'Shit for brains.'

'She loves this show,' Vic said. 'Never misses.'

The room smelled of bacon fat and other odours Francesca did not recognise. A row of chipped plaster ducks flew across a mantelpiece and along a deep dado rail ran a line of grimacing ceramic faces: eighteenth-century gentlemen in cocked hats, their hollowed-out heads forming small jugs.

'Here's your tins, dear,' said Mrs Audrey Shapiro. 'Luncheon meat, spam, peas, baked beans, cling peaches, condensed milk, I got some Pot Noodles for the girls.'

'Oh, lovely, lovely, I'll have such a tea. Where have they gone? Where are the little bitches?'

'Don't go calling them that; you'll have the police round, you silly billy.'

'Let 'em come. They'll get a piss pot all over them.'

'No piss pots any more. Enjoying your programme?'

'Ain't they mugs? The fortune they spend to live in a *barn.*'

'I quite agree,' said Francesca, pleased to meet someone, however unlikely, who shared her distaste for country living.

'Who's she?'

'Local. She's got a shop where my shop used to be.'

'Have you got any pills on you? Pills for my head.'

'Not that kind of shop.'

'What *do* you sell?'

'She sells knick-knacks, nice things young people like.'

'Oh well, if it's knick-knacks she'll be bust by Christmas.'

'We're past Christmas.'

'So she's bust, or what's she doing in my parlour when she should be behind the counter?'

'It's the snow,' Francesca said defensively, 'people aren't going out.'

'Pay her no attention, dear, it's just the tongue in her head. Now, Maureen, we're going to have a little rummage around in your drawers.'

'Please yourself.'

Francesca was repulsed by the old woman and by this stifling back parlour or whatever it was called with its piggy smells and leering china faces. She might back away through the kitchen and retreat into the yard if she was sure that she would be able to get out again to the familiar world of the waterway. She kneaded her hands together and pulled her hair.

'Don't do that, dear,' said Vic. 'You look for all the world like Thora Hird. If the wind changes direction you'll be stuck, come along.'

She looked through the kitchen towards the door, still wide open despite the freezing air. The comic-book twins were fighting, they rolled over each other like squabbling dogs. The visitors began to troop next door and Francesca reluctantly followed them, too unsure of herself or the girls to make a break.

'This is the front parlour,' said Mrs Shapiro. 'Spick and span and kept for show more than living,' speaking as if she was a tourist guide shepherding visitors through a National Trust property.

They were in an icy room with a sixty-inch TV resting on a sideboard.

'She'll damage her eyes watching that portable,' Vic said. 'But she just won't turn on the radiators in here. The kids watch it, they don't mind the cold.'

'Have a look, dear,' said Mrs Audrey Shapiro, opening the doors of the sideboard which dominated the party wall.

She pulled out a wooden monkey that climbed a stick and packs of strange old playing cards bearing pictures of occupations, some defunct – Dyer, Chimneysweep, Milkman, Brewer, Barber. The images on them were compellingly old-fashioned, probably, Francesca thought, Victorian, grotesque and slightly frightening. Cardboard boxes held games of tiddlywinks and snakes and ladders. Some pursuits were baffling: a cotton spool into which four nails had been hammered. Audrey showed her how the wool was woven round them to produce at the bottom of the hole a long, pointless coil. In biscuit tins bearing the faces of the newly engaged Prince Charles and Lady Di, dozens of snakes of the stuff were bound together with rubber bands. Audrey pulled out old cigarette cards, books of Green Shield stamps, postcards from holidays in Margate and plastic toys that had once been free gifts concealed in packets of Sugar Pops.

'I thought you might be interested, my dear, in the old ways, how we used to live and what we had to make do with when we were young. We were poor and all we had were these little things to amuse ourselves. Nothing had a plug on it in those days, electricity came late to these houses.'

'Did you grow up here?'

'Me? There were never any Jews; we wouldn't have been tolerated. Things were very different in those days, very different, men were different and so were women, but mostly the men. My late husband used to say they were Saxons and Danes living here, or their descendants.'

'Doubt it,' Vic said. 'Probably potato famine Irish era.'

'My grandparents—' Francesca began, then felt a sudden circumspection, not necessarily in front of her companions who had met the old people at the opening party, but as if these damp walls might grow ears like cauliflowers. Being in a place, she intuited, which did not hold with foreigners and really there was so much of that about at the moment, one might be wise to keep one's mouth shut. This backwoods environment seemed to her to be so unfamiliar, so distrustful, that she felt quite rattled, as if she was Alice who having slipped down the rabbit hole was going to have to explain herself to a Cheshire cat. And there was a cat, next door, dozing by the oven, a common tabby with a malevolent face, as all cats had, to her.

'Come on, put that stuff away and we'll show you around,' Vic said.

Like mountaineers roped together, she felt the urge to hold on to Audrey's coat collar, but managed to leave through the front door with a display of dignity, thinking how Alan's face would appear confronted with such a situation: alert, eager, curious, puzzled, slightly smiling.

In the street the row of terraced houses blazed on to the snow. They were of a bog-standard late-Victorian construction, two-storey with bay windows on the ground floor, but the brick had been painted in emerald, tangerine, duck-egg blue. The thrilling if garish appearance of the houses to Francesca bore the signs of artists, of an installation of some kind, something she should have known about, read up on. That she did not know seemed an indication of a slippage, a failure of attention. How could she have been living so close to – but what? She had no idea. Looking round, the painted frontages seemed inartistic, sloppily executed. Or maybe that was the point? Could the old woman in front of the TV set and the bounding twins at the back gate be a temporary performance piece and she would soon come across other members of the audience trooping from house to house?

'I see your face,' Vic said. 'You're trying to make sense of it. It's not what you think. This is what we call the Island, it's a geographical anomaly. In the old days you paid a penny to come through their yard, it's a shortcut to and from the marshes, otherwise you'd have to go round miles. Of course, they don't advertise that any more, only a few people know about it now. Audrey does, and she told me.'

'When my husband first opened our chemist,' said Mrs Shapiro, 'I'd come and deliver the medicines myself, they were very insular. They had a shop and a school and a café but no

221

chemist or doctor so we'd use the backyard door to get in and they'd use it to get to us.'

'But they're not really an island.'

'No. But in those days they kept a very separate way of life. I remember one of the women saying she'd been to Chingford and it was the other end of the world. Of course all that changed when they put in the television aerials. And then in the sixties the council wanted to knock the whole place down and build flats.'

The snow had touched the Island as it had touched everyone. If anything it was more compacted. A snowman resembled in its apparel an approximation of a semi-familiar woman.

'Is that—'

'Yes, haven't they got her to the life?'

She was being fucked up the backside by a snow dog.

'Very crude,' said Mrs Shapiro. 'They've no sense of proportion, these people.'

Vic said, 'They never did have. My late wife tried to civilise them, it was a losing battle.'

'So why wasn't the place pulled down?'

'Ah, well, that's another story, a lot of them worked for the council, not in the offices wearing a collar and tie, but on the bins. Working on the bins was a good job in those days and you could only get it if you were connected, it was handed on from father to son. Very tight they were and they could make anyone's life a misery if you got on the wrong side of them, the police couldn't seem to help. I think even they were afraid of the binmen. Especially if they lived in the borough, because whatever you did for a living you could still find your bins upended over your flower beds and all your rubbish hanging off the roses. So they never really needed a campaign, they just got a stay of execution until the whole thing blew over and a lot of them are still here, though, quite a few moved out to Kent and Essex or like Jean they came to our neighbourhood, that's her aunt you saw in front of the telly just now. Where we live is full of the old ones, but the ones who stayed behind are very stubborn and they won't adapt.'

'How long have they been here?'

'The Island families go back generations, to when these houses were first built when the old Queen was on the throne, that's what they call her, Victoria, the old Queen, they used to paint the faces on the pennies and hang them from the windows, they don't do that any more, but it was funny seeing those heads with their crowns on and blue lips and green hair and dabs of rouge. The council let them pass the houses on to their children and their children did the same, and they didn't like newcomers, so the place got a reputation for unfriendliness.'

The air was rent with the same trumpeting she had heard on her first fruitless discovery of the back-door tollgate.

'What is that?' she cried.

'It's the elephant, dear. In the old days a few of the families had a deal with the circus, they stabled the animals here and the women used to make the circus performers' costumes, they curled feathers and sewed on sequins and what have you. It was a family tradition. Do you want to go and see it?'

Yes, she wanted to see an elephant grey and wrinkled and vast looking into the bedroom windows of the terraces. But the elephant was at the end of the street in a lock-up garage, it resided in there in the dark, its days as a performing act in the circus were long gone. It had been abandoned several years ago, and lived here now, sluiced with buckets of water and fed on carrots, potatoes, grass mowings and twigs. Its tusks had been filed down. The elephant stared at her with a hating dark eye.

It seemed very old, resigned to the cold and the absence of company from its own species. She was fairly sure that there must be laws against keeping wild animals in such conditions.

'Something should be done about this,' she said. 'It should be reported to the RSPCA.'

'It'll die soon enough. It must be fifty years old, it was already here when I moved to the area,' Vic said.

'Older. I saw it at the circus myself before that.'

'And then what? How do you dispose of the carcass of a dead elephant?'

'The bin men will take care of it. I'm sure they have a plan,' Vic said.

Francesca had forgotten that she was cold, that everything was cold. The cold seemed now to be a condition of the air, like breathing oxygen. The icy wind on her skin felt not cutting but fresh. Her body seemed to be recalibrating its own thermostat. It was all so very odd. And it seemed to her that she was through the looking glass into another England, one that was half in this time, half in an older age in which kids played in the streets and women in turbans scrubbed their front steps and men drank without female company in the pubs. She had seen an exhibition depicting this way of life at the Photographers' Gallery, striking figures in inky blacks and snowy whites looking as much like ghosts as lines of helmeted young men in the trenches who would be all dead shortly after the camera's shutter closed. A woman her mother's age was saying that she remembered shops in Newington Green when she was already in her twenties that still sold single cigarettes, or you could save up for a packet of five. The past was monochromatic and faintly absurd. It was impossible for her to imagine how they lived like that. But here they had television sets, modern cars were parked on the pavements, they probably had the internet, she must ask if they had it. Vic and Mrs Audrey Shapiro were turning the corner, and she ran to catch up with them.

'So now you know,' said Mrs Audrey Shapiro. 'It was always poor, very poor and very closed-minded. I brought my Indian friend here once, they didn't like it, didn't like it one bit. One of the ladies said to me, "We have to see them when we go to the shops, what you doing bringing one of them nig-nogs here?" But that was years ago, they're probably more up to date now.'

Vic said, 'The salt of the earth can poison it, I believe.'

They passed through the last of the five streets, the colour palette of the houses fading slightly, patches of apricot and peach and violet and moss-green tinting the shadowed snow in their front gardens. Then the Island gave out altogether, abruptly, as if the houses had stopped short and were prepared to move on no further, recoiling at a vast space in front of them they could have no hope of populating. The snow was crossed with lipstick lines of a dying February sun. Vic said they were called marshes but the wetlands lay deep under the deposited rubble from thousands of bombed houses of the Blitz.

Football posts reared in square iron hoops, like letter Es missing their central thrust and she was reminded sharply and unpleasantly of a journey she had once taken.

Her grandfather had surprised his granddaughter with the present of a visit to Poland, a group tour for Jewish teenagers organised by his synagogue. Or not to Poland itself but to a territory which was transnational: the concentration camp. The coach journey from the airport directed them to the museum. This part of the visit was fairly interesting. There was a film and a gift shop and a café and photographic exhibits to look at. In one picture a teenage guard had twisted his whole body into a corkscrew in order to emit a howl of something in German directed at a line of recoiling naked women. He was a spiralling column of hatred and resentment and power over people who might have once been, like say her parents, dentists.

Francesca asked, 'But what is going on in his mind?'

The guide said, 'Nothing is going on, his mind is destructed.'

'I don't believe that,' she said. 'He had an *ideology*.'

'Yes, he had one, that is what made his mind to stop working.'

After the museum they drove a couple of miles to the second camp. The visitors had been advised to dress warmly, where they were going next there was nothing audiovisual to look at or discuss and no café or toilets. They would see fewer visitors, hardly anyone came. Parking by the gatehouse the troupe of teenagers climbed down from the coach jabbering, and walked into a formless dun-coloured wilderness under a lowering sky. From horizon to horizon it extended and Francesca, confined for most of her life to London and its parks, could only compare it to, say, Hampstead Heath where her parents sometimes took her to look at the Rembrandt and the Vermeer in the gallery and allowed her to deliver a little lecture about them which actually drew a small crowd of smiling, attentive strangers gathered round this dark-haired self-possessed child who already, as they remarked, had 'such an eye!' Then lunch in the café before walking a few metres into damp woodland smelling of leaf mould and turning back, her father ridiculously ill-shod in his gold-snaffled loafers and Francesca in a kind of party dress and patent shoes she had insisted on wearing.

Unlike the heath, here hundreds of brick structures rose, fingers pointed accusingly upwards. Their Polish guide explained that they were the chimneys of the wooden huts (repurposed horse stables) which had been burnt to the ground by the liberating Soviet forces. The teenagers had stared out, their high spirits temporarily dampened by the absence of anything to read, look at or be explained. They gazed solemnly at the vista. Some of them felt that a response of some kind was needed or why were they here? It was disrespectful to just look around in silence and they began to say prayers or sing songs, mournful or defiant. One girl sang 'Bridge over Troubled Water'. It was all terribly sad and difficult to understand.

The singing and praying faded away into a desultory hanging

around in the rain, waiting to be told they could get back on the bus. Later, in Krakow, they would hear a talk from a survivor, and would listen with the same bored solemnity with which they had toured the camp.

Now the marshes reminded Francesca of that expanse of land punctuated by its bricky fingers. Which was ridiculous because what could be more benign than football posts? But here, she thought, you could do anything and no one would know. You might fence or wall off the whole expanse of snowy grassland and make a camp. But a camp for what exactly?

As she stood there, a faint hallucination rose in her mind: grey, misty, vague in form in which she saw the whitened grassland covered in temporary structures, a wooden city of sheds housing people no more solid than wraiths dressed in modern clothes, wheeling luggage, holding children, talking on phones, checking screens. Through the last street of the Island they were arriving at their destination and looking round, some assessed the situation accurately. She could see they were deportees, hemmed in on all sides awaiting future arrangements for their permanent departure. From art history she knew of the palimpsest, derived from the Greek παλίμψηστος, to be 'scraped again'. The palimpsest was something she had studied at university, a surface such as a canvas bearing the traces of many layers of record, re-inscribed over time. Beneath the paint lay the trace of other paint, or a chalk mark, a fingerprint. The landscape had been scraped, it had been overlaid, it had reformed itself. Medieval peasants had trudged through this watery land, had got lost in the fog, had drowned, bones deep in boggy occluded earth. The Blitz had brought the rubble and debris of the East End, peace had brought ruled football pitches and weekend playtime.

The marshes collected in pools of greyness. *One can get lost,* she thought, *one can easily go missing.* The lowering sky, the misty indecision between land and air, the formless wilderness of the marshes compacted with ice and patches of grey grass struggling above the frozen surface, the absolute silence and the absence of any birds or planes above – and why should there not be planes, all of London was a flight path – induced a feeling of evaporation, as if by no longer noticing the cold, she was becoming of the cold.

It was a hypnagogic image, she decided, rising up in the border between waking and sleep. Something had short circuited. Perhaps the blankness of the snowy wastes had confused her brain, taking them for white sheets and a pillow. And despite this reasonable explanation, she felt a deep fear, as if she was finally dead and would never wake.

She took out her phone.

'Ringing someone?' Vic said.

'I'm just checking to see if there's a signal.'

'Put it away, dear,' said Mrs Audrey Shapiro, 'you'll find nothing like that here.'

'We'll be off now,' Vic said. 'Enough excitement for one day.'

Back on the Island the twins came running towards her holding a cardboard monkey climbing a stick.

'It's for *you*,' they said.

'Perfect,' she replied faintly, as if reminded of who she was supposed to be.

'*Paarfect paarfect paarfect.*' They squawked away satirically like a pair of parakeets in green jerseys and green ribbons in their hair.

If I linger, I will be lost, she thought. *I'll never get home.* Her companions had disappeared from sight. What colour was the door she had come from? If she followed the girls where would they take her? The children would lock her up with the elephant; she would never be found.

'Where are you, dear?' called Mrs Shapiro's voice. 'Hurry along, hurry, hurry.'

She saw the flash of her silk scarf appearing round the corner and the old woman's face with the oddest of expressions. Were they all ghosts? Were the twins, the old woman, the houses themselves a figment of her imagination or visitors from the other world?

'Is this real?' she cried, not able to overcome her anguish.

'Of course it is, what are you thinking? That you're time travelling? No, it's perfectly real. If you take out your telephone you'll find you can ring your nice husband now, that is if you want to. Go on, try it.'

Francesca could not help but take out her phone and with freezing fingers examine the signal, four rising bars of the network. It was true. She was in the real world. They ushered her through the house. The old woman had sunk far into sleep, the crusts of her Welsh rarebit were cold on a plate on the floor. Vic opened the back door and they were once again on the bank by the aqueduct. The tracks they had made on their journey out were hardening into icy indentations. It was difficult not to slip. Vic took her arm. 'You'll be back in your house soon, don't worry. And then you can make what you like of where you've been.' He smiled. 'Funny old day, eh? I hope you got something out of it.'

At home things were as she'd left them. Alan was inside now, sitting on the sofa watching TV. He was watching one of his own documentaries, he was watching the one about the people who dressed as if they lived in the forties. She had not yet told him about her experience. She needed to sound rational. She knew her husband would pick holes in anything she told him, or be consumed by such curiosity that without even remembering to put on his coat he'd grab a camera and go straight down there to see for himself. Then the day would no longer be hers, it would be turned into a project, a pitch.

'Let me tell you where I have been.'

She described the – what was it, exactly, an hour? Time had

not stood still, it was no fairy tale. The sky had grown leaden with approaching sunset, the clock on her iPhone had gone on advancing. But Alan sitting next to her listening to what sounded like a film or a dream was unconvinced by anything she told him. His wife was prone to embroider and exaggerate. Once, he'd found it adorable.

And it was true, she agreed, that the whole day *had* been garish and unconvincing. Even trying to describe the contents of the sideboard proved harder than she expected for the debris in the drawers was not, as she had thought when she first looked at it, charming, artisan examples of pre-plastic authentic working-class pastimes which could be revived and sold (the climbing monkey was delightful, the coil of knitting put to some contemporary purpose) but seemed to her now just rubbish, smelling of mothballs and death. She began to doubt herself. And she had not shared her thoughts yet about the expanse of marshes and the uses they might be put to.

She picked up his hand and kissed it. She had never told him how she loved his narrow hands, their waisted thumbs, the sign of a sensitive soul, and hands that could also saw planks and do things with electrical wiring. But now the hand felt lifeless. There was no exchange with hers.

'Was it mad, was it all mad? Tell me.'

He could not immediately respond. Why was she pouring out this unbelievable narrative? What could she possibly expect him to make of it? What did she want him to say? Was it some fantasy from the *Thousand and One Nights*? He touched and stroked her fingernails, then let them go.

'I don't know. I don't really understand what you're saying. I don't know what's true or what you're making up.'

'Making up? I'm not making up anything.'

'Then perhaps you've misremembered.'

'It was only an hour ago.'

'Memory isn't—'

'Oh, for fuck's sake, don't give me one of your lectures on memory. I know what memory is. And I know what I saw. Ask Vic, ask Mrs Shapiro, get them to take you; I'm sure they will if you ask, it's ten minutes' walk away, it's just over there.'

She pointed out of the window with a wild imprecise gesture.

'I don't really understand. The topography is wrong. Look, I'll show you on a map, we're just not that near the marshes.'

He reached for his phone. She watched him follow the line of the aqueduct with his slim finger. The marshes lay much further to the east, across the reservoirs.

'I don't know where they took you, or if you fell asleep and dreamed all this—'

And she thought that this was how men drove their wives mad, gaslighting them, but why would he do such a thing, who loved her? It was true, she was imaginative, she had been such a little storyteller when she was a child. And her sense of reality wavered, as heat on tarmac on a summer's day appears to melt the road.

'I was there, I was there! We'll go tomorrow, I'll take you myself. All we you have to do is knock.'

'If you say so.'

But he looked as lifeless as a stick.

'What are you thinking about?' she said from the far end of the sofa, that old intimate question. The light outside had almost died. The room was lamp-lit, warm, serene and the sense of unfamiliarity had completely evaporated.

He smiled. 'We haven't asked each other that for ages, have we?'

'Well, go on.'

'I don't know, I'm not really thinking, more worrying, uselessly and free-floatingly attaching anxiety to everything. It's ridiculous.'

'Perhaps you're right to be worried. Maybe we *should* both worry.'

'No. I don't want you to. Leave all that to me.' He needed her to remain his high-stepping woman, even though her extravagance had started to annoy him. She had no idea of their real budget. It was humiliatingly low.

Then she began to speak again of the strange day she had had, she must make him understand. 'I was there, you know; I was. I don't care what the map says. Or at least I was somewhere. I can't say where. But I was there.' And she described the place once again, so vividly that eventually he thought he could actually see it. He probably should take a camera and try to get in. It sounded, at the very least, quite odd. He had no idea what she meant by the marshes, but she was so urban she could mistake a park for the Pennine Way. Yes, it had to be an unknown park, unknown at least to them. She had taken some kind of turn out there in the snow, a kind of brainstorm perhaps. The claustrophobia of the winter, shut up at home when the shop was closed, had caused her mind to expand to fill the places vacated by the real world.

'Mrs Shapiro said no one has invaded the Island.'

But this observation was what it took to push him over the edge.

'Oh God, life is just all bloody metaphors these days, isn't it? I'm going to bed for a bit.'

And he did not return downstairs that evening, leaving Francesca to eat chicken chasseur all alone at the dining table and study the monkey climbing the stick, up down, up down, reaching, falling.

30

I am the king of wack, I am the dean of deng.

31

William was looking at a snail, he'd picked up the slimy thing by its shell with his little fingers and was turning it upside down. The horns retracted. 'That's disgusting,' said his brother, 'throw it away.' William said couldn't he keep it as a pet? Neil said, 'Don't be stupid, it doesn't even do anything.' He picked the snail up and threw it at the fence. It hit a concrete post and the shell shattered, a soft residue slid down into the earth. This was like the business with the rabbit which Neil had nagged for but forgotten to feed, it had died of starvation in the darkness of the shed. They had buried it in the flower beds marked with a wooden cross made of ice-lolly sticks. When he went to look at the grave a week later, the marker was gone and the earth seemed to have been moved. In later life he learned that soon after the funeral, about half an hour, their cleaner had by agreement dug it up and taken it home for the pot. She was Welsh and terrified him. Her hands were red like meat. On the other hand, she cooked amazing chips.

He had felt terrible about the rabbit, which his dad had named Whiskeynsoda on account of its colouring which was peat brown and white, but a snail was nothing, it had no feelings, could not aspire to be called anything. William was looking at him like he was Hitler though neither of them were sure who Hitler was, apart from being a bad word. 'What?' said Neil. 'It's only a stupid snail. The garden is full of them. They eat Mum's dahlias. We should kill some more.' He knew they were not to eat the pellets she put down in her flower beds, though nothing would tempt him to do so, but William was just a kid and lacked normal common sense.

William was walking back along the side of the house. He was going in through the back door to his room to sulk. Later he'd tell some tittle-tattle tale to Mum about his big brother being horrible to him and his mum would give him a ticking-off because he was older and should know better than William who was just a little boy. Neil was left in peace with his comic. Peace didn't come. He should go in and have a word with Wills, talk it all through with him. Their bedrooms overlooked the garden; he raised his head expecting to see his brother's face at the window, his eyes red with babyish tears. The kid was nowhere to be seen. He went into the kitchen. His mother was chopping carrots for shepherd's pie and half-watching a chat show on the countertop portable.

He had thrown a snail against the fence and William had walked off in a huff, to the front garden, maybe to find another pet snail, but how he came to have gone through the gate and out on to the pavement and into the road was a mystery that the business with the snail could shed no light on. Maybe, he thought, for many years, he'd tried to get *on* the bus, had run for it, not understanding that it wasn't going to stop because there wasn't a bus stop, it was on diversion, they never stopped, just went in a weird loop until they came back to a further point along the route. Was he running away? Did he think he could go into town, away from the safety of their suburb of detached houses with integral garages and front lawns and some already extended-out with conservatories?

In bed that night he couldn't believe his brother's room was empty and he wasn't coming back, ever. He was crying as quietly as it was possible to weep. His mother, hesitating on the landing, held open a crack of the door to watch him lying under the Power Rangers duvet, his face wet. She thought she should go and comfort him, put as much of herself as she could on the narrow mattress and give him a cuddle, tell him it was not his fault. Frank came up the stairs. 'I'll go in to him,' he said. For earlier his wife, in her grief, had said she would throw herself out of the upstairs window, not meaning it, but under such duress she might do anything to escape from the overwhelming strain of her situation with a boy lying in the hospital under a sheet and another crying alone in the dark.

'It's not your fault, Neil,' his father said. 'It was the bus; it must have come out of nowhere, along one of the side roads. He didn't know. He was being naughty, running out like that.'

Neil thought his brother would come home the next day, that he would come down from the bathroom to the breakfast table in the morning room and there would be William, maybe with a bandage round his head and pointing an accusing finger at his brother. Eventually they'd have a laugh about it. A *snail*, of all things. He did not go to school. He sat watching cartoons under a special dispensation. He saw *Caspar the Friendly Ghost*; William was a ghost now, white-sheeted and playful.

He knew he had been wack from the word go, it was just that months would pass and he would forget all about the snail and the garden and the bus. William's possibilities had not even been promised let alone fulfilled. He was forever a little boy aged seven with Neil's eyes and his mother's lighter skin, a bruise on his shin from something at school, a knock, a fall, and went into the ground like that.

Neil had been bought a new jacket for the funeral, a heather tweed he would get a couple of years' wear out of before shooting up and the sleeves became too short.

32

He remembered someone throwing whole bottles of Evian water in his face, the stuff was being passed from the bar along a chain of hands.

He remembered thinking he was blind, then his left eye started to open, his vision patchy and dotted, eventually it cleared.

There had been several operations, major facial reconstructions. Skin from his thigh had been grafted on to his cheeks and forehead and nose. His thigh was his face, the skin smooth and sparsely haired, he would never be able to grow a beard again. He had the urge to touch himself, to be reassured that the skin was still there, that patches had not fallen away while he was distracted. He had become fidgety again having years ago mastered stillness, because a composed man is one who displays no anxiety; now he had to make an effort to stop his hand from going to his face, drawing attention to it.

He worried that he was emitting a constant odour, a chemical stench from all the operations, a hospital stink that Chrissie, he remembered, had brought home in the fibres of her uniform: the smell of the wards and the operating theatre, bloodied bandages, bed pans, infection, decay, topped with the ammonia fragrance of urine and a top note of disinfectant.

He wanted an axe to split him transversely and a new fledgling Marco to arise from the abandoned carcass.

33

They had rung her up and begged her but she said no, no she was so busy at the hospital and anyway he didn't even *want* to see her, she'd heard nothing since they took him home, first to the burns unit then back with them after his treatment, she'd heard it was going grand and in time he could look not too bad, not his former handsome self but maybe he'd been too perfect at that.

But his mum said, 'He *wouldn't* ask you, he's too proud. He's turned against everyone, you know he wouldn't let a soul come and see him in the hospital, not a living soul. None of his friends, nobody. Not that Agatha, she sent him a few texts then nothing, the callous little toff. I'd wring her neck, so I would, if I saw her. His colleagues from work they've been terrific, they wouldn't let up with their messages and trying to visit, but he turned them all down flat. You see, you're the only one who saw, you know what he was like in those first days when he had the worst of it, and you're not shocked or squeamish, you wouldn't be, would you? Can't you put the past behind you? It would mean so much to him, I know it would, honestly. Times change, everything changes, the country isn't the same, is it, and the best of us have got to stick together.'

It was bound to be a mercy mission they were after because he was depressed and trapped at home with his mum and dad during his recovery and why did it have to be her, just as her life was going great? When the Jamaican girls went back to their island, saying enough was enough they didn't like the atmosphere any more, Rob said why didn't she move into his spare room, for they got along fine, which was surprising since they were so very different and he said he liked having her around, because she understood, she'd been there.

She'd told him the flat was great but she didn't think much of his bathroom and he said she was right and he'd have it done up though there wasn't much you could do about the water pressure. Did she still want a bathtub in there? He liked them himself, good to wallow in hot water when you weren't feeling great, and she told him he could put in anything he liked as long as she could get her hands on her shampoo and conditioner and gel when she was in the shower without having to feel around for everything, one of them caddies she wanted and storage for all her bits and bobs, her body lotions and deodorant and make-up bag. And somewhere to sit when she shaved her legs and did her fake tan, so he said he'd get one of those basket chair things with a cushion, Lloyd Loom, which made a nice change from a hard stool. He'd shown her the shower he planned to put in with one of those huge chrome heads which made you feel like you were in a rainforest.

She had no idea what to take. Marco was long past the flowers stage and he was the type you wouldn't dare buy a present for because he was so fussy and wanted stuff she didn't even know existed or if she did know then the brand was something she'd never heard of. A book? He read books on his iPad but she didn't know what they were called or what they were about because you couldn't see them. If he was a girl you could pick up something with a nice smell, a scented candle or bubble bath, or a scarf or a hair ornament but fellas were so hard, especially ones like him. In the end she settled for expensive chocolates. You couldn't buy them in a supermarket you had to get them at their very own shop, there was one at the station. Rob wrote down the name. She had never seen Marco eat chocolates before, but maybe that was what he was craving now, it was impossible to have any idea. The box looked great, though, with a big black ribbon round it and reminding him, no doubt, of his old life so she must surely have got that right.

The south of England was getting over the snow. The white stuff was finished but the rivers had gone mad. All over the country there was flooding, people losing their homes – her dad said, 'Well you build on a flood plain and you're asking for trouble, aren't you? But that's the English for you, all greed, no sense.' Out of the window of the train: fields, animals grazing, everything looking a bit wet and sorry for itself but life coming back when there'd been days, she'd admit it, when she thought they'd all gone to Narnia and there would never be anything but winter for the rest of their lives. 'Who's the Snow Queen?' said Rob. 'The prime minister,' she replied, quick as a flash. 'Yes,' he agreed, 'it's all her fault.'

But they were coming out the other side into mud and rain and sodden grass and birds going mad in the branches of the trees with their nests, singing their beaks off into the skies.

The last time she'd seen him they were on a train. No, she'd seen him in hospital, but the old Marco, the undamaged Marco, that was in the long-ago past before so many things had come out different and not how you expected. Don't watch the news, her mum said, there's nothing good or useful to hear coming out of those lying mouths, but her dad was on top of the whole thing, he'd seen it coming, wasn't fretting, said the conditions had been created for a united Ireland now, wouldn't be all that long and the English left all by themselves in the little whites-only rump state, which was all they deserved, yes. And if she came home she'd be soon enough living in a young country again like in his grandfather's day. The Queen would die and then it was finished, everyone knew that, old jug-ears wouldn't last five minutes on the throne, now would he?

Should she call him Neil? In the hospital he hadn't responded whatever name she used, just lay there looking like he was sending up a message from Hell itself. The Hell of the priests with the toasting forks prodding at your flesh like they tried to show you in pictures at Sunday school until the parents told them to cut it out.

The box of chocolates was in a smart little bag of stiff paper with fabric handles and that was in her handbag. The thing held the kitchen sink, she'd never get rid of it until it was on its last legs even if her phone did keep falling out. She tried to imagine what she was going to say to him – she saw terrible sights the whole time, nothing shocked her, it wasn't his face she was worried about – it was what was going to happen when she said, 'Oh, hello there, long time no see.' And then what? Where would they go from there? Because she had no idea if he actually knew she was coming or if she was a surprise they were springing on him and she had never managed to persuade them that he hated her guts, well maybe not that, but it wasn't like they'd ever been friends. She was on this train for their sake not his, because they were desperate and she'd a reputation to live up to that had taken hold these past few years, that nurses on the NHS were all angels, and not girls of easy virtue who were all after a doctor for a husband.

34

'The thing about Neil is he doesn't let the grass grow under his feet, never has done. One of the things that makes us proud of him is his work ethic. He went to uni knowing exactly what he wanted to do and what he wanted to get out of it. Sorted out all his internships himself and was taken on full time by the third one he completed, and I hear some are interning for years, and for no pay at all, not even their travel expenses. In my day you had management traineeships straight out of college but now they expect them to work for nothing, which is disgraceful. Anyway, since he's been out of hospital he's started his own business, he's doing it from our house, from the spare room. Neil was always what they call a self-starter, he knows what he wants and how to get it, we've tried to give him as much space as we can manage, it's more like a little flat he has up there with a bedroom and an office and his own bathroom. In the old days even executive houses like ours only had the one with maybe a downstairs cloakroom to wash your hands and freshen up but we have the two as well as the downstairs loo so we hope it doesn't make him feel like he's back in his old childhood bedroom because apart from no kitchen it's self-contained. We don't even shout up to him or knock, it's all done on our phones through that messaging app same as when he lived in London. Sometimes he has his meals with us, sometimes he orders a takeaway, or he'll come down and make something for himself, but in general he's got as much freedom and privacy as he had before. The main thing is, he's running his new business, getting it off the ground and it turns out he'd built up an awful lot of goodwill over the years, because people are falling over themselves to help make a go of it.'

They had passed quickly from the station to the suburbs. Her foot was pressed hard against the well of the car as if there was an invisible brake down there she could apply to delay arrival. The father was talking on and on, he was talking himself into Marco being okay up there above the ceiling doing whatever it was he was doing, but you could see the man was in bits because he kept lifting his left hand from the wheel and scratching his neck, though there was no mark there, no bite, but some nervous tic he hadn't had when she had met him in the hospital. It was all an easy flow coming from his mouth but the fella was in a hole, she could see that, more nervous than she was about this visit and if he'd made a mistake even asking her, but probably he was desperate, both of them must be. Months now since the attack and still Marco was walled up in his parents' home with no visitors like those nuns who withdrew to the convent and took the veil. And that was a strange thing, wasn't it, that if he'd been a girl and a Muslim he could have covered his face and no one would think anything of it, just his eyes showing through a slit like she'd seen on women shopping in the Edgware Road.

'Oh, now what kind of business is that?' she said.

'It's a very clever idea, club nights in the comfort of your own home.' He outlined the project, which was now moving towards the beta stage.

Chrissie said, 'The what, now?'

'I think he's going for a soft launch, you know, when you invite your mates to test-run it, iron out the flaws.'

'Okay.'

'Is it the kind of idea that would appeal to you?'

And would the party be shite?

Jesus, this sounded like the shitest party she could imagine, she never would, she'd queue at Fabric if she had to and endure not being let in, turned away because her look was all wrong then go off somewhere and find a pub where they didn't care and you didn't even have to pay to get in and they'd do you a cocktail if you asked them nicely.

Now Marco was in charge of this shite. She turned her head to the side window and laughed, silently, as one suppresses a sneeze.

'Well, you know, I prefer the pubs, the drink is cheaper.'

'I understand.'

He had embraced her at the station, took her in his arms in his warm overcoat and pressed her head to his chest though they were close to the same height. The sight of her coming through the ticket barrier with her long hair to her shoulders and the raw-boned Irish face, the pink plastic handbag slapping at her thighs, off-duty but looking no different than in her nurse's uniform – she evoked the same feeling he'd had when he'd first seen her, *she's a coper*, she's the type you can't shock. And it was a mystery then as it was now that she and his son had ever been flatmates, but that was the oddity, he had heard, of life in London which shoved ill-suited types together, like it or not. He had thanked her for coming. She had said it was no bother at all, wasn't the train quick, she'd no idea they were so close. When he dropped her off he would have a small gift for her, just some supermarket vouchers in a gift pack to use any time she needed. She had not taken up his offer of paying for her train ticket.

His son knew she was coming. He had nodded, for Frank was not going to back down. 'And will you be polite, son?'

'Of course, Dad. Why wouldn't I be?'

'It's true, you're never rude.'

'I like to keep calm. It's useful in business. Some people enjoy playing the prima donna, not me.'

'I know.'

When William was killed he had drawn back into himself. Some spark had been put out that made him quiet and watchful and self-interested.

The garden where the child had run out into the road had been redesigned. The rose bushes were gone, the lawn paved over. A stone cat stood in one corner, curling its tail, underneath it was a plaque memorialising the dead boy. Obviously they would never be able to move. The road had been designated off-limits to buses on diversion after a petition by the residents. It was a terribly quiet road, Chrissie thought, the houses seemed asleep in the winter light, that slumbering quality of the suburbs where a car door slammed in the middle of the afternoon is a fright like a burglar alarm. Her uncle had built roads of houses like this in Wicklow but nobody bought them, they were torn down again, he shot himself by the shed.

After she'd had a cup of tea with them in the lounge and eaten a coffee-cream éclair, and gone to wash her hands in the cloak-room they showed her upstairs to fortress Marco. Oh God, she thought, you've faced worse than this, but I'd rather be tending to a terrorist's victim with her arm blown off than saying hello to him now.

He had quite a set-up in there, three computer screens and a printer and everything stacked up, all his paperwork. Yes, he'd made himself a proper office looking like it was in Shoreditch not Aylesbury because he always had that taste, didn't he, everything finely judged according to rules she didn't know anything about.

Like it was a picture from a magazine, he was a slim guy sitting on an executive chair in beautiful jeans and a navy cable-knit sweater, black hair perfectly groomed with product but then he turned round and Marco was ruined.

'Well now, don't you look a sight better than I saw you last?' she said, lunging towards him holding out the chocolates. 'I bought you these, I don't know if you eat them or not, but I'm reliably told they're the tops.'

'Thank you, Chrissie. That's very kind. You shouldn't have come all this way.' His voice was quiet and soft, the same voice he'd used that time on the train.

'Shall I sit here? You had this chair in the old flat, I recognise it.'

'Yes.'

'I always wanted to try it out to see if it was comfortable but I never sat down in your bedroom, did I?'

'It was a long time ago.'

'I know. A lot's happened since then. Your dad told me about your new business, your club nights at home. What's that then?'

He explained to her his concept in full detail to push through to the moment when she'd be safe to think she'd done enough and could go. He had told his parents he didn't want her there all afternoon. An hour was plenty.

'Well, isn't that grand?' Chrissie said. 'I bet you'd save a ton of money too, not going out, with your tube fares and your taxis.'

'It's definitely good value. And of course there are different levels depending on your budget. I'm organising pick-up points for the cocktails and canapés at supermarkets, but you could have home delivery if you want. We can do custom packages for VIP clients where we charge a lot more so that subsidises the economy brand.'

'Great.'

'We advise a minimum of sixty-inch TV screen, preferably wall-mounted to get the best experience out of it.'

'Who's we?'

'It's just myself at the moment, I'll probably take on staff after the launch. They won't be working from here, they'll be London based.'

'I get you.'

'I'll give you a free package, as a thank-you.'

'You don't need to do that.'

'I insist.'

'And I'm to do no blow jobs at these parties, am I?'

It surprised him now that though he associated Chrissie with her running off from him on the train and going missing and all the business that followed he had half-forgotten what he had said, and it surprised him even more to remember now that he had actually said it aloud to her, instead of just thinking it and smiling to himself. But she had rubbed him up the wrong way once too often and he had just come out with it, to shut her up when she was blathering on about the party – *if the party's shite* – not thinking, not realising she could be hurt, when after all, it was true what he said. He didn't imagine it or make it up, she'd told him. One night, at home with a curry and a bottle of wine, she'd started talking about her social life and all the parties she had been to since she came to London and how things were at a party when you were half-cut. She had thought it was funny and hadn't noticed his face. In his head he'd been counting them up, all those blow jobs, all those cocks in her mouth. Would she give him one if he asked her? Would she say, 'Oh, sure, get it out,' and be on her knees, her mouth smelling of chicken biriyani and then swallowing or going to the kitchen sink and spitting out his cum? Or would she have laughed, or taken offence? But he would never know because the thing was, however accomplished she was with her tongue he would have to think very hard about something else, knowing she of all people was down there sucking him.

This information had been filed, the number of blow jobs she had given at parties, and actually he knew it was seven, not eight, so the question was a bit more hurtful as if she had lost count. But had he asked it to get rid of her, to cause her enough pain that she'd leave the flat? He couldn't remember. That life was a long time ago and the start of it all was forgotten now. Things had gone wrong, you couldn't remember the beginning, you certainly couldn't see the finish either. In the street they had cried wop or was it wog? And he'd dropped his phone and the fire had begun, the torture in the bottle.

It was not so much to put right old wrongs as to please his father's wish for him to be a good host to a guest who had come a long way to see him that he answered, 'I shouldn't have said that, I apologise.'

'Never mind, it all worked out for the best in the end.'

'Did it?'

'Oh, Jesus, no, it didn't. I just meant you and me were never simpatico, were we? You found a better flatmate, did you not?'

'Yes.'

'And we lost sight of each other for a while.'

'That happens.'

He thought how you could share a flat with someone and never see them again. Sharing a space as intimate as a bathroom and you could pass them on the street in twenty years and not recognise them, a stranger sitting opposite you on the tube looking at his phone to whom you used to say goodnight, sleep tight.

'But you've got that boyfriend, haven't you?'

'Yousef? No, he was deported.'

'I'm sorry to hear that.'

'That's what's happening to all of them. And look what happened to you, born here. What was it they called you?'

'I'm not sure.'

'Racially motivated, it said on the news.'

'Yes.'

'Did they ever catch them, the ones who did it?'

'No.'

'Awful. The police don't give a spit, do they? When do you ever see one when you need one?'

She was no different from when he had last been with her on the train, sun-reddened from the park, sitting now on his Mies van der Rohe chair, the gold cross at her throat, with too much claggy black mascara and concealer she'd not blended in properly.

His father messaged him from the lounge downstairs. Was it all going okay? Did they need to stage an intervention or was the visit drawing naturally now to a close? They had no need of a tea tray. Marco had a kettle and a small fridge in his office where William's Lego sets had once been stacked.

Chrissie, thinking she'd never see him again, said, recklessly, 'So what do you do about the other?'

'Why? Are you offering me one of your famous blow jobs?'

She thought, *I should, it would only be polite really, now wouldn't it?* But she said, 'I don't think you'd want my dirty mouth on your nice clean thingy.'

'Oh, Chrissie, you're—'

'What am I now?'

'Unchanging. Everyone changes, you're just the same. Thank you for what you did for me in the hospital.'

'It's just my job, everyone does their job, unless they're lazy.'

'It suits you, that work. Did you always want to nurse?'

'My auntie says it's a calling, she says God picks you.'

'Did God pick you?'

'Maybe, when he came back from having a break and had lost his place on the list.'

'Don't be so self-deprecating.'

'What does that mean?'

'Hard on yourself.'

'Me? I've got the best self-esteem in the world.'

He tried a stiff smile.

'Where are you living now?'

'You'll never believe it, with an old gay guy, a university professor but he's on sick leave at the mo.'

'That's an interesting ménage.'

'A what now?'

'Never mind. How do you get on?'

'Famously. He's badly in need of a laugh. We watch the telly together, he doesn't want anything too challenging, he says; it's all old reruns of *Friends*. Did you ever see that the first time? I never did.'

'You get around, Chrissie, you seem to get around more than anyone. Listen, don't come again. It was nice of Mum and Dad to ask you, they meant well, but get on with your life, make a life for yourself. Please, you're wasted on me.'

'Don't be silly, what are you saying now?'

'Look after yourself, Chrissie. I mean it. No hard feelings.'

She raised herself from the chair and picked up her bag. 'You're all good on that. You're golden. Don't forget the chocolates, I hope you like them.'

He ushered her out and closed the door, went back into his own wack-world. For he was, she had said, golden.

On the landing she hung around to look at a framed picture of a foreign harbour. Frank came up the stairs, his son must have signalled him.

'That's Beirut, that is, where the war used to be.'

'Oh, wars are a terrible thing.'

'My father came over from the Lebanon in the fifties, it's where Neil gets his colouring from.'

'I used to think he was Italian.'

'Yes, that's the impression he liked to give.'

'He'll surprise you yet, you know; he'll come out of this all guns blazing.'

'Oh, we're well aware of that.'

Frank ran her back to the station. She felt she was never going to be able to forget about Marco, he had receded in her mind for months, then again he would rise back up. How far would she have to go to never hear of him again with his shite club nights? Her pink bag was coming apart at the seams; she should get a new one, something smarter she had seen in a magazine, but this bag had stood by her for years, and gave her comfort and courage even though she'd lost not one but three fucking phones that in their time had fallen out. But yes, she'd buy a new bag, she'd nip into Primark and see what they had, she fancied red this time, the colour of traffic lights and the old phone boxes you never saw any more, though they were green back home and England to her had always been those boxes you see on old films.

The train felt itself along the thread of the rails back to London. The sun was low and ruddy. The city had risen, shifted, shrugged, become displaced in some way she didn't understand. Was it time to move on? Not just yet, there was a little length left on the spool.

35

With the thaw, Alan spent even more time sitting alone at the end of the garden, his ear cocked for the thrumming on the rails of the occasional deportation trains diverted along their branch line, the filthy engines spattered with mud coming down from the north-east. The carriage windows were blacked out, desperate fingers scratched away at the paint. Terrible things were done. He subscribed to a WhatsApp alert cataloguing incidents of random raids, possessions uncoupled from their owners, children separated accidentally from their parents and assigned to complete strangers in a clumsy tidying-up of the mess they had made. Rows of human monitors along the tracks held up placards of protest and solidarity. Most days he joined them on the bridge.

Inside the trains the deportees raised their palms, pleading at the glass. The deportation infrastructure formed a network of cross-hatching across the eternal landscape of England, its woods and remaining patches of forests, its indigenous trees and its invaders, oaks, rills, brooks, ditches, barrows, mountains, faint vestiges of enclosed commons. Across all this solid lines of track were moving towards temporary detention centres and on to airports and sea ferries.

Several months ago prison ships had appeared in the Thames estuary confining illegal immigrants before they were floated back to mainland Europe. A few times a month a poor wretch would fling himself off and try to swim to shore. One or two disappeared along the strand at low tide, others drowned or were recaptured by the river police. A newspaper proposed that if they were that desperate, one might as well throw them overboard on a receding tide to make their way back to their countries of origin. When it started snowing the marooned illegals froze and starved, no increase of rations had been arranged for them. The Filipino crew disappeared into the white wastes.

But Alan had no idea how to engage with this single, large, remorseless fiasco. His dad, of course, was in his element, bellowing into the microphone every weekday morning – 'Floating concentration camps, let's give them their right name.' And, 'The heinous expulsion of good people, golden men and women who had come to this land only to make a living and better lives for themselves.' It was what the people wanted, someone taking their side, making it all clear. Moral clarity was what everyone was after, and why not?

The lives Alan and Francesca had aspired to were getting away from them. Those planned futures seemed to be just beyond reach, chased, not caught up with. They had the house but house prices were falling, soon they would be in negative equity. Discreet sums were deposited in their joint bank account by Francesca's parents, whose dental practices continued to thrive, for everyone still needed their teeth, as they did not need a Persian carpet or a sensitive, thoughtful documentary. Alan came off the phone to his father his face so concave and pressed in, distorted from its usual watchful self, that Francesca asked him, 'What's he said now?' She would ring the old man one day, she would give it to him with both barrels. She would tell him he was a bully. And one day she did make that call, and George

McBride listened in silence. 'Okay, he said, 'I get you.' He tried to write a letter of apology to his son but could not bear to send it. One morning Alan received a text from him. All it said was, *You're a good man.* 'What does this mean?' Alan asked his wife. And was it too little, too late? Perhaps.

He would go to his office in Victoria and make calls and send emails to commissioning editors and have occasional meetings about an idea he had for a film about urban legends. Their origins and the fruitless search for the final friend of a friend who lay like the pot of gold at the end of a rainbow, for he too had heard the story of the Pakistani gentleman who had issued a warning to stay away from a certain place as thanks for returning his wallet. Skyping from Hungary Johanna advised him to try Netflix or Amazon, she would help him with the budgets. Her Airbnb business was going very well both in Budapest and in London. He pitched, but what TV wanted these days was a long, gripping story in parts, a Dickensian novel with strong characters, hopefully rooted in a cold-case crime of some kind. He gave up the office in Victoria and took a shop front on the high street.

Francesca's shop had re-opened, she was trying her best. She had demoted her ideas about what to stock, included more children's toys and children's books. Middle-class parents could always be persuaded to at least come in and look at something in the window clearly screaming 'educational'. She was promoting the shop on the neighbourhood Facebook group and on Mumsnet.

One afternoon Alan tried to visit the weird enclosed streets she had told him about, as implausible as the story had sounded. He had found the tunnel, the bridge, the door, had knocked, no answer had come, no footsteps in the yard, no sign of children. He might go round the other way, via the marshes, but the map made no real sense. Did the place even exist? He wasn't sure. Then he forgot about it, as if the whole conversation between them that frozen afternoon when she had come back and sat next to him on the sofa and taken his hand and he had not been able to respond, not even to her touch, not even that, had been something he had dreamed and half forgotten on waking.

The country was being emptied of its unwanted population. Paperwork must be in scrupulous order to avoid being picked up and forcibly removed. Francesca, waiting for a bus by the park, had been briefly rounded up into a holding pen by the boating lake, the children's playground cleared, the detainees lined up by the swings and differently sized slides for babies, toddlers and older dare-devil exuberant children and the tumbling seesaw.

The whole of her family was now on its mettle. Their instinct for self-preservation had risen up like iron filings. They were alert and starting to make plans.

As a result of this encounter her father told his parents not to leave their building, except for the few steps from the front door to his Audi. He did not want them loose on the streets, pleading in painful English, without a phone in their pockets. Groceries were delivered now by van. Walks were restricted to the rear garden. Amira missed her visits to the hairdresser, her son said it was safer to try to manage herself. He did not realise how major a loss this was, how the sensation of strong young fingers shampooing her hair in the sink soothed her, and the tint applied to her roots reflected back from the mirror a face that at a certain angle was not that of a woman over the age of eighty. When her son came to pick them up in the car she would say, 'No, go without me. I can't leave the house looking like this. I'm ashamed.'

Younis would try to comfort and flatter her. She would shake her head and stamp her foot like an old and semi-broken doll.

It took only two months of house arrest for her to die. She was sitting on the edge of the high bed putting on her tights (in their old flat she had had a chair upholstered in oyster satin).

257

Sometimes she struggled and Younis would help her, nestling her feet inside the filmy mesh and easing them over her ankles until they reached her knees and she would say, 'No, I am fine, I can do it.' But she had not struggled and he had not heard her totter, then fall backwards on the counterpane. He was in the bathroom brushing and flossing his teeth. He came back into the bedroom to find her apparently dozing. *Perhaps she is having a short rest before she attends to her brassiere*, he thought, and tactfully left the room. He made coffee and called her from the kitchen. When he knew she was dead he felt something rise in his throat and in a histrionic gesture reached for the breadknife to plunge it into his own heart. But then, he thought, they might at first deduce that she had murdered him and dropped down dead herself in shock. He put the knife back in the drawer and went in to look at her again. The bedroom was small, but her shrunken frame fit the scale of their reduced surroundings.

'And you were born in a villa,' he whispered, 'a *villa* with rose gardens, for the rose is a Persian flower, there is nothing English about it.'

He had heard that the face relaxes after death and returns to its younger self. He looked for the girl Amira and could not find her. He smoothed her forehead with his finger and straightened her hair. She continued to look like the corpse of his eighty-two-year-old wife. This made no sense, he thought. *What are you doing, exactly?* And he went into the hall and called out to the warden to come, come straight away.

Mrs Hubbard explained the process of dealing with what she called 'a passing'. First she would ring the doctor who would come and sign the death certificate. The undertakers would discreetly bring the body out by the rear entrance, through the garden and along the side gate. He or his family must go to the council to register the event. She understood that he would want all this to happen quickly, that there was not to be an open coffin or dates for funerals set two weeks in advance. Younis wished he had discussed these matters with his wife, talked to her about where they had wanted to rest together. They had avoided the subject because neither wanted to lie for eternity in London's clammy clay where they would rot. In dry climates the body withered and fell away to dust. Yes, they would have preferred a desert burial, but he had to face it, it would be Golders Green, a neighbourhood which meant nothing to him, full of men in flapping coats whose heads were burdened with ridiculous fur-trimmed hats like an animal had dropped from the sky and landed on them ('the beavers,' he called them) and whose women wore preposterous unflattering wigs.

Inside Francesca a few cells were clumping together, they had reached the size of an apple pip. She was not yet sure if she was pregnant, her periods were reliably erratic. In a day or so she would become suspicious. She would leave the neighbourhood to find a chemist. She would wrap the pregnancy test in a cocoon of toilet paper and take it outside to the bin. She would think how fat she was going to get, how she would grow blowsy and bloated and tired.

It wasn't the right time to bring a kid into the world, it was almost hysterically wrong. She thought that Alan's face might grow blank with fear, that his mouth would say the right words while inside he was in shock. In such moments, he became unreachable, he seemed unplugged from life at the mains, his blue eyes drained, even his fingers grew cold, it was neurologically fascinating, she thought, but alienating, as if he was a robot not a husband. Of course, he would eventually revive, ask, with a detached formality as if he were her GP, how she came to be pregnant when such an event had neither been planned nor even discussed. She would have to tell him that she was pregnant because she had forgotten to pick up a new supply of the Pill. She had missed four days. She had not mentioned this oversight to him because of an optimistic certainty that it would be fine. And why should it be fine, he was bound to say, calmly (without the stress on the *why* that she would have placed on it, on the edge of raising her voice to a shriek). Then she would have to reply well, how it was is, look, you see, I – and then confess that she assumed it would be fine because, as he knew, all their friends had to *try* to conceive, they had to monitor the days of their fertility, plan their sexual intercourse and when they failed, as they usually did, succumb to humiliating, expensive treatment. They would learn the husbands' sperm was insufficiently motile. She didn't know what this meant, and no, she had no suspicions of any defects in *his* sperm, of course not, but getting pregnant in your thirties seemed to require so much diligent effort and endurance that the likelihood of it happening accidentally when you weren't even trying was absurd. Who *would* worry about that? They weren't teenagers.

What would he say then? He might, she thought, point out that while he was worrying about finding anyone to commission his films and her shop was hardly taking any money, was it not beyond her to shoulder the worry of avoiding getting pregnant? And yet it was impossible to have a row with him, you might as well be shadow-boxing, for he just sat there, his mouth a tight letterbox, snapping open and shut to release short, well-crafted arguments. Her father told her once about a woman who had come in to the surgery with her dentures spilt in two. How did this happen? She had been so incensed by her husband's implac- able reasonableness over the breakfast table that she had seen red, taken the dental plate from her mouth and thrown it in his face, from where it ricocheted on to the marmalade pot, cracked and sailed in halves into his cup of coffee.

Francesca was annoyed that her own parentally cared-for teeth were so flawless that she had not a single filling. She had no replacement parts she could throw at her husband. So she wondered with whom she could share the news of her pregnancy, which seemed at the moment purely tentative, though confirmed. For as long as she sat there, the clump of cells kept multiplying and in a matter of days would begin to resemble a curled humanoid form.

Across London the widower Younis had no one left apart from his son to whom he could speak his native language with fluency and intimacy. The days passed, he watched television. He had no idea what anyone was talking about, or what they wanted, or why they were so angry or so acquisitive. One day he went out with his stick, dressed in a jacket and tie and polished shoes, to sit in the lobby waiting not for his son, but for company, for someone to pass by and notice him, take an adjacent seat and begin a conversation. Bars of sunlight fell across his face, lighting up the hairs inside his nose. On a console table a vase of artificial flowers gathered a light film of dust. Younis wished he had brought a book, so he could appear more nonchalantly at ease, less needy for companionship, but the sight of its alphabet alarmed the others. Was it Arabic? And if it was, what incendiary messages might those squiggles convey?

Eventually a woman emerged from the lift on her way out and nodded to him. She was dressed in a smart camel coat and a beret secured with pins to the back of her hair. He had seen her before, a tall horse-faced, raw-boned old bird, Miss Jenner, who had at first seemed too well to be housed here, but, rumour spread, was 'eaten up with cancer' and the flush on her face which appeared at first to be a symptom of good health – for she said that she felt 'well, terribly well' – was a deceptive veil over the advance in her condition. She wished him a brisk, school-marmish good morning (she was a retired deputy head teacher) while passing across the hall. Maybe she was going to an appointment, might she sit and linger with him when she came back? But how much stamina did he have to maintain his upright posture in the armless vinyl chair waiting for company?

He spent an hour in the lobby, he timed it by his watch. The lobby was a featureless inoffensive territory the residents simply passed through. The longest time anyone spent there was waiting for the lift. Forty minutes in it started to remind him of the anteroom of death. Yes, this was how he imagined life in a hospice when you were morphined into a painless haze: fawn-coloured walls decorated with watercolour prints of subjects his eyesight wasn't good enough to make out, stain-resistant oatmeal carpets, beige easily-wiped chairs in case of sudden accidents of the bladder or bowels. Then black-out, into the soundless total dark where his wife now was. Death must be nothing to write home about, as no one ever had.

No one sat down, no one exchanged more than a short greeting. It was a hopeless exercise. He gave up.

Returning to the flat he made coffee. The long day had many hours to run before it reached its close at nine o'clock when he could decently take off his clothes, change into his pyjamas and climb into the wide territory of the bed. There was nothing for it but to watch television again. He removed his jacket, loosened his tie and sat on the sofa, holding for comfort as a child clutches a favourite toy a rabbit-coloured cashmere blanket his grand-daughter had given them a couple of years ago. On the screen foolish people expressed foolish thoughts and others dangerous ones. He was not sure which category worried him more. The fools would believe any nonsense, their brains had been softened and made malleable for irrational ideas.

With a pang of loneliness he at first confused with an attack of angina, panicking he rang his granddaughter. She was not very busy in her shop and usually available to chat, however limited their conversation. With volleys of love, Francesca greeted him and within a few minutes she had blurted out a secret. No one else knew, not her mother and father, not her husband. What should she do? He did not understand the question. A woman was pregnant, a baby came some time later. There was nothing *to* do but wait it out and buy the necessary items for the child's wellbeing, the cot, the pram, all the other paraphernalia. The woman was sick, the woman was in pain, then comes the baby, these were the necessary conditions for existence.

Once again Younis missed his wife; what did he know about babies or pregnancy that he of all people should be having this conversation? Had she been alive he would have passed over the phone and said, 'Talk to her, this is women's work.'

In his ear, Francesca's voice spoke rapidly and in a circular manner of her fears and anxieties. Would they have enough money? How could she go on running the shop? Was this a time to bring a child into the world? Supposing –

Younis replied in the only way he knew how, to remind her that they had come to London as tourists, were staying in a very nice Kensington hotel, that they arrived with only suitcases and though the revolution had not taken them completely unawares, they really had thought that they would have enough time to go back and put their affairs in order before the exile. That when they moved out of the hotel, and the theatre and restaurant visits had come to an abrupt end, then they were in a *room*, just a room, did she understand? This was all before she was born. It was what was known as a bed-sitting room. No kitchen, and they must even share a bathroom with strangers. This was what it meant to be thrown off the edge of the world. They slept on a mattress on the floor. But at home in Iran there was a cousin who was arrested by the Revolutionary Guards, taken somewhere, presumed shot, maybe tortured first. In those days people disappeared, no grave. So with his fate in mind they had soon got up from their knees and found their feet again in a foreign country. Drove taxis, started businesses. If it came to it they could do the same again, and even again.

And had she forgotten that she had resources, liquid assets?

'What do you mean?'

'Have you taken your jewellery to be valued?'

'Not recently, not since before I got married.'

'Find out.'

'Of course, I should have thought of that. But don't tell anyone, please. You're the only one who knows. Don't breathe a word, it might all come to nothing.'

Younis hoped he would be able to remember that he was sworn to secrecy. In the mornings it took a couple of hours for the fug of sleep to pass. If his son rang too early he could blurt it out, feeling around for something to say and the memory piercing the coddled density of forgetfulness.

Francesca terminated the call with a tap of her finger. Talking about the situation had given it the outlines of a solid and permanent reality she didn't yet believe in. She was still surprised that she had conceived so easily, so conversely in a few days she might as easily have a silent miscarriage. If she told Alan now there would be spreadsheets with the family finances drawn up for her to study, all for nothing, for an abrupt ending. Speck-like life, just a few clumped cells, gave up all the time, often because it was never going to be viable, damaged and doomed. Plenty of time to have an abortion, Alan would never know. Still, her grandfather was quite right about getting the jewellery valued, she should have thought of that herself. The opal necklace, the platinum and emerald ring, the pearl choker with its diamond clasp, the gold necklaces from Jerusalem, the bracelet from Antwerp – on and on she counted, the whole brilliant store laid out in front of her on the dining table, resting on a clean tea towel.

In ignorance of all this, the baby was getting on with it, increasing in size with obstinate determination. Soon it would have the same measurements as a blueberry.

36

They had decided (or Rob had, and Chrissie had sent a thumbs-up emoji into his phone which he received first with a wince, then a giggle) on navy and dove-grey tiles and a replica cast-iron freestanding bath resting on claw feet. The outside of the bath would also be painted navy. It would look, he thought, very smart, in contrast with the clinical, featureless American bathrooms of his recent past and the bathroom at home in Horsham with its flapping plastic shower curtain, rubber hose extending from the taps to wash one's hair and the mauve towelling apron in front of the toilet to protect the carpet from accidental splashes. Here his father had strained against his bowels for twenty minutes in the mornings, his mother had tried with patchy success to home-tint her hair, and his sister painted her toenails silver. In the bathroom, the door locked, he had set out on his epic wanks accompanied by his pop magazines, staring with semi-closed eyes at his dream man, Jimmy Somerville.

He said to Chrissie, 'I think actually it's going to look really nice. And I'm glad you moved in, I'd have endured that dingy porcelain without ever really noticing and the modern toilets of course are better for the environment. Something to do with the flush or the cistern; anyway, they use less water and I like those little buttons you push.'

'Yes, it'll be grand and those tiles you chose, that effect on the blue ones, what is that called now?'

'It's crackle glaze. I'm guessing it's rather out of fashion because I got such a smile from the man in the shop, not that kind of smile, more of a sneer, but he was happy enough to price up an order.'

'I love it, it's very glam, like a movie star's boudoir.'

'Are you saying I'm camp? It would be the first time if you are. I'm supposed to be a bear, you know. We in the bear community pride ourselves on our beards.'

He could not decide if she was a bit simple or more knowing than she made out. She played little tricks on him, rudimentary practical jokes. Once she had made an apple-pie bed, he'd not heard of such a thing since those two terms at the boarding house of his school when he had told his parents that he *wanted* to board like all his friends, then had to backtrack after the incident with Stewart Henry. Returned home to the serenity of the family bathroom and like a good little boy assiduously doing his homework in the lounge while his parents watched TV in the morning room. I have been good all my life, he told Chrissie, apart from depriving my mother of a wedding and a daughter-in-law. Last week she had rung him up and asked him the date of the wedding. 'What do you mean?' he had asked her. 'Who is getting married?' After a few minutes she withdrew, agreed with him that she was muddled, was thinking of someone else, oh yes, it must be Auntie Phyllis's daughter. But his cousin Alison, who ran a Weight Watchers group in Hove, had been married for thirty-four years to Ryan. Perhaps, he suggested, it was her daughter Abigail who was indeed getting married to Lyndsey, but his mother said, 'Don't be ridiculous. How could that be? Lindsey is her flatmate, very nice girl, pretty too, must have a string of boyfriends, not like poor Abigail who's never been out with anyone as far as Phyllis knows.' 'You mean Alison. Phyllis died years ago.' 'Who did I say?' The next week she said she'd been shopping for a hat 'and found such a nice one in the Sue Ryder, a straw boater with a black ribbon. Fits like a dream.' 'Well, that doesn't sound very *weddingy*,' he had replied. 'Who said anything about a wedding?'

When he told Chrissie these stories, she laughed. The more she laughed, the easier he found it to see the funny side himself, and the burden of his mother was relieved. Justin had made such a meal of it, insisting on hospital referrals, cat scans, social workers. He did not understand that the sole load of managing all of this would fall on him and him alone; his sister with her troublesome weed-addicted son and her daughter with her Downs baby had enough on her plate. He wanted to wait a little longer until the inevitable arrived: a phone call from a neighbour. She was lost. A missing persons alert would have to be put out. Old people with dementia were always straying off. Sometimes they were never found.

One had to make one's mind up about Chrissie, he told his friends, either she got on your fucking nerves or you saw the essential goodness in her, for she really did have that kind heart one heard so much about and rarely actually encountered in anyone who did not drag after it some mission or cause like an air-borne kite signifying one's principles. Life for her was all tra-la-la or blood and amputations and cancer. Tra-la-la? Yes, happy as the day is long. Shallow? She is, he said, you should see her awful celebrity magazines, reality TV stars, people I've honestly never heard of. *Love Island?* Me neither. But not when it comes to avoiding unpleasantness, pain or death. It was odd, but then, he thought, why not just take her as she came? And she had come with a couple of suitcases full of cheap clothes and her washbag with shampoos and make-up, her mascara wand sticky with clumping fibres and her eyebrow pencil and her glitter blusher and her three lipsticks.

This bathroom renovation was easing him back to – what? Life? More a case of being able to leave the house. There was no avoiding going out to visit bathroom fitting supply companies, tile shops, pick up the expensive paint he had chosen. He asked if they could recommend a bathroom fitter. He was handed a card with the name Alexandru Radu. Looking him up online he found his website and its impressive list of recent testimonials. He had done some rather grand work in central London and might not wish to take on an ex-council flat. Rob sent him a text. Received a reply. *Would come Tuesday morning if this good. Alex.* This good.

Alex walked in, commanding the whole of the recently installed engineered oak floor in the hall with his tan Timberland boots, sucked his breath through his teeth. Laughed. 'This is what the English workman does, no? It means I haven't got the parts, or it'll cost more than I estimated. Really it means he is playing for time, does not know. Does not know how to do the work.'

Men of Alex's physical type always provoked in Rob a mental exploration of where they had decided to place their tattoos, and what the tattoo depicted. There would be a tattoo. He would bet on it. Years ago, working-class men all had a gold earring. Now it was ink. His own was on his bicep, even he thought that was unimaginative but he had cried from the pain and not gone any further.

Alex was also a bear, if Rob thought about it, he was so beary he was ursus major. Lit by sunshine his blond beard would look like the gates of heaven.

By the window Alex looked down on the passing river. 'This is an incredible place. All day you can watch it, the boats, the barges. I wish I had a flat like this. You wake up, you make your coffee, you just sit and look at the whole scene. I would not be able to go to work, every day would be lazy, listen to music, make some lunch, beer later. Beautiful. I will never afford. How much you pay for it?'

Rob, flustered, was suddenly unable to remember anything about the transaction. 'It was – look, come and I'll show you the bathroom.'

'Okay, I am coming.'

In the bathroom, getting up from a supine position on the floor shining a torch at the plumbing and muttering to himself in his language, Alex said, 'Good. I don't like an easy job, it's boring. This is not so easy. If we put in this bath you like, we move the sink here. That's fine, plenty of space, but then pipes are going the wrong way, you get a slow-draining sink. Blockages. If I take this job I have to redo the pipes. Will you pay for this? I will give you estimate, with, without pipes, but if you want without, you go to someone else and show them. We say goodbye. You ask for a better price from them, you fix your sink yourself.'

With the other estimates Rob had received, the tradesmen had not bothered to get down on the floor and look under the vanity unit. And would one have wanted the view they offered? Alex's jeans pulled down slightly. The blond hairs on his back gathered in a golden fuzz. The others had speeded in and speeded out and given him a price which he suspected might rise as the job went on. One guy who had come highly recommended, Derek Alcott, said he could do it, but not for another three months, he was going to his villa in Spain for a rest. Rob didn't like to imagine him with his shirt off and his beer belly suspended over his shorts.

Rob said, 'Well, okay, I accept that but I do want someone who can start right away. How busy are you?'

'I have ten guys, all from my country. On this job I put three guys. I have a degree in engineering from the University of Bucharest. I could build a bridge if someone asked me. These guys they just want to work and be given orders. They will work all day, it will be fast, no breaks.'

'How do you retain them; surely they keep on being deported?'

'Yes, this is what they call the occupational hazard. Maybe I will have to think of something else soon, use English guys, but this job will be Romanians.'

They left the bathroom and went into the living room. Alex said, 'Very nice. I like what you have done. And many books.'

'I suppose you're wondering if I've read them all.'

'No. I'm wondering why you don't arrange them by the colour.'

'Why would I want to do that? How on earth would you know how to find them?'

'It depends on your memory. I have a very good visual memory. In my head I took a picture of your bathroom. Later, when I do your estimate, I will pull it out and look.'

'How useful, in your line of work, I mean. I'm good at remembering conversations, my friends are always telling me I throw their words back in their faces.'

'You would be an excellent witness in court, then.'

'I suppose I would.'

'Then I am careful what I say, eh?' He winked.

At the bookshelves he examined the fiction. 'This one I read.'

'The Hollinghurst?'

'Yes, it was a famous book in Romania for a while.'

'Really?'

'We all read it. Poor guy. Parts of it I didn't understand. The railings, what did that mean? The family, bad people, but was he really so good?'

'And do you read a lot?'

'Some, just this type of book.'

It was boarding school and Stewart Henry all over again,

teetering on the cusp of uncertainty and hope and terrified of getting it completely back to front, and exposure.

'Well, if there's anything you'd like to *borrow*.'

'Let's see if you like my estimate and I work for you. Then maybe I take a book.'

'I'll get back to you straight away.'

'You can pay by bank transfer. No cash. I pay tax. One woman in Muswell Hill, she wants me to work in exchange for psycho-therapy sessions. I say thank you, I do not need.'

At the door Rob held out his hand. His father had been an inveterate hand-shaker and taught his son always to offer his mitt, a habit he had acquired in childhood and quickly got out of. It was absurdly old-fashioned. But now he wanted to feel Alex's hand. He needed to flatten his palm against another man's for a moment, it was always a thrill. Alex took his hand, gripped it. Rob experienced the dry skin as if he'd received an electric shock.

'See you again, I hope,' Alex said.

In the corridor the lift opened and took Alex away, to his van, his tools, his ten Romanians, and more where they came from. Rob thought of having Alex in his flat every day, kneeling on the bathroom floor, his jeans riding down his back, talking about lines of beauty. He could not wait to accept the estimate.

37

But the other Romanians were always there. They looked nothing like Alex, they were squat, dark, unfanciable and spoke almost no English. Alex came in each morning, delivering his crew like supplies of meat, giving them their orders to which they listened carefully. He pointed at pipes, drew diagrams on scraps of paper. 'They understand,' he said to Rob. 'They know exactly what to do.'

While the work was going on, and it was scheduled to take six days, Rob had to go out. The noise and the dust were intolerable, no peace, and as promised they seemed never to take a break, let alone eat. He had no real understanding of their situation, if they were illegal immigrants or if in fact they might be some type of modern slaves. He didn't like to ask. They disturbed him in several ways, their dirty clothes, their smell, their black inexpressive eyes. He went to the British Library and read all day. He prepared the classes he would teach on his return to work, he drew up a reading list on literary terrorism.

He would try to come back before Alex returned to pick up his workers but sometimes he missed him altogether and the place was silent, the dust-sheets folded, the coffee mugs washed up in the sink. He thought Alex might be the cleverest fellow he'd ever met, getting work by assessing the contents of a bookcase and resorting to flattery or pretence.

When the bathroom was finished, when the navy crackle glaze tiles were glowing faintly in the light from the frosted-glass windows, Alex took away his Romanians in his van and said he would return the next morning for a closer inspection.

'Don't worry, if the job is no good I send them back Saturday. They like to work weekends. They have nowhere else to go.'

Alex arrived at eight o'clock. The bathroom met with his satisfaction.

'They're good boys, they do what I tell them. I am happy. You happy?'

'Yes, I am. I'm very pleased. So is my flatmate.'

'Him I never met.'

'It's a she. She's around here somewhere, getting ready for work.'

'You have girlfriend?'

'No, not at all, very much not.'

'Okay,' Alex said. 'No girlfriend.'

Do it/don't do it, say it/don't say it. They say act like you have nothing to lose, but there was always plenty to lose, starting with one's self-respect. The flood of rejection, the clang of disappointment, how could one have been so *stupid* as to think— He knew men who didn't care. A particularly ugly barber once told him, 'If I ask a hundred times, ninety-nine will say no, but one will say yes. I win.' But you could be beaten up. It hadn't happened to him, not yet, but it could.

A fold in the day, a man with a map. A fold, a crease, an indentation, a page turning. The before, the after, the dead, the injured, the walking wounded.

It was odd, Rob thought, how you could say that you didn't know, how something could appear one way and it could also appear another, like those optical illusion drawings that might be an old woman or a vase. Somehow the brain did a switch and you saw clearly what had not been present a moment before. That internet thing, the dress, for example, was it blue or was it gold? It had taken him ages to see it as gold. The shades were so different he didn't believe it was possible to view it any other way.

Now he remembered he had seen Alex before, dancing in very tight jeans and spotlights glancing off his beard, a sun-god at the Vauxhall Tavern. But why had that image been suppressed? Why hadn't he recognised him? It was preposterous. His memory must have been affected by the attack. And now he might be on the brink of fucking ursus major if he could formulate the right words when Chrissie came out of her bedroom in her nurse's uniform and her comfortable white nurse's shoes.

'So this is the famous Alex.'

'Me? You are the famous person in this room. I see you on TV and on YouTube.'

'He tells me he has an almost photographic memory,' Rob said. 'It's amazing.'

'Crazy time, eh?' Alex said. 'Funny you should end up here and I meet you. Coincidence.'

'Why a coincidence?'

'Two people I know from that TV show.'

'Who was the other?'

'The woman in the river.'

As if Little Dorrit or Lady Dedlock had themselves walked into the room, made of flesh and blood not paper and printer's ink, Rob thought that he was hearing things, an auditory hallucination. The casual admission that she was known, had always been known, was philosophically too taxing to a mind on furlough since the fold. Or were there more folds he did not know about?

'What? But why on earth didn't you tell the police? She's still unidentified, as far as I know.'

'Nobody is going to go to the police about that lady. It would be crazy.'

'Was she in some sort of trouble?' Far from resembling a character from a Victorian novel, the woman now seemed more like a person from a true-crime Netflix boxset.

'Not big trouble, ordinary trouble, she is a type who you see for a while at parties, Romanian parties, then you don't see her, she falls in with a new crowd, you forget about her. New people come to the country, maybe she becomes friends with them, she keeps her life in what do you call it, cupboards?'

'Compartments.'

'But you knew she was dead when you saw her on TV. Why didn't you contact the police then?'

'I already told you, no one will talk to the police. People who know her are not stupid. It's not their business.'

'I don't understand.'

'Of course. You are nice Englishman, a professor. You buy nice little ex-council flat. I am guessing you started out your life in a house with garden and flowers and shit. You have nothing to fear except random things no one can avoid, just bad luck, no point worrying about it. Now me, I go to the police and say, "This woman, I can tell you her name and who she worked for. Why she does not want to live any more I cannot say, I haven't seen her for a while." They start asking questions and then I am involved and they start asking questions nothing to do with this woman because now it is me who is being investigated. So the people she worked for hear that their name is in police hands. Where did they get this information? Who touches their name with the *police* and then—'

'You know what,' said Chrissie. 'Just tell me what you know and I'll tell Alan. He can deal with it.'

'Who is Alan? What does he have to do with this?'

'The guy who made that TV show. He can pass it on to the police if you don't want to be involved.'

'Look what is happening here. I get a text. Give estimate for bathroom. I do bathroom. I like the guy, the guy likes me, nice Englishman. I see straight away we are going to do something together.'

'What?'

'Of course. You know this. Why do I tell you about that stupid book if I am not telling you something else? I never read it, I saw it on TV, not all of it, it was boring. Not enough sex. But I am getting established in this country, maybe soon I have English boyfriend, educated man. You think I will talk to the police now?'

'Oh, don't make such a drama out of it,' said Chrissie. 'Just tell me her name and let's be done with you. I'm due at work in a minute.'

'It's not as easy as that. You will see.'

'Fine.'

They were all fucking useless, they played their games, the lot of them, and these gay guys were no different. She didn't give a stuff about the woman who drowned herself. People were dying on every shift; who cares about one who doesn't even want to live? But no one deserves to go to God without a name, and when she remembers, maybe every couple of weeks or so, she does believe in God and even thinks that when she's got a Sunday off one day she could drop into church for Mass, and tell the priest about those 'seven or was it eight?'. The little gold man round her neck reminds her when she takes him off in the shower that she believes in the Father, the Son and Holy Ghost but she does not know how she would find the words because she'd go bright red with the shame of it, and so she could be going to Hell. For death can come any second; moment by moment death is waiting, she's seen that in the wards, don't think you have a whole life ahead of you or so many years till old age.

So in repentance for her sins and for the love of Jesus and her immortal soul, she will save this unknown woman from an anonymous eternity and maybe that will count in her favour when it comes to the final score without having to confess any blow jobs.

38

At home in Aylesbury the proteins in the cells of Marco's skin had undergone a permanent alteration. As an egg that is exposed to heat, its yolk solidifying, its transparent albumen becoming white and rubbery, can never revert to the liquid that sloshed around in a shell, so the proteins had lost their complex structure and could no longer function properly. Lying in hospital immediately after the attack while his face was being swabbed with cold water, Marco's body had done its very best to heal the injury quickly using its own resources: inflammation. Inflammation is a mechanism to bring in food for new cells to grow and the building blocks for essential molecules to form but its secondary contribution is to trigger scar tissue, excessive scar tissue. Light scars, he had been told in the burns unit, could be treated by specialist camouflage make-up, but the raised welts, the patchy discoloration, the puckering of his right eyelid, could not be concealed by a pot of beige foundation. The scars would cause him misery, persistent and relentless. They were, according to their mood, hot, tight, painful, itchy, raised or angry. Often they were all of these.

The nights were filled with cats and foxes and owls making

out in the garden. He lay in his teenage boy's single bed and heard them be their nocturnal selves, hunters and scavengers and hunted. They were almost on the edge of town, one of the last few houses before the suburb gave out to the countryside. They were in a grey zone, neither one thing nor another, a village had expanded into the landscape and keeping its boots on, kept going. When he arrived back from the burns unit for the first night in his old bedroom, his mother had said, 'You're home now, darling.' He knew what she meant, he was prepared to be generous, and try to kiss her and say, 'I know, Mum, it's good to be back,' as his imprisoned feet walked up the stairs. To be home was to be captured in a former life, but he had no other place, this was the thing that scared him. Agatha sent him occasional texts. She evidently thought this constituted keeping in touch. He replied, often goading her into a sense of her abandonment of him, but her responses did not acknowledge his sarcastic little barbs. Perhaps she was too thick to notice. The thought of being married to her seemed now both piercingly unobtainable and a lucky escape from a life of country pursuits and watching her get fat in dowdier and dowdier clothes. He had only been in love once, at university, but she had returned to Rome at the end of the course. He could hardly remember the sensation of rapture and despair and did not miss it.

Days were broken up with messaging his app developer and fiddling around with interfaces and Spotify playlists. The stay-at-home club nights, like a new-born foal, were shakily getting to their feet. He had a couple of packages ready to go, had run soft launches with mates. In a month or two he'd be ready for the roll-out with press and PR. He was assured that he had such goodwill behind him, he had a story, he *was* the story, but how that narrative was to be told without him as the pathetic victim was up to himself to devise. He had transitioned abruptly and not of his own desire. He did not self-identify as a mutilated man.

If he did not recast himself then his club nights were going to be seen as something to do for freaks and monsters too unsightly to leave the house.

The attack was just a symptom of these times they were living through, times which his father said felt like being on a plane during a long bout of severe turbulence with a bunch of half-trained amateurs in the cockpit and no guarantee that you were ever going to land. You sat there with your seat belt fastened, switching between films and old TV shows on the in-seat screen, and drank your glass of wine and ate your tasteless chicken and unidentifiable cream dessert while the cabin lunged and plummeted and righted itself for a moment and people in the row behind you were screaming and others were being sick and the seat belt sign seemed to have been on for ever so someone had peed their pants.

In these strange times, Marco thought, strange things were going to have to happen. There was no way round it. He had been thinking for a long time how he could conceal his face. The tricky part was that the functions of sight, speech, hearing and smell were all collected on that small oval at the top of your body. He thought at first of some kind of plastic mask that would resemble flesh, but it was trying too hard to be natural and you would never get away with it, it would look gross and fake. A young gentleman as he aspired to be was always easy, correct and understated in his appearance unless you were, say, out on the hunting field, when you could wear a pink coat and not worry about alarming the already excitable hounds. On the hunting field all was noise and commotion, horns, hooves, cries. If he covered his face it would need to make a statement, flamboyant and unnatural. Precious metal must be his medium.

After weeks of research, he contacted a goldsmith in Birmingham. He had in mind a delicate object with articulated lips. She studied his proposal and said she got what he wanted.

In the Middle Ages the crafting of protective clothing such as helmets, visors and metal gloves was an art form, she had studied it, stared at suits of armour in the V&A with their iron beaks and leather straps. What he wanted was very exciting and interesting, somewhere between armour and a pharaoh's tomb – she would love to take on the commission. She sent him preliminary sketches; it would require measurements and fittings and adjustments to mould it exactly to the contours of his face so it felt like a warm, rigid skin. She thought she might line it with thin removable muslin to prevent the discomfort of chafing. It would be held on with a light curved apparatus that would sit neatly round his ears. In mechanical as well as aesthetic terms it was a complex undertaking, she advised him. He agreed, it would be a difficult commission, but all the more rewarding in that it would be the only one of its kind. He did not imagine other victims of facial disfigurement would want one, nor did he regard it as a form of therapeutic aid; its purpose was to make people look, but look with gasps of what he hoped were admiration and even awe, recognising that he did not accept what had been done to his face, but it having happened, he would draw attention to the calamity, force people to be aware of what had been done to him (because he was a wop or a wog, he was still not certain which).

He noticed her very slight flinch when she came into the room accompanied by his mother with a pot of coffee and an uncut coffee-walnut cake on a tray. His mother entered first, her body interposed between him and Jenni, moving slowly to one side as if she was sympathetically aware of the sudden shock of seeing him all in one go. Jenni's flinch as his face, like the moon, waxed to full features from the left, which wasn't too bad, to the right, which was the worst, confirmed that he could not live with a series of revulsive twitches on the face of every stranger he met or passed on the street.

She measured the circumference and length of his head, the horizontal span of his mouth, the width of his nostrils, cupped in her palm his ears. The business of her calm, precise hands about his face reminded him of hospital. He kept his eyes fixed on his mother in the garden pegging out washing in her jeans and Breton top. Life went on with its usual merciless frenzy in the lawn and flower beds but there fell upon him a kind of transitory peace, as if he could stay in this chair for ever, looking out on to the bird feeder, the squirrels, his mother's arm rising and falling to pick up his shirts and hang them out on the line. Sometimes out of the corner of his eye he thought he saw the shadow of his brother falling across the border of the rockery. He would be twenty-seven now if he had lived.

'And we're all done,' Jenni said, shocking him back into this unfathomable present in which he had forgotten for a moment why she was here and what ambitious plans he had for his resurrected future.

On her final visit when the mask was completed he picked it up, felt its lightness, attached it to his ruined face, looked in the mirror.

'Oh yes', she said, 'oh, that is *marvellous*. Is it comfortable?'

The cheeks smooth, the eyebrows tooled and etched, the furrows between the mouth and nose lightly indented, his nose faithfully copied. He was magnificent and apart, slim, graceful, his dark hair curling round the beaten edges of the golden face. He tried to smile beneath the gold lips but this movement had not been part of the design. He had forgotten about smiling.

'This is fantastic,' he said, his words only a little muffled, perhaps if there was ever to be a Mark II he might take advice from a speech therapist on the exact construction of the mouth with a greater understanding of the operation of the tongue.

'Are you really happy with it?'

'I am. It's everything I wanted.'

'I'm so pleased. I've made you a velvet bag to keep it in. I'll show you.'

When she returned home she remembered the blaze of gold on his face in the sunshine from the garden, the long garden leading to another suburban long garden and downstairs his mother calling up the stairs, 'Are you ready for a refill yet?'

The gods in a domestic setting, Zeus in suburbia.

That evening, when his father came home, Marco nonchalantly entered the kitchen wearing the mask. 'My baby!' his mother cried, unable to help herself, ashamed, knowing she had said precisely the wrong thing without meaning to. *How will I kiss him now?* she thought, on the hand like the Queen?

Frank, for whom years of customer relations had helped him develop a neutral expression, thought it was just weird and must be uncomfortable and hot to have on for an extended period.

'Are you going to wear that all the time now?'

'No, Dad, I'm wearing it to show you. What do you think?'

'It's very special. So is it, like, for best?'

'I don't know. I'm going to do a trial run in town.'

'In Aylesbury? We've got one of those living statues now in the market square. People are up for anything.'

'Of course not, I'm not trying to *parade* myself. I'm going to London to gauge reaction. I'm pretty pleased with it, actually.'

'I can see why. She's done a marvellous job. Very artistic but functional at the same time. But – now hear me out for a minute – wouldn't you say that people who are your real friends will take you whatever you look like? You really shouldn't have to hide your face like this.'

'Oh Dad, you're sweet. That's not the way it works.'

'Not the way what works?'

'Well, could you run a supermarket with a face like this?'

'Why not?'

'Interfacing with the public?'

'I don't know, we've got a check-out girl who's, what do you call it, a midget?'

'A what?'

'There's probably a better word for it these days I'm just not up on. Everyone thinks the world of her; she has to stand on a box, mind you.'

'It's just not the same thing at all. Mum, what do you say?'

Avril struggled for words. She thought the blankness of the mask's expression was off-putting rather than inspiring awe, if that was the intention. She felt the urge to take him in her arms and breastfeed him again. She and Frank had known about the bullying at school, how he had carried on cleaning toilets, steadfast in his goal of those ridiculous expensive shoes from the magazine. He could take it, she knew that, but why should he have to? Couldn't the world just . . . But she didn't know what she expected the world to do. Be nicer? Be less squeamish? Perhaps he had the right idea to protect himself from the nastiness he was going to have to endure. One noticed birthmarks, a strawberry stain on the skin, a scar, even botched cosmetic surgery or an excess of Botox and filler, it was impossible not to look, to stare, for the mind to calibrate new information. Turning quickly away seemed rude.

'It's beautifully made, a lovely thing, she's done a very nice job. Did it cost a lot?'

'Of course it did. But it was worth it, I think; you get what you pay for.'

Bending to fill the dishwasher, his mother silently wept among the plates and glasses and cutlery. She asked herself what she had done to deserve such torments. Why had bad luck attacked the bodies of her sons and not her own? Her lost boys.

'Can I borrow your car, Dad, just for a couple of days?'

'You're driving to London, then?'

'That's the idea.'

Frank really needed the car for work but did not want to let him down. He said he'd take his wife's Honda run-around if that was okay for her and she could manage with the bus.

'So what are you going to do up there? Meet up with old friends?'

'Dad, don't ask questions.'

'No, crumbs,' said his mother, which was all she could think of that would tell him she was still his mother.

'Crumbs?'

'I don't know what I'm saying.'

'Get hold of yourself, Avril.'

'All will be revealed,' Marco said, returning upstairs to his room. 'Don't worry.'

'Neil is a survivor,' Frank said. 'We should admire him for what he's doing.'

'But who will love him if he carries on like this?' she cried.

'I don't know. He'll have to find a way through it. Let's hope this gold thing is just a phase.'

If you're going to do gold, he thought, *you might as well really do gold*. He had weighed his fingers down with gold rings, put on a midnight-blue mohair suit that seemed to him retro without advertising exactly to which era it was paying homage. Below the jacket sleeves his shirt was trimmed with gold lace cuffs, at his neck a gold bow tie. His mum had stitched the gold cuffs on for him, borrowing Mrs Hendricks's sewing machine. Arriving in London he moved from Soho to Dalston to Shoreditch, spending enough time in each bar to gingerly sip a drink and stand apart from the throng, while around him people asked each other how does he eat, how does he kiss? Does he kiss anyone? Who *is* he?

Gods are forged by fire, he thought. He had emerged from the anvil of suffering to immortal life.

He drove home the next morning. Road signs pointed to Aylesbury. Aylesbury was a stronghold of the Ancient Britons, then taken by the Saxons, then the Norman king seized the manor for himself. The town was decimated by the plague and became a Puritan stronghold in the Civil War. Louis XVIII's wife died in Aylesbury, the only French queen to be buried on English soil. Its crest is a duck, after the Aylesbury ducks that used to be a standard of the fifties English restaurant meal. The rearing of ducks has declined in Aylesbury itself and now there is only one flock left in the whole country. Marco's Lebanese grandfather, the chef, opened a restaurant in Aylesbury in 1969, moving from London with his English wife Sue and their English-born son Frank and two daughters. Though not Italian, he reproduced the dishes he had worked on in the kitchens of Soho. Everyone assumed he was from Naples or Sicily.

Marco knew this shit because when you grow up somewhere you're taught in school all the tedious local history whether you want it or not. It could have been anywhere, it happened to be Aylesbury which was his home town. *Gods don't come from Aylesbury*, he said to himself, *but they do now,* and parking the car in the drive, the front door was opened by his mother who cried out, 'Neil, come quick, you're all over the internet.'

Part Six

39

What has delayed Gaby's mother picking her up from school? Why is she not at the gates waiting for her daughter? Why must Gaby walk home with her violin case, crossing the road very carefully, waiting for the green man to appear before she steps out into the traffic? She is eleven years old and next year she will start at the big school wearing a burgundy-coloured uniform, white shirt, burgundy and grey tie, grey pleated skirt, lace-up shoes and a special round-brimmed hat she is excited about (though with a pre-pubescent sensitivity to her appearance, worries it will not suit her). It is a school for clever gifted children, particularly those good at music; she has taken a scholarship examination to be admitted and she will travel on the bus all by herself. She will have to change buses, the school is quite far away on the other side of what her father calls the orbital road. It is a big change in her life and one she is being prepared for by her father putting her on the bus at one stop and her mother waiting for her a mile away, as if they were flinging her between themselves like a ball. Over the summer the practice runs will intensify. It's all planned and has been explained to her, she is not frightened, she knows she will be okay. Actually, there is also a school bus but they prefer her to start taking steps towards her independence from day one.

None of her friends are going to this new school with her, she will have to make new ones. When she thinks of this she feels a little sick and worried, but as her father has pointed out, everyone likes her, she is a nice girl, a kind person as well as clever and talented and she has made friends every step of the way, from nursery onwards. She will not lose touch, they live in the streets all around her, she will see them at the weekends. Playdates will continue. They will not be lost to her.

Her parents do not know she has fallen out with her best friend Olivia over a German book she brought to school and lent to her to take home which is a story about a little girl who – but Olivia's mother has said, and Olivia has repeated when she brought the book back next morning, that it was barbaric and so typical of that dark Black Forest strain in the German heart. All these stories about gingerbread houses and witches and children being eaten, not to mention that boy whose thumb was cut off because he sucked it, it's all cruelty. 'But it's my favourite storybook!' cried Gaby. 'My grandmother gave it to me.' Olivia has said, 'You shouldn't bring it to school, you should keep it at home, nobody wants to see it.'

She has not told her parents about this rift, which took place yesterday, and so she has not walked home with Olivia and her mother, which was what Elfriede expected and hoped would happen when the tube train she was on broke down in the Piccadilly Line tunnel and its passengers have been trapped there for an hour and a half, something having gone wrong with the engine or the electrics, she can hardly hear the crackly announcements explaining what's happening. Claustrophobic, suffocating, eventually having to actually get off and walk down the tracks to Arsenal station where the emergency services are waiting with bottles of water and first-aid teams.

Gaby is one of the few children in her class who does not have a phone, not even the simple type with just a few buttons. Caspar and Elfriede have never seen any point to it, and to their surprise Gaby has never asked for one. She says she finds the noise of them ringing unmelodic. Yes, she is special, both precocious and naive. She has decoded the password to unlock her mother's iPad but only used it to watch videos of songs and stories; she does not know that Elfriede is tracking her search history (Gaby does not know about search histories, she is something of a digital illiterate) and her mother is happy with how she is using the internet. She does not want her to discover chatrooms where children goad each other to suicide.

It is so unusual for her mother not to be there that Gaby, sensibly, thinks that something has happened to her to cause her to be delayed. It is not the first time. Once, when her mother did not turn up, the teachers had phoned her. She had tripped over a loose paving stone on the way and her knee was bleeding and her wrist maybe sprained or even broken but she would be there in a few minutes. And there she was, limping into the playground.

But that was when she was little and other children her age now go home on their own from school though they do not have to cross the scary big dual carriageway which brings traffic off the orbital down into North London.

She sets off by herself without anyone noticing, lost in the crowd. She navigates the journey with all its treacherous obstacles, no one pays her any attention, no paedophiles or child abductors are out today patrolling the vicinity, she is safe and arrives home safe, but there is nobody there and she does not have a key.

But my dear Gaby, she says to herself, not at all worried, still not anxious, not knowing that her mother is in an Uber coming from Arsenal station delayed further by the start of the early rush hour. *Gaby,* she says, *you are a grown-up young lady now,* which is what she has heard her doting grandmother say on Skype when she described her new school uniform.

It is time to take a few risks, time to make her own way in the world, to leave the front door and to walk with her violin in its case (she does not think Mummy would be pleased with her if she left it in the porch, however well hidden) along the street to the railway-line alley and make her way across the bridge by the babies' and toddlers' nursery and enter the street of friendly shopkeepers where she feels safe. And now she is walking past Francesca's shop, Mummy's friend who had given them a funny thing to make lemon juice with which they never used because Mummy said, better to look at than try and squeeze anything with that useless object.

Francesca has a new plan. The shop is being remodelled as a children's bookshop with story-time, remedial reading sessions, puppet shows and what she calls, 'all that middle-class yummy-mummy crap that actually sells in a neighbourhood like this'. She's still into selling carpets but that's all now done on her online site and she is back to taking taxis to the remaining wealthy foreigners and rolling out her merchandise on their marble floors. Francesca, glancing up at that moment, sees Gaby on her own and thinks it only a little odd, for the child has a long leash these days and no doubt Elfriede is at this very moment buying something in the charity shop that has taken over from the long-gone Greek delicatessen.

At twenty-one weeks pregnant Francesca is round like a semi-inflated beach ball. All of her is round now. Alan loves this. He cannot keep his hands off her. Because, let's face it, Alan likes fat women. Fleshiness turns him on. He has no idea how hot this would have made him on Tinder, but he met Francesca before that innovation existed. He is both terrified and looking forward to being a dad, for whatever happens, he will do things very differently and not be on any account the overbearing father of his own childhood, but will be up for all the feeds and the nappy changes and with the advent of this kid, things are kind of back to normal at home.

In these motionless months of her pregnancy, each day strung at intervals like cloudy pearls, Francesca has been to Hatton Garden and had her jewellery valued. It comes to an eye-watering sum; she had no idea. She has sold a couple of pieces already and banked the proceeds in a separate account she has not yet told Alan about. It will buy the £1000 buggy she wants and other paraphernalia. She has her eye on a luxury highchair in rose gold she has seen on the John Lewis website, but would not be able to explain such a purchase to him. The sale has made a very small dent in the value of her easily-liquefied assets. She feels better about the pregnancy already.

The baby knows nothing of all this. It has its own secrets and devices. All will be revealed in a few months' time, whether it will look like its mother or its father, whether it will have any congenital conditions, prone to walk or talk early or late. Parental anxiety lies ahead of them, when they will be unable to stop themselves studying baby development apps which monitor the development of their little girl. Making notes in the diary for three weeks hence. SHOULD BE ROLLING OVER BY NOW. IS SHE SITTING UP THIS WEEK? IS SHE READY FOR SOLIDS?

Gaby is making for the aqueduct. She has never been allowed to walk here, her mother isn't interested. It is too dirty and difficult to make your way along the bank and you don't get very far before you have to turn back so what is the point, when in the other direction there are beautiful parks and playgrounds with swings and slides and climbing castles and a café where the young mothers have coffee and cake and watch over the nest of children all around them, crawling, hopping, running on the grass?

The aqueduct is a green-tinged sluggish waterway of some

historical interest, and not even forbidden ground for Gaby, just a place her parents had almost forgotten was there though they had seen the old Jewish lady and the man with the dogs entering from time to time and Francesca had told Elfriede a far-fetched story which involved an elephant. Caspar had said to his wife, 'Either she is very imaginative, or you have misheard her.'

'*Elefant*, the word is almost the same in English,' she said, 'of course I did not.'

The entrance to the aqueduct is protected by a kind of metal stile to prevent vehicles being driven down there. First you turn to the right, then you turn to the left, and you are through! You are on the bank.

Gaby is perfectly well aware that she should go no further than a few metres along the grass, she can see that there's no path, that the bank is steep, her mother's voice is in her head saying, *It is easy to slip, watch your step.* But her loyalty to her mother is a little undermined this afternoon by the feeling that she did not come, she has failed her. It is probably not her mother's fault, but anyway, she's not here. Not at home either. And she is such a big girl now, so close to the burgundy uniform with its crest and badge. Maybe this is a test, an examination she is being set to challenge her resourcefulness? That is always possible, knowing her parents.

'Where *are* you, Mummy?' she says aloud in English, having not forgotten that now they speak German only at home.

She turns and expects her mother to be following her, calling her name, but Elfriede's Uber is still crawling past the park, the safe park. She has rung the school, but they say, 'Oh, we think she must have gone home with her friend Olivia, they're inseparable.'

In defiance of her absent mother Gaby walks on a few more steps. The smell is not pleasant. She stops to look at the water, thinks maybe she should turn back but coming towards her along the bank are two children her own age, they are twins, she sees that, and they both have plaits. She does not recognise them, she does not think they go to her school, but she is a child renowned for being friendly and making friends, so smiling she carries on, thinking they can tell her all sorts of things about this little river which is not a river, before she turns back and Mummy will be home.

Francesca receives a call from Elfriede who has arrived at the house and is saying that Gaby is not here and she has rung her friend Olivia's mother who has not seen her and has Francesca seen her at all?

Francesca says she will go straight out and look for her. It was only a few minutes ago that she saw her walk past. She follows the direction of Gaby's movements along the street until she reaches the entrance to the aqueduct and thinks it must look like forbidden territory, and if she was an eleven-year-old that's where she would go if she was exploring.

It's a warm June afternoon, the waterway looks very different to that icy February day when she had last come here with Mrs Audrey Shapiro and Vic Elliott. She has never returned to the Island, the place gives her the heebie-jeebies. She does not think Gaby could have gone far, she is a naturally sensible, intelligent, cautious child without much spark of adventure or disobedience. Almost preternaturally mature, though hopelessly backward in other ways. The child might get as far as the iron structure on the bank, and stop and stare at it, trying to make her developing brain find a function for this bizarre sight, not knowing how impossible it was to guess.

Could she slip in the water? Unlikely. The grass is very dry, it has not rained for ten days. But really, she hopes that this incident will teach Elfriede and Caspar to give the kid a phone, it was one thing trying to keep her pure and apart from the dangers of technology, but now she was about to go to secondary school and travelling on her own, she really needs to be contactable, anything could happen.

Elfriede has left the house, she is following a few minutes behind Francesca and has had the same idea, because she knows how often Gaby has nagged to go for a walk along the aqueduct and how often she has been brushed off with the excuse that it is not very clean and the way is uneven and doesn't lead anywhere. She is also sure that Gaby will not have ventured too far because her mother has embedded her cautious practicality in her daughter's brain, she *is* her mother.

On the surface of the water, Gaby's violin case is floating. Francesca thinks she's dropped it, she must be trying to retrieve it. She runs now, a lumbering lope, quite like an elephant herself, and sees a child on the bank, but it's not Gaby, it's one of those weird twins who is standing there laughing and pointing while the other twin is lying on the edge holding Gaby's head down under the water.

'Paarfect paarfect paarfect,' the girl screams at her.

And Francesca, running, running with her twenty-one-week foetal development inside her, grabs the kid and using her fist with as much force as she can manage, the whole big fatness of her pregnant state behind her arm, punches the child in the face. She tries to pull Gaby out and behind her the air is full of the sound of Elfriede screaming like the heavens have been rent and the sky is full of lamentations.

40

One morning of blurry rose-pink skies in this, his second winter alone in London, Pete rented a boat at Putney Bridge. His aim was to take it out as far as the Thames Barrier and turning back, have a pint and a plate of whitebait at the Trafalgar in Greenwich. At home he had a shelf of books handed on from his dad who read nothing else but tales of the Thames, a one-note hobby his son had inherited. He had read that in olden times it had been possible to cross from one bank to another simply by stepping from deck of a ship to deck of a ship, which was obviously one of the myths of the city, an exaggeration, but he liked these hoary old yarns, he enjoyed them for what they were. The Thames was an old lady with an expensive facelift and new clothes, robed in cloth-of-gold and ermine in the form of luxury apartments and Michelin-starred restaurants.

When he was a kid he had aspired for a few months to the position of captain of the Woolwich Ferry. In his twenties he had found another more awe-inspiring ambition. The day the barrier opened in 1984, he and his brother had sailed to Charlton where they sighted from afar the still-slim figure of the Queen in an apple-green coat and matching hat with what looked like asparagus fronds waving about her head. From their bobbing boat on the water they saw the silvery armadillo-plated gates open and close, thwarting the flood tide. A lump of pride stuck in Pete's throat as the city was saved from rising waters that would threaten fifty square miles of London, drowning the Houses of Parliament and Buckingham Palace and the hospitals and the tube tunnels and all the houses and parks and schools and universities, the gentlemen's clubs and the pubs and shops. It kept up its magnificent industry (incapable of being privatised, really, Pete thought, for how could you monetise it?), opening and closing a few times a year under the guidance of a mathematical matrix which measured the river flow, the tide and the surge. But it was a human hand that pushed a button and held back the North Sea. Over thirty years later, the barrier and its grandeur and its purpose had faded from public recollection replaced by small rectangles of light held in the hand, strangely old-fashioned by virtue of its behemoth size, a maximist enterprise in times of miniaturisation.

The Thames was tidal as far up-river as Teddington Lock. After that it meandered through countryside and was of no interest to him. If DB27 had thrown herself off on a high-tide day when the barrier was closed, and had her body not met the chains of HMS *Belfast*, she might have been pushed down past Greenwich as far as Charlton and then held there, impeded by the gargantuan machinery before finally being released and taken out to Europe and total physical annihilation on the bed of the sea. Without a body, there would be no missing person, no police investigation, no funeral, no documentary. He could not believe she had evaporated from all human thought, that she did not exist in somebody's memories, she had to, how was anything else possible? There must be photographs in a frame on a mantelpiece, or at least caught in the background in someone else's snapshots.

298

As he passed under London Bridge he looked up at the balustrade she had thrown herself from. They were lucky to have found her so quickly. The lungs fill up and the body goes down and stays down until it starts to putrefy, then the stomach swells and it rises back up to the surface. The colder the water the slower the process and the longer it stays on the bottom; in the winter it could be three weeks or more, particularly if they get stuck under something, in which case the corpse slowly disintegrates and bits of them come up. In warm water in the summer the drowned will re-emerge fairly quickly, only two or three days max, a floating substance on the surface of the river.

This is what he had explained in repugnant detail to Alan when he was filmed in the empty lounge of the West End hotel. All of it had been cut. As was his explanation of the process of pulling people out. If you grabbed hold of a limb there was a good chance of it simply coming off in your hand so you tried to roll them into some kind of net and scoop them up, or a body bag if you had one, and try to bring them out in a complete state.

But this was too gory, and unnecessary, Alan said, for his theme. Pete felt differently. For her beauty, if that was what it was, had been preserved by the chains of the river, by not going down, by being found before she began to decompose. Mudswaddled as she had been, it was still possible when the body was washed, her hair dried, and she lay chilling in the morgue freezer, to see that once there had been a person, not a swarm of maggots and flies and only the rigid structure of the spine, skull, limbs, feet, fingers left.

These morbid thoughts did not bother him, he had seen too many corpses in his time, they were never pleasant, but he was inured to the physical manifestations of mortality. Leaves did it better, he thought, lying in golden drifts on pavements and gardens, crunching away to dry fragments before the street-sweepers came and cleared them away.

Puttering along the river, his boat upset for a few moments by the uproarious swell of a sight-seeing rib, he looked from side to side at the new London. The skies had cleared, white bars of cloud looked painted on to an ice-blue heaven. For several minutes he experienced what Marie said she felt: that the river, like the city, had been taken away from him, this down-at-heel waterway lined by derelict warehouses was in the hands of billionaire Russian Jews. They were not welcome to what was rightly his, as a Londoner whose great-granddad had come down from Lancashire and fought the fuzzy-wuzzies in the Boer War. But thoughts like these led to where they had led Marie, who somewhere in the Orkneys was sitting beside her VW camper van brewing a cup of tea on a primus stove and looking out at what he could only think of as *scenery*.

The postcard she had sent him was of a desolate wasteland whose supposed beauty he did not respond to. There was nothing human to get a visual purchase on. She had survived the second season in the café, she had made a real go of it. He knew this because most nights he had gone online and studied her TripAdvisor page where she was currently running at four stars, held back by a spattering of one-star reviews from customers with complaints that there was no outside seating area, the cakes were not baked on the premises, they'd been given the wrong change, they'd waited too long for a table, there weren't enough highchairs and the décor had been inappropriate for a traditional tea room. This was not the complete list. Marie had replied to all of them politely. She had told him that it always paid to be responsive. But most of the reviews were warm, and Marie herself came across ('the smiling owner') as a transformed person from the wife he had known going off to work at HM Customs and Excise in her navy suit and patterned tights – now a fantasy countrywoman in floral Boden wrap dresses and ditsy pink and yellow Doc Martens which reminded him of measled skin.

He had believed she would not last the first winter on her own there when it rained and rained. Most businesses in town were shut up until the spring, the grey village lay silent under louring skies, nothing to do, days too long. But she had lit out for even lonelier places, had actually made the promised journey to the far north and loved it. Had 'met people', she said in her occasional emails, which he took to be couples or other café owners, but could be single men.

The summer had come round again, she had gone back to Windermere after her Hibernian tour and opened up for a second season and that had come to an end and she had returned to Scotland. This annual pattern of exchanging one godforsaken place for another was incomprehensible. Better the Sino-Russian banks of the Thames and the blinking pyramid roof of Canary Wharf, the whole blood-red skyline of sinister implacable seductive towers than the empty pub, the swan-infested river.

One day he would take a boat out past Canvey Island and the Isle of Grain. Years ago there'd been a big snowstorm that cut Kent off from London, the power failed, helicopters airlifted sacks of potatoes to starving residents. The Isle of Grain was isolated for twelve days, he had never forgotten that, watching at home on telly, not even knowing where it was, then his dad taking out his Ordnance Survey map and showing him. It was in the mouth of the bloody Thames, for God's sake. And this had given him a respect for the climate and an expectation of natural disasters.

They were in two separate spheres now. He had no idea how to get this rubbish out of her system. He thought it might have to do with some mood that had overtaken people, nostalgia. He was nostalgic for being a punk, for Johnny Rotten before he went weird and fat and tweedy, for the leather jacket that did not fit him, for all the years of fancying Marie and waiting for her. He was not nostalgic for toasted crumpets and the old pound notes.

On the foreshore he saw figures bending on the strip of wet strand. Mudlarks. He and his brother had done it for a few summers when they were kids. The steep, slippery stone steps down to the river seemed to them a portal to another city, that it was possible to ease your body through a crack in time while above your head Londoners marched to and fro across the bridges. They found Tudor clay pipes, and eighteenth-century buttons, Edwardian bottle-stoppers, a pewter token which might be medieval, and foreign coins with old heads and strange designs dropped, their dad said, from the pockets of the sailors from foreign ships. The historic rubbish from the foreshore should remind the boys, he had said, that London had once had an empire.

If you lived in a coastal port, you had to expect people would come in as well as go out. Some of them would be bad'uns. He'd tried to explain that to Marie. You couldn't have London without foreigners, it wouldn't be the same place, would it? It would be some lily-white National Trust mock-up with volunteers dressed in mob caps and packets of shortbread in the gift shop. That wasn't London, nor had it ever been. And yet she took some perverse pride in being salt-of-the-earth English, though he had heard that if you took a DNA test you found you were all sorts. He laughed at her stubborn naivety.

He should call her from the boat. He should tell her everything he had been thinking since he set off from Putney and if she heard his voice echoing on the water, if he told her that at this very moment he was sailing under Tower Bridge, now he was past Rotherhithe, now the Blackwall Tunnel was under his hull – then the tidal pull of London would haul her back in, the chains of the Thames would catch her.

But when he pulled off his gloves and found his phone in the inside pocket of his fleeced jacket, and hoisted up his feet and braced his back, and hit her number, there was no plaintive cry of connection from one end of the country to the next, only the anonymous voice of O2's answering service, which meant the phone was turned off or, more likely, there was no signal. Or, if he was going to be neurotic, she was lost somewhere. Fallen into a loch, or blinded by sunlight had driven off the edge of the road, or the van broken into or stolen, or just gone. The wind was very fresh. He was sailing past a floating Chinese restaurant, he could see waiters in there doing the place-settings for lunch. He could cry and no one would see a middle-aged man in a tweed cap weeping in the middle of the river. He could do anything out here, throw himself off, watch a porno on his phone, call a friend and give up all his misery in the kind of rant you only managed when you were drunk. Something had ripped in his life, torn it. He didn't really understand what had happened. Everything was coming to pieces. (But still he wanted his whitebait and pint, he thought he deserved it.)

He steered his boat past the prison ships. He thought it was a disgrace and a blot on the face of the river that these hell-holes were still moored there, with deteriorating conditions and far too many suicides from the decks. The deportees were kept locked up now in the hold, the poor wretches. Barbaric, Magwitch territory, one of the great books of his childhood, his dad had made him read it, the chained convict looming up through the marshes from the hulks. The poor devils were to be transported, not to Australia but back to chemical weapons and nerve gas and aerial bombardment, hiding with your kids in a basement while hell was above your head. Nothing to be done about it. Nor was it just refugees from war zones but anyone whose visa had run out or had the wrong paperwork, or just filled out a form with a single error, because that was what they were trying to do: catch you out over a mistake. Getting your date of birth wrong by a day, or misspelling the name of your place of work, or missing a question. The officials had targets and they combed the paperwork looking for excuses to get rid of you. The barrier had been built to keep back the sea. Next, he thought, they'll pour concrete through the Channel Tunnel. And all for want of a passport. He had one. He got his first when he was seventeen, a holiday with mates to Minorca. He had a nationality, he could prove it, everything was in that. Just an accident that he was born on the Surrey side of the Thames and not in the middle of a war. He had no idea who he would be without a passport.

But now he had arrived, taking in the barrier as one of the seven wonders of the world. What a feat of engineering, what poetry in mechanisation! Long ago he and his brother had sat on the same spot and felt that surge of pride as if they were about to burst out singing 'God save the Queen' without being able to help themselves, having only a year ago said that if it was up to them they'd turf her out of Buck House and see how she got on in a council flat on the Isle of Dogs.

How one had changed. How the years took it out of you.

Who was DB27? If they had met would they get on, would they be attracted to each other, would she be interested in him? What did she smell like? What perfume did she use? Was she a good dancer? Was she another one like Marie who was dreaming of the old life, the old England? Or a lady who had endured too many of life's blows, a brutal husband, tearaway kids, knocked-about, prone to depression and other mental health problems? How could she be depressed, though, in newly bought clothes? For when he was down he didn't care what he put on.

Sharing these thoughts with the river, calling down into the deep over the side of the boat – *Who the fuck are you? Why won't you leave me alone and why did you even do it, you silly slut?* – he let his words spread and mingle with the stream from passing craft and turning, headed back upstream to Greenwich.

It was a few years since he'd been to the pub, a Union Jack flew over its bosomy bow windows. Whitebait was still on the menu. He ordered it and went and sat with his beer by the window.

I walk my beat before London Town,
Five hours up and seven down.
Up I go till I end my run
At Tide-end-town, which is Teddington.

Banging poem, they'd all learned it at school when he was a kid, though they wouldn't teach it any more he supposed. It was Rudyard Kipling for a start.

Norseman and Negro and Gaul and Greek
Drank with the Britons in Barking Creek.

No way would that be on the national curriculum. Still it twanged in his mind.

He tried Marie's number again. She picked up, but her voice was tinny and fragmented, he began to say something about his love for her but he heard her laughing. She was telling him some funny story whose elements he would never connect together, the string they hung on was broken. It was all so fucking ridiculous and it seemed to him that there was no way there couldn't be a resolution between them, a compromise, maybe summer in the Lake District, winter in London. He'd put himself out, he'd go along if he could just talk her into it. Then his whitebait arrived. It looked brilliant, the tiny fish turning their dead eyes up at him, crisply fried. The good city, the lovely river, the smell of the fawn-coloured water, the mudlarks wading in the fore-shore, the beat of oars and a golden canopy, a regal face.

41

Valentina Popov, aged forty-three at the time of her death, who had lain anonymously in a pauper's grave for four years.

A double helix ran through her. A speck of what was left of her body would be sent away to a laboratory and the long chains and sequences and codes of her Valentina-ness identified.

To Geoff Stott's mind came the vivid flash of remembrance, as if a switch had been thrown, of an olive and cactus Triumph Herald he had once bid on but failed to win and was irked to be reminded of it. He was thinking that nothing much had happened in the intervening years since they had buried her, apart from his taking over the business when Kevin Redmond retired.

He and the vicar were conducting a funeral in another part of the cemetery, an avenue away. The number of paupers' funerals at the cemetery had increased in recent years. They were doing them all the time now, the council had to expand its budget to cover the expense of people dying and the family had no money to pay for the disposal of the body, let alone services, hymns, readings, a headstone. These events took place without formality or ceremony, as one disposed of unrecyclable rubbish in the public incinerators. The children were dispatched in cardboard coffins, a dozen at a time, bleak little boxes going into the flames. The cremated ashes belonged to the council and were used to fertilise the public parks. Parents who begged for them back to spread their child in a special place were refused. 'Well, that's your austerity for you,' Geoff said. 'Though they won't cremate an unidentified body in case someone comes forward so they can test the DNA. Which is exactly what's happened here.'

'I'm glad it all worked out in the end,' said Father Cutler. 'Poor woman.'

'Valentina, eh? Nobody's valentine, though.' A pause. 'Very sad.'

'Yes.'

For the past hour in another part of the cemetery mechanical diggers had been working away at the clay soil. The paupers on top of her came up briefly into the light, looked about at the world they'd left, were piled around the grave and soon would be returned back to their hole. DB27s transient soul had unearthed them. She was resting now on the ground on two planks but there was something in her that belonged to motion, to the river and the sea she had tried to return to. Father Cutler had said all along that God knew who she was. Now everyone did.

Valentina Popov, born in a town called Ungheni, a border post between Moldova and Romania. Until independence it had been part of the Soviet Union. The EU was on the other side of the bridge across the river. Geographically it was *in* Europe, but it must be galling, he thought, to look over the bridge and there was your freedom to travel all over the continent, get on a train, be in Paris or Rome. And if you looked in the other direction, then you had Mother Russia; now that was what you call drawing the short straw.

Moldova's Wikipedia entry was a long story of land grabs and futile independence movements; swallowed up by imperial powers and then rising, gasping for air, to the surface for a

307

while. These fluid countries were beyond Alan McBride, filming the scene once again, to understand, even though he was an Ulsterman and should have felt some affinity with their contested status, but he didn't, not really. Even though he was now living in a country which had been one thing and was in the process of becoming something else, making him feel as if the landmass was tipping up and emptying him into the sea. Younis had said once that Persia had never been conquered, was always Persia. 'That's nice,' he had replied, and Younis had looked at him as if he had realised in this moment that his granddaughter's husband was an idiot. For no, he had not understood the big picture. People were moving about in all directions, they were in the middle of a vast perpetual motion experiment. Countries rose and fell. Languages withered into disuse until there was only a single native speaker who must talk to herself. Tyrants appeared, ascended as marble and iron statues and were deposed, their images torn down. And Valentina Popov was on the wrong side of a border a few metres away and did not have the right to live and work in the EU, though that was what she had been doing until her suicide.

The DNA tests would have to be carried out but there was little doubt that they had found her at last, knew who she was, a mystery like an irritant finally solved, even if the story of that sad end in the river was not yet explained and maybe would never be known exactly. But she was real and no longer a poster, a set of tagged clothes, some empty holes in her ear lobes.

She worked as a cleaner for wealthy Russians who were unconcerned about legalities and who existed like a row of expensive cigars in a climate-controlled vacuum from the city. Alan knew they were there and even, more or less, where they lived (white wedding-cake mansions in Mayfair and Notting Hill and Hampstead), but he didn't understand the first thing about them. They occasionally appeared in Francesca's magazines holding glasses of champagne, wearing prohibitively expensive clothes and watches, flat-coloured papery people with names ending in *itch* and *osky* and *ov*. They bought and sold power stations like sweeties, they moved money about the world, owned newspapers and football teams. Their wealth was so abstract in its size they seemed to him more like banks than human beings, even though they had grown up in towns such as Ungheni, learned their letters in schoolrooms with Lenin's photograph fixed to the wall like a classroom monitor to inspire them with collectivist thoughts.

When she wasn't running the vacuum cleaner over the parquet floors of ballrooms and cleaning the sunken marble baths, Valentina was passing through the Romanian party scene like a hand riffling a pack of cards. She liked to dance, she drank white wine, she did not do drugs, she had terrible taste in music (loved Kiss and Iron Maiden), she was an okay cook, she had some boyfriends. The plumber had come forward, he had all the right paperwork and still the information had to be squeezed out of him like a hand choking a throat. His account of her life in London was reduced to a few predictable elements.

She had a dog, it is not easy to be a servant when you have dog, God knows how she kept it all that time. Did the owners allow it? I don't know. Some places she lived in, servants' rooms, were very nice, all the luxuries. But she was not EU so she was illegal. She fell in love with some bad guy and he said, give me all your money or I go to the police. We all heard this. The man was a shit, but a good-looking shit, used a lot of product in his hair, very good jeans, smelled nice, this crap a woman likes. She gives him a thousand pounds. Of course, it was not enough. He was bleeding her. He tried to take everything she had. We told her go home. Your situation is bad, very difficult. She said she was too ashamed. To go home with nothing, no money for her daughter. One day, she said, my daughter will get married, I want to make her a beautiful wedding. She thought

309

maybe she would steal a necklace from a women she is working for but she didn't know how to sell it. She wanted to come back with a suitcase full of presents. But she had nothing left. Just her clothes, she thought she could sell them when she got home, she mentioned this. Very proud of Marks and Spencer. But I think the dog died, went missing, ran away maybe, that's what I heard and she was broken-hearted for the dog. When she lost the dog she was finished, the dog was the end. This is all I know.

Alan saw the policeman walking quickly along the avenue of trees, saw Pete Dutton falter as he approached the party, for he had taken in the tight cold pale face of the daughter standing with her boyfriend and thought that it would not be made prettier by the soft focus of sadness.

Daria, shimmery pink lipstick, both frail and proud in skinny jeans and white puffer jacket, like an egg held up by two cocktail sticks, expressing no tears or grief or tenderness but speaking in okay, hotel receptionist English, pointed at the coffin and told what she considered a few home truths to the Englishmen gathered round her to whom her fucking mother was some kind of film star, mysterious and tragic.

'She was a bitch, she abandoned me when I was a kid to come to London, she never even sent me a plane ticket to see her.'

'Why do you think she took her own life?'

'Who knows? Maybe she got sick of being a bitch.'

Listening to this, Pete supposed that it was more than a dog and a dodgy boyfriend that had finished her off. There was a mother-and-daughter story one would never get to the bottom of. Some epic of resentment and slights and crossed lines and the feeling that you were not loved or it was not the right kind of love. Or the *fiery feeling* had got hold of Valentina as it took women all the time and they were lost to those who were close to them.

There was a case in Devon he'd heard about, of a housewife

310

and community volunteer, ran jumble sales for the RNLI. She made her family their Christmas lunch, tidied away the paper wrappings, hoovered up the pine needles, loaded the dishwasher, told her husband she was staying up a while longer to watch a programme on the telly, then when he was in bed walked out of the house, a mile and a half to the cold beach as the clock ticked into Boxing Day and disappeared into the sea. In that case they had the CCTV from a café on the sands. No fuss, no note, nothing to indicate she'd been depressed and unhappy and her bewildered grown-up children left with hands full of water.

Valentina had wanted to be erased from life. Life is not for everyone, he supposed. The thought was more mysterious than anything: never to drink a really good pint, listen to music, sit on the banks of the Thames with a plate of whitebait and watch the river wash down to the sea. In place of that, eternity in the dark until the suns all went out and there was nothing *but* dark. He didn't get it. If it was up to him, he'd live for ever.

A lot of elements had come into play in the breakdown of his marriage, irreconcilable differences about where they would live, the types of people they were prepared to allow themselves to be but he admitted that Marie had never quite had the fullness of his attention after he found the body. He had made up stories about her as he was going to sleep, a girl from a farm, a lady running away from her husband, but always a person who took care of her appearance and who might have been very attractive if you'd seen her when the life was still left in her eyes. A man must be allowed his fantasies. A man must allow his mind to run away with him. A man must surely be allowed to be a perfect fool for once in his life, even when he's found cancer in a woman's body with his own hand. Maybe men too should be allowed a fiery feeling once in a while.

Now he knew the outlines of her story and it was nothing like

311

he had thought so this whole business would teach him not to be so imaginative.

Alan was asking Daria if she had any photos of her mother. The girl took out her phone. 'See.'

Her finger flickered through Valentina with straight brown hair, a little dumpier and younger than the woman in the artist's impression. In the first photo she is outdoors, there are blurred trees in the distance at the side of the frame. She is on a stool by the wall of a house. The little girl is sitting rigidly on her knee staring at the camera, half a man's leg appears on the left, he seems to be walking away from the shot. It is posed and a little tense. Her expression is tired, and she seems uncomfortable with her situation. Next, she's holding the child's hand as she toddles forwards trying to ascend a shallow step, held back by leading reins attached to a harness round her chest. Once again, she looks exhausted and distressed. Then Valentina in a kitchen, lifting a glass of wine, as if raising a toast, and in front of her a disembodied hand with a lighter moving towards the candles of a birthday cake. In this photo she has the animation, the vivacity which can allow Pete to believe she was the London party girl of Alex's statement. In later pictures, presumably as the child was growing up and giving her mother more freedom, she keeps changing her hairstyle and its colour, getting ready for flight to London, to all those maid's rooms, to all those parties. She's nobody special, except to Daria. Unfortunately for Valentina, Daria is claiming, her daughter was not special enough to be loved by her.

No, she was nothing unusual after all, Pete thought. She lacked Marie's eccentricity, her spark. He'd thrown everything away for a Moldovan cleaner. And he didn't even like dogs.

Daria put her phone away. 'Have you seen? Do you want more? I have no more. Better you should have left her in the river.'

The boyfriend was holding her upper arm as if she was a jug or a pint pot. He said, 'You know it's not true she didn't love you.

She wanted a better life for you, you deleted all her messages, you never even read them, I saw you do it.'

'If she loved me she would have stayed in our town. Don't tell me she had a hard life in London, she had the best of everything, beautiful clothes, good food to eat. I know, she texted me pictures of what she buys. She was going to parties, she was always meeting new people, she was all over the city with that stinking dog on a leash, laughing, while I am at school and coming home to my dad telling me to clean the house.'

'I'm sorry,' Alan said.

'Yes, you are sorry. Everyone says, but no one is sorry when she is going to parties and I am at home watching TV with my father in our town which was too shit for her. When she went to London and sends me a picture outside Buckingham Palace my uncle says, "You should be proud of your mother, look where she is." But why should I be proud? You take all our best people, everyone wants to come here. She wasn't even the best, just a scrap, you did not even leave us that.'

The couple then spoke to each other. They were deciding that there was enough time left to go sightseeing before their evening flight home, but where would they go? The boyfriend said he would like to visit the British Museum, Daria said she wanted to go to the famous Hard Rock Café. He told her only tourists went there, she said fine, they were tourists. They walked off, disappeared into London, following raggedly and briefly Valentina's footsteps in her long pilgrimage.

'So there you have it,' Pete said as they walked back to the car park. 'I see you've brought your camera gear. Will you do a follow-up?'

'I'll try. I don't know if anyone will want to be interviewed. The daughter will but she says she wants to be paid. The plumber says he won't talk, not even for money. I can't say I blame him, not with this atmosphere.'

'That's a shame. Will she take the body back home?'

'I don't think so. Too expensive.'

'So she'll go back into the ground again.'

'Yes, London's daughter, after all that.'

'I suppose you're right. Do you need a lift up west?'

'No, I'm okay. I rented a car.'

They got into their respective cars. Pete felt he was far from home. He would head east, there were plenty more hours left in the day. He would go as far as he could until the river ran out then turn back to Gunnersbury and his flat above the nail bar. He knew by now that this was the last of London, he'd seen it through. He would ring Marie tonight. He would undertake voluntary exile from the city, from the good city that nourished him. He would starve of his real life in a seaside town. It was inevitable, always had been. So that was that.

And driving home to his wife and kid, Alan was assessing the question of whether they should sell the house.

More dead rats were being found in the alley at the end of the road, three or four a day. On one weekend Vic Elliott's dogs had sniffed eleven and gone mad with the rodent smell, bounding in the air, running at the fence, escaping from their leashes. Pest control had been out and suggested that the increase in rail traffic through the station must be accounting for the numbers being hit. There had been no increase in the commuter service, it was the deportation trains which came through in the night, carrying their cargo of the removed, deported, departed, banished, transported, expelled, exiled, exported. These days of human waste.

The German family had left voluntarily, with smiles and dignity and farewell presents and exchanges of email addresses and not, in any way, thought Alan, in the manner of a retreat. They had simply adjusted to a new set of circumstances. The girl was fine, she had recovered from her brief underwater experience, but

Caspar had said, 'We won't take the risk, our safety is too important, words at school are nothing, but we must be sensible.' 'Of course,' Francesca said, 'I would do exactly the same.' (Though without knowing where exactly she would be able to withdraw to.) The two women held each other, Francesca kneeled down to give Gaby a kiss. She smelled the sweet scent of rose soap on her skin.

Mrs Audrey Shapiro and her friend Mrs Simarjit Kaur Khalistan had stood on the doorstep and watched the taxi turn at the end of the road, taking them to the airport, to a plane whose destination was, it was believed, Frankfurt.

Mrs Shapiro was surprised to find that she was sad to see them leave, having overcome a prejudice so innate that she had, all those years back, had to return to the shop a German alarm clock. The flash of their Hawaiian Fire lips brightened the day, indomitable old ladies going nowhere.

London is vast, very vast, Younis and Amira had often said so. 'When we first came here we could not believe how long it took us to get to our hotel from the airport.'

Younis was under instruction never to leave the building without being accompanied. The risks of assault out on the street were too great for a frail old man. He stayed indoors and watched TV and listened to Persian music. He is at home in Isfahan, happy with his days. He is in the bazaar, he is with the merchants, he is trading, buying, selling. His memory is prickly with old transactions. He is drinking mint tea and holding out a palm full of rose petals. He is a man of wool and gold and ink and perfumes. The place of prices under a vaulted roof.

He had never penetrated the huge territories east of the North Circular, out at Wanstead Flats and Tower Hill and Stratford, the whole city seeping outwards and upwards until the Green Belt stops it, a girdle of landfill, golf courses and untilled fields. Through this landscape Alan drove, back to his wife whom he had first seen wearing a violet trilby hat with an emerald feather in the gift shop of the National Gallery and had instinctively known that the high-stepping woman his father had described was to be his salvation from a more narrow constricted existence. Francesca, spoilt, vain, so superficial in her preoccupations with appearance, like all her family had an instinct for self-preservation. A nose for it. A big brown nose for changes in the atmosphere.

She had foreseen, with that awful joke about the attic, that the German child would at some point need saving. It was pregnant Francesca who had pulled the girl coated in a green slime from the shallow water. Had called the police and the ambulance though Gaby was unhurt, just wet and slippery and screaming. Months later, she had given birth in good time without complications. The baby emerged with a full head of light brown hair and light eyebrows, emitting a piercing scream as if she was immediately offended by the décor of the delivery unit.

A week before she went into labour Francesca had pulled out an envelope and slid it across the dining table to him.

'What's this?'

'I had my jewellery valued.'

'Jesus.'

'I know. I was surprised.'

'I'm glad you never showed it to me before we got married, it feels like a bloody dowry.'

'But it means we'll be all right.'

'We can still sell the house if you want. You never really liked it. You were right about the rats. They were always there, and getting worse.'

'The shop is here, the shop is doing okay.'

She felt defensive about her little business and how the young mothers had taken it over as a kind of drop-in centre, so that she had installed a coffee machine and begun to serve lattes and flat whites and Americanos. Someone asked if she could sell slices of her home-made cakes. Now, she was always sweeping up sugary crumbs of lemon drizzle and some kind of vegan carob loaf with a mortar-like texture in the roof of the mouth. The mothers sat on the last of the ghost chairs sipping and nattering. The buggies stood out on the pavement and inside, their children on their knee or running around or quietly reading, the mothers spoke of sore nipples, of pouches of organic puréed quinoa with Mediterranean vegetables, of first shoes, of late talking, of whether the crawling stage was strictly necessary for Tommy was already getting to his little feet and clinging on to the coffee table, sidling round the edges without having learned to coordinate the complex crawl manoeuvre of hand forward, knee back. There was an unspoken understanding that in return for what was effectively a support group for harassed women, no one would leave without making a purchase of some kind, so two-year-olds were building libraries of books, both for their own age and for later, occupying whole bookcases.

This mammary world bored her. Yes, the shop was an unexpected, accidental, unwarranted success but it wasn't who she was but something she did.

And was it a misstep? Can you get back to where you started and right yourself? When she thought of that afternoon on the Island – the old woman snoozing by the fire, the twins (now in foster care while their fate was decided by the courts), the painted houses, the dying elephant, the wide expanse of the territory that lay beyond the last street, whatever it was – she understood, as she always had, that you could not choose your period of history. Whether or not she was lucky she had no idea. And what about the infant on her lap, just learned this very week to hold her head up, not to need the protective cupped hand? She would, if things worked out, still be alive at the end of the century. Would she be a drone for the master race of artificial

317

intelligence, humans downgraded to the status of animals, and think it normal? Francesca clicked away these thoughts, for they were like staring at the sun.

Now in the garden surrounded by roses she pointed upwards. 'Look at the plane,' she told the baby. 'Look at the aeroplane in the sky. We'll go somewhere some day, you and me.' The baby waggled her fingers and flapped her hand against her breast. Her mouth opened in an optimistic O.

'And have we been paying attention?' she asked the child. 'Have we?'

The anti-Brexit marches they didn't go on, the houses they didn't buy and the one they did, the prizewinning novel she bought and left on the bedside table only half read, the petitions she signed without really reading them, the thirty-four-degree London days and the twenty-eight-degree London nights, the new iPhone, the new dress, the new shoes, the dying trees in the streets, geraniums still flowering on Christmas Eve ('the seasons are broken'), another election, a by-election, a new prime minister and me, me too, she said to the child in her arms who stared up with unfocused eyes at the blue sky and a plane's white streak, banking, returning.

My soul is unprepared, thought Alan, still driving home.

42

There was a girl at school who one day said, 'I'm going to Bangkok, you'll see,' and she went to Bangkok, and later you told everyone you're going to London and you went, surprising them all and no trouble getting a job.

You had served your time in their hospitals and sat by the beds of the dying and comforted the families and gave the correct dosage of the medicines and the injections and turned them gently, even big fat fellas, and flirted with the doctors and kept your uniform neat and sweet and your hair always clean and on your face the smile that came naturally. Rob says you're an uncomplicated person and that's what he likes about you. You have told him when to get that cut seen to or it's going to go septic, and no, he doesn't need antibiotics for that chesty cough it's just a virus, for he's a little bit of a hypochondriac and his mind races ahead with any symptom, thinking always the worst, and you've kidded him out of it.

But the country isn't what it was and your dad and your brother are telling you to come home, the place is finished, the English are withdrawing back into themselves like a mollusc to its shell. All those centuries a great empire with its pink map and now they're turning their backs on the world, the world is not wanted. Of course, when you can get the world on the screen of your iPhone without meeting it in person it's not that surprising that flesh-and-blood strangers can be way too much. The immigrants are off back home, some will stick with it, but outside London they're emptying out and you've heard of an Indian restaurant in Manchester with Mancs serving the curries and Mancs playing the sitar, like Rob told her about a place in Poland where the locals got dressed up as Jews and cooked Jewish food and sang the old Jewish songs because the Jews were long gone.

Home to your country of origin, it's quite an idea, isn't it, this new thing, that we'll all go back into our original boxes like we're not mongrels from here there and everywhere. But it's all everyone talks about. Going home.

Chrissie will not go back to Ireland. She isn't even thirty yet and her youth is still singing in her veins. Her heart is an aeroplane, and no, she tells her daddy, no plans to settle down yet, not with anyone. But it is a long time since she's gone down on her knees at a party, she doesn't do that any more.

These years in London and the people she has met and known, the patients recovered or passed away, the flat-shares made and broken, Marco who is famous now with his gold face and back in London, living in a beautiful flat in Shoreditch, she saw it in a magazine and doing those club nights that get all the write-ups in the papers. He won't be beaten and now she's read he's thinking of taking the thing off altogether and becoming what is it now, an ambassador for acid attack victims, the public face, the poster boy. And next he's said he's talking about giving up the fashionable life to become a counsellor or therapist, whatever he called it, and she'll believe that when she sees it, but you never know, people can change. At least he hadn't done himself in, she'd been half-expecting that bad-news call from his parents but maybe now it would never come. For things can turn out okay for some people, and Marco is made of some stuff that will make everything all right. She should send him a card or something, to wish him well, when she arrives at her destination, won't he be surprised!

At the gate everyone has said goodbye, all aboard all aboard, anyone who is not coming is left behind, their farewells are over. Her mum has sent her a text, a heart emoji, *are you on the plane yet, are you in the air?* A whole day will pass and then she'll step off in Australia. In the old times an Irish person went off to the new world and never came back, never saw their family again, committed to a new life. Maybe she'll meet an Aussie and get married, but before that she wants to learn to surf at Bondi Beach, which she had always imagined like some great deserted strand with waving palm trees but when she saw a picture it seemed a lot like Bournemouth, just a boring suburb on the sea.

And she thinks of a summer evening when she was on the phone to her mate saying the party might be shite, whose party that was now she can't even remember, or where they had just been, it must have been the park, yes, there was a festival in a park.

But they're calling her row. She's walking along the tunnel on to the plane, showing her boarding pass and passport and settling into her seat, they've got seat-back tellies and the screen is currently showing the world with her plane on it. Still earth-bound, a winged creature ready to leave when the pilot has completed his checks and the crew have completed their cross-checks and they are waiting for air traffic control to tell them they can begin to taxi down the runway. Goodbye, goodbye.

Departure, take-off, ascent. From the air the Thames is a wiggling serpent. It has not always had this shape, it will not in the future. The seas will rise, the barrier will not hold them. Like everything, London is a temporary place, a temporary condition.

It takes only minutes to leave the English coastline behind

and soon they make landfall again in France. The air is loud with engines. A few rows behind her a passenger is taken ill, the crew are getting out the defibrillator. They look like they know what they're doing, she probably won't have to get out of her seat with its little bottle of wine on the table and do some emergency nursing.

'God, I hope we don't have to turn back,' says the woman next to her. But they're turning back. The plane is revolving through the sky.

Look at the wings dipping now, banking, turning, the announcement that despite the successful departure of the flight a passenger needs urgent treatment, and apologies, and drinks cleared away, and tray tables to upright as England reappears and the great web of the capital stretches out along its river, its mouth wide open to the sea.

'London is some bloody place,' Chrissie says, 'you can never get away from it. Now is this a sign, or what?'

For she might leave her seat and step back out into the departure hall and return to everything she knows, she isn't sure. She has choices and chances. The sky unites the exhumed body of Valentina Popov, on her way back to the morgue for tissue analysis, and Pete Dutton on his last journey to the river's mouth, and Alan McBride driving home to his wife and daughter, and Francesca in the garden with the baby, looking up at the jet's white tail, thinking for the first time that the small domestic gods should be able to save you, that carpets, for example, could actually fly.

Acknowledgements

The origins of this novel go back to 1992 when I stood at the grave of an unknown woman who had drowned herself in the Thames. I was there because she was the subject of a TV documentary about paupers' funerals and I was writing about the programme for *The Times*. To pass through life leaving no trace seemed the most mysterious condition: the woman was evidently a rough sleeper in middle age but no one on the streets recognised the artist's impression of her. I've never forgotten that Christmas Eve burial and its unmarked grave. My foremost thanks go to the director Ann Pariso who made the film, for responding so generously to my request to see it again twenty-five years later, and who confirmed that the woman buried that desolate morning was never identified. Thanks, too, to Rose Wild of *The Times*, who very kindly went to the trouble of recovering my original piece.

My thanks to Simarjit Kaur Khalistan who was the winning bidder at the auction for the charity Freedom from Torture to have a character named after her. Also to Audrey Anand whose generous donation to Authors for Grenfell Tower brought Mrs Audrey Shapiro into being.

The poem 'A London Plane Tree' is by Amy Levy (1861–89).

My heartfelt thanks, as ever, to my editor Lennie Goodings, my publicist Susan de Soissons and my agent Jonny Geller.

To my family, particularly the millennial generation assaulting the high cliffs of London's housing market, and obviously most of all to two-year-old Talah, my love and my hopes.

Linda Grant is author of five non-fiction books and seven novels. She won the Orange Prize for Fiction in 2000 and the Lettre Ulysses Prize for Literary Reportage in 2006. *The Clothes on Their Backs* was shortlisted for the Man Booker Prize in 2008 and went on to win the South Bank Show Award. *The Dark Circle* was shortlisted for the 2017 Women's Prize for Fiction. Linda Grant lives in London.